# Praise for Philip Pullman

'Philip Pullman. Is he the best storyteller ever?'
*Observer*

'Pullman is in a league of his own'
Jon Snow, Chairman of the Whitbread judges

'Once in a lifetime a children's author emerges who is so
extraordinary that the imagination of generations is altered.
Lewis Carroll, E. Nesbit, C. S. Lewis and Tolkien were all
of this cast. So, too, is Philip Pullman' *New Statesman*

'Philip Pullman, capable of lighting up the dullest day or greyest
spirit with the incandescence of his imagination' *Independent*

'A comic genius of children's fiction' *The Times*

'A masterly storyteller' *Independent*

'Pullman's genius is to invest the weirdest beings, the most
outlandish events, with their own inner logic and provide a
connection to a recognisable reality' *Mail on Sunday*

'One of the most successful children's authors writing today'
*Daily Telegraph*

'A remarkable writer, courageous and dangerous:
he reminds us that this is what an artist should be, after all'
*The Times*

'Pullman is a master at combining impeccable characterizations
and seamless plotting' *Publishers Weekly*

D1324929

*Selected Works by Philip Pullman*

THE BOOK OF DUST TRILOGY
*La Belle Sauvage*

HIS DARK MATERIALS TRILOGY
*Northern Lights*
*The Subtle Knife*
*The Amber Spyglass*

HIS DARK MATERIALS COMPANION BOOKS
*Lyra's Oxford*
*Once Upon a Time in the North*

THE SALLY LOCKHART QUARTET
*The Ruby in the Smoke*
*The Shadow in the North*
*The Tiger in the Well*
*The Tin Princess*

OTHER BOOKS
*Count Karlstein*
*How to Be Cool*
*Spring-Heeled Jack*
*The Broken Bridge*
*The Wonderful Story of Aladdin and the Enchanted Lamp*
*Clockwork, or All Wound Up*
*The Firework-Maker's Daughter*
*Mossycoat*
*The Butterfly Tattoo*
*I Was a Rat! or The Scarlet Slippers*
*Puss in Boots: The Adventures of That Most Enterprising Feline*
*The Scarecrow and His Servant*
*The Adventures of the New Cut Gang*
*The Good Man Jesus and the Scoundrel Christ*
*Grimm Tales: For Young and Old*

GRAPHIC NOVELS
*The Adventures of John Blake*

# PHILIP PULLMAN

## FOUR TALES

*Illustrated by Peter Bailey*

PUFFIN

PUFFIN BOOKS

UK | USA | Canada | Ireland | Australia
India | New Zealand | South Africa

Puffin Books is part of the Penguin Random House group of companies
whose addresses can be found at global.penguinrandomhouse.com.

www.penguin.co.uk   www.puffin.co.uk   www.ladybird.co.uk

Penguin
Random House
UK

This collection first published by Doubleday 2010
This edition published 2019
001

Typeset in Bauer Bodoni
Printed in Great Britain by Clays Ltd, Elcograf S.p.A.

A CIP catalogue record for this book is available from the British Library

ISBN: 978-0-241-41004-2

All correspondence to:
Puffin Books, Penguin Random House Children's
80 Strand, London WC2R 0RL

# CONTENTS

# PROLOGUE

'Now come on, Pullman,' my publisher said. 'You need to write a Prologue for this book, so as to tell the readers something about the stories in it.'

'But my readers don't need that sort of thing,' I said. 'They're quite clever enough to work it out for themselves.'

'It's not a matter of being clever,' said the publisher. 'It's a matter of basic information. You've got four stories here, and they're all quite different. What the readers will want to know is what they've got in common, why you call them fairy tales and why you wrote them.'

So off I went to think about it. The last question was the easiest: I wrote them because I wanted to, and because nobody stopped me. Some of my readers aren't as free as I am, and have to write stories because someone told them to. To them I say: Never mind! One day you'll be free, and you'll be able to write nothing at all if you don't want to. You can sit and twiddle your thumbs till the moon falls down.

But I like my readers, and I admire their excellent choice of reading matter. And if it will help them to get started with the stories in this book, I'm glad to say something about how and why I wrote them. The title first: we decided to call the book *Four Tales*, but what these stories really are is fairy tales. If you get as far as the Epilogue, you'll find that I say a little more about fairy tales there.

I wrote *The Firework-Maker's Daughter* as a play before I changed it into a book. I had to change quite a lot of things, but I haven't got the script any more to check what they were. Recently it came full circle and turned into a play again, and this time there were real fireworks on the stage. Because I think fairy tales ought to have some truth in them if they're going to be any good, I was quite serious when I wrote about the Royal Sulphur and what it means, and the Three Gifts that Lila had to bring in exchange for it. She thought she didn't have them, but she did. If you want to gain the Royal Sulphur you have to offer them up yourself, but two of them are no good without the third: you need all three.

'*I Was a Rat!*' is the title of the next story. Not *I Was A Rat*. There's a difference. It began for me with the picture in my mind of the ragged little boy in his torn and stained uniform standing in the moonlight on the doorstep of the best two people in the world to look after him, and saying those words. In a fairy tale you're allowed to use ideas that have often been used before, and the one I used here is that of the old couple who had always wanted children, but had never had any. I once had a letter from a father who'd been reading this story with his little daughter, and he told me there was a point in the middle of the story when they said at the same time: 'Oh! It's –' and they both said aloud one of the most famous fairy-tale names of all. And, yes, it is, but you'll have to see who it is for yourself.

In *Clockwork*, or *All Wound Up*, the same idea crops up, oddly enough. I suppose you could write a million stories about someone who wants a child but never has one. In European fairy tales they usually go on to say they want a child as red as blood and as white as snow, but I thought I'd change that formula in keeping with the clockwork theme. This story took a lot of writing. I tried it this way and I tried it that way, and I kept on fiddling at it till it all fitted together. The *All Wound Up* part of the title has several meanings, and one of them is 'Brought to a pitch of tension', which some of the characters in this story certainly are. Sometimes you can put words in a story hoping they'll be seen out of the corner of the reader's eye and not really thought about, but that they'll unconsciously affect the way things around them are understood, and here are three of them. They have yet another meaning as well, as those who reach the final sentence will discover.

I'm sometimes asked which is my favourite book. Well, I love them all equally, of course, but if there was ever a story I felt happy writing, it's *The Scarecrow and His Servant*. I've got an old pack of cards called the Myriorama, and on each card there's a picture of a bit of landscape that joins on perfectly to whichever card you put down next. There are people wandering along a road, or pulling a cart out of a ditch, or going to market, or watching soldiers march along, and it all makes one long, endless story. I was thinking of the Myriorama when I wrote *The Scarecrow and His Servant*, because it's one of those stories that could go on for ever, with the Scarecrow and Jack wandering over a sort of Italian landscape and encountering brigands and enchanters and pirates and giants and people in distress without ever coming to the end of their adventures, and perhaps in another world that's exactly what they're doing.

But books have to come to an end, even if stories don't, and the fireside in that comfortable old farmhouse in Spring Valley, with Jack and his family and their beloved Scarecrow sitting around after supper telling stories themselves, was the place to stop.

It's a good place to stop the prologue too. The stories can speak for themselves now.

*Philip Pullman*

# PHILIP PULLMAN

## The Firework - Maker's Daughter

Illustrated by Peter Bailey

# CHAPTER ONE

A thousand miles ago, in a country east of the jungle and south of the mountains, there lived a Firework-Maker called Lalchand and his daughter Lila.

Lalchand's wife had died when Lila was young. The child was a cross little thing, always crying and refusing her food, but Lalchand built a cradle for her in the corner of the workshop, where she could see the sparks play and listen to the fizz and crackle of the gunpowder. Once she was out of her cradle, she toddled around the workshop laughing as the fire flared and the sparks danced. Many a time she burnt her little fingers, but Lalchand splashed water on them and kissed her better,

3

and soon she was playing again.

When she was old enough to learn, her father began to teach her the art of making fireworks. She began with little Crackle-Dragons, six on a string. Then she learned how to make Leaping Monkeys, Golden Sneezes, and Java Lights. Soon she was making all the simple fireworks, and thinking about more complicated ones.

One day she said, 'Father, if I put some flowers of salt in a Java Light instead of cloud-powder, what would happen?'

'Try it and see,' he said.

So she did. Instead of burning with a steady green glimmer, it sprayed out wicked little sparks, each of which turned a somersault before going out.

'Not bad, Lila,' said Lalchand. 'What are you going to call it?'

'Mmm . . . Tumbling Demons,' she said.

'Excellent! Make a dozen and we'll put them into the New Year Festival display.'

The Tumbling Demons were a great success, and so were the Shimmering Coins that Lila invented

next. As time went on she learned more and more of her father's art, until one day she said, 'Am I a proper Firework-Maker now?'

'No, no,' he said. 'By no means. Ha! You don't know the start of it. What are the ingredients of fly-away powder?'

'I don't know.'

'And where do you find thunder-grains?'

'I've never heard of thunder-grains.'

'How much scorpion oil do you put in a Krakatoa Fountain?'

'A teaspoonful?'

'*What?* You'd blow the whole city up. You've got a lot to learn yet. Do you really want to be a Firework-Maker, Lila?'

'Of course I do! It's the only thing I want!'

'I was afraid so,' he said. 'It's my own fault. What was I thinking of? I should have sent you to my sister Jembavati to bring you up as a dancer. This is no place for a girl, now I come to think of it, and just look at you! Your hair's a mess, your fingers are burned and stained with chemicals, your eyebrows are scorched . . . How am I going to find a husband for you when you look like that?'

Lila was horrified.

'A *husband*?'

'Well, of course! You don't imagine you can stay here for ever, do you?'

They looked at each other as if they were strangers. Each of them had had quite the wrong idea about things, and they were both alarmed to find it out.

So Lila said no more about being a Firework-Maker, and Lalchand said no more about husbands. But they both thought about them, all the same.

Now the King of that country owned a White Elephant. It was the custom that whenever the King wanted to punish one of his courtiers, he would send him the White Elephant as a present, and the expense of looking after the animal would ruin the poor man; because the White Elephant had to sleep between silk sheets (enormous ones), and eat mango-flavoured Turkish Delight (tons of it), and have his tusks covered in gold leaf every morning. When the courtier had no money left at all, the White Elephant would be returned to the King, ready for his next victim.

Wherever the White Elephant went, his personal

7

servant had to go too. The servant's name was Chulak, and he was the same age as Lila. In fact, they were friends.

Every afternoon Chulak would take the White Elephant out for his exercise, because the Elephant would go with no-one else, and there was a reason for this: Chulak was the only person, besides Lila, who knew that the Elephant could talk.

One day Lila went to visit Chulak and the White Elephant. She arrived at the Elephant House in time to hear the Elephant Master losing his temper.

'You horrible little boy!' he roared. 'You've done it again, haven't you?'

'Done what?' said Chulak innocently.

'Look!' said the Elephant Master, pointing with a quivering finger at the White Elephant's snowy flanks.

Written all over his side in charcoal and paint were dozens of slogans:

**EAT AT THE GOLDEN LANTERN**

**BANGKOK WANDERERS FOR THE CUP**

**STAR OF INDIA TANDOORI HOUSE**

And right at the very top of the White Elephant's back, in great big letters:

## CHANG LOVES LOTUS BLOSSOM
## TRUE XXX

'Every day this Elephant comes home with graffiti all over him!' shouted the Elephant Master. 'Why don't you stop people doing it?'

'I can't understand how it happens, Master,' said Chulak. 'Mind you, the traffic's awful. I've got to watch those rickshaw-drivers like a hawk. I can't look out for graffiti artists as well – they just slap it up and run.'

'But *Chang loves Lotus Blossom True* must have taken a good ten minutes on a stepladder!'

'Yes, it's a mystery to me, Master. Shall I clean it off?'

'All of it! There's a job coming up in a day or two, and I want this animal *clean*.'

And the Elephant Master stormed off, leaving Chulak and Lila with the Elephant.

'Hello, Hamlet,' said Lila.

'Hello, Lila,' said the Elephant. 'Look what this obnoxious brat has reduced me to! A walking billboard!'

'Stop fussing,' said Chulak. 'Look, we've got eighteen rupees already – and ten annas from the Tandoori House – and Chang gave me a whole rupee for letting him write that on the top. We're nearly there, Hamlet!'

'The *shame*!' said Hamlet, shaking his great head.

'You mean you charge people money to write on him?' said Lila.

'Course!' said Chulak. 'It's dead lucky to write your name on a White Elephant. When we've got enough, we're going to run away. Trouble is, he's in love with a lady elephant at the Zoo. You ought to see him blush when we go past – like a ton of strawberry ice cream!'

'She's called Frangipani,' said Hamlet mournfully. 'But she won't even look at me. And now there's another job coming up – another poor man to bankrupt. Oh, I hate Turkish Delight! I detest silk sheets! And I loathe gold leaf on my tusks! I wish I was a normal dull grey elephant!'

'No, you don't,' said Chulak. 'We've got plans, Hamlet, remember? I'm teaching him to sing, Lila. We'll change his name to Luciano Elephanti, and the world'll be our oyster.'

'But why are you looking so sad, Lila?' said Hamlet, as Chulak began to scrub him down.

'My father won't tell me the final secret of Firework-Making,' said Lila. 'I've learned all there is to know about fly-away powder and thunder-grains, and scorpion oil and spark repellent, and glimmer-juice and salts-of-shadow, but there's something else I need to know, and he won't tell me.'

'Tricky,' said Chulak. 'Shall I ask him for you?'

'If he won't tell me, he certainly won't tell you,' said Lila.

'He won't know he's doing it,' said Chulak. 'You leave it to me.'

So that evening, after he'd settled Hamlet down for the night, Chulak called at the Firework-Maker's workshop. It lay down a little winding alley full of crackling smells and pungent noises, between the fried-prawn stall and the batik-painter's. He found Lalchand in the courtyard under the warm stars, mixing up some red glow-paste.

'Hello, Chulak,' said Lalchand. 'I hear the White Elephant's going to be presented to Lord Parakit tomorrow. How long d'you think his money'll last?'

'A week, I reckon,' said Chulak. 'Though you never know – we might run away before then. I've nearly enough to get us to India. I thought I might take up Firework-Making when we got there. Nice trade.'

'Nice trade, my foot!' said Lalchand. 'Firework-Making is a sacred art! You need talent and dedication and the favour of the gods before you can become a Firework-Maker. The only thing *you're* dedicated to is idleness, you scamp.'

'How did you become a Firework-Maker, then?'

'I was apprenticed to my father. And then I had to be tested to see whether I had the Three Gifts.'

'Oh, the Three Gifts, eh,' said Chulak, who had no idea what the Three Gifts were. Probably Lila did, he thought. 'And did you have them?'

'Of course I did!'

'And that's it? Sounds easy. I bet I could pass that

test. I've got a lot more than three gifts.'

'Pah!' said Lalchand. 'That's not all. Then came the most difficult and dangerous part of the whole apprenticeship. Every Firework-Maker –' and he lowered his voice and looked around to make sure no-one was listening – 'every Firework-Maker has to travel to the Grotto of Razvani, the Fire-Fiend, in the heart of Mount Merapi, and bring back some of the Royal Sulphur. That's the ingredient that makes the finest fireworks. Without that, no-one can ever be a true Firework-Maker.'

'Ah,' said Chulak. 'Royal Sulphur. Mount Merapi. That's the volcano, isn't it?'

'Yes, you pestilential boy, and already I've told you far more than I should. This is a secret, you understand?'

'Of course,' said Chulak, looking solemn. 'I can keep a secret.'

And Lalchand had the uneasy feeling that he'd been tricked, though he couldn't imagine why.

# CHAPTER TWO

Next morning, while Lalchand was at the paper merchant's buying some cardboard tubes, Lila went to the Elephant House to see Chulak. When she heard what Lalchand had told him, she was furious.

'Mount Merapi – Razvani – the Royal Sulphur – and he wasn't going to tell me! Oh, I'll never forgive him!'

'That's a bit drastic,' said Chulak, who was busy making the Elephant ready for his new job. 'He's only thinking of you. It's dangerous, after all. You wouldn't catch me going up there.'

'Huh!' she said. 'It's all right to let me make Golden Sneezes and Java Lights, I suppose – little

15

baby things. But not to let me become a real Firework-Maker. He wants me to stay a child for ever. Well, I'm not going to, Chulak. I've had enough. I'm going to Mount Merapi, and I'm going to bring back the Royal Sulphur, and I'll set up as a Firework-Maker on my own and put my father out of business. You see if I don't.'

'No! Wait! You ought to talk to him—'

But Lila wouldn't listen. She ran straight home, packed a little food to eat and a blanket and a few bronze coins, and left a note on the workshop bench:

*Dear Father,*
   *I have completed my apprenticeship.*
*Thank you for all you have taught me.*
*I am going to seek the Royal Sulphur*
*from Razvani, the Fire-Fiend, and I s*
*hall probably not see you again.*
   *Your ex-daughter, Lila*

Then she thought she should take something to show Razvani her skill, and packed a few self-igniting Crackle-Dragons. One of the last things she had invented was a new way of setting them off: you just had to pull a string instead of setting light to them, because the string was soaked with a solution of fire-crystals. She put three of them in her bag, took one last look around the workshop, and slipped away.

✳

When Lalchand came back and found her note, he read it with horror.

'Oh, Lila, Lila! You don't know what you're doing!' he cried, and ran out into the alley.

'Have you seen Lila?' he asked the fried-prawn seller.

'She went off in that direction. About half an hour ago.'

'She had a bundle on her back,' added the batik-painter. 'Looked as if she was going on a journey.'

Lalchand hurried after her at once. But he was an old man with a weak heart, and he couldn't run fast,

17

Philip Pullman

and the streets were crowded: rickshaw-drivers
jostled with bullock-carts, a caravan of silk-traders
was pushing its way through the market, and in the
Grand Boulevard, a procession was going past. The
crowd was so thick that Lalchand couldn't move
any further.

The reason for all the excitement was that the
White Elephant was being led to his new owner.
Chulak was leading Hamlet at the head of
the procession, and with them came musicians
playing bamboo flutes and banging teak drums,
and dancers swaying and snapping their fingernails,
and a troop of servants with tape measures, ready
to measure Hamlet's new home for the silk curtains
and velvet carpets the owner would have to

buy. Flags flapped and banners waved in the sunlight, and the White Elephant shone like a snowy mountain.

Lalchand forced his way through the crowd to Chulak's side.

'Did you tell Lila about Razvani and the Royal Sulphur?' he panted.

'Course,' said Chulak. 'You should have told her yourself. Why?'

'Because she's gone, you wretch! She's gone off by herself to Mount Merapi – and she doesn't know the rest of the secret!'

'Is there more, then?'

'Of course there is!' said Lalchand, struggling to keep up. 'No-one can go into the Fire-Fiend's Grotto

without protection. She needs a flask of magic water from the Goddess of the Emerald Lake – otherwise she'll perish in the flames! Oh, Chulak, what have you done?'

Chulak gulped. They were nearly at the house of the White Elephant's new owner, and they had to slow down to allow all the dancers and musicians and flag-bearers to get through the gate first and form two lines for the White Elephant' to walk between.

Then Hamlet whispered, just loud enough for Chulak to hear:

'I'll find her! Help me get away tonight, Chulak, and we'll go and take Lila the magic water.'

'Good idea,' whispered Chulak, beaming. 'Just what I was going to suggest.' He turned to Lalchand and said, 'Listen, I've got a proposition. Me and Hamlet'll find her! We'll get out tonight. Emerald Lake – Goddess – magic water – Mount Merapi! Nothing to it.' Then Chulak turned to the servants. 'Mind out the way,' he called, 'we've got to get him round the corner – dear, dear, what a narrow gate! That'll have to come down. And what's this? *Gravel?* You want the White Elephant to walk on *gravel?*

Fetch a carpet at once! A red one! Go on! Hurry!'

He clapped his hands, and the servants bowed and scampered away. In the background the new owner was tearing his hair. Chulak whispered to Lalchand once more:

'Don't worry! We'll get away tonight. All we need is a tarpaulin.'

'A tarpaulin? Whatever for?'

'No time to explain now. Just bring one to the gate tonight.'

And Lalchand had to make do with that. He went back to the workshop feeling heavy-hearted.

All this while, Lila had been making her way through the jungle towards the sacred volcano. Mount Merapi lay far to the north, and she had never seen it until, late that afternoon, she came to a bend in the jungle path, and found herself beside the river.

The size of the great mountain made her gasp. It was far away on the very edge of the world, but even so it reached halfway up the sky, with the bare sides rising in a perfect cone to the glowing crater at the top. From time to time the fire-spirits who lived there rumbled angrily underground and threw boiling rocks high into the air. A plume of eternal smoke drifted from the summit to join the clouds.

*How can I ever get there?* she wondered, and felt her heart quail. But she had chosen to make the journey, and she could hardly turn back when she'd barely begun. She shifted her bundle from one shoulder to the other and walked on.

The jungle was a noisy place. Monkeys gibbered in the trees, and parrots screeched, and crocodiles snapped their jaws in the river. Every so often Lila had to step carefully over a snake sleeping in the sun, and once she heard the roar of a mighty tiger. There was no-one to be seen except some fishermen laboriously rowing their boat across from the other side of the river.

She stopped and watched as they brought their boat in towards the bank where she was standing. They weren't making very good progress. There were six or seven of them, and all their oars were getting in one another's way. As she watched, one of the fishermen missed the water completely with his oar, which swung round and clumped another fisherman on the head. That fisherman turned around and punched the first one, who fell off his seat with a squeal and dropped the oar in the water. One of the others tried to grab it, but instead he fell out of the boat, which rocked so violently that the others all cried out in alarm and grabbed the sides.

The man who'd fallen out was splashing and spluttering as he tried to climb back into the boat, and all the crocodiles basking in the shallows looked up, interested. Lila caught her breath in alarm, but the fishermen were so helpless that she could hardly stop herself laughing; because when the man in the water leaned over the gunwale, all the men in the boat leaned over that side to help him, and the boat tipped over so far that they nearly fell in too. They suddenly realized what was happening and let go, and then the boat tipped back the other way and they all fell on their backs.

And the crocodiles slid off the sandbank and began to swim towards them.

'Oh, pull him in, you stupid creatures!' Lila cried. 'Over the end, not over the side!'

One of the fishermen heard her, and hauled the man over the stern to lie in the bottom flopping and gasping like a fish. Meanwhile, the boat had drifted in to the side, and Lila put out a hand to stop it bumping.

As soon as they saw her, the fishermen nudged one another.

'Look,' said one.

'Go *on*,' muttered one of them. '*You a*sk her.'

'No! It was your idea! *You* do it.'

'It wasn't me, it was Chang!'

'Well, he can't say anything, he's still full of water . . .'

Finally one of them snorted with impatience and stood up, making the boat rock alarmingly. He was the stoutest man in the boat, and by far the most impressive, for he wore an ostrich plume nodding in his turban, an enormous black moustache, and a tartan sarong.

'Miss!' he said. 'Would I be correct in supposing that you were hoping to cross the river?'

'Well, as a matter of fact, I was,' said Lila.

He tapped his fingertips together with pleasure.

'And would I also be correct in supposing that you had a little money?'

'A little, yes,' said Lila. 'Could you take me across? I'll pay you.'

'Look no further!' he said proudly. 'Rambashi's River Taxi is at your service! I am Rambashi. Welcome aboard!'

Lila wasn't sure why a river taxi should have the name *The Bloody Murderer* painted on the bow, nor why Rambashi should be wearing no less than three daggers in his belt: one straight, one curved, and one wavy. However, there was no other way to cross the river, and she stepped aboard, trying to avoid the man who'd been saved from drowning, who was still lying dripping in the bottom of the boat. The others took no notice of him at all, but rested their feet on him as if he was a roll of carpet.

'Cast off, my brave lads!' cried Rambashi.

Lila sat in the prow, and held the sides apprehensively as *The Bloody Murderer* swayed out into the current. Behind her she could hear the clash of oars as the blades banged together, the cries of pain as one man's handle struck another man's back, and the groaning and cursing as the half-drowned man tried to regain his seat; but she didn't take much notice, because there was plenty to look at on the water.

There were dragonflies and hummingbirds, and a family of ducks out for an afternoon cruise, and crocodiles practising looking like logs, and all sorts of things; but presently she noticed that the rowers had stopped talking, and the boat wasn't rocking unsteadily as it had been when they were rowing. In fact, it was drifting.

And the oarsmen weren't entirely silent, either. She could hear whispers:

'*You* tell her!'

'No, I don't want to. It's your turn.'

'You've *got* to! You said you would!'

'Let Chang do it. It's about time he did something.'

'He's not fierce enough. *You* do it!'

Lila turned round.

'Oh, for goodness sake,' she said, 'what are you—?'

But she didn't finish the sentence, because of the sight that met her eyes. All the rowers had put down their oars, which were sticking out in all directions, and each rower had tied a handkerchief over his nose and mouth, and they were all holding daggers. Rambashi was holding two.

They all jumped slightly when she turned round. Then they looked at Rambashi.

'Yes!' he said. 'Fooled you! Ha, ha! This isn't a River Taxi at all. We are pirates! The fiercest pirates on the whole river. We'd cut your throat as soon as look at you.'

'And drink your blood,' one whispered.

'Oh yes, and drink your blood. All of it. Hand over your money, come on!'

He waved his dagger so vigorously that the boat rocked and he nearly fell out. Lila almost laughed.

'Pay up!' said Rambashi. 'You're captured. Your money or your life! I warn you, we're desperate men!'

# CHAPTER THREE

Rambashi and his pirates managed to get *The Bloody Murderer* to the other bank of the river, but Lila had to fish another oar out of the water when one of them dropped it, and promise to sit still and not joggle the boat.

When they hit the bank, everyone fell off their seats.

'All right,' said Rambashi, picking himself up. 'Tie the boat to a good bit of tree or something and take the prisoner ashore.'

'Are we going to eat her?' asked one of the pirates. ''Cause I'm hungry.'

'Yes, we've had nothing to eat for days,' grumbled another. 'You promised we'd have a hot meal every evening.'

'That's enough of that!' said Rambashi. 'You're a pack of scurvy dogs. Take the prisoner up to the cave and stop complaining.'

Lila wasn't sure if she could run away *just* yet. Some of those pirates did look fierce enough to run after her. Though now she looked more closely, she saw their daggers were made of wood wrapped in silver paper, so they wouldn't be able to do her much damage.

'I hope you don't mind this little transaction,' Rambashi said, as they walked along a jungle trail. 'It's purely business.'

'Have you kidnapped me, then?' asked Lila.

'I'm afraid so. You're going to have to hand over all your money in a minute, and then we'll tie you up and hold you to ransom.'

'Have you done it before?'

'Oh yes,' he said. 'Lots of times.'

'What happens when you don't get any money?'

'Well, we . . .'

'We eat you,' said the hungry pirate.

'Ssh,' said Rambashi, waving his hand vaguely.

'You're not cannibals,' said Lila.

'We're blooming hungry,' said the pirate.

31

'Have you always been pirates?'

'No,' said Rambashi. 'I used to keep hens, but they all died of melancholy. So I sold the business and bought the boat . . . Oh no! Ssh! Stop! Don't move!'

The last pirates in the line, still grumbling, bumped into those in front, who stood behind Rambashi, transfixed with fear.

For there on the path ahead of them was a tiger. It swung its tail lazily from side to side, and raised its golden eyes at them, and then opened its mouth and roared so loudly that Lila thought the very earth was shaking. One of the smallest pirates put his hand in hers.

So there they stood, and the tiger was just gathering its strength to spring, when Lila suddenly remembered her self-igniting Crackle-Dragons. She took her hand back from the small pirate, reached into her bag, and took out the three she'd brought with her.

'Mind,' she said to Rambashi, and, pulling the string of the first one, she threw the firework in front of the tiger.

The mighty beast had never been so surprised in

its life. First one, then another, then yet another Crackle-Dragon snapped and flashed and sparked and leapt at him, and that was too much: with a whimper, the tiger turned and fled.

The pirates cheered.

'Magnificent!' cried Rambashi. 'Congratulations! I was about to stab him to death, of course, but never mind.' (Lila wondered how he would have done that with his silver-paper-covered knife, but she didn't say anything.) 'And of course,' Rambashi went on, 'this changes everything. We can't keep you hostage if you've just saved our lives. You'll have to be our guest instead. Stay with us overnight, why don't you?'

'We've got no food,' said someone. 'What's she going to eat?'

'We'll send Chang out to catch some fish,' said Rambashi cheerfully, shaking his head at the protests that arose. 'No, no, fish is *good* for you. Go on, Chang! Don't just stand there!'

'I can't,' said Chang. 'Look.'

They looked back at the river bank. *The Bloody Murderer* was drifting away, with the painter drifting in the water.

'Who tied it up?' said Rambashi.

One of the pirates looked down and tried to rub a hole in the ground with his big toe.

'Hmm,' said Rambashi. 'Fine pirates *you* are. I hope you're ashamed. But never mind! I've got a better idea. Miss!' he said to Lila, rubbing his hands. There was a bright gleam in his eye. 'Can I interest you in a little investment?'

'Well,' Lila said, 'I ought to be getting on.'

'No, really, this is a *much* better idea than piracy,' Rambashi said. 'It came to me in a flash, just as I saw the boat floating away. (I can't be cross with those fellows, they're like children really). Yes, all my best ideas come in a flash. And this one's a corker! Can't fail!'

'Is there any food in it?' said a pirate sourly.

'My dear boy! It's *built* on food! Just wait till you hear – I say! Miss! Just a little money – the safest investment you'll ever make—'

But Lila had walked away. As she went along the path she could hear his voice behind her.

'No, listen, boys – I know where we went wrong last time. I saw it in a flash. But this is an idea that'll suit your talents down to the ground. Look, let me draw you a picture . . .'

Lila would have liked to know what Rambashi's next plan was, but she was eager to hurry on. Mount Merapi was smoking and rumbling in the distance. She felt her heart lift when she saw it again, so powerful and dominating, and she thought, *I belong to that mountain, and it belongs to me!*

And on she went, with no other thoughts in her mind but that, and excitement putting a spring in her step.

Meanwhile, Chulak was getting ready to smuggle Hamlet out of his new home. The master had gone to bed early, groaning, but the slaves were still awake, and Chulak had to distract them.

'Now listen,' he said to them in the kitchen. 'You know you've got to do all you can to please the great White Elephant, or else the King'll be cross?'

They all nodded.

'Well, the Elephant's a bit restless. He never sleeps well the first night in a new place, so we'll have to play a game of Elephant's Footsteps to cheer him up. You have to go and hide your eyes in the garden, and when you think you can hear him coming, turn around. He likes playing that. Go on, go and wait in the garden, and I'll tell him when you're ready.'

The slaves all streamed out of the back door, and as soon as they were hiding in the garden with their eyes shut, Chulak unlocked the front door and led Hamlet out to the gate.

'It's a good thing they put down that carpet I ordered,' he whispered. 'You don't half make a row on the gravel.'

'Can we go past the Zoo?' Hamlet whispered.

'No, of course not! Never mind Frangipani.

It's Lila we've got to think about. And stop breathing so heavily . . .'

They tiptoed out of the gate, and found Lalchand waiting there with a tarpaulin, just as Chulak had asked.

'What's it for?' Lalchand whispered.

'For this,' said Chulak, and made Hamlet kneel down to have it laid over his back. 'So he doesn't show up so much in the dark.'

'Huh,' grumbled Hamlet. 'It's hot and scratchy and it smells like a marquee. Couldn't you find a nice blanket?'

'I don't think you realize your own size,' Chulak said.

'Do be careful!' said Lalchand. 'I ought to come with you – it's not a safe journey at all— Oh, I should have told Lila everything from the start! I should have trusted her! What a foolish old man I am!'

'Yes,' said Chulak. 'Still, never mind. We'll find her. Come on, Hamlet!'

And they set off. Lalchand stood watching them for a minute, until they'd disappeared in the dark streets.

But someone was watching Lalchand.

One of the slaves who'd come to play Elephant's Footsteps was hiding under a bush nearby; and as soon as he realized what he'd seen, he began to tremble. Helping the White Elephant to escape was a terrible crime. There'd be a terrible punishment – and there might be a great reward for the person who pointed out the criminal.

So when Lalchand began to trudge homewards, the slave silently followed him to find out who he was and where he lived.

Chulak and Hamlet walked all night, and when morning came they slept in a little valley under some thick trees. They woke up in the afternoon and, while Hamlet browsed on the leaves, Chulak went to the nearest village to ask the way to the Emerald Lake. He came back with an armful of bananas and some news.

'Guess what, Hamlet?' We're in luck! This is the night of the Full Moon. The Water Goddess comes out of the lake and grants people's wishes. Couldn't be better, my boy! Finish your leaves and let's be moving.'

They weren't the only people going to the Emerald Lake. The jungle paths were busy with families carrying picnic baskets, and even a troop of monkeys was heading in the same direction. Just before the sun set, Chulak and Hamlet saw a young man busily pinning up notices on the trees beside the path.

Chulak was about to read one when the young man caught sight of him.

'Hey! I know you!' he said. 'And him . . .'

'We know lots of people,' said Chulak. 'Is this the right way for the Emerald Lake?'

'Just along there. Here, can I . . . ?' The young man looked bashful.

Chulak knew what he wanted.

'Kneel down, Hamlet,' he said. 'Customer.'

Hamlet couldn't say anything with the young man there, but he gave Chulak a severe look as he knelt down. The young man daubed something on Hamlet's side with a stick and some mud, and gave Chulak a coin.

'Thanks!' he said. 'Wait till I tell the boss!'

And he ran off. Chulak read what he'd written:

EAT AT RAMBASHI'S JUNGLE GRILL

'Rambashi?' Chulak said. 'I've got an Uncle Rambashi. He used to be a chicken farmer.'

The notices on the trees were advertising the Jungle Grill as well. It was opening that very night, and there were meals at half-price if you brought in a voucher from one of the notices.

'It'll be nice to see Uncle Rambashi again,' Chulak said. 'Come on, it'll be dark in a minute.'

They hurried on. Soon they came out on the shores of the Emerald Lake. Under the trees at the edge of the water there stood some houses on stilts, with cooking fires and coloured lanterns, and as the tropical darkness covered the sky in less than five minutes, Chulak and Hamlet entered the village.

Naturally, a white elephant with an advertisement written on him caused a sensation, and soon Chulak and Hamlet were being followed by a crowd of excited children and some older people with nothing else to do. Even the troupe of dancers getting into their costumes for the ceremony couldn't resist, and the dancing-mistress had to run after them with her mouth full of safety pins to pull them back and scold them.

'Which way to Rambashi's Jungle Grill?' Chulak asked, and someone pointed along the shore to where a wooden building stood on stilts over the water. There was a terrace with coloured flags, and tables with checkered tablecloths, and lamps made out of wine bottles, and a cloud of smoke was coming from the kitchen, with the sounds of sizzling and bubbling and the smell of grilling meat and fish and spices.

'Just in time, Hamlet! What d'you think of that? And that's Uncle Rambashi!' said Chulak.

Rambashi, wearing a white apron over his tartan sarong, was ushering some customers on to the terrace when he saw Chulak.

'Chulak! My boy! How delightful to see you! And your – your friend – your pet – this excellent mobile advertising billboard! Come in, dear boy! Voucher? Oh, don't bother with that. Free food for everyone, in honour of the Ceremony of the Full Moon! (Of course I'll lose money on it, but we'll soon make it up. Wonderful publicity). Yes, that's right, ladies and gentlemen! Free meals tonight!'

'What about us?' said a waiter. 'When do we get our supper?'

'Customers first,' said Rambashi. 'You and the boys can have as much as you like later on.'

'I thought you were in the chicken business?' said Chulak, tucking in to a big plate of prawns and rice in satay sauce.

'Yes, but I had to give that up. I felt sorry for the hens, Chulak. So we took to the transport business for a while – river taxi, you know, with some freelance work on the side – but then came the opportunity to invest in the restaurant trade – where my talents truly lie, Chulak! – Yes, madam, our grilled lake trout is exquisite tonight – may I suggest some saffron rice to accompany it? And a flask of jasmine wine? Yes, all free! No charge! Compliments of the house . . .'

The Jungle Grill was certainly doing good business – or would have been, if Rambashi had been charging for it.

'I hope he knows what he's doing, Hamlet,' Chulak said, as the elephant browsed quietly on the banyan tree that overspread the terrace. 'He reckons it'll be such good publicity that they'll come back when he starts charging. I'm not so sure. Still, the food's good. Smoky, but tasty.'

Rambashi's cook was having trouble with the grill, which he kept having to throw water over when it got too hot. Clouds of smoke and steam kept billowing out, and the waiters rushed to and fro with full plates and dirty plates and flasks of wine and menus and coconuts full of ice cream.

Meanwhile, the village elders were preparing the lakeshore for the Full Moon ceremony. Chulak and Hamlet, full of supper, wandered along to have a look. The sand was swept and smoothed, lanterns were hung in the trees, and blossoms of all colours were scattered on the water. The path from the temple to the lake was crowded several deep on either side, and Chulak had to climb on Hamlet's back in order to see.

Then the ceremony began. A great drum sounded three times, and an orchestra began to play: gongs and xylophones and drums and cymbals and flutes. A line of dancers came out of the temple and swayed down the path towards the lake, their fingernails snapping and flicking like fireflies and their golden skirts shimmering in the lantern light.

The headman of the village struck a light and lit a scented candle in a paper boat, which he floated out onto the lake. The incense made the air sweet and rich. Very soon other paper boats were floating out to join it, and then a little child pointed at the treetops on the far side of the dark lake and said: 'Moon!'

The full moon was rising. And as it rose the music rose too, the gongs and the xylophones and the cymbals all summoning the Goddess from the lake.

And then she was there, though no-one had seen her arrive; it was as if she'd come when they were looking away, and when they looked back they saw her; though no-one had really looked away. She was floating to the shore on a raft of water-lilies, a beautiful lady in a robe the colour of the moon, with silver rings and amulets, and a necklace of jasmine flowers.

One after another the villagers bowed to her and asked her help: this woman for a sick child, that man for a good harvest, these lovers for a blessing on their marriage. The Goddess rebuked some for asking too much, though she never refused anyone in need. When they had all finished, and the Goddess was about to depart, Chulak gathered his wits and shook his head, because he was a little dazzled by

her beauty, and he thrust his way to the water's edge and knelt down.

'Goddess!' he said. 'Please hear me, too!'

But before the Goddess could answer, hands took him roughly and hauled him away.

'What are you doing, stranger?'

'Away with him! Defiling the lake!'

'Who is he? Who gave him permission?'

'Stone him! Turn him out!'

Chulak struggled. He could see Hamlet raising his trunk and shifting his feet, and he knew the elephant was getting angry.

'No!' he cried. 'Listen! I've got a special request! Let me just ask the Goddess!'

The high priest looked down, frowning. His face was shadowed and stern.

'How dare you come to this sacred place?' he said. 'The Goddess of the lake is not to be disturbed by your frivolous requests. Take him away! No! She shall not hear you! Be thankful we let you go with your life. Take him to the village boundary, and if he comes back, kill him!'

# CHAPTER FOUR

O ver the noise of the shouts and the struggle there came a sound like a mighty trumpet, and everyone fell still in fear. Chulak was frightened as well, though he knew what it was; for when Hamlet trumpeted, it meant he had nearly lost his temper.

But before anyone could move, the Goddess herself spoke. Her voice was soft and low, like the murmur of waves on a beach at night.

'What is the cause of all this commotion? Stop fighting at once. It is good of you to protect me from embarrassment, High Priest, but I should like to hear from this young man, and to see his friend the elephant. Come down to the water, both of you.'

49

Chulak looked at Hamlet, and saw that the great beast was embarrassed as well. Hamlet stepped through the crowd, being very careful not to tread on any toes, and knelt down next to Chulak on the sand. The slogans daubed on him were very clear in the moonlight. The Goddess read them, and asked Hamlet to turn around and show his other side.

' "Eat at Rambashi's Jungle Grill" . . . "Chang loves Lotus Blossom" . . .'

'I thought I'd washed that one off,' Chulak said.

'I think it's charming,' said the Goddess. 'But you mustn't do it any more. Your friend is too wise and noble to be written on, and if he could speak I'm sure you'd realize that yourself.'

And she looked at Chulak in such a way that he knew exactly what she meant, and felt ashamed.

'However,' she went on, 'I can see that your request is not a frivolous one. Tell me what you seek.'

'We've got a friend,' Chulak said eagerly, 'and she wants to be a Firework-Maker, you see. And she's done all the apprenticeship, but she wants to get some Royal Sulphur from Razvani the Fire-Fiend so as to qualify properly. So she's gone off by herself to Mount Merapi, only she didn't know about getting a flask of magic water for protection, and we don't want her to get hurt, so we've come to ask, please, as a great favour, if you could give us some, and then we'll chase after her and see if we can catch her up.'

The Goddess nodded. 'Your friend has good friends,' she said. 'But Mount Merapi is far away, and the journey is dangerous. You had better set off at once. And take great care!'

And as if she had known what they wanted all the time, she held out a little gourd fastened with

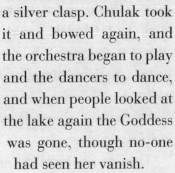

a silver clasp. Chulak took it and bowed again, and the orchestra began to play and the dancers to dance, and when people looked at the lake again the Goddess was gone, though no-one had seen her vanish.

Before they left, Chulak washed Hamlet clean in the lake. Some of the village children helped, but they didn't help for long, because soon there was something else for them to see: a great cloud of smoke and flames coming from the Jungle Grill.

'Oh dear, oh dear,' said Chulak. 'There goes Uncle Rambashi's latest plan, Hamlet. I could tell that cook was having trouble. I hope he's all right.'

'They're all safe,' said Hamlet. 'And the children are enjoying the fire.'

Squeals of delight and excitement were coming from the crowd as the roof fell in with a shower of sparks. Buckets of water were being passed from the lake, and Chulak could hear Rambashi saying, 'What a spectacle! What a splendid sight! D'you know, my boys, that gives me my best idea yet. All we have to do—'

'We haven't even had our meal!' cried one of the waiters.

'Time to go, Hamlet,' said Chulak, and they set off along the lakeshore towards the mountains in the distance.

By this time, Lila had come to the end of the jungle. Climbing all the time, she moved on and on, as the trees thinned out and the path became a mere track and then vanished altogether. All the jungle sounds, the clicking and buzzing of the insects, the cries of the birds and monkeys, the drip of water off the leaves, the croaking of the little frogs, were behind her now. When she had heard them she had enjoyed their company, but now there was nothing except the sound of her foot on the path and the occasional rumble from the mountain, which was so deep that she felt it through her feet as much as she heard it through her ears.

When night fell she lay down on the stony ground beside a rock and wrapped herself in her one blanket. The full moon shone right in her face and kept her awake, and she couldn't get comfortable because of the stones on the ground. Finally she sat up in annoyance.

But there was no-one to share her annoyance with. She'd never felt so lonely.

'I wonder . . .' she began to say, but shook her head. She hadn't come on this journey in order to wonder how things were at home. It was the way things were at home that had made her come on the journey, after all.

'Well, if I can't sleep, I might as well keep walking,' she said to herself.

She folded her blanket away, and re-tied her sarong and tightened her sandals, and set off again.

The ground became steeper and steeper. Soon she could no longer see the top of Mount Merapi, so she knew she must be climbing the side of it. There were no plants at all here, not even shrubs or grass: just bare rock and loose stones. And the ground was warm.

'I'm close,' she said to herself. 'It can't be far now—'

But as she said that, she set her foot on a stone and it rolled under her weight and she fell, and a dozen other rocks rolled down with her.

All the breath was knocked out of her, and she had none left to cry out with as the rocks pummelled and battered her.

The rocks bounded on down the mountain until finally they came to rest a long way below. Lila sat up gingerly.

'Ow,' she said. 'That was silly. I wasn't looking where I was putting my feet. I must be more careful.'

She got up, and found that one of her sandals had come off, and had tumbled down the mountain with the stones. It was nowhere to be seen. Very delicately she put her naked foot down, and found the ground hot beneath it.

Well, there was nothing she could do about that; and hadn't she come seeking fire? And hadn't she burned herself time and again as an apprentice? And what did she need delicate feet for anyway?

On she climbed, higher and higher. Before long she came to a part of the slope where all the stones were loose, and where she slid back two steps for every three she took upwards. Her feet and legs were bruised and battered, and then she lost her other sandal; and she nearly cried out in despair, because there was no sign of the Grotto – just an endless slope of hot rough stones that tumbled and rolled underfoot.

And her throat was parched and her lungs were panting in the hot thin air, and she fell to her knees and clung with trembling fingers as the stones began to roll under her again. She let go her little bag of food and her blanket; they didn't matter any more; the only thing that mattered was climbing on. She dragged herself on bleeding knees up and up, until every muscle hurt, until she had no breath left in her lungs, until she thought she was going to die; and still she went on.

Then one stone bigger than the rest began to shift above her as the little stones beneath it tumbled down. It slid and rolled towards her and she had no strength to move; but at the last second it bounded over her and rolled on down the mountainside in a cloud of dust and pebbles.

Where it had been, there was a great hole as tall as a house. The moonlight shone into it a little way, but the hole went deeper still, right into the heart of the mountain. A gust of sulphur-laden smoke came billowing out, and Lila knew she had found her goal: it was the Grotto of the Fire-Fiend.

# CHAPTER FIVE

She pulled herself up with shaking arms, and stepped inside. The floor was baking hot and the air was hardly breathable. She walked on, deeper into the earth, deeper than the moonlight went, and heard nothing but silence, and saw nothing but dark rock.

Harsh barren walls rose to left and right; she felt them with her bleeding hands. Then the tunnel opened out into a great cavern. She had never seen anything so gloomy and empty of life, and her heart sank, because she had come all this way and there was nothing here.

She sank to the floor.

And as if that were a signal, a little flame licked

out of the rocky wall for an instant, and went out.

Then another, in a different place.

Then another.

Then the earth shook and groaned, and with a harsh grating sound the rocky wall tore itself open, and suddenly the cavern was full of light.

Lila sat up, astonished, as red fire and flame licked and crackled at the rocky roof. All of a sudden the Grotto was alive with movement, as a thousand fire-imps swarmed upwards to dash themselves against the rock and smash into a thousand more, as a wide carpet of boiling lava spread from side to side, as the clang and clash of mighty hammers and anvils rang with the rhythm of a great fire-dance.

The cavern was full of light and noise. Thousands upon thousands of little fire-spirits toiled and blazed and swung hammers, and ran to and fro with handfuls of sparks, and swarmed against the rocky wall till it melted and slid downwards like soft wax. Then the greedy creatures plunged their red hands into it and lifted up the bubbling sulphur to their tiny mouths and ate and ate until another mass of rock slid down and smothered them.

And then into the heart of the light, and the fire and the noise leapt Razvani himself, the great Fire-Fiend, whose body was a mass of flame and whose face a mask of scorching light.

Thousands of fire-imps scattered as he landed, and even the blazing flames bowed down to him. And so did Lila.

In a voice like the roar of a forest fire, Razvani spoke.

'By what right have you come to my Grotto?'

She swallowed hard. It was difficult to breathe, because she seemed to be taking fire into her lungs as well as air.

'I want to be a Firework-Maker,' she managed to say.

He laughed a great laugh.

'You? Never! and what do you want from me?'

'Royal Sulphur,' she gasped.

At that he slapped his sides and laughed even harder, and a chorus of jeers and shrieks of merriment burst from all the fire-imps.

'Royal Sulphur? Did you hear that? Oh, that's good! That's funny! Well, speak, girl: have you the Three Gifts?'

Lila could only shrug and shake her head. She could hardly speak.

'I don't know what they are,' she said.

'So what were you going to exchange for the Royal Sulphur?' he roared.

'I don't know!'

'You were going to give *nothing* in exchange?'

She had nothing to say. She bowed her head.

'Well, you've come this far,' said the Fire-Fiend, 'and there's no going back. Now you're here you must walk in the flames, like every other Firework-Maker. I expect you've brought some magic water from my cousin the Goddess of the Lake? You've brought nothing for me, but I don't suppose you've forgotten to take care of yourself. Better drink it quickly!'

'I've got nothing!' Lila gasped. 'I didn't know about magic water or the Three Gifts – I just wanted to be a Firework-Maker! And I'll be a good one, Razvani! I invented self-igniting Crackle-Dragons and Shimmering Coins! I've learned everything my father could teach me! It's all I want – to be a Firework-Maker like him!'

But Razvani merely laughed.

'Show her the ghosts!' he cried, and clapped his blazing hands.

Instantly a crack shivered its way down the rock wall, and out of the opening came a procession of ghosts, each attended by fire-demons. The ghosts were so pale and transparent that Lila could hardly see them, but she heard them wailing.

'Beware! Look at me! I came without the Three Gifts!'

'Alas! Take warning from me! I hadn't worked at the craft and I wasn't ready!'

'Maiden, turn back! I was arrogant and head-strong! I didn't seek the water from the Goddess, and I perished in the flames!'

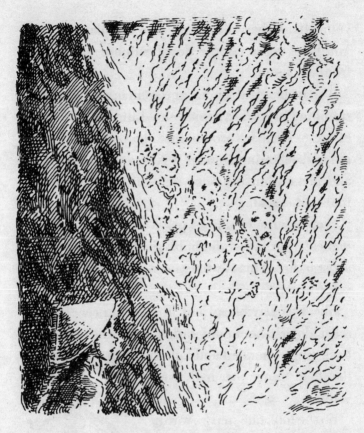

Wailing and weeping, the ghosts passed across the lake of fire, and vanished into a crack in the opposite wall.

'That's what happens to those who don't come prepared!' said Razvani. 'But now you must submit yourself as they did. Walk into my flames, Lila! You have come for the Royal Sulphur – receive it from my hands!'

And he laughed louder, and spun in a rapid dance, stamping his feet in a wide circle and causing a ring of fire to blaze up around him. Through the lashing red and yellow and orange, his face seemed to waver and flicker, but his voice rang out clearly over the roar and crackle:

'You want to be a Firework-Maker? Walk into my flames! Your father did in his time, and so did every artist in fire. This is what you've come for! Why are you waiting?'

She was terribly afraid. But she knew that she must do it; she would rather be a ghost than go back empty-handed and fail at the one thing she had ever wanted.

So she took one step forward, and then another, and her poor feet burned and blistered so that she cried out loud. Then she took another step, and when she knew she could bear it no longer she heard a great sound behind her, like a mighty trumpet. And through the blaze a voice was shouting:

'Lila! The water! Take it, take it!'

And there was a small figure beside her, thrusting something into her hands: a gourd! A drinking gourd with a clasp that she tore off, before lifting it to her parched lips and drinking, drinking, drinking deep.

All at once a marvellous coolness spread through her body and down to the tips of her toes. The pain vanished and the dryness in her throat and lungs was soothed and moistened. At the entrance to the cave behind her she could see Chulak, shrinking back and covering his face from the heat; and she could see Hamlet fanning him with his ears.

But she was in the heart of the fire, facing Razvani once again, and the flames were harmless now. They played like fountains of light; they rushed up her legs and arms and across her face like darting birds and she felt light and joyful as if she were a flame herself, dancing with pure energy and joy.

'So you have done it!' Razvani said to her. 'Welcome to the flames, Lila.'

'And . . . the Royal Sulphur?' she said.

'Ah, when you reach the heart of the fire, all your illusions vanish. Didn't your father tell you that?'

'Illusions? I don't understand!'

'The Royal Sulphur doesn't exist, Lila. There is no such thing!'

'Then . . . how can I be a Firework-Maker? I thought every Firework-Maker needed some Royal Sulphur to become a true artist!'

'Illusions, Lila. Fire burns away all our illusions. The world itself is all illusion. Everything that exists flickers like a flame for a moment, and then vanishes. The only thing that lasts is change itself. There is no Royal Sulphur. An illusion . . . Everything outside the fire is illusion!'

'But the Three Gifts – I don't understand! What are the Three Gifts, Razvani?'

'Whatever they are, you must have brought them to me,' he said.

And that was the last thing she heard from him, for as he said that he dwindled away, and the lake of fire darkened and became red rock, and then just rock, and all the myriad fire-imps became little feeble sparks that floated aimlessly for a second, and sank, and went out at once.

The grotto was bare again.

Lila turned away from where the fire had been. She was dazed and disappointed, calm and curious, pleased and puzzled; in fact she didn't know what she felt or who she was, for a moment. But then she saw Chulak and ran to him.

'Chulak, you saved my life! And you're hurt – you're burned – let me help you!'

He was shaking his head and tugging at her hand.

'Don't waste any time,' he said. 'We've got to hurry. Tell her as we go, Hamlet!'

They stumbled out of the grotto into the pale light of dawn, and Hamlet said:

'I'm sorry, Lila. I heard the birds talking at the foot of the mountain, and they said, "Look! The White Elephant! That's the very one who escaped from the city!" And I asked the bird what he knew, and he said, "The Firework-Maker helped you to escape. Someone saw and told the King, and now Lalchand has been arrested, and he's going to be executed!" Then he flew away to tell the other birds. Lila, we've got to go back as fast as we can. Don't waste time blaming anyone! Get on my back and hold tight.'

So, in a torment of fear that put Razvani and the Royal Sulphur and the Three Gifts completely out of her mind, Lila clambered up next to Chulak on the Elephant's back, and held on tight as Hamlet began to slither down the mountain in the light of dawn.

# CHAPTER SIX

How they did it Lila never knew – they stopped only for Hamlet to drink deeply from the river while Lila and Chulak snatched some fruit from the trees overhanging the bank – but after hours and hours of pounding and trudging and half running on blistered feet, they came to the outskirts of the city. The sun was setting.

Of course, Hamlet attracted a lot of attention as soon as he was seen, because everyone knew that the White Elephant had escaped. Soon they were surrounded by a curious crowd, all trying to touch Hamlet for luck, and before they'd got anywhere near the palace, they could move no further.

Lila was nearly weeping with fear and impatience.

'Have they killed my father yet? Is Lalchand still alive?' she asked, but no-one knew.

'Move out of the way!' Chulak shouted. 'Clear a space there! Make room!'

But they could only move forwards an inch at a time. Chulak could feel Hamlet getting angry, and he feared he wouldn't be able to control him. He stroked the elephant's trunk to try and keep him calm.

Then they heard shouts and the clash of swords from somewhere ahead, and the crowd parted at once. Word had reached the Palace and the King had sent his Special and Particular Bodyguard to escort Hamlet back to his royal home.

'About time too!' said Chulak to the General in charge. 'Come on, we're in a hurry. Clear the streets and stand aside.'

So the three of them, burnt and blistered and dusty and exhausted, were escorted into the Palace by the splendidly uniformed Bodyguard, who tried to look as if they'd found Hamlet all by themselves.

Poor Lila's heart was beating like a bird caught in a net.

'Prostrate yourselves!' said the Special and Particular General. 'Grovel! Faces to the ground! Especially yours, boy.'

They knelt on the stones of the courtyard in the light of flaming torches, and the Special and Particular Guard lined up to present arms as the King came in.

His Majesty stood in front of them. Lila could see his golden sandals, and then her anxiety got too much for her, and she knelt up and said in anguish, 'Please, Your Majesty – my father Lalchand – you haven't – he isn't – is he still alive?'

The King looked down sternly. 'He will die tomorrow morning,' he said. 'There is only one penalty for what he has done.'

'Oh, please! Please spare his life! It was my fault, not his at all! I ran away without telling him and—'

'Enough,' said the King, and he was so frightening that she stopped, just like that.

Then he turned to Chulak.

'Who are you?' he said.

Chulak got up at once, but before he could begin to speak, a Special and Particular Guard forced him down again.

'I'm Chulak, your Majesty,' he said. 'Can I look up? It's not easy to speak with a foot on my neck.'

The King nodded, and the guard stood back. Chulak knelt up beside Lila and said:

'That's better. You see, Your Majesty, I'm the Elephant's Special and Particular Groom, in a manner of speaking. He's a delicate beast, and if he's handled wrong there's no end of trouble. And as soon as I found out he'd escaped I set off at once, Your Majesty. I swam across the river and I climbed mountains and fought my way through the jungle and—'

Suddenly all the breath was knocked from Chulak's body and he sprawled on the ground again. Something soft had knocked him in the middle of the back, and he knew it was Hamlet's trunk. Hamlet had never done that to him before, and he rolled over in surprise to see the Elephant giving him a special and particular look, and then he realized what he must do.

He struggled up again and faced the King.

'Your Majesty, the Elephant has just made a

request. He and I have got this unusual way of communicating, you see. He is asking for an audience alone with Your Majesty.'

Even the Special and Particular General could hardly restrain a snigger at the idea of an animal asking to speak to the King, but he changed it into a cough when the King glared at him.

'Alone?' the King said to Chulak.

'Yes, Your Majesty.'

'The White Elephant is a rare and wondrous beast,' the King said. 'For his sake I shall grant his request. And if it turns out that you are playing a joke on me, you may be certain that tomorrow morning you will have very little to laugh about. General, take these two outside and leave me alone with the Elephant.'

The guards hauled Lila and Chulak out of the courtyard and into the kitchen compound where the smell of grilling meat and spices reminded them both that they hadn't eaten for twenty-four hours.

'Don't worry,' said Chulak. 'Hamlet will explain everything.'

'Is he going to *talk* to the King, then? I thought his talking was a great secret!'

'These are special and particular circumstances. Oh, that rice! Oh, that plum sauce! Oh, the smell of those spices!'

And even Lila's fear couldn't prevent her mouth from watering, she was so hungry.

And then they waited. Minutes went by, and more minutes, and poor Lila was so stiff and tired she nearly fell asleep standing up, as worried as she was. But finally there was a stir of movement by the door.

'Prisoners!' barked the General. 'Fall in and follow me!'

Two lines of Guardsmen all stamping proudly, with Chulak and Lila between them followed the General back to the courtyard.

When they had bowed properly the King said, 'Firstly, as for you, Chulak, I am suspending my judgement. I have it on good authority that you have never sought to harm the Elephant, but I am not convinced that you are the best person to look after him. You are dismissed.'

Chulak swallowed hard, and looked at Hamlet.

Then the King turned to Lila and said, 'I have considered your case very carefully. It is highly unusual, and this is my decision. I shall spare the life of Lalchand the Firework-Maker, but only on one condition. Next week, as the whole city knows, we celebrate the Festival of the New Year, and I have invited the greatest artists in fireworks from all over the world to contribute to a display.

'Now here is my plan: I shall announce a competition for the final night of the Festival. A firework display will be put on by each of my invited artists, and Lalchand and Lila will take part as well. The prize of a golden cup will be awarded to the artist whose display receives the longest applause. That is all that the other competitors will know.

'But you and Lalchand will know something else as well. If your display wins, Lalchand will receive the prize and go free; but if you lose the competition, he loses his life too.

'That is my decision, and there will be no appeal. You have a week to save your father's life, Lila.

'Guards, see them out, and release Lalchand the Firework-Maker into the care of his daughter.'

And Lila barely had time to think before she found herself at a little side-door of the Palace, where a servant held up a flickering torch for her to wait by.

But she didn't have to wait long; from behind a door came the sound of a chain falling to the ground, and then the door opened and there was Lalchand.

Neither of them could speak, but they hugged each other so tightly that they could barely breathe. When they'd had enough, they realized how hungry they were, and hurried home.

'We'll get some fried prawns from the stall in the alley, and eat them as we work,' said Lalchand.

'Have they told you what the King decided?' Lila asked.

'Yes. But I'm not worried. We'll have to work as we've never worked before, but we can do it . . .'

And Lila forgot all about the Royal Sulphur and

the Three Gifts. There was no time to wonder about them now. She hurried into the workshop with some dishes of rice and prawns and fried vegetables, and they scooped them up absent-mindedly as they worked.

'Father,' said Lila. 'I've got an idea. Supposing . . .'

She took a stick of charcoal from the bench and drew some quick sketches. Lalchand's eyes lit up.

'Aha! But begin slowly. Build up to it.'

'And on the way back from Mount Merapi,' she said, 'when we stopped by the river, I saw how some vines had twisted around each other, and I thought of a way of delaying the fuses. Making them burn at different rates.'

'Impossible!'

'It isn't. Look, I'll show you . . .'

And so they set to work.

# CHAPTER SEVEN

The invited Firework-Makers arrived the very next day, together with all the other famous artists and performers: the Chinese Scout and Guide Opera Company, Señor Archibaldo Gomez and his Filipino Mambo Orchestra, the Norwegian National Comedy Cowbell Players, and many others. They all disembarked from the *S.S. Indescribable* with their luggage and their instruments and their costumes, and began to rehearse at once.

The first Firework-Maker was Dr Puffen-flasch, from Heidelberg. He had invented a multi-stage rocket which exploded at a height of two thousand feet into the shape of a gigantic Frankfurter sausage, while a huge instrument he'd invented played *The Ride of the Valkyries*. Herr Puffenflasch had gone to immense trouble to prepare something just as spectacular for the New Year Festival, and he supervised the unloading of his enormous equipment with scrupulous care.

The second visiting Firework-Maker was Signor Scorcini from Naples. His family had been making fireworks for generations and his speciality was noise. For this display he had invented a full-scale representation of a battle at sea, featuring the noisiest fireworks in the world, and with King Neptune emerging from the water to see fair play and declare peace.

The third and last Firework-Maker was Colonel Sam Sparkington from Chicago. His display was called *The Greatest Firework Show in the Galaxy*, and it usually featured Colonel Sparkington himself, wearing a white Stetson hat and riding a horse. This time, it was rumoured, he had invented an especially exciting display, involving something never before seen in the art of pyrotechnics.

And while the three visiting Firework-Makers were assembling their displays, Lalchand and Lila

were working on theirs. Time flew past. They barely slept, they scarcely washed, they hardly ate. They mixed vats of Golden Serpents, they ordered a ton and a half of flowers of salt, they invented something so new neither could think of a name for it until Lila said:

'Foaming . . .' and snapped her fingers.

'Moss?' said Lalchand.

'That's it!'

Lila showed Lalchand her delayed-fuse method, but it didn't work until he thought of adding some spirits of saltpetre, and then it worked magnificently. It would let them set off fifty or a hundred fireworks at once, which had previously been impossible. Then Lalchand came up with a spectacular finale, but it depended on something even more impossible: burning a fuse underwater. Lila solved that by thinking of caustic naphtha, and they tried it, and it worked.

And before they knew it, the day of the Festival arrived.

'I wonder where Chulak is?' Lila said vaguely, but her mind was really on the Foaming Moss.

'I hope Hamlet's being treated well,' said Lalchand, but he was really thinking about the caustic naphtha.

And neither of them said anything about the King's decision, but they couldn't get it out of their minds.

After a hasty sleep and a hurried breakfast, they

loaded up the fried-prawn seller's cart (he'd lent it to them because he was taking the day off) and trundled it through the streets to the Royal Park, where the displays were going to take place. The batik-seller followed behind with another cart, and behind him came the sandalwood-carver from down the street with a third, all laden with fireworks.

But when they reached the ornamental lake, Lila and Lalchand stopped in dismay.

For there was Dr Puffenflasch supervising the final stages of putting together about fifteen tons of equipment, all swathed in a neat tarpaulin, and swarmed over by a dozen pyrotechnicians in white overalls, with clipboards and stethoscopes.

And next to him there was Signor Scorcini clambering about on a model galleon even longer than the Royal Barge, all bristling with cannons and flares, while his Neapolitan crew were arguing and gesticulating in a Neapolitan dialect as they lowered a vast, nodding, bearded model of King Neptune below the water.

And next to him Colonel Sparkington was rehearsing his display. There was a gigantic red, white, and blue rocket with a saddle on the back of it, and on a scaffolding platform high above the treetops there was a model of the moon, with dozens of craters all being loaded with exciting-looking things . . .

It was too much. Lalchand and Lila looked at the vast displays being prepared by the other artists, and then at their three little cart-loads, and their hearts sank.

'Never mind,' said Lalchand. 'Ours is a good display, my love. Think of the Foaming Moss! They've got nothing like that.'

'Or the underwater fuse,' said Lila. 'Look, they're having to light that sea-god by hand. We can do better than that, Father!'

'Of course we can. Let's get to work . . .'

They unloaded their materials, and the batik-painter and the sandalwood-carver took their carts back, with the promise of free tickets to the show.

The day passed quickly. All the Firework-Makers were very curious about one another's displays, and kept wandering over to have a look, with the excuse of borrowing a handful of red fire powder or a length of slow fuse. They came to look at Lalchand and Lila's, and they were very polite, but it was plain that they didn't think much of it.

And all of them were desperate to look under Dr Puffenflasch's tarpaulin, but he kept it tightly tied down.

Promptly at seven o'clock the sun went down, and ten minutes later it was dark. People were beginning to arrive already, with rugs to sit on and picnic baskets, and from the Palace nearby came the sound of bells and gongs and cymbals. All the Firework-Makers were busy in the dark, putting the finishing touches to their displays, and they all wished one another good luck.

Then came a roll of drums, and the Palace gates were thrown open. By the light of a hundred flickering torches, a great procession made its way to the grandstand by the lake. The King was being carried in a golden palanquin, and the royal dancers were swaying and stepping elegantly alongside. Behind them, decorated with gold cloths and jewels of every colour, with his tusks and toenails painted scarlet, came Hamlet.

'Oh, look at the poor thing!' said Lila. 'He looks utterly miserable. I'm sure he's lost weight.'

'He's missing Chulak, that's what it is,' said Lalchand.

Hamlet stood disconsolately beside the grand-stand as the King declared the competition open.

'A prize of a gold cup and a thousand gold coins will be awarded to the winner!' the King proclaimed. 'Only your applause will decide who has won. The first contestant will now begin his display.'

The Firework-Makers had drawn lots to see which order they would perform in. Dr Puffenflasch was first. Of course the audience had no idea what to expect, and when his mighty rockets whizzed up into the night sky, and his gigantic *Bombardenorgelmitsparkenpumpe* began to play *The Ride of the Valkyries*, hurling out great lumps of Teutonic lava, they all burst into oohs and aahs of excitement. Then came the highlight of his display. Out of the darkness arose a tribute to the King's favourite dish: a gigantic pink prawn, fizzing and sputtering, which began to revolve faster and faster until it all went out in a shower of salmon-coloured sparks and a sonorous chord from the *Bombardenorgelmitspark-enpumpe.*

The applause was colossal.

'That was good,' said Lila apprehensively. 'That big prawn. Really . . . *big.* And pink.'

'A bit too obvious,' said Lalchand. 'Don't worry. Nice pink, though. Must ask him for the recipe.'

The next to go was Signor Scorcini with his Neapolitan Pyrotechnicians. Red, green and white rockets whizzed up in the air to explode with enormous bangs that echoed all round the city, and then the galleon came ablaze with sparklers and Catherine wheels, and a chorus of galley-slaves made of Roman candles moved their oars stiffly to and fro. Suddenly a giant octopus rose up out of the water, waving ghastly green tentacles, and attacked the ship. The sailors fired all kinds of Jumping Jacks and Whizzers and Incandescent

x

Fountains at it, and then they tipped cascades of Greek Fire over it from barrels lashed to the masts. The noise was indescribable. Just when it looked as if the ship was about to tip over, up came King Neptune, waving his trident, accompanied by three mermaids. The band struck up, and the mermaids sang a jolly Euro-song called *Boom Bang-a-Bang*, the octopus waved its tentacles in time, and more rockets went off in rhythm with the music.

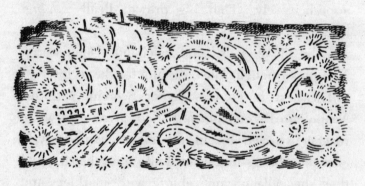

The audience loved it. They roared with delight.

'Oh dear,' said Lalchand. 'That was very exciting. Oh dear, oh dear.'

'But didn't you see how they had to light the sea-god?' Lila said. 'They had to wait till he was right out of the water and a little man in a boat reached up with a match. Just wait till they see our underwater fuse!'

When the applause had died down, Colonel Sparkington's display began. First a lot of saucer-shaped fireworks whizzed down from the darkness and landed on the grass. That got a round of applause on its own, because fireworks usually went up, not down. Then the famous moon swung into view, way up above the treetops, and Colonel Sparkington galloped in on a white horse made of tiny Catherine wheels, waving his Stetson hat to the audience, who were in such a good mood that they cheered and cheered.

Lila could see an official beside the King, carefully counting the seconds that each burst of applause lasted. She swallowed hard.

Then came the climax of Colonel Sparkington's display. After stamping out the flying saucers with his Catherine-wheel horse, the gallant Colonel jumped aboard the red, white and blue rocket. A Cherokee chieftain galloped in on a Palomino pony and fired a blazing arrow at the tail of the rocket, which ignited at once and whooshed up along a wire to the moon, with Colonel Sparkington waving his hat all the way.

As soon as it landed, a dozen craters flipped open and out came some little round-faced moon people with big eyes and pointed ears.

The audience went wild. The moon people waved the flags of all nations and bowed to the King, Colonel Sparkington distributed rockets to them all, and they whizzed off in all directions, singing a song called *Sparkington For Ever*. You could hear the clapping, the cheering and whistling and stamping, for miles around.

Lila and Lalchand looked at each other. There was nothing to say. But then they hugged each other very tightly, and ran to their places, and as soon as the audience was settled again, they began their display.

The first thing that happened was that little lotus flowers made of white fire suddenly popped open on the water, with no hint of where the fire had come from. The audience fell silent, and when the flowers began to float across the dark lake like little paper boats, they were completely hushed.

Then a beautiful green light began to glow beneath the water, and rose slowly upwards to become a fountain of green fire. But it didn't look like fire – it looked like water, and it splashed and danced like a bubbling spring.

And while the fountain played over the lake, something quite different was happening under the trees. A carpet of living moss seemed to have spread itself across the grass, a million million little points of light all so close together that they looked as soft as velvet. A sort of 'Aaah' sound came from the audience.

Then came the most difficult part. Lila had designed a sequence of fireworks based on what she had seen in the Grotto of the Fire-fiend, but it all depended on the delayed-action fuses working as they should – and of course they hadn't had time to test them properly. If some of the fireworks went off a second too early or a second too late, the whole show would make no sense.

But there was no time to worry about that now. Quickly and expertly she and Lalchand touched fire to the end of the master fuses, and held their breath.

First came a series of slow dull explosions like the beat of a muffled drum. Everything was dark. Then a red light shivered downwards, leaving a trail of red sparks hanging in the air, like a crack opening in the night. The solemn drumbeats got louder and louder, and everyone sat very still, holding their breath, because of the irresistible feeling that *something* was going to happen.

Then it did. Out of the red crack in the night, a great cascade of brilliant red, orange and yellow lava seemed to pour down and spread out like the carpet of fire in the Grotto. Lila couldn't resist glancing up very swiftly at Dr Puffenflasch, Signor Scorcini, and Colonel Sparkington, and saw them all watching wide-eyed like little children.

When the lava carpet had flowed down almost to

the edge of the lake, the speed of the drumbeat got faster, and sharp bangs and cracks beat the air between them. And suddenly, dancing as he had in the Grotto, Razvani himself seemed to be there, whirling and stamping and laughing for joy in the play of the eternal fire.

Both Lila and Lalchand forgot everything else, and seized each other's hands and danced as well. Never had they produced such a display! No matter what happened, it was worth it, everything was worth it, for a moment of joy like this! They laughed and danced for happiness.

But their fire was not Razvani's, of course, and it couldn't last for ever. The great red firework-demon burnt himself out, and the last of the red lava poured slowly into the lake, and then the little white lotus-boats, now scattered over the water like the stars in the sky, flared up and burnt more brightly than ever for a moment before all going out at once.

Then there was silence. It was a silence that got longer and longer until Lila could hardly bear it, and she gripped Lalchand's hand so tightly it nearly cracked.

And when she thought it was all over, Lalchand was doomed, everything was ruined, there came a mighty yell from Colonel Sparkington.

'*Yeee-haa!*' he cried, waving his hat. And—

'*Bravissimo!*' shouted Signor Scorcini, clapping his hands above his head. And—

'*Hoch! Hoch! Hoch!*' roared Dr Puffenflasch, seizing the cymbals from his *Bombardenorgelmitsparkenpumpe* in order to clap more loudly.

The audience, not to be out-applauded by the

visiting Firework-Makers, joined in with such a roar and a stamping and a clapping and a thumping of one another on the back and a whistling and a shouting that four hundred and thirty-eight doves roosting in a tree ten miles away woke up and said, 'Did you hear that?'

Of course the court official timing the applause had to give up. It was obvious to everyone who had won, and Lalchand and Lila went up to the Royal platform where the King was waiting to present the prize.

'I keep my word,' the King said quietly. 'Lalchand, you are free. Take this prize, the pair of you, and enjoy the Festival!'

Hardly knowing what was happening, Lila and Lalchand wandered back to the darkness of the firing area under the trees. And he might have been going to say something, and she might have spoken too, but suddenly the air was filled with the sound of a mighty trumpet.

'It's Hamlet!' said Lila. 'Look! He's excited about something!'

A moment later they saw what the elephant had seen, and Lila clapped her hands for joy. A little figure came strolling onto the grass in front of the Royal platform and bowed elegantly to the King. It was Chulak.

'Your Majesty!' he said, and everyone stopped to hear what he was going to say. 'In honour of your great wisdom and generosity to all your subjects, and in celebration of your many glorious years on the throne and in the hope of many even more glorious ones ahead, and as a tribute to the splendour of your courage and your dignity, and in recognition . . .'

'He's on the verge of being cheeky,' Lalchand said, as Chulak went on. 'I can see the King tapping his foot. That's a bad sign.'

'. . . So, your Majesty,' Chulak finished, 'I have the honour to present to you a group of the finest musicians ever heard, who will sing a selection of vocal gems, for your delight. Your Majesty, my lords, ladies and gentlemen – Rambashi's Melody Boys!'

'I don't believe it!' said Lila.

But she had to, because there were Rambashi's ex-pirates in person, wearing smart scarlet jackets and tartan sarongs. Rambashi himself, beaming all over his broad face, gave a deep bow and prepared to conduct them – but before he could begin, there was an interruption.

One of the dancing-girls who had accompanied the royal procession from the Palace suddenly squealed and cried, 'Chang!'

And one of the Melody Boys held out his arms and cried, 'Lotus Blossom!'

'What did he say?' said Lalchand. 'Locust Bottom?'

The young couple ran to each other with their arms outstretched, but stopped, embarrassed, as they realized that everyone was watching.

'Well, go on,' said the King. 'You might as well.'

So they kissed shyly, and everyone cheered.

'And now I'd like an explanation, please,' said the King.

'I was a carpenter, Your Majesty,' said Chang, 'and I thought I ought to seek my fortune before I asked Lotus Blossom to marry me. So I went off and sought it, and that's what I'm doing here, Your Majesty.'

'Well, you'd better start singing then,' said the King.

So Chang ran back to the Melody Boys, and Rambashi counted them in, and they began to sing a close-harmony song called *Down by the Old Irrawaddy*.

'They're very good, aren't they?' said Lalchand.

'I'm amazed!' said Lila. 'After all the trouble they've had finding the right thing to do! Who would have thought it?'

The song came to an end and the King led the applause. While Rambashi was announcing the next, Lila went to talk to Chulak, and found him stroking Hamlet's trunk. The Elephant looked happy, but of course he couldn't say so with everyone around.

'Have you heard?' said Chulak. 'Hamlet's going to get married! Oh, well done, by the way. We heard the racket they made when you won. I always knew you would. And I've got my job back!'

Hamlet cuffed him gently around the head.

'So Frangipani said yes?' said Lila. 'Congratulations, Hamlet! I'm so pleased. What made her change her mind?'

'Me!' said Chulak. 'I went and told her about his gallant deeds up on Mount Merapi, and she was conquered. Actually she said she'd loved him all the time, but she hadn't liked to say so. Old Uncle Rambashi's doing well, isn't he?'

The audience was clapping and cheering as Rambashi announced the next song. When the Melody Boys were singing and swaying to *Save The Last Mango For Me*, Lila wandered back to Lalchand, who was deep in talk with the three other Firework-Makers. They all stood up politely and asked her to join them.

'I was just congratulating yer pa on that mighty fine display,' said Colonel Sparkington. 'And half the credit goes to you, Miss. That trick with the little bitty boats that all went out at once – that's a lulu. How d'you work that stunt?'

So Lila told them about the delayed action fuses,

because there are no secrets among true artists. And Dr Puffenflasch told them the art of pink fire, and Signor Scorcini told them how he made the octopus's legs wave, and they all talked for hours and liked one another enormously.

And very late, when they were extremely tired and when even Rambashi's Melody Boys had run out of songs to sing, Lila and Lalchand found themselves alone in the great garden, on the grass under the warm stars; and Lalchand cleared his throat and looked embarrassed.

'Lila, my dear,' he said, 'I've an apology to make.'

'Whatever for?'

'Well, you see, I should have trusted you. I brought you up as a Firework-Maker's daughter; I should have expected you to want to be a Firework-Maker yourself. After all, you have the Three Gifts.'

'Oh yes! The Three Gifts! Razvani asked if I had them, and I didn't know – but then he said I must have brought them after all. And what with rushing back to the city and preparing the display, and worrying about whether we'd manage to save your life, I forgot all about them. And I still don't know what they are.'

'Well, my dear, did you see the ghosts?' said Lalchand.

'Yes, I did. They didn't bring the Gifts, and they failed . . . But what *are* the Three Gifts?'

'They are what all Firework-Makers must have. They are all equally important, and two of them are no good without the third. The first one is talent, and you have that, my dear. The second has many names: courage, determination, will-power . . . It's what made you carry on climbing the mountain

when everything seemed hopeless.'

Lila was silent for a moment, and then said, 'What is the third?'

'It's simply luck,' he said. 'It's what gave you good friends like Chulak and Hamlet, and brought them to you in time. Those are the Three Gifts, and you took them and offered them to Razvani as a Firework-Maker should. And he gave you the Royal Sulphur in exchange.'

'But he didn't!'

'Yes, he did.'

'He said it was illusion!'

'In the eyes of Razvani, no doubt it is. But human beings call it wisdom. You can only gain that suffering and risk – by taking the journey to Mount Merapi. It's what the journey is for. Each of our friends the other Firework-Makers has made his own journey in a similar way, and so has Rambashi. So you see, you didn't come home empty-handed, Lila. You did bring back the Royal Sulphur.'

Lila thought of Hamlet and Frangipani, now happily engaged. She thought of Chulak, restored to his job, and Chang and Lotus Blossom, restored to each other.

She thought of Rambashi and the Melody Boys, happily snoring in the Hotel Intercontinental, dreaming of the triumphant show-business career that lay ahead of them. She thought of the other Firework-Makers and how they'd welcomed her as one of them.

And then she realized what she had learned. She suddenly saw that Dr Puffenflasch loved his pink fire, and Signor Scorcini loved his octopus, and Colonel Sparkington loved his funny moon-people. To make good fireworks you had to love them, every little sparkler or Crackle-Dragon. That was it! You had to put love into your fireworks as well as all the skill you had.

(And Dr Puffenflasch's pink fire really was very pretty. If they combined some of it with a little glimmer-juice, and some of that doubling-back powder they'd never found a use for, they might be able to—)

She laughed, and turned to Lalchand.

'*Now* I see!' she said.

And so it was that Lila became a Firework-Maker.

# PHILIP PULLMAN

## I Was a Rat!
### or The Scarlet Slippers

Illustrated by Peter Bailey

# The Daily Scourge

## LOVE AT THE BALL

*by our Court Correspondent*

Yes – it's official!

Hunky Prince Richard has found a bride at last!

At midnight last night, the Palace announced the engagement of His Royal Highness Prince Richard to the Lady Aurelia Ashington.

'We are very happy,' said the Prince.

It is understood that the Royal Wedding will be celebrated very soon.

*Our Romance Correspondent writes:*

It was like something out of a fairy tale. The charming prince, the mysterious girl who seemed to vanish into nowhere only to be found by the merest chance . . .

They met at the Midsummer Ball. To the music of a shimmering waltz, they danced like thistledown, and they only had eyes for each other.

'I've never seen him so in love,' said a close friend of the Prince. 'I think this time it's the real thing.'

It was certainly fast. By midnight, they were head over heels in love, and it only took another day for the engagement to be made official.

## PRINCE RICHARD – THE LOVER

A fact-file of the playboy prince's previous girlfriends – *page 2,3,4,5,6,7,8*

## LADY AURELIA – WHERE DOES SHE COME FROM?

Our reporters investigate the background of the lovely young Princess-to-be – *page 9*

*Stars in their eyes!*

# I Was A Rat!

Old Bob and his wife Joan lived by the market in the house where his father and grandfather and great-grandfather had lived before him, cobblers all of them, and cobbling was Bob's trade too. Joan was a washerwoman, like her mother and her grandmother and her great-grandmother, back as far as anyone could remember.

And if they'd had a son, he would have become a cobbler in his turn, and if they'd had a daughter, she would have learned the laundry trade, and so the world would have gone on. But they never had a child, whether boy or girl, and now they were getting old, it seemed less and less likely that they ever would, much as they would have liked to.

One evening as old Joan wrote a letter to her niece and old Bob sat trimming the heels of a pair of tiny scarlet slippers he was making for the love of it, there came a knock at the door.

Bob looked up with a jump. 'Was that someone knocking?' he said. 'What's the time?'

The cuckoo clock answered him before Joan could: ten o'clock. As soon as it had finished cuckooing, there came another knock, louder than before.

Bob lit a candle and went through the dark shop to unlock the front door.

Standing in the moonlight was a little boy in a page's uniform. It had once been smart, but it was sorely torn and stained, and the boy's face was scratched and grubby.

'Bless my soul!' said Bob. 'Who are you?'

'I was a rat,' said the little boy.

'What did you say?' said Joan, crowding in behind her husband.

'I was a rat,' said the little boy again.

'You were a – go on with you! Where do you live?' she said. 'What's your name?'

But the little boy could only say, 'I was a rat.'

The old couple took him into the kitchen, because the night was cold, and sat him down by the fire. He looked at the flames as if he'd never seen anything like them before.

'What should we do?' whispered Bob.

'Feed the poor little soul,' Joan whispered back. 'Bread and milk, that's what my mother used to make for us.'

So she put some milk in a pan to heat by the fire and broke some bread into a bowl, and old Bob tried to find out more about the boy.

'What's your name?' he said.

'Haven't got a name.'

'Why, everyone's got a name! I'm Bob, and this is Joan, and that's who we are, see. You sure you haven't got a name?'

'I lost it. I forgot it. I was a rat,' said the boy, as if that explained everything.

'Oh,' said Bob. 'You got a nice uniform on, anyway. I expect you're in service, are you?'

The boy looked at his tattered uniform, puzzled.

'Dunno,' he said finally. 'Dunno what that means. I expect I am, probably.'

'In service,' said Bob, 'that means being someone's servant. Have a master or a mistress and run errands for 'em. Page-boys, like you, they usually go along with the master or mistress in a coach, for instance.'

'Ah,' said the boy. 'Yes, I done that, I was a good page-boy, I done everything right.'

'Course you did,' said Bob, shifting his chair along as Joan came to the table with the bowl of warm bread and milk.

She put it in front of the boy and without a second's pause he put his face right down into the bowl and began to guzzle it up directly, his dirty little hands gripping the edge of the table.

'What you doing?' said Joan. 'Dear oh dear! You don't eat like that. Use the spoon!'

The boy looked up, milk in his eyebrows, bread up his nose, his chin dripping.

'He doesn't know anything, poor little thing,' said Joan. 'Come to the sink, my love, and we'll wash you. Grubby hands and all. Look at you!'

The boy tried to look at himself, but he was

reluctant to leave the bowl.

'That's nice,' he said. 'I like that . . .'

'It'll still be here when you come back,' said Bob. 'I've had my supper already, I'll look after it for you.'

The boy looked wonder-struck at this idea. He watched over his shoulder as Joan led him to the kitchen sink and tipped in some water from the kettle, and while she was washing him he kept twisting his wet face round to look from Bob to the bowl and back again.

'That's better,' said Joan, rubbing him dry. 'Now you be a good boy and eat with the spoon.'

'Yes, I will,' he said, nodding.

'I'm surprised they didn't teach you manners when you was a page-boy,' she said.

'I was a rat,' he said.

'Oh, well, rats don't have manners. Boys do,' she told him. 'You say thank you when someone gives you something, see, that's good manners.'

'Thank you,' he said, nodding hard.

'That's a good boy. Now come and sit down.'

So he sat down, and Bob showed him how to use the spoon. He found it hard at first, because he would keep turning it upside down before it reached his mouth, and a lot of the bread and milk ended up on his lap.

But Bob and Joan could see he was trying, and he was a quick learner. By the time he'd finished, he was quite good at it.

'Thank you,' he said.

'That's it. Well done,' said Bob. 'Now you come along with me and I'll show you how to wash the bowl and the spoon.' While they were doing that, Bob said, 'D'you know how old you are?'

'Yes,' said the boy. 'I know that all right. I'm three weeks old, I am.'

'Three weeks?'

'Yes. And I got two brothers and two sisters, the same age, three weeks.'

'Five of you?'

'Yes. I ain't seen 'em for a long time.'

'What's a long time?'

The boy thought, and said, 'Days.'

'And where's your mother and father?'

'Under the ground.'

Bob and Joan looked at each other, and they could each see what the other was feeling. The poor little boy was an orphan, and grief had turned his mind, and he'd wandered away from the orphanage he must have been living in.

As it happened, on the table beside him was Bob's newspaper, and suddenly the little boy seemed to see it for the first time.

'Here!' he said, delighted. 'That's Mary Jane!'

He was pointing to a picture of the Prince's new fiancée. The Prince had met her just the other day and they'd fallen in love at once, and the royal engagement was the main story of the week.

'She's going to marry the Prince,' said Bob, 'but she ain't called Mary Jane. That ain't the kind of name they give princesses.'

'I expect you must have got confused,' said Joan. 'And you can't go anywhere else tonight, that's for sure. We'll make you up a bed, my love, and you can sleep here, and we'll find the proper place for you in the morning.'

'Ah,' he said. 'I didn't know that proper place, else I'd have gone there tonight.'

'Look, we'll have to call you something,' said Bob.

'Something,' the boy said, as if he was memorising it.

'A proper name,' said Joan. 'Like . . . Kaspar. Or . . .'

'Crispin,' said Bob. 'He's the saint of shoemakers, he is. That's a good name.'

'I bet there's a saint of washerwomen, too,' said Joan. 'Only no-one's ever heard of her.'

'Well, if it's a her, it'd be no good as a name for him, would it?'

'No, probably not,' she said. 'I don't suppose . . . I don't suppose we could call him Roger, could we?'

Roger was the name they would have called a son of their own, if they'd ever had one.

'It's only for tonight,' said Bob. 'Can't do any harm.'

'Little boy,' said Joan, touching his shoulder. 'We got to call you by a name, and if you ain't got one of your own, we'll call you Roger.'

'Yes,' said the little boy. 'Thank you.'

They made up a bed in the spare room, and Joan took his clothes down to wash. They gave Roger an old nightshirt of Bob's to wear, and very small he looked in it, but he curled up tightly, looking for all the world as though he were trying to wrap a long tail around himself, and went to sleep at once.

'What are we going to do with him?' said Bob, squeezing the page-boy uniform through the mangle. 'He might be a wild boy. He might have been abandoned as  a baby and brung up by wolves. Or rats. I read about a boy like that only last week in the paper.'

'Stuff and nonsense!'

'You don't know,' he insisted. 'He as good as told us. "I was a rat," he said. You heard him!'

'Rats don't have page-boy uniforms,' she said. 'Nor they don't speak, either.'

'He could have learned to speak by listening through the walls. And he could have found the uniform on a washing line,' Bob said. 'You depend on it, that's what happened. He's a wild boy, and he was brung up by rats. You can read about that kind of thing every week in the paper.'

'You're a silly old man,' said Joan.

# THE PRIVY

Next morning Joan found the little boy lying in a heap of torn sheets and a terrible tangle of blankets and feathers, fast asleep.

She was going to cry out, because she feared that something had come in at the window and attacked him in the night; but he was sleeping so peacefully among all the destruction that she couldn't bring herself to wake him, though she was in despair over the damage.

'Come and look,' she said to old Bob, and he stood open-mouthed in the doorway.

'It looks like a hen-run after a fox has been in,' he said.

There wasn't a sheet or a blanket that hadn't been

torn into strips. The pillow was burst open, and feathers lay like snow over the whole bed. Even Bob's old nightshirt lay in tattered strips around the thin little body on the mattress.

'Oh, Roger,' said Joan. 'What have you done?'

The boy must have learned his name, because he woke up as soon as she said it, and sat up cheerfully.

'I'm hungry again,' he said.

'Look at what you've done!' she said. 'What were you thinking of?'

He looked around proudly.

'Yes, it was hard, but I done it,' he said. 'There's a lot more that needs chewing and tearing and I'll do that for you later.'

'You shouldn't tear things up!' she said. 'I've got to sew them all together again! We don't live like that, tearing things to pieces! Dear oh dear!'

The more she looked, the more damage she saw. It was going to take hours to repair.

Bob said, 'Did you do that because you was a rat?'

'Yes!' said Roger.

'Ah, well, that explains it,' the old man said, but

121

Joan was in no mood to listen.

'That's got nothing to do with it! Never mind what he *was*, it's what he is *now* that matters! You shouldn't tear things up like this!' she cried, and she took his thin little shoulders and shook him, not hard, but enough to startle him.

'You come down the kitchen with me,' said Bob, 'and I'll tell you a thing or two. But first let's have some more manners. You've upset Joan, so you have to say sorry.'

'Sorry,' said the boy. 'I understand now. Sorry.'

'Come along,' said Bob, and took him by the hand. He could see Roger fidgeting, and guessed what he wanted to do, and took him to the privy just in time. 'Whenever you want to do that, you come in here,' he said.

'Yes, I will,' said the boy. 'That's a good idea.'

'Now come and have your breakfast. Wrap them pieces of nightshirt around you, you can't walk around naked, it ain't decent.'

Roger sat and watched Bob cut two slices of bread and prop them on the range to toast.

'I'll cook you an egg,' the old man said. 'You like eggs?'

'Oh, yes,' said Roger, 'thank you. I like eggs a lot.'

Bob cracked it into the frying pan, and Roger's jaw dropped as he saw the white spitting and bubbling and the golden yolk glistening in the middle.

'Ooh, that's pretty!' he said. 'I never seen the inside of an egg!'

'I thought you'd ate 'em before.'

'I ate 'em in the dark,' Roger explained.

'What, when you was a rat?'

'Yes. Me and my brothers and sisters, we ate 'em in the dark, yes.'

'All right then,' said Bob peaceably, and slid the fried egg onto a plate, and buttered the toast.

Roger could barely hold himself back, but he remembered to say, 'Thank you,' before he put his face right down onto the plate and drew it back at once, gasping at the heat. His eyes brimming with tears, yellow yolk dripping off his mouth and nose, he turned to Bob in distress.

'Oh, I forgot you don't know how boys eat eggs,' the old man said. 'You probably thought you was a rat still, I expect.'

'Yes,' said Roger unsteadily, wiping at the mess with his fingers and licking them hard. 'I couldn't see the spoom, so I used me face.'

'It's a spoon, not a spoom. For eggs, you got to use a knife and fork. Here, do it like this, you copy me.'

Ignoring the tears and the egg on his face, Roger tried hard to do as Bob showed him. It was much harder to eat the egg with a fork than it had been to spoon up the bread and milk, but whenever he got discouraged, Bob told him to take a bite of toast. Roger held it up in both hands, and chewed it swiftly with his front teeth.

'I like toast,' he said. 'And egg.'

'Good. Now listen. We got to find out where you come from, and if there's someone who ought to be looking after you. Because you can't look after yourself, you're too little. And you can't stay here, because . . . Because you don't belong to us, see?'

'I want to stay here. I don't want to go anywhere.'

'Well, we got to do what's right. There's clever folk in the City Hall, they know what's right. We'll go along there by and by.'

'Yes, that's right,' said Roger.

# THE CITY HALL

The office they needed was at the top of a grand staircase and along a panelled corridor. Bob and Joan had to hold the boy's hands, because he kept making little twitching movements as if he wanted to run away.

'D'you want the privy again? Is that it?' said Bob, and Joan hushed him for using a rude word in an important place, but he said, 'There's times when the privy is the most important place.'

'No,' said Roger, 'I just want to see what the wood on the walls tastes like.'

'He's an odd one, all right,' said Joan.

But she looked down at him fondly all the same, and he did look smart, with his brown hair brushed neatly and stuck down with water, and his uniform washed and pressed, and his vivid black eyes gazing around.

In the office where they deal with lost children, they had to sit down while a lady filled in a form. Bob was anxious to get things right.

'Properly speaking, we oughter gone to the Found Children Office, because this is a found child, only there ain't one as far as we could see,' he told her. 'So we come here instead.'

'You'd better tell me the details,' said the lady.

She took one of a dozen very sharp pencils out of a jar.

Roger watched her hand move to the jar, but he didn't watch it go back to the paper. As soon as he saw the pencils, he fell in love with them. His whole heart longed for them.

So while the lady and Bob and Joan leant across the desk talking, Roger's hand crept off his lap and slowly, carefully, over to the jar. He couldn't help it any more than a dog can help tiptoeing round the corner to eat the cat's food.

Bob was puzzled by what the lady was saying, which was why he was leaning over the desk to peer at the form she was filling in.

'No, no,' he said, 'that can't be right. He's got to come from somewhere. Someone must be missing him.'

'I can assure you,' she said, 'our records are very thorough. There are no lost children in the city. Not one, boy or girl.'

'But what about found children?'

'There's nothing we can do about found children. We deal with lost ones.'

'Gor,' said Bob, 'I'm baffled.'

'Have you asked him where he comes from?' the lady said.

And they all turned to Roger.

He looked up, pleased to be noticed, but a little guilty too. The stump of the pencil was just sticking out of his mouth, and he quickly sucked it inside and pressed his lips together; but the lead had marked his mouth, and there were little flecks of red paint all round it too.

Joan said, 'Child, what have you been doing?'

He tried to answer, but his mouth was full of pencil.

The lady said, 'That pencil was the property of the City Council! I shall have to ask you to pay for it!'

Bob paid up. It seemed a lot of money for a pencil. Roger could see he'd done something wrong, and as soon as he'd swallowed the last of it, he said, 'Sorry.'

'That's all very well, but you don't mean it, you bad boy,' said Joan, 'that's the trouble.'

The little boy was bewildered. Did he have to do something else as well as say sorry? What did *meaning it* mean? He looked from one grown-up to another, but they were all talking again.

'He must have said *something*,' the lady said. 'I'm trying to help you, though it's not my job to. I've shown you a lot of patience.'

Roger looked for the patience, but since he didn't know what they looked like, he supposed she meant the pencils.

'He said he was a rat,' Bob said. 'Not now, I mean he didn't say I *am* a rat, he said I *was* a rat. That's all he said.'

129

The lady looked at them all with distaste.

'I've got plenty to do without listening to non-sense,' she said.

'Well,' said Bob, 'all right. We won't trouble you any more.' And he got up, as massive as a hill beside the little boy. 'All I can say,' he went on, 'is that you ain't been much help. Good day to you.'

And with Roger between them, the old couple walked out of the City Hall.

'Ain't I going to stay there?' said the boy.

'No,' said old Bob.

'Is that because I'm a bad boy?'

'You ain't a bad boy.'

'But Joan said I was.'

'She was muddled,' said Bob, frowning. 'And now I'm muddled too.'

# THE ORPHANAGE

S ince it wasn't far away, they decided to go to the orphanage, just in case. But when they stood outside it, and looked at the broken windows and the cracked brickwork and the missing tiles on the roof, and smelt the orphanage smell drifting out of it (stale cigarette smoke, boiled cabbage, and unwashed bodies were the better parts), and heard someone crying steady sobs of misery through an upstairs window, Bob and Joan looked at each other and shook their heads.

They didn't need to speak. Holding Roger's hand, they turned and walked away.

# THE POLICE STATION

There was a blue light outside the police station and a stout sergeant on duty at the desk. Roger looked at everything: the poster about Colorado beetles, the pictures of wanted criminals, the notices about bicycle safety. Since he couldn't read, he liked the picture of the Colorado beetle best. It looked very tasty.

'Well?' said the duty sergeant.

'We found this little boy last night,' said Bob. 'He don't know where he comes from. We thought we ought to bring him here.'

'I *do* know where I come from,' said Roger. 'I come from down under the market. There's a broken gutter behind the cheese stall and we had a nest in there. I was a rat,' he added, to make it clearer for the policeman.

The sergeant gave him a long cold look.

'Did you know there's such an offence as wasting police time?' he said.

'No, he's confused,' said Bob, anxious to explain. 'That's all it is. He probably had a bang on the head. He'd forgotten his name and all.'

'I know it now though,' said the boy. 'I'm Roger.'

'Surname?' asked the sergeant.

'My surname . . .' said Roger, then worked it out. 'My surname is Sur Roger,' he declared, nodding firmly. 'That's who I am all right.'

'And we been to the City Hall,' Joan said, 'but they couldn't help, and—'

'And you're the only other place we could think of,' said Bob.

'If he's had a bang on the head,' said the sergeant, tapping a pencil on the desk, 'he ought be took to the hospital.'

'Ah, we didn't think of that,' said Joan.

Roger was watching the sergeant's hand.

'That's a nice patient,' he said to him.

'Eh?'

'That patient you got. You been chewing the flat end. I like chewing the pointy end first.'

The sergeant gaped, and then recovered his wits.

'Did you notice that?' he said. 'When I said *hospital*, he said *patient*. That proves it. He's had a bang on the head. Either that or he's an escaped lunatic. But in any case he ought to be at the hospital. We can't take him here, we haven't got the facilities for lunatics, and in any case he ain't committed an offence. Yet,' he added, glaring down at Roger.

# The Hospital

'No,' said the receptionist, 'he's not one of ours.'

They were very busy. People with broken legs or saucepans stuck on their heads sat waiting to be dealt with; doctors in white coats rushed about listening to heartbeats or taking temperatures; nurses emptied bedpans or bandaged cuts and grazes. It was the best place Roger had been in yet.

'But he might have had a bang on the head!' said Joan. 'Poor little boy, he thinks he was a rat!'

'H'mm,' said the receptionist, and wrote *rodent delusion* on a pink slip of paper.

'You got a lot of patients,' said Roger, looking with great interest at her desk.

'Got to be patient here,' she said, and passed the slip to the nearest doctor.

That puzzled Roger, but he soon forgot it. The doctor was an important-looking man with a smart black beard, and he said, 'Follow me.' So Bob and Joan took Roger into the consulting room, and watched anxiously as the doctor examined him.

First he felt all round Roger's head.

'No cranial contusions,' said the doctor.

Roger was fascinated by the rubber tube the doctor had round his neck, and when the doctor put the two hooks on the end into his own ears and placed the other end against Roger's chest, he could hardly hold himself back. His mouth was watering so much that he dribbled.

'Good appetite?' the doctor asked.

'Very good indeed,' said Joan. 'In fact—'

'Good,' said the doctor, twiddling Roger's knees.

Joan thought she'd better keep quiet.

The doctor examined Roger all over, and seemed to find only a healthy little boy.

'So what's this rodent delusion?' he said finally.

'Well, he says he was a rat,' said Bob. 'He's convinced of it.'

'A rat, were you?' said the doctor. 'When did you stop being a rat, then?'

'When I turned into a boy,' said Roger.

'Yes, I see. When was that?'

Roger twisted his lips. He looked at Bob for guidance, but the old man couldn't help, and neither could Joan.

'Dunno,' the boy said finally.

'And why did you stop being a rat?'

'Dunno.'

'Do you know what you are now?'

'I'm a boy.'

'That's right. And you're going to stay a boy, d'you hear?'

'Yes,' said Roger, nodding seriously.

'No more of this nonsense.'

'No.'

'Mustn't worry your . . .' The doctor hesitated. He'd been about to say 'your parents' but he looked at Bob and Joan again and said, 'Granny and Grandpa.'

Joan sat up a bit sharply. Roger looked puzzled.

Bob took Joan's hand.

'He's no worry to us,' he said. 'As long as he's all right.'

'He's perfectly all right,' the doctor said. 'A normal healthy little boy.'

'But what should we do with him?' Joan said.

'Send him to school, of course,' said the doctor. 'Now I'm busy. Run along. Good day to you.'

# The Daily Scourge

# PALACE MAKE-OVER!

To celebrate the royal marriage, the palace is to be spectacularly redecorated.

OUT go fuddy-duddy antiques and dusty old pictures.

IN come designer furniture and a new, bright, up-to-the-minute look.

The redecoration is being carried out by attractive blonde, Sophie Trend-Butcher, 23, the brilliant young designer. The wallpaper is being hand-printed in gold.

While the work is being carried on in the palace, the royal family is staying at the Hotel Splendifico.

*The old...*

*...and the cool*

## THE SCOURGE SAYS:

Yes, the redecoration is costing a fortune.

Yes, the money is coming from you and me.

## BUT THIS IS OUR ROYAL FAMILY!

*For Heaven's sake, where is our national pride?*

We have the finest designers and craftspeople in the world – and here is a chance to show what they can really do.

And don't let's forget Prince Richard and his radiant bride-to-be.

*Are they supposed to live in a museum?*

Let's get behind the royal family in their attempt to bring the palace up to date!

# School

Since they hadn't had any luck, Bob and Joan took the little boy back home with them. He was perfectly content to trot along holding their hands, looking this way and that, for all the world as though he did belong to them.

'Granny and Grandpa,' said Joan scornfully.

'Well, that's not so bad,' said Bob. 'He might have thought *we* were rats, and all.'

'But what are we going to do with him?'

'Blowed if I know. But I don't want to spend another day trailing about and getting nowhere. I shall have to work late tonight, and I'm blooming tired.'

Roger didn't eat his bedclothes that night, though

Joan thought the wooden bed-posts looked a little gnawed, and there was a damp splinter or two under his pillow the next morning.

'There's a good boy,' she said, cooking him some porridge on the range. 'You eat this and I'll take you down the school.'

Bob stayed at home to catch up with his cobbling. 'Listen carefully and do what the teacher says,' the old man told him. 'That's the way to learn.'

The school was a big building smelling of children. Roger liked it at once. There were boys and girls running about outside and throwing balls and fighting each other and shouting, and he thought this would be a fine place to spend a day.

'But you're not in fact his, er, any relation at all?' said the Head doubtfully to Joan as she stood holding Roger's hand in front of his desk.

'No. But we're looking after him for the time being, and the doctor said we had to bring him to school,' she said.

'I see,' said the Head. 'Well, Roger, how old are you?'

'Three weeks,' said Roger.

'Don't be silly now. That's not a good way to start.

141

If you were only three weeks old you'd still be a baby. How old are you? Answer me properly this time.'

Roger shifted uneasily and looked up at Joan.

'He's not sure,' she said. 'I think he's lost his memory, poor lamb. He wouldn't know a thing like that.'

'He looks about nine,' said the Head. 'He can go in Mrs Cribbins's class. She won't stand any nonsense.'

A bell rang loudly and all the children stopped running and shouting and fighting and came inside. Roger was disappointed that the fun seemed to have stopped, but he sat where the teacher told him to, next to a boy with a runny nose.

'Now get out your pencils,' said Mrs Cribbins, 'and we'll have some arithmetic.'

Roger hadn't got a pencil, of course, or he'd have eaten it already. So he just watched as the other children took out theirs, and he knew he'd learned another word: *arithmetic* meant *snack*.

But to his absolute amazement the other children put the tasty ends of their pencils onto pieces of paper and drew lines with them. Roger had no idea you could do that, and he was so surprised and delighted that he laughed out loud.

'What's the joke?' snapped Mrs Cribbins. 'What's so funny? Eh?'

'They're making lines with their patients!' Roger said, eager to share his discovery.

'You're playing a dangerous game with *my* patience,' said Mrs Cribbins. 'Haven't you got a pencil?'

'No,' said Roger.

Mrs Cribbins couldn't believe that any pupil would come to school so badly prepared, and thought he was being cheeky.

'Go and stand in the corner,' she snapped.

Roger was happy to do that. He could smile at all the other children. But she made him face the wall, and that wasn't so interesting. And then the boy with the runny nose found a rubber band in his pocket and flicked it hard at Roger's neck.

Mrs Cribbins's back was turned, so naturally when Roger shouted and jumped and rubbed his neck she thought he was being naughty.

'I'm warning you,' she said, 'one more piece of nonsense and you're going to the Head.'

All the other children were enjoying it no end, and as soon as she turned away, someone else flicked another rubber band. Roger shouted again, and spun round to find Mrs Cribbins making for him with her hand raised.

Whether she would have smacked him or not no-one knew, because she didn't get any closer. Roger, seeing a threat, leapt up to bite her hand.

He got a good mouthful of it and shook hard, and Mrs Cribbins shrieked and whacked him with her other hand, and the two of them struggled back and forth while the other children gasped with delight. Of course, the more she struggled, the more frightened Roger became and the tighter he bit, until at last she tugged her hand away. Roger, wild-eyed, was trembling and panting with his back to the wall, and no-one was laughing any more.

'Right,' said Mrs Cribbins, 'that's it for you, my lad.'

The door opened. There was the Head.

'What is all this noise?' he demanded.

'Look!' said Mrs Cribbins, holding up her hand. 'Look what this child has done! He's drawn blood! I'm bleeding!'

Actually she had to squeeze quite hard to force a drop of blood out, but it was real blood, sure enough.

The room was full of wide-open eyes, staring at the Head, at Mrs Cribbins, at Roger.

The Head seemed to get bigger and bigger, and Roger to get smaller and smaller.

'Come with me,' said the Head in a dangerous voice.

All the children knew that voice. It was the voice that meant he was going to use the cane. He didn't use it very often but the occasions when he did were terrifying. There would be a deep silence over the whole school, and a sick feeling in everyone's stomach, and no-one would dare to look at the victim before he went into the dreadful place where he'd be beaten, or to speak to him after he came out, sniffling and limping. And everyone would be quiet and unhappy for a day or so afterwards.

And now Roger was going to be caned, and

everyone knew it but him.

He thought the Head was taking him away from the cruel woman who'd frightened him, so he smiled up at him and said, 'You can make lines on paper with them things. I thought they was called patients at first but they got other names too. I never knew you could make lines with 'em.'

All the children sat open-mouthed. How could this new boy dare to speak to the Head in this familiar friendly way? It was the cheekiest thing they'd ever heard. Some of them felt shocked, and some felt gleeful at the thought of the extra punishment he'd surely get, and some felt admiration.

'This way,' said the Head.

Roger followed.

Silence fell over the classroom. Mrs Cribbins ran some water over her hand and dried it on her handkerchief and took a plaster from her handbag and carefully placed it over the bite, and the children watched her solemnly without making a sound.

Then, just as she was opening her mouth to tell them to turn back to their work, there came a wild scream from down the corridor.

No-one had ever heard a scream like that. When

a boy went to be caned, he tried as hard as he could to make no noise at all, and some of the toughest ones managed to stop themselves even from whimpering, and were greatly admired for it. But not even the most babyish victim would have screamed as long and as wildly as Roger was screaming. The sound seemed to drill into everyone's head and scrape round and round in their skulls. Some of them put their hands over their ears.

Those who didn't block off the sound soon heard other sounds too: the Head's voice raised in anger, furniture crashing, doors banging, footsteps running down the corridor – it was the most exciting arithmetic lesson they'd ever had.

'Look, he's running away!' shouted a girl, and pointed out at the schoolyard.

Roger was racing for the gate, with the Head in red-faced pursuit. All the children crowded to the window to watch, ignoring Mrs Cribbins's efforts to make them sit down. They jumped and clapped and

laughed with shocked delight as Roger fought and screamed and bit and kicked and finally tore himself free, leaving the Head flailing at the empty air behind him.

Then Roger scrambled up and over the gate in a second or so, and vanished round the corner.

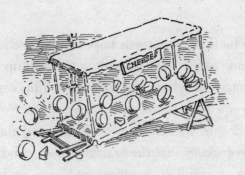

# No Escape

Roger ran in terror through the streets and alleys till he came to the market-place, where he ran up and down between the stalls, looking this way and that, and gulping and shaking with sobs. His face was wet and his nose was running and he looked a thorough mess.

Finally he got down on all fours and crawled under the cheese stall and made for the drainpipe in the corner; but that was a bad mistake. He wasn't quite as small as he thought he was, and

before he knew what was happening, he'd knocked away one of the trestles holding the stall up.

At once the whole top fell down. Cheeses rolled, slid, flopped and bounced in all directions. Somehow, every dog in the area suddenly learned that there was free cheese in the market-place, and within seconds a yapping, barking mob was making for the overturned stall. Roger was terrified of dogs, and when he saw them coming he screamed and cowered in the corner, where it was easy to catch him.

And five minutes later Roger was in the police station again.

'Who's that?' said the sergeant, as the constable came back to report his arrest. 'Little boy in a page's uniform? Let me look at him.'

Roger was crouching in the corner when the sergeant opened the cell door, and as soon as he saw daylight he tried to dart out, but the sergeant grabbed him.

'Ah, I thought it was you,' he said. 'Born trouble-maker, you are. As soon as I heard the words "market" and "cheese", I remembered you, just like that. Good thing I made a record of your address. See how your old auntie and uncle feel about coming down here to bail you out.'

When Bob arrived, he wasn't pleased at all.

'Well, Sergeant?' he said, across the counter. 'What's the boy done? Last thing I knew, he was at school.'

'Ah,' said the sergeant triumphantly, 'well he ain't any more. And he's in real trouble, your lad. Mayhem and criminal damage. I shouldn't wonder if it amounted to riot. Bring him out, Constable.'

'Riot? How can one little boy have a riot all on his own?'

The constable came out with Roger firmly in his grip. As soon as the boy saw Bob, he smiled up with happy relief.

'Ah, I was worried,' he said. 'It was all because I started to worry. But I wouldn't have got worried if the Head hadn't hit me.'

'He hit you?' said Bob. 'Why?'

'I don't know. It's mysterious,' said Roger. 'She just called him a Head, but he wasn't only a head. I thought he was just a head, on a table maybe, or he might have had a little stand, and I wanted to see it work. But he had arms and legs and everything. And I didn't know what he was going to do. He made

151

me bend over and I thought he was going to play leap-frog like I seen 'em in the playground, only suddenly whoosh! He hit my tail with a blooming stick! Ooh, that hurt awful. I wished he *was* a head with no arms and legs, then he wouldn't be able to hurt boys like that. So I ran away and I got in a muddle with the cheese. Then they caught me and put me in that room in there. Can we go now?'

'Sergeant, this ain't a desperate criminal,' said Bob. 'This is a little boy who don't know what's what. You ain't going to use the whole majesty of the law to punish a little boy for a bit of mischief, are you?'

'What about the damage to my stall?' demanded the cheesemonger, who had just arrived. 'And all my cheeses! Who's going to pay for them?'

Bob's heart sank. 'I suppose I'll have to pay for the damage,' he said. 'Make up the account and send it to me. I'm not a rich man, mind.'

'Sergeant,' said the constable, 'ain't this the boy who had some tale about being a rat?'

'Yes,' said Roger eagerly. 'I had a tail all right. It was a good 'un.'

'Be quiet,' said the sergeant sternly. 'Rats don't

belong in decent society. They ought to be exterminated.'

Roger didn't know what exterminated meant, of course, but he didn't like the sound of it. He clung tight to Bob and said nothing.

They agreed that Bob would pay for the cheese, and that Roger would behave himself in future.

'And if I see you back here,' the sergeant said, 'you'll be in terrible trouble. Don't you forget it.'

# The Daily Scourge

# SIX OF THE BEST

Six MPs are standing out against the proposal to ban the cane in schools.

'It made me the man I am!' claimed Sir Bernard Brute, MP. 'Children today are getting out of control. They must be beaten hard and often.'

*Sir Bernard Brute, MP, demonstrating the strength of his convictions*

Some teachers claim that the cane has no place in the caring and compassionate society they want to bring about.

'It is a relic of the Middle Ages,' said a teacher yesterday. 'We no longer need to rely on torture to encourage good behaviour.'

But other teachers disagree.

'There is a hard core of violent hooligans in our schools,' said Mr George Hackett, Head of St Lawrence's Primary School. 'If we take away the cane, we will leave teachers without the power to defend themselves.'

## THE SCOURGE SAYS:

### KEEP ON WHACKING!

These feeble so-called 'experts' who say that the cane is cruel are helping no-one.

A quick smack never did any child any harm.

And in today's schools there are some little brutes and bullies who could do with a taste of the cane to keep them in order.

*Support the six of the best!*

Vote in our readers' poll on *page 10.*

# A Curious And Interesting Case

It was a fine sunny morning, and the Philosopher Royal was taking a nap.

Normally at this time of day the King liked to chat with the Philosopher Royal over a cup of coffee and a biscuit, discussing things like why toast always fell on the buttered side or whether flies looped the loop before landing on the ceiling, but with the royal family away at the Hotel Splendifico while the palace was being decorated ready for the royal wedding, there was little call for philosophy.

The servant who woke the Philosopher Royal up for lunch was a cousin of the constable who'd arrested Roger, and he told him all about it, knowing the old man's curious turn of mind.

'Said he was a rat?'

'Said he *used* to be a rat, sir. He was ever so sure about it. My cousin said it give him a creepy feeling all up his spine. He don't like rats.'

The Philosopher Royal made a note of the policeman's name, and after lunch he went to the police station to ask about the case. The sergeant was very impressed to see his card.

'Now when I see the word "Philosopher" in connection with the word "Royal",' he said, 'I wonder whether I'm right in guessing that you might have met the Prince's fiancée. What's she like? Is she as pretty as she looks in her pictures?'

The Philosopher Royal told him. 'But this boy who said he was a rat,' he went on. 'Have you got his address?'

'Not *was*,' said the sergeant. 'He said he used to be, but he wasn't any more. Oh, yes, it's all on file.' The sergeant read out Bob and Joan's address. 'But you be warned by me,' he said, 'that boy's a bad influence, rat or no rat. He'll come to a bad end.'

'I am most grateful,' said the Philosopher Royal. 'Good day to you.'

In the cobbler's shop Bob was waxing some thread. 'Morning, sir,' he said. 'What can I do for you?'

'You are Mr Bob Jones? Guardian of a boy called Roger?'

Bob looked alarmed. Then he looked careful.

'What's he done now?' he said.

'I would like to see him. Is he at home?'

'He's in the laundry room, helping my wife. You got to keep an eye on him, else he eats the soap. But who might you be, sir?'

'My interest is purely philosophical. May I see the boy?'

'Well, I don't see why not. Step this way, sir . . .'

Bob led the Philosopher Royal into the laundry room, which was full of warm steamy air. Joan was stirring some sheets in hot water with a big stick, and Roger was feeding a pillowcase into the mangle and squeezing the water out, tasting it from time to time.

'Mrs Jones?' said the Philosopher Royal. 'And Roger?'

Joan dried her hands and gathered Roger close to her. He peered up at the Philosopher Royal with his bright black eyes wide.

'Did you want some washing done, sir?' said Joan.

'No, no. My washing is done by the palace laundrymaids. I was hoping for a brief talk with your, er, with the young, with Roger.'

'He's not in trouble, is he, sir?' she said anxiously.

'No, no,' said the Philosopher Royal, 'this is a purely philosophical investigation.'

'Well, I suppose you could talk in the parlour if you liked . . .' she said, and led them through to a little room that smelled of furniture polish. 'I'll leave you to get on with it,' she said, 'because I've got a lot of washing to get through. Now, Roger, you be a good boy, and answer the gentleman politely. No nibbling.'

When Joan had left, the Philosopher Royal sat down and looked at Roger: a little boy of eight or nine, perhaps, dressed in a uniform.

'Now, Roger,' he began, 'why are you wearing a page-boy's uniform?'

'I dunno. I expect I forgot, but I'm not sure. If I could remember whether I'd forgot it I'd know if I had, but I probably forgot without remembering it.'

The Philosopher Royal was used to problems of epistemology, so he made sense of that with no trouble at all.

'I see,' he said. 'Now, would you let me examine you properly? It won't hurt,' he added.

'I expect so,' said Roger.

The Philosopher Royal was thinking of the book he'd write about this. What a discovery! There'd been children brought up by wolves before, but no-one had ever studied a child brought up by rats. It would make him famous! Rubbing his hands together, the Philosopher Royal left Roger chewing one of the tassels off the lampshade and went to speak to Bob.

'You want to take him away?' said Bob, frowning.

'Just to make some tests, you know – weigh him, measure him, that sort of thing. To see how a human child is affected by being among rats. It's a question of exceptional philosophical importance.'

'But when he was among the rats he weren't a human child,' said Bob. 'He's a human child *now*.'

'Well, of course, he wasn't really a rat,' said the Philosopher Royal, thinking how simple these people were.

'H'mm,' said Bob. 'You bring him back here this evening, and don't you hurt him. I don't know what legal responsibility we got, but he come to us and knocked, and that's enough for me. And he's a lovely little feller, for all his chewing. You look after him proper.'

'No question about that,' said the Philosopher Royal.

Roger had finished off all the tassels except one. Bob sighed and snapped off the last one and dropped it into the little boy's hand.

'I dunno how you digest some of this, I really don't,' he said.

'No,' said Roger. 'It's a mystery to me.'

'Now you go along with this gentleman and do as he says, all right? And he'll bring you back home in time for supper.'

Roger bowed goodbye to Bob and went out happily with the Philosopher Royal.

# A Philosophical Investigation

On the way up the palace staircase, Roger said, 'I been here before.'

'Are you sure, my boy?' said the Philosopher Royal.

'Oh, yes. I slid down them banisters.'

The Philosopher Royal thought: *Cannot distinguish truth from fantasy.*

Once in his study the first thing he did was to weigh Roger, and then he measured him, and then he listened to his heart, and then he counted his teeth. He didn't learn much, but he did notice that Roger had perfectly human teeth, not a bit like a rat's. There was no point in looking for a tail: the boy was human all the way down, no doubt about it.

'Now then, Roger,' said the Philosopher Royal, 'let's do some mental tests. What is two and three?'

'Two and three what?' said Roger, very puzzled.

'Well, if you have two things, and you add three more, how many have you got?'

'Ah, that depends. If they're really little things you still wouldn't have very much, but if they're big things you couldn't even carry 'em,' Roger explained.

'Yes, I see. What's half of four?'

'Cheese,' said Roger. 'Cheddar. Quarter of four's Cheddar too. Quarter of five'd be Stilton. One is Lancashire, two is Wensleydale—'

'I don't understand,' said the Philosopher Royal, writing everything down.

'Well, they come to the stall and they ask for a half pound of number four, and that's Cheddar, or a quarter pound of number five, and that's Stilton. I likes that one. You get worms in it. Only sometimes they say just half instead of half a pound, that's how I knew what you meant. You got to keep your wits about you,' he told the Philosopher Royal.

'Oh, indeed. Now tell me, when did you learn to speak?'

163

'When I changed into a boy.'

'Yes, but you didn't really *change*, did you? You were a boy all the time. Perhaps you *thought* you were a rat. But rats can't—'

'I never thought at all when I was a rat! I just was! So I never thought I was a rat. I never started thinking till I was a boy. Now I think I'm a boy. But it's making me confused. I hope I don't get irritated.'

'All right,' said the Philosopher Royal nervously. He wasn't used to dealing with children, after all, and he might have expected them to be irrational. But even the King was more rational than this child. 'Don't get upset,' he went on. 'Now I'm just going to ask you some questions about the world we live in. Do you know the name of the Prime Minister?'

Roger laughed as if the Philosopher Royal had made a joke.

'No!' he said happily.

'And the name of this city?'

'I never knew it had a name. I thought it just was, like a rat.'

'What is the name of the King?'

'Ah, I know that,' said Roger. 'He's called King Henry.'

'And the Queen?'

'No. She's not Henry. She's Queen Margaret.'

'And the Prince?'

'No, he's not Henry nor Margaret. He's Richard.'

'Good. You know all their names. Well done.'

'And I know the name of who the Prince is going to marry. She's called Mary Jane.'

'Mary Jane?' said the Philosopher Royal. 'No, no. She's called Aurelia.'

Roger looked doubtful. 'She might be called Aurelia as well,' he admitted, 'but in the kitchen they calls her Mary Jane. I do know that.'

The Philosopher Royal wrote down: *Fantasy-identification with figures of glamour. Common among lower classes. Indicates humble origin for boy.*

'What's that mean,' said Roger, 'what you just wrote?'

'I'm making notes,' said the Philosopher Royal. 'To remind me of our conversation.'

'Ah,' said Roger. 'You're probably a bit forgetful, then. Once you've learned to remember things you won't need to do that. You can keep 'em all folded up in your head. They don't take up much room,' he went on. 'As long as you fold 'em flat. I seen Joan do that with the sheets, and I thought, there's a good idea. 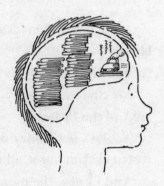 So now I folds and irons all the things in my head and I stack 'em neat. I know where they all are.'

'Remarkable,' said the Philosopher Royal, and wrote: *Insane. Sensory-intellectual delusions, paranoid in nature.*

Roger was eyeing the bell pull in the corner.

'Excuse me,' he said, 'but you know that rope? Well, there's a loose bit of thread at the bottom. That could be dangerous, someone could trip over that and hurt theirselves. So maybe I ought to chew it off, just that little bit of thread. If it would help,' he added.

'Well . . .' said the Philosopher Royal, and then, 'Yes. Why not?'

He turned a page and wrote: *Gross and unnatural appetite.*

Roger nibbled off the bit of thread, which was almost as long as his fingernail, and then found that he'd accidentally pulled loose a longer piece, so he had to chew that too; and that brought with it a very tasty knot, flavoured with a length of gold thread from the tassel, and before a minute had gone by Roger was blissfully eating his way up the bell pull itself.

Seeing him eating so well, the Philosopher Royal turned his mind to thoughts of food and nourishment, and what rats eat, and then by a logical process to the question of what eats rats.

'Aha!' he said. 'Wait here, my boy. Don't go away.'

And he left the study and hurried to his sitting room, where he scooped up his cat Bluebottle and hurried back. Bluebottle was not a philosophical cat; she was lazy and greedy and exceptionally stupid. She had no objection to being picked up and carried somewhere else, because there was very little in her head to object with. So, tucked under the Philosopher Royal's arm, she just dangled her back legs and stuck out her front ones and half opened her eyes . . .

Until they went into the study.

As soon as Roger saw the cat, he shrieked and leapt away. The window was open, and he dived out and into a flower bed and then scrambled to his feet and ran, and Bluebottle chased after him, automatically.

But she was a lazy cat, and when she saw she'd have to run further than the edge of the lawn she slowed down and gave up. She forgot about him almost at once and sat down to groom herself, while the Philosopher Royal stared out of the window, amazed, and Roger vanished out of the palace gates.

# MR TAPSCREW

In the market that day there happened to be a man from a fair. The fair was in the next town at the time, and it moved around, as fairs do, but this man had come to Roger's town because he'd heard a rumour that he wanted to investigate. He was the proprietor of one of the shows in the fair, and his name was Oliver Tapscrew.

Early that evening, Mr Tapscrew was standing at the bar of the Black Horse, a pint of bitter in his hand and a fat cigar in his mouth, talking to the owner of the jellied-eel stall from the market.

'I heard tell of something odd recently,' said Mr Tapscrew. 'I dunno if I heard it right – something about a boy who was really a rat. You ever heard of anything like that?'

'Rats?' said the jellied-eel man. 'No. Used to be a plague of 'em. But the Mayor and Corporation got a first-class firm of exterminators in. They exterminated everything in sight: rats, mice, cockroaches, fleas, lice, you name it. Wiped 'em out. Clean as a whistle. Place is so clean now I don't even have to wipe my stall down. Thanks, I'll have another.'

Mr Tapscrew reminded himself not to eat any jellied eels while he was here.

'They ain't really been exterminated,' said a horse-dealer. 'Rats and mice. You couldn't. They're cunning, they are, they got cunning blood. They take samples of the poison and they learn how to digest it. I shouldn't wonder if there's a race of super-rats down the sewers. With fangs like *that*. And a hatred for the whole human race. The rats' time is coming, you mark my words.'

Mr Tapscrew listened, and bought more pints of beer, and noticed with satisfaction that although nobody *knew* anything about rats, or boys who'd been rats, they all enjoyed a good shiver when they thought about them. Good shivers were good business.

He sipped his beer, while his fertile brain played with the notion of rats: super-rats, rat-boys, a whole freak-show of rat-humans, owned and trained and exhibited by Oliver Tapscrew – no, Professor Tapscrew – that would look good on the sign. He'd have it painted as soon as he got back.

Then he felt a hand on his arm, and turned to see a small greengrocer with a dapper little moustache.

'Excuse me,' said the greengrocer, 'that rat-boy you was talking about – I just seen him.'

'My dear fellow!' said Mr Tapscrew. 'D'you know him, then? Where is he?'

'If he's who I think he is,' said the small man, 'he's been took in by neighbours of mine. You wouldn't think he was a rat, really, he looks just like a boy. But he's got an unnatural appetite. There's something uncanny about it, mark my words.'

'Did you say you'd seen him?' said Mr Tapscrew.

'Yes. Just going down that alley over there, looking furtive.'

'Thanks,' said Mr Tapscrew. 'Have a drink, old man!'

He thrust some money into the greengrocer's hand, and hurried off down the alley.

It was a grubby little place between the municipal workhouse and the Hotel Salmagundi. At first Mr Tapscrew couldn't see a living creature there, but hearing a soft clatter, he stopped to look behind a mound of empty cardboard boxes, wine bottles, and soggy vegetable crates.

There he saw a small boy, crouching by a tipped-over dustbin, scooping something creamy out of a carton. He looked up, and Mr Tapscrew noted with pleasure the boy's quick-moving jaws, the appalling stink from the dustbin, and the bright black eyes that looked back at him.

172

'Tell me,' said Mr Tapscrew, 'I wonder if by any chance you might happen to be the boy who used to be a rat?'

'Yes,' said Roger. 'Only now I'm—'

'Good! Excellent!'

'I didn't mean to knock the dustbin over, only I—'

'Don't worry about it, dear boy. Come with me!'

Reluctantly abandoning the last of the smoked salmon mousse that had been in the dustbin for six days, Roger took Mr Tapscrew's hand and walked away with him, because he thought he ought to be a good boy.

# WHERE'S HE GONE?

When Roger didn't come back, Bob and Joan weren't sure when they should start to worry. On the one hand he was with the Philosopher Royal, who was sure to be looking after him properly, but on the other hand the man had said he'd bring Roger back, and he hadn't.

And on the third hand there was the fact that Bob and Joan had never had a child to look after before, and didn't know what to expect or whether they ought to worry. And on the fourth hand there was the fact that they were worrying about him already, because they were very fond of him, strange as he was.

It was a good thing they only had four hands

between them, or they'd have been even more worried. Joan even snapped at Bob, a thing she hardly ever did.

'What are you wasting your time with them silly slippers for?' she said. 'No-one's got feet that small, and what that leather must have cost I can't imagine.'

Bob was putting the last stitches in the scarlet slippers he'd been making. He looked up over his glasses and said, 'If a cobbler can't do something for the pure craftsmanship of it, it's a poor thing. They'll come in useful one day, don't you fret.'

He wasn't cross; he knew she was worried. When the old cuckoo clock struck nine, Bob put the slippers away and took off his glasses.

'Well, that's late enough,' he said. 'I'm not going to wait any more. I'm going down the palace to see what that man's been up to.'

'I'll come with you,' said Joan. 'I can't bear sitting waiting.'

'Funny, innit,' said Bob, 'we been sitting by this fire for thirty-two years, but it never seemed like waiting before.'

They put on their hats and coats and went to the tradesmen's entrance of the palace. Some soldiers were playing football in the courtyard, and another was smoking and reading the paper in a sentry box, and took no notice. Bob and Joan could hear giggling from somewhere inside, and the sound of glasses clinking.

'Yeah?' said the maid who opened the door, and hiccuped. 'Oops!'

'We come for the little boy,' said Bob firmly. 'It's his bedtime. The gentleman who wanted to investigate him must be finished by now.'

The maid vanished, shutting them outside. After a few minutes, during which Bob and Joan had to blow on their hands and stamp up and down to keep warm, she came back.

'Dr Prosser says he ran home,' she said, and was about to close the door when Bob put his foot in it.

'No he didn't,' said Bob. 'I want a word with Dr Prosser.'

The maid reluctantly opened the door. There was a party going on in the servants' hall, and she hurried them past and along to the door of the Philosopher Royal's apartment.

'Oh dear, oh dear,' said the Philosopher Royal when he opened the door.

'Where's our Roger?' said Joan.

'He ran away. Couldn't concentrate. Just leapt out of the window and ran home.'

'Ah, but he didn't,' said Bob. 'He never turned up.'

'And what did you do to him?' said Joan.

'A number of tests. They showed quite clearly that the boy is deranged. A psychotic personality disorder, with paranoid delusions combined with fantasy-identification with figures of glamour. Marked retardation of intellectual development. In short, he has a hopeless future, though he might find a useful occupation in some humble manual activity.'

'Never mind that,' said Bob, who was getting hot and bothered. 'We didn't send him to you to be tested because we wanted it. *You* wanted it. You come and took him, and now you've lost him, and we want him back. What are you going to do about it?'

'Ah,' said the Philosopher Royal cleverly, smiling and shaking his head, 'no, no, no. I think you're making an elementary error about the nature of language. When you say, "You've lost him," that seems to imply the notion of fault, of blame, of the whole discredited apparatus of causality. We don't talk in those terms any more. As a matter of fact, meaning itself is a problematic concept when nothing is final and everything is a matter of interpretation into terms which themselves—'

'I don't understand a word of that,' said Bob, 'but I tell you what, it makes me feel sick. You lost that little boy, and there's an end of it. When did he go? You can say that, I suppose?'

The Philosopher Royal gulped.

'About three o'clock,' he said.

Bob turned and walked away, but Joan hadn't finished.

'Someone oughter smacked you when you still did believe in things,' she said. 'It's too late now, else I'd do it myself.'

And she took Bob's arm and they went down the silent stairs, past the

laughter in the servants' hall, past the soldiers playing football in the moonlight, and out of the palace grounds.

'Where to now?' said Bob, as they looked down over the chilly rooftops in the frosty air.

'Don't know,' she said. 'We ain't just going to give up though, are we, Bob?'

'You're a silly old woman,' he said. 'We'll find him, never mind how long it takes. We just need a clue, that's all. But I'm blessed if I know where to start.'

# You Want 'Em Nauseated

'That's it! *Professor Tapscrew's Amazing Rat-Boy! The Wonder of the Age! See this subhuman monster wallow in abominable filth!* That's it, paint him as ferocious as you can. You got all those words written down? Get on with it, then,' said Mr Tapscrew, slapping the sign-painter on the back. 'Now, Martha, how's that costume coming on? Let's have a look at that tail. Dear dear dear, that's not nearly scabby enough. Make it six foot long and all covered with pustules. We could bung a few pustules on his face, come to think of it. Oh, and whiskers.'

In Mr Tapscrew's caravan, Roger sat peaceably chewing a leather belt and watching all this activity.

These people didn't mind him eating anything.

'Here! Ron! Make that cage a bit smaller. We can get more punters in the tent then, and the rat-boy'll look all the bigger. Rig up a sort of sewer-looking thing – big round pipe kind of effect for him to squat in – yeah, like that. Do they have nests? Do rats have nests? Here, you,' he said, nudging Roger with his foot, 'do rats have nests?'

'Yeah,' said Roger. These questions were much easier than the philosophical ones. 'Nice and cosy,' he added.

'You heard him,' said Mr Tapscrew. 'Get some rotten old bones off the lion-tamer and bung 'em in. Now – lights. We want to go for a sort of ghastly look. We want him to sort of emerge from the shadows. A pool of light near the punters, so he can come up front and do a bit of snarling when it gets quiet. Here,' he went on, struck by a sudden thought, 'd'you think he ought to have a name?'

'I got a name,' said Roger. 'It's new, I ain't hardly used it. It's Roger.'

'No, no, no. A wild sort of name. Like . . . Rorano, the Rat-Boy. What d'you think?'

181

'That's daft,' said his wife Martha, sewing on a pustule. 'If he's got a name, they'll only sympathize. You don't want that. You want 'em nauseated.'

'You know,' said Mr Tapscrew with admiration, 'that's why I married you. What a brain! Rat-Boy he is, then.'

'And he mustn't speak, neither,' she said. 'Just snarl and grunt. Here, you, Rat-Boy, come here and try this on.'

Since Roger hadn't been listening, he didn't know who she meant, and went on chewing his belt.

'Give him a clout, Ollie,' she said. 'He's got to learn.'

Mr Tapscrew bent very close and said, 'Now you listen careful, else you'll be sorry. You ain't Roger any more. You're Rat-Boy, understand? Don't forget it. Now try this costume on.'

Roger was puzzled, but he did as he was told. It was fun wriggling into the rat-suit, and then squirming on the floor as Mr Tapscrew instructed. Martha watched critically.

'It's a bit on the loose side,' she

said. 'I'll have to take it in. And he ought to swing that tail around. Here, Rat-Boy, swing your backside, get that tail swishing.'

Roger tried, but it just trailed limply on the floor. She shook her head.

'He'll have to practise,' she said. 'Can't go in front of the public like that. He looks too tame altogether. We'll have to do something about that.'

# THE WEDDING OF THE YEAR!

His Royal Highness Prince Richard and the Lady Aurelia were married yesterday in the magnificent surroundings of the cathedral.

The bride was radiant in her white lace and satin wedding dress.

'She looks like a fairy princess!' was the verdict of the crowd, who had stood all night long to see the ceremony.

As the coach rolled back bearing the Prince and Princess, thousands of happy well-wishers waved flags and cheered.

*Their eternal love sealed with a kiss*

one's hearts by turning to her Prince and giving him a long kiss.

'You can tell they're really in love,' said Dorothy Plunkett, the *Scourge*'s royal expert. 'It's the real thing this time for the playboy Prince.'

## A KISS ON THE BALCONY

Outside the Palace, the crowd had something else to cheer about when the royal couple appeared on the balcony to wave to their loyal subjects.

Princess Aurelia won every-

## GETTING MARRIED?

### WIN...

- **A replica of the royal wedding dress**
- **A fortnight's honeymoon at the Hotel Splendifico**
- **A right royal make-over for your dream house!**

*See page 5*

# A Load Of Old Cod

Bob and Joan decided that after their experiences with the police, they'd be better off not going to them again, and they weren't very impressed with the other officials they'd spoken to on Roger's account, either. As they wandered home through the market square they felt sorely puzzled.

'You don't think he's run right away, do you?' said Joan. 'I think he was feeling that we were his home. I *think* he was.'

Just then the door of the Black Horse opened, and out came their neighbour Charlie, the dapper little greengrocer, staggering slightly.

'Evening, Bob,' he said. 'Hello, Joan. Here – you know that little boy . . . Where's that sleeve gone?' He was having trouble with his coat.

'Go on,' said Joan at once, helping him into the sleeve, 'what about a little boy?'

'Aha,' said Charlie. 'I'm getting to that. Lot of talk about rats in the pub today. There was a flash-looking feller with a big cigar asking about 'em. Seems there's a monster about,' he added, stepping alongside very carefully, as if he wasn't sure the ground was there.

'Get away,' said Bob. 'What sort of a monster?'

'Half child,' said Charlie solemnly, 'and half rat.'

Joan's hand tightened on Bob's arm. Charlie was having trouble finding the end of his scarf, because it was inside his coat at the back. Bob pulled it out for him.

'Thank you,' he said, bowing to him and staggering a little.

'Well, what about the little boy?' Joan said.

'Ah,' said Charlie, trying to lay a finger alongside his nose and nearly poking his eye out. 'Coming to that. This man Stewtap – Plumbscrew – summing – he was looking for this rat-monster because he was going to put him on show, Eric reckoned. Eric seen the man before, in a fair, exhibiting a mermaid in a tank. And Eric – he paid his money and went in to see the mermaid, and you know what he says? He says – ooh Lor, listen to this – he says the top half was prime, but the bottom half was a load of old cod! Lor! What d'you think of that, eh?'

He was nearly doubled up, choking with laughter.

'On account of her tail,' he wheezed. 'A load of old cod!'

'Very funny,' said Bob, 'yeah, that's a good 'un. What was the feller called again?'

'And what about the little boy?' said Joan, stamping her foot. 'I swear, Charlie Hoskins, you're driving me mad. *What about the little boy?*'

'I seen him,' said Charlie, 'and I told the man about him.'

'What? Where? When?'

'This afternoon. Down the alley. Wossisname again – Tapstew – Thumbscrap – can't remember – he was looking for him, and I showed him where he'd gone. Ooh, I feel ill. Ooh, I feel awful . . .'

'Well, there's one consolation,' said Joan. 'You'll

feel worse in the morning.'

'Oh, good . . . oh, Lor . . . Here,' said Charlie, clinging to Bob's sleeve, 'I'll get his name in a minute. Tap – Snap – Screwfish – 's no good, 's gone. Goo'night.'

'Well,' said Bob to Joan once they'd helped Charlie inside his front door and seen it safely shut, 'I suppose that's a start.'

# THE WONDER OF THE AGE

Two days later, and many miles down the road, St Matthew's Fair opened for business. It was always the same fair, but in this town it opened on St Matthew's Day, so it was St Matthew's Fair; in that town it opened over Michaelmas, so it was the Michaelmas Fair; and it reached another town on May Day, so it was the May Fair. The stall-owners and merry-go-round proprietors, and the man who ran the ghost train, and the owner of the Death-defying Wall of Doom all knew what time of year it was by what town they happened to be in.

They arrived late at night and by the light of many lamps and lanterns they set up their stalls and assembled their roundabouts and bolted together their rides in the cattle market, under the old town castle.

Mr Tapscrew was putting the final touches to his stall as the sun rose over the market cross.

'No,' he said, 'we still need a bit more filth and squalor. It looks almost respectable in there. We need mud and rotten vegetables. We need dung, really, but there's a limit to what the public will stand, more's the pity. A good show ought to be a little ahead of the public, but not too far, and I think they'd draw the line at dung.'

'So would I,' said his wife. 'We've got to live with him, remember. Here – what about charging 'em extra to feed him? We'll have a feeding time, every hour on the hour, special price. And the beauty of it is,' she went on, 'we don't have to supply the food! They bring it theirselves!'

# THE WONDER OF THE AGE!

Professor Tapscrew presents

### The World's only genuine living

## !! RAT-BOY !!

This half-human, half-rodent
altogether ABOMINABLE Creature
*discovered living in the Filth of the Sewers*
will demonstrate his

### Loathsome and Unnatural Appetite

by *Eating Anything*

put before him by the Public.

Feeding Time: every Hour on the Hour.

 # WARNING:

The Rat-boy's Savage and Ferocious Instincts
make him

## DANGEROUS TO APPROACH.

# Wonder! Marvel! Shudder!

He looked at her fondly. 'Genius,' he murmured.

'Rig up a sign,' she said. 'Make it fancy, with all toothsome words. You're good at that.'

Less than an hour later, everything was ready.

'Smashing,' said Mrs Tapscrew.

The first visitors came soon afterwards. Seven people, grown-ups and children, crowded into the little booth and stared down into a pit lined with crumbling plaster and rotten planks. The floor was covered in dirty straw, cabbage-stumps, and bits of vegetable too decayed to recognize.

'Eurgghh,' said a girl.

'Look!' said a boy. 'He's coming out! Yuk!'

As the little boy pointed, something stirred at the back of the pit, and first there appeared a hand, then skinny arms, then a face—

'Eeeuuurrgghh! Yuchh! Eurghhhh!'

Roger had been thoroughly decorated with scabs and pustules and a couple of great red boils for good measure. His rat-suit had been taken in to fit him tightly, and as he scrambled out he swung his horrible leathery tail in the way he'd practised.

Cries of revulsion and disgust greeted him. He was delighted. He smiled up happily, showing the blacked-out teeth Mrs Tapscrew had painted.

'Here, Rat-Boy! Eat this!' someone called, and threw in a rotten potato.

Roger hadn't eaten anything that day. The Tapscrews had kept him hungry on purpose, and although he'd chewed a bit of wood and swallowed some straw, there was no nourishment in that; so he seized the potato at once, and remembering what

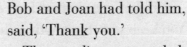

Bob and Joan had told him, said, 'Thank you.'

The audience goggled. They looked more closely.

Then someone said, 'That's a boy.'

'He's got a costume on!' said someone else.

'He ain't a rat-monster at all!' came the voice of a third person, and with cries of disappointment and anger they called for their money back.

Mr Tapscrew, who was busy outside drumming up another crowd, came in hastily.

'Hush – yes – all right – understood – money back, certainly – just keep your voices down, ladies and

gentlemen – here, Mrs Tapscrew'll give you the
money out the back here – hush now . . .'

He ushered them grumbling and muttering, out
of the booth, and then went back in to find Roger
munching his rotten potato.

Mr Tapscrew bent down and hit him so hard the
potato flew out of his hands, and he fell full length
to the floor.

'What'd you do that for? Ain't you got no sense?
You keep your bloody trap shut, you little fool! How
can a rat say "thank you"?'

Roger, his head ringing, didn't know what Mr
Tapscrew meant about the trap. He had a vague
idea that traps were bad for rats, but he couldn't
make any sense of it. One thing he was sure about,
though.

'I'm not a rat any more,' he said, struggling to sit
up. 'I'm a boy now. Old Bob told me that good boys
say thank you, so—'

'Damn your Bob, and damn your thank yous!
You'll do as I tell you, you ungrateful skellum! After
all I done for you – I pick you out the gutter – I give
you a home and a useful occupation – you go and
spoil it with your niminy-piminy "thank you"! You

ain't supposed to *thank* 'em! You're supposed to snarl and snatch and threaten! You're supposed to be a Rat-Boy, not a choir boy!'

'Ah,' said Roger, his head beginning to hurt now, 'if I'd knowed that I'd've done it. When I got changed into a boy, that's when I found out about being good, so I was doing that. When I was a rat I never knew about being good. So now I got to be a good Rat-Boy, only that's hard.'

'Oh, shut up, you sanctimonious little mumper! Just remember – snarl and snatch and threaten. Else I'll pull your bloody nose off. Now the next lot of punters'll be in any minute, and I want 'em horrified and disgusted. See?'

He kicked Roger for good measure, and went out. Roger felt a choking sensation in his throat, almost like a hiccup, and it might have turned into a sob except that he thought Mr Tapscrew wouldn't approve. And he did want to be a good rat-boy, so he gathered up the biggest bit of the potato and crawled back into the sewer-pipe to wait for the next audience to come in.

All that day and all through the evening he snarled and snatched and threatened, and the people threw him bits of mouldy bread and chicken heads and scraps of rancid pork and banana skins and potato peelings and rotten fish, and exclaimed with revulsion when he ate them.

# GOOSE WEATHER

After being St Matthew's, the fair moved on to a town fifty miles away to become the Goose Fair. At this time of year there were a lot of geese being fattened for Christmas, and autumn was getting on, so the evenings were longer and darker.

Mr Tapscrew was looking forward to good business, because people were more willing to come in out of the cold and look at an exhibition of curiosities than they were in the long summer evenings, when the rides and the merry-go-rounds did their best business. He paid for a new sign showing the Rat-Boy with an expression of savage malevolence, dripping green venom from hideous fangs. He even had special leaflets printed, and travelled ahead and distributed them in all the pubs.

As for Roger, he took to being a Rat-Boy quickly enough, once he realized what he had to do; and he didn't mind what he ate, so the fish-heads and rotten carrots went down easily enough; but there wasn't any goodness in them, and presently he began to feel a little listless. He didn't enjoy swishing his tail any more, and the rat-suit was getting loose.

Mrs Tapscrew cursed, and took it in half an inch.

'He ain't eating his scraps,' she said to her husband, as they sat in their caravan. The lamplight was golden, the stove was warm, the kettle was singing. Outside, the rain was lashing at the windows, and the autumn wind was howling.

'Mmm,' said Mr Tapscrew, applying a match to his cigar and puffing luxuriously. 'Think we ought to feed him proper, then?' he said once it was nicely lit. 'Bit of soup of an evening?'

'Don't be daft. You know how the takings go up at feeding time. If he's full of soup and stuff, he won't be worth watching. No, I think you ought to hit him.'

'Well,' said Mr Tapscrew reluctantly, 'I could.

The thing is,' he went on, examining the glowing tobacco, 'I don't think he's normal. I don't think he understands the meaning of things.'

'You're too soft,' she said, snapping off a thread between her teeth. 'You're getting attached to him. That's your problem. Like that blooming mermaid. You were too interested in her by a long way—'

'All right, all right,' said Mr Tapscrew hastily. 'I'll do as you say, dear. I'm sure he'll settle down.'

Roger was trying to settle down at that very moment. He slept in his pit, curled up in the sewer pipe, and it was cold and draughty, and Mrs Tap-screw was sewing up his rat-suit, so he only had his tattered old page-boy uniform to keep out the cold. But he piled up some straw to keep out the worst of the wind, and nibbled a twig that someone had thrown in, and whispered the words he always whispered each night before he went to sleep: 'Bob and Joan – bread and milk – nightshirt – privy – patience.'

And soon afterwards he fell asleep.

But he hadn't been asleep for long when a knocking sound woke him up. It was coming from the wooden wall of the wagon, at the back of his sewer pipe. He turned round and pressed his ear to the wall, and there it was, knock-knock-knock – pause – knock-knock-knock.

And then there came a whisper through the cracks in the planks:

'Psst! Rat-Boy!'

Roger woke up properly.

'Yes?' he whispered back.

'Listen,' said the voice, 'I'm going to help you escape. In a minute I'm going to heave this plank out the way, and you can wriggle through.'

'Oh,' said Roger. 'Does Mr Tapscrew know?'

'No, and it's better if he doesn't,' said the voice. 'Keep it quiet now, Rat-Boy. Here goes.'

There was a crack and a splintering noise, and all of a sudden a cold wind blew in on Roger from a plank-wide gap in the wall. Amazed, he peered out and saw by the flickering light of a hurricane lantern a boy a little bigger than himself, with very pale hair that hung like a curtain over his forehead. Roger admired him enormously at once.

'Come on,' said the boy. 'Wriggle through. I bet you can.'

Roger was naturally a good wriggler, and his diet had left him so thin that he had no trouble at all in squirming through the gap.

He fell on the muddy ground and got up at once.

'Come on,' said the boy. 'Let's run. We got to get away!'

'Yeah!' said Roger, joining in at once.

They ran along between the stalls, and then the other boy turned and crouched in the shadows beside the ghost train, waiting to be sure the way was clear.

'Are you helping us all escape?' said Roger.

'Why, who else is there?' said the boy. 'I thought you was the only freak.'

'There's them,' said Roger, pointing up at the painted ghosts and skeletons of the ghost train. 'They're all locked in there like I was. We could let them out too.'

'You're a downy card, aintcher?' said the boy, looking both ways carefully. 'Right, come on!'

And he set off. Roger followed, looking back reluctantly at the still-imprisoned phantoms. Once they were safely in the darkness of the alleys under the castle, the boy stopped.

'Now,' he said. 'You call me Billy, understand?'

'Oh, yes, I understand,' said Roger. 'That's your name, Billy.'

'Yeah. Now I been watching you, Rat-Boy. I been in to look at your pit three times today, watching you wriggle. You probably didn't see me, but I was there. I'm on the look-out for a good wriggler, see, and I admired your style. I thought you wriggled like a champion. I got a job for you, Rat-Boy. So now you got to do as I tell you. Because I rescued you, and it's like you belong to me, you got to do everything I say.'

'Oh,' said Roger, nodding, 'I'll remember that.'

'Yes, you better. You're the lowest of the low, you are.'

'The lowest of the low,' said Roger proudly.

'That's right. Now listen, and I'll tell you something you never heard about. You listening?'

'Oh, yes,' said Roger, eager to learn.

'Look over there then,' said Billy, and pointed

across the alley. Opposite them was a rusty iron gate with some broken spikes at the top, and through the gate the dismal gleam of a feeble gas lamp cast a glow over some weed-covered graves and broken tombstones.

'See that in there?' Billy whispered.

'Yeah. Looks nice. I bet there's—'

'Shut up. It don't look nice. It looks horrible. Scary, that's what it looks. That's where they bury all the dead people. Now real people, like me, we die natural. But rats, like you—'

'Ah,' said Roger, 'I ain't a rat any more. I'm a proper boy.'

'Once a rat, always a rat,' said Billy, and he said it with such simple certainty that it impressed itself on Roger profoundly. He struggled with it, but the words wouldn't go away. He said them to himself to make sure they were right, and Billy nodded.

'That's it,' he said. 'Now you interrupted me, and I don't like that. Don't do it again. I was going to say that rats like you never die natural.'

'Don't we?'

'No. You got to be sterminated. If people think there's rats about, they send for the Sterminator.

203

And if they even so much as suspect you're a rat underneath, watch out. The Sterminator'll be on his way.'

It sounded horrible. Roger gulped, and remembered the police sergeant: he had mentioned the Sterminator, too. He trembled and managed to say, 'What's it like?'

'It's not an it. It's a him. No-one's ever seen what he's like. He comes along with his apparatus and—'

The word 'apparatus' filled Roger with a deep and horrible dread. Terrifying pictures of a faceless man armed with some shadowy engine kept thrusting themselves into his mind, and he couldn't keep them out.

'No! Don't tell me!' he begged.

'Oh, I've got to, Roger,' Billy said gently. 'It wouldn't be right if I didn't tell you about the Sterminator. What he does with his apparatus' – Roger shivered and moaned – 'no-one knows, but when he's been sterminating, there ain't a single rat left to tell the tale. They find 'em with blood on their whiskers and their faces twisted with a nameless horror.'

'I ain't got whiskers,' said Roger, in faint hope.

'Wouldn't make no difference. The Sterminator, he can tell if someone's a rat underneath, even if they look like a boy in every particular.'

'Has there been other rats turned into boys, then?'

'Yeah. Doesn't happen often, but it has been known. The Sterminator's very hard on those cases. They're the ones he wants to sterminate most of all.'

'Like me,' whispered Roger, clutching himself with both arms.

'Just like you. It's a good thing you got me to look after you, innit? You do as I say and I'll keep the Sterminator off you. But you disobey me and I'll be so upset I'll forget. And the Sterminator'll have you while my back's turned, he's that quick.'

'Oh, no, don't forget,' Roger begged.

'Don't upset me, and I won't. Now you come along o' me and we'll find something good to eat. You hungry?'

Roger was now shaking so hard he felt his teeth chatter and his knees knock. He clenched his jaw and nodded, and gripped his knees to stop them, in case the sound attracted the Sterminator. There was

205

a loose and swimmy sensation all around him.

'Follow me, then,' said Billy.

He led Roger down another alley, into a courtyard lit only by the gleam on the wet cobbles, and lifted the lid of a coal chute. A faint glow came up, accompanied by the smell of frying.

'Down you go,' said Billy, shoving hard, and before he knew what was happening Roger had slid and tumbled on the dusty floor of a cellar, where a ring of glittering eyes surrounded him.

A hand reached out and snatched him off the floor a second before Billy tumbled down the chute behind him. Roger saw half a dozen boys, all bigger than he was, and all ragged and dirty. The glitter in their eyes came from an oil lamp and from the red-hot glow of a stove, on which one of

the boys was frying chips.

'This is the Rat-Boy,' said Billy, dusting himself. 'You remember.'

'Oh yes,' said one boy, and, 'Aha,' said another, and, 'So this is him,' said a third.

Roger understood that the boys were glad to see him, and he did what he'd seen other people do, and held out his hand.

'How do you do,' he said to the first boy, and they all shook his hand one by one, laughing. They were so friendly altogether, squeezing his arms, pretending to look for his tail, fluffing up his hair, that he thought he'd never been happier; and then they gave him a hot chip and roared with laughter when he burned his mouth and dropped it on the floor, and he felt so grateful to them that his eyes filled with tears and he laughed even harder than they did.

# WELL, WHERE'S HE GONE?

'**O**h, the wickedness!' said Joan. 'We find him at last, and look at this!'

It was a cold grey morning. She held Bob's arm as they stood in the rainswept fairground, gazing up at the picture of the Rat-Boy and his venom-dripping fangs.

'Hold on,' said Bob, 'what's this?'

Joan peered closely at the notice pinned on the door of the wagon.

'*Due to unforeseen circumstances the world-famous Rat-Boy will not be appearing today. Exhibition closed until further notice. Open again SOON with even more amazing wonders. O. Tapscrew, Proprietor.*' Joan read it aloud. 'I hope

Roger ain't fallen ill,' she said. 'Knock on the door and fetch this Tapscrew out, Bob.'

Bob knocked, and a minute later a harassed Mr Tapscrew opened it.

'Can't you read?' he said. 'The performance is cancelled.'

'Where is he?' said Bob.

'None of your business,' said Mr Tapscrew, and would have shut the door, except that Bob had his foot in it. 'Oy!' he went on. 'Go away!'

'You better listen to us,' said Bob, 'else we're going to the police.'

'Let 'em in,' said a voice from inside, a voice that sounded to Joan like lemon marmalade with too little sugar in it.

Mr Tapscrew opened the door, and Bob and Joan went in after him.

'Well?' he said.

'We want to know what you done with our Roger,' said Bob firmly.

'How d'you know he was yours?' said Mrs Tapscrew at once.

'We found a witness,' said Bob. 'We know you took him. You can't deny it. So where is he?'

'Wait a minute,' said Mrs Tapscrew. 'What's your interest in the Rat-Boy? You claiming to be his owners? You'd have to prove it.'

'Course we ain't his *owners*!' said Joan hotly. 'What d'you think he is, a slave, or a dog, or something?'

'Not his owners,' said Mrs Tapscrew. 'Then I don't see what business it is of yours. Show them out, Oliver.'

'Oh no,' said Bob, and when he stood still, nothing on earth could budge him. 'You listen to me, and don't you talk till I've finished. That little boy come to us and we took him in. He didn't hardly know nothing, but he was a good little boy, and he tried hard to learn. But then he got lost, and that's the last we knew till we heard of you asking about Rat-Boys. He may be a Rat-Boy to you, and a handsome living, I don't doubt, but he don't belong here, he belongs in a home where he's going to be properly looked after. So where is he?'

'He's a freak,' said Mrs Tapscrew. 'Half rat, half human. He needs a profession. We was training him for a fine career. He could have been the best freak of all time. He could've been famous. He had the finest career in front of him that any freak's ever had. He could've—'

'What d'you mean, "freak"?' said Joan.

'What I say. He wasn't properly human. He couldn't have eaten all that filth otherwise. He was a—'

'Filth? What filth? What are you talking about?' said Joan.

Bob could feel her losing her temper, and he put his hand on her arm.

'Never mind the details,' he said. 'We want the main question, and the main question is, where is he?'

'He's gone,' said Mr Tapscrew.

'When?'

'Last night. He bust out of his wagon. Lovely warm wagon,' Mr Tapscrew said bitterly, 'with every sort of convenience, and he goes and smashes a plank out the side. That's going to cost me, that is. If you're responsible for him I shouldn't wonder if it ought to be you as pays for it.'

'You lock our little boy up and send us a bill when he escapes?' said Bob. 'Don't be daft. Let's go and look at this wagon.'

Joan was feeling strange. It was Bob saying 'our

little boy'. He'd never said that before, and she'd never thought it, but now it was as if she was connected to Roger with the same sort of deep connection that joined her to Bob, and she felt herself saying it again in her head: our little boy.

Mr Tapscrew was reluctant to show them the wagon, because he had the idea that they wouldn't think it was quite as comfortable as he'd said, but he couldn't argue with Bob.

So grumpily he took his bunch of keys, and with Mrs Tapscrew coming as well to argue, they all trooped round to open the Rat-Boy's pit.

Joan waved her hand in front of her nose.

'You didn't keep him in here!' she cried.

'He wasn't very fastidious in his habits,' said Mrs Tapscrew.

'He didn't have anything to be fastidious in!' said Joan. 'And what's this? Is this what you gave him to eat?'

'No, no,' said Mr Tapscrew, shoving a piece of mouldy bread under a pile of straw with the side of his foot. 'We gave him lovely food – soup, stew – ever so nourishing. This was just professional food. A prop,' he added. 'That's what we call it. Props.'

'Slops, more like,' said Joan.

Bob was peering at the broken plank.

'He never done that,' he said to Mr Tapscrew. 'You're no workman, else you'd see in a moment. There's no leverage in here. Come outside.'

They went round the back, and Bob bent down and pointed to some marks on the next plank down.

'See that?' he said. 'That was a crowbar as done that. He never broke out. Someone broke in, and let him out.'

And he straightened up and faced Mr Tapscrew, and then suddenly prodded him in the chest with a forefinger that felt like a battering-ram. Mr Tapscrew staggered backwards.

'Oh – ah!—' he gasped. 'No need for assault—'

'You're responsible for this,' Bob said, and now his voice was like a battering-ram too, a very heavy one made of solid oak.

'No, not at all! Not a bit of it!' Mr Tapscrew blustered. 'We did everything we could to keep him safe and secure!'

'Well, *where's he gone?*'

# THE SHARP ARTICLE

The boys in the cellar slept for most of the day, and so did Roger. When he woke up, he found Billy shaking him and holding some new clothes.

'Here,' said Billy, 'I got you some duds.'

'Did you just buy 'em?' said Roger, amazed at this generosity.

'You're a sharp article, and no mistake,' said Billy. 'I requisitioned 'em, that's what I did. Now slip them old togs off and put these on.'

When Roger proudly stood there in his new shirt and jacket he looked quite different from the tattered little page-boy he'd been. He looked like a sharp article, or a downy card.

'Now,' said Billy, 'you got to start earning a living. Me and my associates, we had a prime wriggler in the company, only he got too fat. And one day he set out a-wriggling and he got wedged. Course, there was nothing we could do. He was beyond our help. We had to leave him there.'

'Did the Sterminator get him?'

'I couldn't say. Maybe he didn't and maybe he did. But that wriggler weren't as good as you. You wouldn't get wedged.'

'No,' Roger agreed, shaking his head vigorously.

'Well, that's why you caught my eye in the fair. And when you wriggled out the wagon last night, that just made me even surer. You're a world-class wriggler, no doubt about it.'

Roger glowed.

'Am I going wriggling today?' he said.

'This evening,' said Billy. 'We're nocturnal. Like you, Rat-Boy. You're a nocturnal wriggler.'

'Yeah,' said Roger. 'That's what I am.'

The associates were just waking up. They all admired Roger's new duds, and soon there were eggs and slices of ham frying on the stove, and Roger was allowed a chunk of cheese as big as his two fists together, which kept him blissfully gnawing for a long time.

After they'd eaten, and when it was dark outside, Billy said, 'All right, lads. Line up.'

The associates stood in a row, and Billy inspected them carefully. He checked their shoes (to make sure they didn't have metal bits on the heel that made a noise, or broken shoelaces that would trip them up), their clothes (to make sure they wore nothing light-coloured that would show up and give them away), and their sacks. Each boy carried a sack, and he had to hold it up and show Billy there was no hole in it.

'All present and correct,' Billy said. 'Good lads. Now we got a new wriggler, so we won't have the trouble we had last time. And as soon as we're done, straight back here by different routes. Just go through 'em, to show you remember. Dozzer first.'

A boy recited, 'Through the garden over the fence turn right along the canal over the bridge round the castle through the market and back home.'

'That's right,' said Billy, and each of the other boys recited his route, all different. Billy turned to Roger and said, 'That's the power of organization, see. As for you, you stick by me and you won't go wrong.'

Normally, he explained, they left the cellar by climbing a rope Billy had fixed by the coal chute, but he wanted to check Roger's wriggling one last time, so he pointed to a tiny window high up in a corner.

'See how long it takes you to get through that,' he said. 'And mind, a good wriggler's got to be as quiet as a worm.'

'I can do that!' said Roger, and got through in less than half a minute, and waited excitedly for the others to climb the rope.

Presently all the boys were standing quietly in the alley. Billy patted each one on the back and sent them off at thirty-second intervals. It was so dark that even Roger's keen eyes couldn't see where they went.

# REMOVALS

Half an hour later they were crouching in the bushes at the edge of a fine big garden looking up at the shuttered windows of a grand house.

'Now this is the problem, Roger,' Billy whispered. 'We got to get in, but there's only one way, and that's a loose airbrick over the scullery. But you could wriggle through there in a second, I bet.'

'Yeah, I bet too,' said Roger.

'Once you're inside,' Billy explained, 'you got to look around and find a key. Most folks are careless, and servants are specially careless. They don't like their masters and mistresses and they don't take trouble for 'em. So you look around, and ten to

one you'll find a key on a hook somewhere, or a nail.
Get that key and come and open the kitchen door.'

'I can do that!' said Roger. 'What are we going to
do then? Are we going to live there?'

'No,' said Billy, 'the owners want us to do a
removal job.'

Roger liked the sound of that, and said it to himself several times.

When everyone was ready, Billy said, 'Now, look
closely at the wall just next to that little window and
up a bit. There's a brick with holes in it there, what's
called an airbrick. You take my crowbar – here it is
– and get up on the window-sill, and jiggle it in
beside the airbrick, and get it loose. When it comes
out, you wriggle in and look for the key.'

Thrilled to be trusted with such complicated
instructions, Roger took the crowbar from Billy. A
few seconds later he was jiggling away at the
crumbling mortar, and presently the air-brick did
come loose. He passed it down to Billy,
and then began to wriggle through.

It was a good thing he was a world-
class wriggler, and probably a good
thing too that he'd lost weight being the

Rat-Boy, because several parts of him nearly got stuck. But even his widest bits were narrow, and what he remembered about being a rat helped too. It took him four whole minutes, but he got through in the end, to fall in a heap on the scullery floor, covered in dust and mortar.

'I done it!' he shouted. 'I got in!'

'Good boy,' said Billy outside, very quiet and calm.

The associates, hiding in the bushes, all heard Roger's shout, and their nerves were all twitching; but they felt a glow of admiration for the coolness of their leader as he just spoke softly and didn't move.

'Now you're in,' Billy was saying, 'you got to move around very quietly. That's the way we do removals. No noise. Now look for that key.'

A minute went by. Billy didn't move. Nor did the associates. Another minute went by. Then there was a little scrabbling noise at the back door, and Billy was there in a flash, turning the handle, and the door swung open.

The associates came tiptoeing over the flagstones, making no more noise than a flock of shadows. Seconds after the door had begun to open, they were all in the big kitchen with the door shut again behind them.

'Well wriggled,' Billy said. 'Now, Roger, you stay here and keep watch. You know what to do, lads.'

The associates flitted away into the dark house. Roger stayed in the kitchen, wondering how to keep watch, but willing to do it, whatever it was.

Then, being Roger, he looked around for something to eat.

Because the family who lived in the house had gone away, and taken their servants with them, there was no fresh food in the kitchen. But he found all kinds of dried food in jars and packets and boxes on the shelves. At first he thought he'd found some very long and very thin patience, but they tasted quite different from the wooden ones and snapped more easily, sending bits of themselves flying all over the kitchen. If he could have read the packet, it would have told him he was eating spaghetti.

When he'd had enough of that, he found some dried figs at the back of a shelf. Then he ate his way through a packet of cream crackers, one old and flexible carrot, half a pound of rice, and some very tasty dried beans.

Then he made a big mistake.

There was a paper bag twisted up in a corner, with some light rattling things in it, and Roger automatically thrust them all into his mouth and chewed and swallowed. Of course, he'd never heard of chillies, and never suspected what these were. They took a moment to hit.

Then he gasped and goggled and began to run around in circles, flapping at his mouth in the hope of cooling it down. He couldn't imagine what it was he'd eaten. His lips and his tongue and his throat and his stomach were all ablaze. Parts of his insides he'd never known about were sizzling. He yelped – he jumped – he squeaked – he gargled – he hooted – and suddenly the thought came to him: Water! Water! Water!

He ran to the tap, but the water was cut off at the mains, and only a hollow rattle filled his scorching mouth. He was making all kinds of noises now – mewlings and whinnyings and yippings and hoickings and gurkings – and then he remembered the big barrel that stood just outside the kitchen door. He'd seen it on the way in.

He tore outside and scrambled up between the

barrel and the wall, only to find a big wooden lid at the top. He hauled it off in desperation, dropping it to the cobbles with a crash, and plunged his whole head into the cold wet delicious moon-reflecting depths.

Gripping the barrel with both hands, feet pressed hard to the slippery sides, Roger swallowed and guzzled and swallowed and gulped. Oh, the relief! The marvellous coolness! The sweet wetness of his mouth! He swallowed till he was just about waterlogged.

As full as he could be, he loosened his grip and slid down the side of the water-butt. And he forgot all about his burning mouth and turned his attention downwards, for something strange was happening inside him. He staggered slightly on the ground and listened to his stomach. All kinds of burblings and gurglings and swooshings and bubblings were taking place, as the cascade of water met the dried beans and the rice and sloshed about among the bits of spaghetti. Roger felt his turbulent belly with apprehensive hands. As the grains of rice began to swell, and the dried beans began to soak up the water and double in size, as the bits of pasta grew plump and fat, Roger's stomach began to strain at the buttons of his new shirt, creaking and rumbling.

'Oh,' he said, staggering a bit, 'ah. Ooh.' Then he said, 'Hic!'

He'd never had hiccups before. He thought he was exploding. He clenched his teeth together to stop it, but the next *hic* simply came out through his nose instead. And all the time his stomach was getting fuller and fuller and fatter and fatter.

He staggered this way and that, gulping, hicking, gasping, snorting, feeling very sorry for himself indeed.

And suddenly a light shone into his eyes, and a hand closed over his shoulder, and a deep voice said, 'What's going on here?'

# Who's That?

Above them, in a window overlooking the scullery yard, several pairs of eyes glittered silently and then withdrew.

Roger, dazed and bloated, could hardly think. But when he looked up and saw the policeman looming against the sky, he knew there was only one person it could be.

'Billy! Help!' he yelled. 'It's the Sterminator! Come and help me!'

And he sank his teeth into the policeman's hand.

The man gasped and let him go, to seize the truncheon at his waist, but Roger was out of reach already and running about in fear, looking up at the house and calling, 'Billy! Billy! Come and fight him!'

'More of you, are there?' said the policeman. 'Like rats in a trap.'

And he blew his whistle. That was enough for Roger. If the man spoke of rats, he must be the Sterminator, and the whistle must be his horrifying apparatus starting up. For all his loyalty to Billy, and despite his waterlogged stomach, the little boy turned and fled into the dark.

He didn't know where he was going. He couldn't remember the way back to the cellar, and even if he could, he didn't dare go there. In fact, everything in his world was soaked in guilt and misery. He had wanted to be a good boy, but it seemed that whatever he did, he was a bad one. He didn't deserve a nice dry place to curl up and sleep; he didn't even deserve to whisper *Bob and Joan – bread and milk – nightshirt – privy – patience* as he used to do. Somehow the words didn't want to come to his mouth. He just moved his lips and tried to hear the little puffs and clicks and hisses they made and pretended he could make out the words.

So he crept through the dark streets until he came to a grating in the gutter, like a proper rat-hole, only human-sized. If he went down there he wouldn't have to bother anyone and he wouldn't do anything wrong. He could stop trying to be a boy and go back to being a rat. 'Once a rat, always a rat,' Billy had told him, and it must be true, because he certainly wasn't any good at being a boy.

So he lifted the grating and slipped down into the dark.

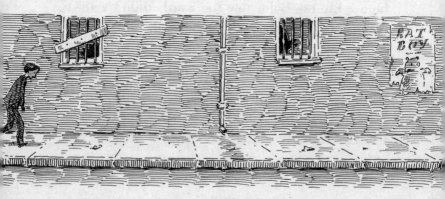

# The Daily Scourge

*Rotten to the core*

## CRIME UP AGAIN

This is becoming a crime-ridden country – and it's official.

Crime figures have risen for the fifth year in succession.

Typical of the sort of lawlessness all too common today is the break-in at the home of the Earl and Countess of Ditchwater by a gang of young boys, all of whom were luckily caught red-handed.

'I blame the teachers,' said the Home Secretary.

## ANARCHY IN THE CLASSROOMS

But teachers are finding it harder and harder to maintain order and discipline over the bullies and thugs in the classroom.

'There is no respect for learning any more,' said a teachers' leader. 'I blame the parents.'

## FAMILY BREAK-UPS

The traditional family is under threat. Family values have crumbled away. Changing working patterns, taxation, and violent entertainment are playing havoc with all the old certainties.

'There's no-one to give a moral lead any more,' said a parent. 'I blame the church.'

*'Ere, 'ere!*

## A MORAL VACUUM

But the church itself speaks with an uncertain voice.

'How can anyone be moral in a world of poverty under the constant threat of war and environmental devastation?' said the Archbishop. 'I blame the government.'

# THE SCOURGE SAYS:

**RUBBISH!**

All our so-called experts are wrong, as usual.

Dripping and moaning about the state of the world and blaming everyone else – is it any wonder that our country is in a mess, with people like that in charge of it?

As for the rise in juvenile crime, it's easy.

The kids are doing it, aren't they?

Then there's no need to look any further.

*BLAME THE KIDS!!!*

**The Daily Scourge** READERS OFFER!

MECHANICAL GUARD DOG

ONLY £499·99!

ELECTRIC FENCE ONLY £2,799!

ONLY £299·99!

HEAVILY ARMED GARDEN GNOME

ONLY £1,599·99!

PATIO TRAP DOOR

# A Pair Of Old Trams

The fair had moved on. Mr Tapscrew had dismantled the Rat-Boy's Pit of Horror, and Mrs Tapscrew, with the aid of some horsehair and glue, had become a Bearded Woman to keep up the cash flow. She'd do it for a week and that was it, she said, it was too itchy for any more than that; so Mr Tapscrew was trying to persuade the Dodgems' sulky daughter to become Serpentina, the Snake-Girl. The Rat-Boy was over and done with.

Meanwhile, Bob and Joan had had to go back home, because there was work to be done, and they'd run out of money. They had to spend a few days earning some more, and then they went back to the town where the fair had been, and looked around.

They spent all day at it. They asked in every shop, they looked in every alley, they even did what they'd been uneasy about before and went to the police.

But the police were no help. The sergeant on duty took down the details and promised to have a poster made up, but without a picture, he pointed out, they couldn't expect much.

Bob and Joan went to sit in the Memorial Gardens to have their sandwiches.

'I feel as if we'll never find the poor little scrap,' she said.

'No,' said Bob, 'we'll find him. Don't fret, old girl. You know what?'

'What?'

'I reckon we got a purpose in our lives now, that's what. We been just trundling along all these years like a pair of old trams. I didn't think about nothing except soles and heels and the price of leather. But when that little boy come and knocked on our door, I got a jolt, I did. And now he's vanished I don't want to go trundling on in a straight line all the way to me grave. I got something better to do. Are you with me, old girl?'

'You're a silly old man,' she said. 'You and your

trams. Who are you calling a tram? How long have we been married now? I bet you can't remember.'

'Thirty-two years,' he said.

'Well all right, you can remember. And you have the nerve to ask if I'm with you. If I wasn't with you all the way to the depot, Bob Jones, I'd have gone off a long time ago. When you were talking to that Tapscrew, and you said – it was when you said – oh dear—'

She cried a bit then, and Bob just held her hand and let her dab her eyes.

'It was when you said "our little boy",' she went on after a bit, 'that's what done it. I'd go anywhere now and do anything to fetch him home, I really would. But oh, Bob . . . Do you really think he was a rat? That ain't possible, is it, for a rat to become a real boy?'

'No,' he said. 'Least, I never heard of it, or read it in the paper.'

'You and your blooming paper. Then what do you think is the truth about it? He wasn't lying, was he?'

233

'No. He's a truthful little soul. I don't think he could ever tell a lie. Even when he done bad things he owned up straight away. And they weren't really bad things anyway, only the kind of things a poor innocent beast would do . . .'

'Like a rat,' she said.

'That's right. I don't like rats any more than the next bloke, but they ain't wicked and cruel like people can be. They're just ratty in their habits.'

'That's Roger, too. Just a bit ratty in his habits,' she repeated, and dabbed her nose. 'There, I'm a bit better now. Oh, it is a worry . . .'

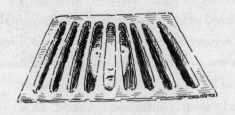

# Hunched And Malevolent,
## Radiating Pure Evil

The paper Bob read was good for sport, Bob said, but he usually read the stories about lottery winners and scandals and murders as well, and so did hundreds of thousands of other people.

The editor of the *Daily Scourge* encouraged his reporters to listen out for every kind of weird, or sentimental, or horrible, or sensational story they could find, and then he printed them, whether or not they were true. The best kind of story was one that went on and on, with a new twist every day, and could be easily understood even by numskulls in a hurry.

The *Daily Scourge* hadn't found much in the way of that kind of story recently. They had tried to whip up some interest in the royal wedding, but as soon as that was over people stopped buying so many papers. The editor was getting impatient.

So when an ambitious young *Daily Scourge* reporter began to hear a strange kind of rumour, he pricked up his ears and started asking questions. Pretty soon, more rumours began to circulate. There were said to be ghosts in the drains: people had heard them whispering. Someone had seen a creepy face looking up at her from a rainwater grating. And the men who cleaned the sewers swore they'd seen something down there in the dark.

The reporter arranged to meet three of the sewage workers in a pub, and bought them lots of drinks.

'So what is all this then?' he said. 'You saw something in the sewers? What sort of thing?'

'Something uncanny,' said one. 'A ghost, I reckon.'

'Or an evil spirit,' suggested another.

'A hobgoblin, even,' said the third man.

'What's it look like?'

'Ooh, evil,' said the first man. 'I couldn't describe it. I been working down the sewers all me life, and I never been frightened till now.'

'I tell you,' said the second man, 'it's not a fit sight for human eyes, what we saw down there.'

'A little figure,' said the third man, 'sort of like a horrible little man, scampering, running, kind of thing. Not like a proper human being. Kind of hunched and malevolent.'

*Hunched and malevolent*, the reporter wrote in his notebook. 'Good,' he said. 'What else?'

'You know where I seen something like that before?' said the second man. 'In the carving on the cathedral doorway showing the sinners being hauled off down the pit. There's a devil there with just the exact same expression. Gives you the shivers. Just radiating pure evil.'

*Pure evil*, wrote the reporter. 'Brilliant,' he said.

'And I tell you something else,' said the first man. 'The rats is back.'

'Rats?'

'Thousands and thousands of 'em. They cleared 'em out not so long ago, but they come back with a vengeance. You can hear 'em twittering in the dark. They're follering this ghost about.'

'Fantastic!' said the reporter. 'Look, lads, I don't suppose I could get down there and have a look around?'

They looked doubtful. He took out his wallet. They nodded.

# The Daily Scourge

## MONSTER FOUND IN SEWERS

*by our Star Reporter, Kelvin Bilge*

A monster, semi-human in shape, has been found living in the city's sewers.

It was captured yesterday after a desperate struggle in which three sewage workers were badly wounded.

### HUNDREDS MORE

Experts believe that the monster is the first of a new breed.

'There could be hundreds more breeding down below us,' said a scientist. 'The only solution is to destroy them before they get too strong for us.'

### EXTERMINATION

The monster is being kept in the custody of the quarantine department so that scientists can examine it before it is exterminated.

*Manhole where daring **Scourge** reporter, Kevin Bilge, entered sewers to confront monster*

The Mayor and City Council were urged last night to waste no more time.

### OUTRAGE AT MERCY PLEA

There was outrage when some politicians urged caution.

'We should not rush to judgement,' said an Opposition spokesman. 'The Monster is a victim too.'

# THE FREEDOM OF THE PRESS

All over the country, people read the *Daily Scourge* and shuddered.

In fact there was such a stir about the Monster of the Sewers that other stories vanished altogether. No-one was interested in the Chancellor's income-tax proposals, or in the Prince's return from his honeymoon with his new Princess, or even in the sports results: everyone wanted to hear about the Monster.

The *Daily Scourge* printed a special weekend supplement, and sold an extra two hundred and fifty thousand copies as a result.

# Special Supplement

## THE MONSTER OF THE SEWERS

Scientists are baffled by this creature. Is it the relic of a lost tribe of subhuman creatures?

Is it a visitor from another world?

Or is it a hideous mutation caused by environmental pollution?

What is certain is that nothing like it has ever been discovered before.

Its evil and bloodthirsty past can only be guessed at.

We must be thankful that the vigilance of the *DAILY SCOURGE* has revealed this horrible threat to the public.

*Artist's impression of the evil monster in his lair in the sewers.*

---

### YOUR VOTE

Fill in this coupon and send it to us:

*Should this evil monster be destroyed?*

# YES     NO

# Don't Be Deceived

At the quarantine department, the Government Chief Scientist looked in at the creature through the bars of the cage. It sat in a heap of straw, looking back at him with an expression which, of course, he couldn't understand.

'Certainly anthropoid,' he said, and his assistant made a note. 'I've heard talk of some connection with rats, but there's nothing rodent in its physiology, to my mind.'

'It's done a fair bit of gnawing,' said his assistant.

'So do chimpanzees. Twigs and things. This is a form of ape, no doubt about it.'

'But what was it doing in the sewers?'

'That's what we shall have to find out.'

The Chief Scientist was there because the Prime Minister had sent him to investigate. The Prime Minister was taking a close interest in the Monster case, because he wasn't very popular just then, and nor were any of the ministers in the government. It was a great help to have something else on the front pages of the papers, and even better to have something new for the public to hate. So the Chief Scientist was under instructions to find the Monster as loathsome as possible, and to spin out the examination for as long as he could.

With two experienced zookeepers at hand, armed with nets and prods in case the Monster became dangerous, the Chief Scientist opened the cage and went inside. His assistant stayed close at hand to make notes.

The Monster didn't look very monstrous, but the Chief Scientist didn't go by surface appearances. It was what lay underneath that mattered. This little shivering naked thing might have had the form of an ape, or even (to be more accurate) a human boy, but that only made it more horrible and unnatural. The Chief Scientist wrinkled his nose and prodded the creature with a pencil.

At once the Monster made a semi-human noise and seized the pencil in its filthy paw. The Chief Scientist let 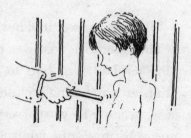 go, alarmed, and the Monster began to nibble the pencil with every appearance of pleasure.

'Remarkable,' said the Chief Scientist. 'Certainly an anthropoid manner of gnawing. Must be conditioned. Couldn't be inborn. Teeth the wrong shape altogether.'

'Excuse me, sir,' said one of the zookeepers uncertainly. 'Did I get it wrong, or did he say *Thank you*?'

The Chief Scientist laughed indulgently.

'No, no,' he said, 'the sound you heard was purely a reflex vocalization. It was your mind that put any meaning into it. I want you to hold the creature still so I can take a sample of its blood.'

'We better use the net, sir,' said the zookeeper.

'Go on then. I shall need a forelimb so I can find a vein.'

The zookeepers threw their net over the Monster,

which struggled violently, uttering lots of reflex vocalizations. But everyone disregarded them now, knowing that they didn't mean anything, and presently the creature was trussed and pinioned on the straw, with its forelimb outstretched.

'Hold it tight,' said the Chief Scientist, and stuck a needle into the skinny little arm and drew off some blood.

The creature howled and kicked and cried, but they found it was easier if they took no notice. The Chief Scientist corked the little bottle.

'That'll do for today,' he said. 'Now as for food: I've drawn up a list here, and I want it fed twice a day according to the plan. Then we'll try different kinds of stimulus to see what it responds to. Firstly we'll try noise. Then we'll lower the temperature . . .'

His assistant wrote all the plans down dutifully.

'He does seem . . . I don't know . . . very human,' she said tentatively when he'd finished.

'Appearances are only superficial. I expect to find the creature quite different, underneath, from what it seems on the surface.'

'Yes,' she said.

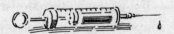

# Our Children Are In Danger

The results of the *Daily Scourge*'s Readers' Poll came in: 96% said the Monster should be destroyed, 2% said it shouldn't, and 2% didn't know, which was clever of them, because there wasn't a box to tick for *don't know*. The publicity campaign was building up. Other papers joined in.

*Every minute this vile and savage monster remains alive*, said one paper, *our children are in danger.*

*When is the government going to act?* said another.

*Make the streets safe for our children!* said a third.

Before long, the Monster was the main topic of conversation and guesswork. Everyone had an opinion, and the less they knew, the more strongly they expressed themselves. Soon politicians began to speak up as well. An MP said in Parliament, 'It is time to do away with old-fashioned scruples! There are choices that are hard, options that are painful, courses of action that require resolution and courage, but we must not shrink from the task, we must not falter, we must be bold and determined! I say to you, we must carry out this duty, and do so with a firm and fearless hand!'

What that meant was: we must do exactly what the *Daily Scourge* tells us to do, and hope it'll be nice to us. And what *that* meant was: we must get someone to kill the Monster. But of course he wouldn't have said it openly, because it sounded rather brutal, put like that.

Even the Government spent most of their cabinet meetings talking about the Monster.

'The public is alarmed!' said the Home Secretary. 'We must do something to calm their fears!'

'Stuff and nonsense,' said the Chancellor of the Exchequer. 'I don't believe this Monster even exists.'

'Well, it does, and I've seen it,' said the Minister for Agriculture.

They were amazed. 'How did you manage that?' said the Foreign Secretary, enviously.

'The quarantine department is my responsibility. And I have to tell you that when you see the Monster in the flesh, it looks uncannily like a small boy.'

'Appearances are deceptive!' said the Minister for Education.

'You can't judge by appearances!' said the Lord Chancellor.

'It's what's underneath that matters, not what it looks like on the surface!' said the Home Secretary. 'And I say the public demand a firm hand! This thing should be exterminated!'

'Well, normally, one would agree,' said the Minister of Agriculture. 'But consider the problem from the point of view of presentation. What would it look like to take what appears to be a small child and, as you say, exterminate him?'

There was a silence at that. They all saw the problem.

'Perhaps we could dress him up to look more like a monster,' suggested the Minister of

Education. 'It wouldn't look so bad then.'

They talked for hours. It was clear that they had to do something, or the newspapers would turn all their fury against them. But whatever they did mustn't seem unjust, because you could never tell what the voters would put up with, and there was an election coming up in a year or so.

Only the Prime Minister kept quiet. And when they asked him what he thought, he had an answer ready.

'I think we ought to set up a tribunal under a High Court judge, and call expert witnesses and so on, and let that decide,' he said firmly.

'Excellent idea!'

'A brilliant solution!'

'Magnificent stroke of imagination!'

They all agreed. So they appointed a judge, and set a date, and announced that the fate of the Monster was going to be decided by law.

# TRIPE

O n the day before the tribunal was going to begin, Bob and Joan were sitting at home, exhausted. They'd just come back from hours and hours of knocking on doors at the other end of town, just asking if anyone had seen Roger, because they couldn't think what else to do; and when they got back there was a load of washing to do and seven pairs of shoes to be re-soled and heeled; and now it was nearly midnight and they were drinking a cup of cocoa before going to bed.

Bob listlessly picked up the paper. He hadn't read it for days, and although he'd seen the headlines about monsters, he couldn't be bothered to read them: all he was interested in was Roger. But in order to take his mind off their trouble, he'd bought a copy on the way home, and he began to read the main story wearily. Then he sat up.

'Here,' he said, 'listen to this.'

He rustled the paper and began to read.

# The Daily Scourge

## FURY OVER MONSTER 'EXPERTS'

There was widespread fury today at reports that some so-called scientists will testify on behalf of the Rat-Monster at the Tribunal tomorrow.

The 'defence' intends to make the absurd claim that the sub-human creature from the darkness is actually a human being and should be spared extermination.

## HELPLESS VICTIMS

Members of the public were quick to condemn this move.

'How can we sleep safely when this hideous evil beast is still alive?' said Mrs Kitty Nettles, 38.

Mrs Nettles is a mother of six.

*Six adorable, helpless children. Children who might be victims of the ravening fiend.*

*Mrs Kitty Nettles, 27, and her family sheltering in an emergency refuge from gigantic, marauding, evil hell-monster*

## EVIL BEYOND BELIEF

Parents' groups were forming protest committees last night.

'This monster is evil beyond belief,' said Mr Derek Pratt, 46. 'Something must be done to protect our kiddies from the monster demon from hell. The government are keeping him safe on purpose. It is a conspiracy to protect the criminal elements and put ordinary innocent people into danger. If the government does not act to destroy this foul beast then we shall keep our children home from school indefinitely.'

## RIOT OVER HUNCHED FIGURE

A 500-strong crowd attacked a police station with bricks and stones after rumours spread that the Monster was inside.

'I saw this horrible hunched figure being taken in the back,' said Mrs Glenda Brain, 57. 'It was entirely covered in a blanket but I knew it was the Monster. I just had a feeling.'

# THE SCOURGE SAYS:

If the government does not act soon there will be bloodshed and it will be their fault.

*KILL THE MONSTER NOW. BEFORE IT'S TOO LATE!*

'What you reading that tripe for?' said Joan. 'That ain't worth using to wipe your feet on, that rubbish.'

'No, listen,' said Bob. 'We been so busy we missed all this. It seems they found this rat-creature in the sewers, and they're going to put it on trial and decide whether or not to kill it.'

Joan realized what he meant.

'You don't think—' she began.

'No, it couldn't be,' he said reluctantly. 'But just suppose—'

'What's it look like?'

'Let's see,' said Bob, turning the page. 'Evil – hideous – dangerous – vile – bloodthirsty – they don't say what it looks like . . .'

'He couldn't *change*, could he? The little one? He couldn't go back to being a proper rat?'

Bob was silent. 'We don't know as he ever was,' he said finally. 'He might have only thought it.'

'Bob, suppose it *is* Roger?' she said. 'And they're going to kill him!'

'Well, we'll have to go and stop 'em,' he said.

# No Room

The court building was crowded, and Bob and Joan had to struggle through packed corridors before they found the courtroom; and then they couldn't get in.

'Quite impossible,' said the usher outside the door. 'We been full up since seven o'clock this morning.'

'Please!' said Joan. 'We *got* to find out what this monster is!'

'So's ten thousand other people. Why should I let you in?'

'All right,' said Bob, 'here, take this. Here's a pound for you.'

'Get away!' the usher laughed. 'A *pound*? You're joking! *Fifty* pounds, and I might look the other way while you slip in at the back. There's some as gave me a hundred for a seat near the front. A *pound*? I'm insulted. Clear off.'

Bob would have had to go home on foot if the usher had taken the bribe, because it was all he had for the bus fare. Now he felt humiliated.

Joan said, 'There's no need to be rude, young man. What are all these people doing here if *they* can't get in?'

'Witnesses,' said the usher, and turned away to keep someone else out.

Joan tugged at Bob's arm and whispered, 'Those scientists must be here then – from the paper – the ones who are going to defend him . . .'

Bob unfolded the page he'd torn from the paper.

'Doesn't say their names, though,' he said.

'Perhaps we could find them,' she said hopefully.

The people in the corridor were arguing loudly and showing one another papers and diagrams and models of bones and skulls.

The door opened, and the usher called loudly:

'Mr Kelvin Bilge! Calling Mr Kelvin Bilge!'

One of the witnesses got up and followed him out.

'They must have started the trial,' said Bob.

He and Joan sat down unobtrusively near one of the loudest-arguing groups, and listened to what they were saying.

'—and it was surrounded by rats! Thousands of them!'

'—carry plague—'

'—assistant swore she'd heard it say *thank you*! I ask you!'

Bob and Joan looked at each other.

'—reflex vocalizations—'

'—studies on the vocal tract of parrots—'

'—particular fondness for pencils—'

Bob and Joan held each other's hand tightly.

'—of course the outcome's all arranged already, they're going to put it down—'

'*Daily Scourge*—'

'—I understand it sleeps curled up very small—'

Bob couldn't sit still. Joan got up with him and they walked to the end of the corridor and back, unable to speak.

Then the door opened. The usher looked out and

called, 'Mr Gordon Harkness! Calling Mr Gordon Harkness to the witness stand!'

No-one responded.

'Mr Gordon Harkness, please!'

Suddenly an idea came to Bob. He squeezed Joan's hand.

'Oh, sorry,' he called out. 'Mr Harkness, yes, that's me!'

'What are you *doing*?' Joan whispered.

'It's the only way to get in!' he whispered back.

'This way, please,' said the usher.

Bob tugged at Joan's reluctant hand. She was sure he'd be arrested for impersonation, and then they'd be in even more trouble, but he was just as solid and fearless as he ever was, and he said to the usher. 'This is my wife, Mrs Harkness. She's a witness too. I can't give me testimony without her. She's got to come in with me.'

'She's not on my list,' said the usher.

'That's because she weren't available. She was away seeing her niece. But she is now, so she ought to be with me.'

'Oh, very well. I don't suppose it matters.'

And the usher showed them into the courtroom.

# THE TRIBUNAL

There was a rustle of surprise all round the crowded court as Bob and Joan walked up to the witness stand together. Joan looked around nervously: there was a judge with a wig and a red gown, and rows of lawyers with wigs and black gowns, and what looked like hundreds of people crammed onto benches and standing at the back. To keep herself from trembling, Joan tried to count the seated ones and multiply by a hundred, and the standing ones and multiply by fifty, and add them together, to see how much money the usher had made.

As soon as Bob and Joan were on the stand, a lawyer stood up clutching his lapels and said. 'You are Mr Gordon Harkness, Lecturer in Comparative Anatomy?'

'No, I ain't,' said Bob. 'I'm Bob Jones, cobbler. And this is my wife Joan, washerwoman.'

'Then what are you doing here?'

'I had to pretend,' Bob went on, 'because you wouldn't have let us in otherwise. We got information about this so-called Monster that you ought to hear.'

The crowd was buzzing with excitement and curiosity. Lawyers passed notes to one another, the reporters scribbled busily, and all the spectators were talking and pointing and standing up to look.

'Silence!' said the Judge. 'I will have order in this court room. If we don't have silence, I shall clear the court.'

Everybody suddenly stopped talking.

'Now, Mr Jones,' said the judge, 'if that is your name, you had better explain yourself. This is a serious matter.'

'All right, your lordship,' said Bob. 'You see, we reckon that this Monster ain't a monster at all. It's a little boy called Roger. And all you need to do is just fetch him here and let everyone look at him,

and if it is him, then we'll take him home and that'll
be an end of it.'

'Is this Roger a relation of yours?' said the Judge.
'A child or a grandchild?'

'Well, no.'

'Then what is your connection with him?'

'He just knocked on the door one night and we
took him in,' Bob explained.

'Did you try to find out where he came from?'

'Yes.'

'Well, what did he tell you?'

'He said he'd been a rat,' said Bob unhappily.

The Judge glared at him.

'He did, Your Honour,' said Joan.

He glared at her too. Some of the people began to
whisper, and some began to laugh. The judge banged
his gavel for silence.

'And what did you do with this child?' he asked.

'We took him to the police, to the hospital, to the City Hall, and none of 'em wanted him. We sent him to school and all they did was thrash him. Then a gentleman called the Philosopher Royal called and took him away for some tests, and he frightened the boy and he ran away. Since then we been looking all over for him.

'And every time we nearly found him, something happened and he ran off somewhere else. He's a friendly little feller but he's very easy to mislead. And when we heard of this Monster nonsense we thought we should come along, in case they exterminated him by mistake.'

'I see,' said the Judge. 'Is the Philosopher Royal due to attend as a witness?'

'Tomorrow, my lord,' said the Clerk of the Court.

'Send for him now,' said the Judge. 'Mr and Mrs Jones, you did a wrong thing in deceiving the court. Nevertheless, I accept that you acted for what you thought were good reasons, and I direct that you shall be found room to sit and listen to the rest of the tribunal. But whether you are called again to the witness stand depends on my judgement.'

'Thank you, my lord,' said Bob.

The usher led them to a bench at the front and made everyone else squeeze up, which led to a lot of grumbling.

By this time the real Mr Harkness had arrived, and he was brought in next. He had examined the Monster, he claimed, and discovered all kinds of ways in which it was non-human. He showed the court diagrams and charts and mathematical tables, and proved by the use of chemical analysis and statistical spectroscopy that the Monster was an unknown and dangerous life-form.

Bob began to fidget. Joan nudged him to keep still.

The next witness was someone surprising: none other than Mr Tapscrew. Bob sat up and clenched his fists.

'You are the proprietor of a fairground exhibition?' said the lawyer.

'I am, sir, and proud to be so,' said Mr Tapscrew.

'Please tell the court of your involvement with the Monster.'

'I have had long experience with the freak trade, my lord. I have exhibited numerous natural wonders, from the famous Sumatran mermaid to the Boneless Wonder of Mexico.

'Now I don't need to explain to you sophisticated ladies and gentlemen that much of the business of a fairground exhibition is in the nature of light-hearted make-believe. My mermaid, for instance – well, whether there's mermaids in the sea I couldn't say, but this one was a girl called Nancy Swillers, and her tail was run up out of satin and sequins by my good lady wife. Mind you, we did good business with her; the patrons got their money's worth, Nancy got a wage, everyone was satisfied.

'But I'm always on the look-out for new and unusual exhibits to set before the public, my lord. And when I heard of a new kind of a monster, half child, half rat, I set out to find it. And—'

'One moment, Mr Tapscrew,' said the judge.

'Where did you hear of this phenomenon?'

'In the saloon bar of a pub called the Black Horse, if I remember right,' said Mr Tapscrew. 'I was passing the time of day, and someone happened to mention that he'd heard tell of a creature very like a child, only different, really a rat, in fact, being looked after or concealed by some neighbours of his. And this creature would gnaw its way through anything – it was wild, it was dangerous, it was probably carrying all kinds of diseases – he wasn't happy about living next to it.'

'Charlie,' muttered Bob.

'Sssh!' said Joan.

'Well, following on from this,' Mr Tapscrew went on, 'I made enquiries and began to investigate, and being a determined and experienced investigator, I soon found the creature in question.'

'Did you take it back to its carers? These neighbours you mentioned?' asked the lawyer.

'No. The fact was, I didn't know this man's name, the chap in the pub, and I forgot where he'd told me he lived. So—'

'I thought you said you were an experienced investigator,' said the Judge.

'You're quite right, my lord,' said Mr Tapscrew cheerfully, not a bit put out. 'So I did. But it was very late at night when I found it, and the rat-creature itself seemed to form an attachment to me. Anyway, he wouldn't leave me, and I took him home out of pure charity and my good lady wife gave him a meal and as we watched him eat, the idea came to me of exhibiting him as an educational display.

'So we went to great expense to fit out a wagon full of all the most comfortable surroundings, and made sure he had the most varied food, and opened it up to the serious-minded and discerning public.

'And I have to say, my lord—' here Mr Tapscrew took out an enormous handkerchief and blew his nose vigorously, '—I have to say we became quite attached to the creature, very fond indeed. It would curl up at our feet of an evening and take food from our hands, and we even taught it a few words.'

He dabbed his eyes, 'But nature will out, my lord,' he said sadly. 'You can take the beast into your home, but you can't make him human. One day the creature treacherously gnawed through the side of his wagon and escaped, and we haven't seen him from that day to this.'

Bob could hardly contain himself. Every muscle in his body was twitching to get up and punch Mr Tapscrew on his lying nose, but he knew that if he did that he'd be thrown out, and Joan was squeezing his hand so tight her nails were digging into his palm.

'From your first-hand observations of the creature,' the lawyer was saying, 'did you draw any conclusions as to its nature?'

'Yes,' said Mr Tapscrew. 'For all his mimicking, he wasn't human. There was a definite scaliness about him. He was covered in scabs and pustules. I dread to think of the health risks, but my dedication to science is so great that I didn't worry about it. And his gnawing: that was the give-away. Just exactly like a giant rat. That and the pustules.'

'And from your experience, Mr Tapscrew, would you say that a creature of this sort could be successfully tamed?'

'No, sir, it could not. As a young one, what you might call a cub or a puppy kind of thing, it might display signs of human-style behaviour and even affection. But let 'em grow up and feel their strength, and soon they start growing wild. They want to dominate, you see, they won't be tamed. They ain't like your dogs, or your cats, what are proper domesticated pets. This is a wild and ferocious creature. Just let it get big enough and nothing'll stop it from tearing your throat out and chewing it up before your very eyes. With relish,' he added with relish.

'And you have no idea what happened to the Monster after it escaped?'

'None, your worship?'

'What are you exhibiting at the moment, Mr Tapscrew?'

'A very fine and unusual display, if I may say so, your lordship. Serpentina the Snake Girl. Half snake, half human, this lithe and sinister creature displays her uncanny—'

'Is she genuine? Or is she like your mermaid?'

'Aha, you're no fool, I can see that. No,' said Mr Tapscrew jovially, 'she's a bit of light-hearted amusement. Half price today, ladies and gentlemen! Half-price admission to the Snake Girl during the trial—'

'Thank you, Mr Tapscrew. You may stand down.'

As Mr Tapscrew left the witness stand, he handed out leaflets to the nearest people, until he saw Bob and Joan glaring at him. Then he looked the other way, and hurried out.

The usher was handing the Judge a note. The Judge read it, and said, 'Very well. Call him in next.'

The usher went out, and Bob muttered, 'The longer they talk, the worse it gets! They oughter just bring the little feller in and put him on the stand, and then everyone'd see he ain't a monster!'

'I don't think they will,' Joan whispered back. 'The longer it goes on, the more silly they'd look if they did. They just can't afford to now.'

The usher came to the court and announced, 'Dr Septimus Prosser, the Philosopher Royal!'

'Ah, they're all coming out the woodwork now,' said Bob under his breath, as the Philosopher Royal took the stand.

'What are your duties, Dr Prosser?' the lawyer began.

'His Majesty the King is a very gifted amateur philosopher. I have the honour to serve as his personal philosophical adviser.'

'Could you tell the court of your involvement with the Monster?'

'By all means. It came to my attention that there was a child who claimed he had been a rat. I was curious, so I traced the child and conducted some tests.'

Here the Philosopher Royal took some papers out of a briefcase and put on a pair of glasses.

'I found,' he went on, 'a remarkable degree of dissociation and denial, paranoid in nature. The creature's cognitive development was abnormally retarded . . .'

Bob was grinding his teeth. The Philosopher Royal talked smoothly on, explaining, demonstrating, defining, and Roger seemed to become less and less real, until he was only a word among a lot of other words.

Eventually the Judge interrupted. 'Dr Prosser, let me see if I understand you clearly. You maintain that the creature is essentially a rat, and not essentially a human?'

'Quite so, my lord. The intrinsic nature of the creature is such that there is no moral continuum between it and ourselves.'

'Again, let me try to clarify this. You maintain

that we, as human beings, have no moral responsibility to this creature? It is not human, and therefore we should treat it as we might any kind of vermin?'

'Yes, that is the case.'

Bob could stand it no more. He stood and shook his fist at the Philosopher Royal, and roared, '*You* never treated him proper, you old fraud! You broke your word to us and you let him run away! Damn all this fancy talk! He ain't a monster or a creature or a rat or any kind of vermin – he's a little boy!'

The Judge was banging on the bench, the usher was hurrying towards Bob, two policemen were rushing in to help.

As they seized Bob's arm he shouted: 'Bring him to the court! Let 'em all have a look! Listen to him speak! Then you'll see! He's a little boy! He's human! He's like us! Bring him out and have a look at him!'

But they'd got him to the door by this time. Joan cried out to Bob that she was coming with him, but no-one could hear in all the confusion. People were shouting, jeering, laughing, standing on the benches to get a better look. It was the most exciting day in court for years.

# The Daily Scourge

## MONSTER CONDEMNED

The Monster of the Sewers is to die – official!

Yesterday, after sensational scenes at the Tribunal, the decision was handed down by the learned judge: **KILL THE FOUL BEAST**.

The Monster will be exterminated tomorrow.

## CELEBRATIONS

There were wild scenes of joy outside the court when the verdict was announced.

Parents who had been keeping their children away from school celebrated with fireworks and street parties.

Seventy-eight people were injured, five of them seriously.

### *Our Philosophy Correspondent writes:*

It was the testimony of Dr Prosser, the Philosopher Royal, that made the difference. **READ HIM TODAY**, only in the *Daily Scourge*.

## THE PHILOSOPHER ROYAL SPEAKS – ONLY IN THE *SCOURGE!*

### Don't believe in what you see!

*by Dr Septimus Prosser*

Wise men and women throughout the ages have said this again and again: appearances are deceptive.

It's not what something looks like on the surface that counts.

It's what lies underneath.

The Monster of the Sewers may look like a little child. He may have the appearance of a normal nine-year-old boy.

*But how often have we been deceived by looks?*

Our senses are limited things. We see very little compared to birds of prey. Next to bats, we're almost deaf. And as for the sense of smell, Fido and Rover have got us well beaten in that department.

**SO WHO IS TO SAY THAT WE SHOULD TRUST THE APPEARANCE OF THIS CREATURE?**

His true nature is what matters. Hidden, secret, dark, deceptive. A cesspool of wild appetites. That's the real truth of the matter.

Then there are those who ask what the Monster has 'done wrong'.

As if that matters!

Wrongness is in his very nature. It's what he is that matters, not what he does.

Philosophy says: **Don't trust your senses. The truth is not what you see. It's what you don't!**

## Scarlet Slippers, Or The Practical Value Of Craftsmanship

To tell the truth, the Philosopher Royal's article had been entirely rewritten by the sub-editor so the readers could under-stand it, but it was more or less what Dr Prosser had said.

Everyone agreed that this was a very effective article, and readers said to each other that of course you should never go by appearances, they never had done, you could never trust what someone looked like on the surface, they were bound to be different underneath.

Joan didn't read it, and nor did Bob. They were far too worried. After they'd been thrown out of the court, they had tried to find a reporter to tell their side of the story to, but no-one would listen. The *Daily Scourge* had decided that the public was more interested in having the Monster exterminated, so that was that.

As the old couple sat that evening in despair about what they could do, Joan caught sight of the newspaper. Bob had thrown it down angrily after reading the philosophy article, and it had fallen in a heap, with one of the inside pages on top. On it was a picture of the new princess.

And something came to Joan's mind, and she said suddenly, 'Mary Jane!'

'Who's Mary Jane?' said Bob.

'D'you remember,' she said, gripping his arm, 'when we was talking about the royal wedding and the new Princess, Roger said she was really called Mary Jane!'

'Oh, aye, so he did. I thought he was just making up a yarn.'

'Well, so did I. But he was ever so firm about it, and it wasn't like him to be stubborn, so I didn't ask him any more – anyway,' she said, 'what about asking her to help?'

'How?' he said.

'I don't know. But she seems a nice kind person, to go by her picture—'

'Shouldn't go by appearances,' Bob said bitterly.

'Oh, that's philosophy. Common sense always goes by appearances. I say she looks nice and she might *be* nice and it's the only thing we can do, isn't it?'

Bob scratched his head. 'Yeah,' he admitted, 'that's true enough.' Then he sat up. 'Here,' he said, 'I know how we can get to see her!'

'How?'

'You know them scarlet slippers I made, with the gold heels?'

She said nothing, but just looked at him, and nodded.

'Well,' he went on, 'we could take 'em to her as a present, and if she can't wear 'em herself she could use 'em for a royal child if one comes along. We'll go right away!'

# Princess Mary Jane

They knew the way to the palace well enough by now, and they found the place much better looked after than when they'd last come. There were no high jinks in the servants' hall, no football in the courtyard, no smoking in the sentry boxes. Now the King and Queen were back from the Hotel Splendifico, and the young Prince and Princess were back from their honeymoon, everything was spick and span and the servants were on their best behaviour.

The footman who came to answer their knock at the tradesmen's entrance listened carefully, and said, 'I shall convey your gift to Her Royal Highness, and I'm sure her lady-in-waiting will send you a note of thanks.'

'Could we see the Princess ourselves?' said Joan. 'It's really important, honest.'

'Not without an appointment, madam. Write to the Office of the Princess Aurelia at the Palace. Her Private Secretary will see to it.'

'But we *got* to see her!' said Bob, desperately. 'It's a matter of life and death!'

'I'm very sorry—' the footman began, but a voice behind him said:

'Who's this?'

It was a young lady's voice. The footman jumped with surprise, and bowed while he was still in mid-air, so he came down already in a crouch.

Bob and Joan could hardly believe their eyes. It was the new Princess herself, dressed in casual clothes, just standing there as ordinary as they were. The footman didn't know whether to fawn and grovel, or to tell her off for being in the wrong part of the Palace.

'Oh, Your Royal Highness,' said Joan quickly, 'we came to bring you a present—'

'How kind! Do come in,' she said.

The footman sagged with shock, but he had to go along with what the Princess wanted, and he held the door open for Bob and Joan.

They felt very shy. They followed the Princess along the corridor and up the stairs into a friendly-looking little sitting room, not at all grand and pompous like the rest of the palace.

'Er – here you are, Your Royal Highness,' said Bob, handing her the shoebox. 'If they don't fit, I expect they'll do one day for a littl'un. Beg your pardon – I mean a young princess. I made 'em meself,' he added.

'Oh, they're beautiful,' she said, kicking off the sandals she was wearing. 'And they fit me perfectly! Thank you so much. You're too kind.'

They did fit, too, small as they were. Bob could hardly believe his luck.

'I'm glad you like 'em, ma'am,' he said. 'But the thing is, we got a terrible problem – I don't like to impose, but we couldn't think of anyone else to ask—'

'Tell me about it,' she said. 'Let's sit down.'

She wasn't at all like you expected a princess to be, they agreed afterwards; just like a real person, in fact, but a thousand times prettier; and so kind and concerned. She listened to their story from the moment Bob heard the knock on the door to the moment they thought of bringing her the slippers.

The Princess listened wide-eyed, and didn't speak till they'd finished. She'd gone pale.

'They're going to *kill* him?' she said.

'It's cruel and wicked,' said Bob, 'but we can't stop 'em. We done everything we could think of.'

'So we came to you,' said Joan, 'as a last resort, and I'm sorry to put this trouble on your doorstep, but the thing is, he said something about "Mary Jane", and—'

The Princess sat up sharply.

'But that's my name!' she said. 'Only no-one's supposed to know it. They said it wasn't a suitable name for a princess, and I had to change it. But tell me again: *when* did he say he changed into a boy?'

'He weren't sure,' said Bob, 'but reckoning backwards, I'd say it were just about the time your

280

engagement was announced, ma'am.'

The Princess put her hand to her mouth.

'I know who he is!' she whispered. 'Please – don't ask any more – I'll help him,' she said. 'I'll do my best, I promise – but you mustn't ask me any more about it! Please! It's a deadly secret . . .'

'We wouldn't dream of betraying any secrets,' said Bob. 'And if you help to save that little boy, I'll keep you in slippers for the rest of your life, ma'am.'

'Do you think you can, Your Royal Highness?' said Joan.

'I don't know what they'll let me do,' said the Princess, 'but I'll try my absolute hardest, I promise.'

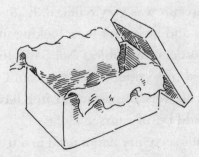

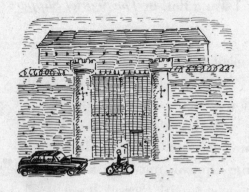

# THE PRINCESS AND THE PRISON

Next day, the director of the quarantine department received an urgent message as soon as he arrived for work.

'Do not proceed with the E-programme for Subject No. 5463. Repeat, do not proceed. Expect Very Important Visitor. Make sure Subject is clean and presentable.'

The Director was very relieved. E stood for extermination, and he hadn't been looking forward to it. He gave orders for Subject No. 5463 to be washed and placed in a comfortable cage, and then he got ready for his Very Important Visitor, having no idea who it could be, of course.

When his secretary announced in a trembly voice,

'Her Royal Highness the Princess Aurelia,' he nearly fainted.

Like everyone else, he was fascinated by the graceful and charming princess. He'd read all the accounts of her whirlwind engagement, he'd been among the crowd cheering on the wedding day, he'd half-fallen in love with her himself, as so many others had done. To find her here, in his own office, almost made him dizzy.

She was wearing something that made her look even prettier than he could imagine. There was a detective to guard her and a lady-in-waiting to accompany her, and through all the bewildered roaring in his ears the director heard her say something about the Rat-Boy.

'I'm sorry,' he said, 'the . . . did you say . . . ?'

'Yes,' she said, 'I'd like to visit him if I may.'

'He's – er – very dangerous, ma'am,' he managed to say. 'He doesn't look it but, as you know, appearances are very deceptive. It's easy to be misled into thinking he's harmless, but—'

'Yes, I understand,' she said. 'But I'm very interested in this case, and I'd like to see for myself.'

'Of course! By all means! Now we'll just call three or four keepers – they'll be armed, don't worry – and then I'll take you along to his cage.'

'Why do you keep him in a cage?' said the Princess.

'Because he is a being of unknown origin, something sinister and dangerous,' the director explained patiently. She was so pretty, he thought, it didn't matter if she wasn't very clever.

'I see,' she said. 'Well, I'd like to see him anyway. And if he's in a cage, I won't need any other protection.'

She was stubborn too. She wouldn't agree to the armed member of staff, and she insisted on her lady-in-waiting and her detective staying in the office. She wanted to see the Monster alone, and that was that.

Well, she was the Princess, and they had to agree, although the idea of this fragrant delicate beauty face to face with the ravening Monster of the Sewers made the director shiver. It was too horrible to think about what might happen, so he tried not to think about anything, and ordered some coffee and made conversation with the lady-in-waiting instead.

# WISH AS HARD AS YOU LIKE

Roger was sitting on the floor of his cage counting his toes, when the door of the room opened and someone came in. He didn't look up; they were all the same, except that some of them were worse.

But his nostrils caught a nice smell, like flowers.

It reminded him of something. He twitched a bit harder – and then he looked up.

'Mary Jane!' he cried.

She was alone. He jumped up with delight, never minding that he hadn't got any clothes on, and ran to reach out through the bars.

She took his hands.

'Hush, Ratty,' she said, 'you mustn't call me Mary

Jane any more. We both been changed, and you're Roger now, isn't that right? Well, I'm Princess Aurelia. So you mustn't tell anyone about Mary Jane, and I won't tell anyone you were a rat.'

'I kept telling 'em,' he said, 'only no-one believed me! First they never believed I was a rat, then they never believed I'm a boy! I don't understand 'em, truly I don't.'

'Bob and Joan came to see me last night,' she said. 'I never knew about any of it till then. Oh, they're so worried about you, Roger. And I told them I'd help, and I'll try, truly I will. It's horrible what these people are doing to you, it's wrong and wicked, and I'll get it stopped, see if I don't. Evil monster from the sewers! I never heard such nonsense!'

'Where's the monster?' said Roger, half-frightened.

'There isn't one,' she said. 'Now listen carefully, because we might not be able to talk again like this, in private I mean. What do you remember about being a rat?'

'Well, I was a little boy rat, and we lived near the cheese stall in the market, just behind your house. And you used to work in the kitchen. And you used to give me scraps and tickle me and call me Ratty. I remember that now, but I forgot it before. Then one day you caught me in a shoebox and brung me in the kitchen too, and before I knew anything else, I was a boy, standing up like this, only with clothes on.'

'Do you remember what changed you?'

'No. When I was a rat I didn't know anything, and when I was a boy it was all over already. But you was all dressed up for dancing, and I had to go with you on the coach and open the door and pull the step down and go with you into the palace. This beautiful lady told me all that, and I done it.'

'And you were supposed to wait with the coach for me to come back.'

'Was I? That must be what I forgot to do. Yes, I remember! I got lost in the palace and got up to

mischief. Me and the palace page-boys, we played football in them long corridors upstairs, and we slid down the banisters, and we crept in the kitchen and ate the jellies and sausage rolls. We done all kinds of things. And then I was supposed to go back on the coach, and put the step up after you and shut the door and all, only when I remembered and went there, you was gone and there wasn't a coach or nothing. And they wouldn't let me back in the palace because all them other page-boys had been whipped and sent to bed, and I didn't belong, I had the wrong uniform, so they sent me away.

'And after that I dunno what I done. All kinds of bad things, I think. Then I found Bob and Joan, only I got lost again, and now I'm in prison. I think

they're going to sterminate me, Mary Jane, and if Bob and Joan knew about it, they wouldn't let it happen. Maybe it'd be best if I went back to being a proper rat. I tried being a rat in the sewers, only nothing went right. I can't go back and I can't go forward, I don't know what to do, Mary Jane, really I don't. Can I go back?'

'I don't reckon you can,' she said, 'any more than I can. You're stuck as a boy, and I'm stuck as a princess.'

'Don't you want to be a princess, Mary Jane?'

'Well, I did to start with. I longed for it. I wished so hard! But I'm not sure any more. I'm so afraid I made a mistake, Roger. I might have been better off staying as Mary Jane. See, I don't think it's what you *are* that matters. I think it's what you *do*. I think they'd like me to just *be*, and not do anything. That's the trouble.'

'We oughter work that magic again, like what changed us in the first place,' he said.

'I wish we could,' she said.

'We could try and wish that lady back!'

'Yes,' she said, 'let's try.'

She was holding his hands through the bars. The

Princess and the Monster closed their eyes and wished, as hard as they could, till they were trembling with it; but when they opened their eyes, nothing had changed, and the only beautiful lady there was the Princess herself.

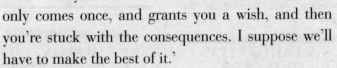

'Well, perhaps we can't,' she said after a moment or two. 'It goes to show. Maybe she only comes once, and grants you a wish, and then you're stuck with the consequences. I suppose we'll have to make the best of it.'

'Well, I *could* go on being a boy,' said Roger, 'if only they'd let me. I can do it quite well most of the time, except when they make out I'm something else underneath.'

'We'll have to see what we can do,' said the Princess.

# MIRACLE OF PRINCESS AND 'MONSTER'

There were extraordinary scenes yesterday outside the Palace as the news emerged of Princess Aurelia's miracle intervention in the so-called 'Monster' case.

As many had suspected, the 'Monster' was nothing of the sort.

## A FAIRY-TALE PRINCESS

It took the clear-sighted vision of a fairy-tale Princess to penetrate to the heart of the matter, and see the astounding truth:

***THE MONSTER WAS ONLY A LITTLE BOY.***

Not a subhuman fiend. Not a venom-dripping beast from the nethermost pit of hell.

Just a normal little fellow like any other. Mischievous, perhaps – but evil?

Not in a month of Sundays!

## LUCKY TO BE ALIVE

The boy is to be released into the care of foster-parents, and apprenticed to a decent trade.

# THE SCOURGE SAYS:

**GOD BLESS PRINCESS AURELIA!**

There's no corner of the world so dark that a little ray of magic from a Princess's heart can't light it up.

As for these self-appointed 'experts' and 'philosophers':

**WHERE IS THEIR COMPASSION?**

Thanks to Princess Aurelia, a little boy can sleep safe tonight.

*How many more innocent children are under threat from our cruel cold-hearted system of so-called justice?*

*Princess or angel?*

Read more about Princess Aurelia on *pages 2–13*

A fairy tale made in heaven, by our Royal Correspondent *p. 14–16*

Private pictures from Princess Aurelia's family collection *p. 17–19*

Special feature: Princess Aurelia's favourite charities *p. 20–21*

Interview with Princess Aurelia's hairdresser *p. 22*

Beauty tips by Princess Aurelia's personal make-up expert *p. 23*

Compassion: the latest health secret *p. 24*

# THE POWER OF THE PRESS

On every front page of every newspaper in the country there were big pictures of the Princess, looking beautiful and concerned, and the stories that went with them were confusing, but they all said roughly the same thing: the Princess, by the superhuman power of her love and compassion, had worked a miracle and transformed the ghastly evil ravening Monster of the Sewers into a normal little boy.

What had really happened, of course, was simple. The *Daily Scourge* had seen an even better story than the one about the Monster of the Sewers. The Princess Aurelia story had everything, and it could run for years, with prettier pictures, too.

## Toasted Cheese

'Well, I never knew the like,' said Bob. 'I tell you this, I'm fed up with them blooming papers. I'll never buy one again.'

'Yes you will,' said Joan. 'You'll buy it for the sports and the crossword, and then you'll just see what's happened in the news, and you'll believe it just as much as you ever did.'

'I won't,' he said, but he didn't want to argue.

In the corner, Roger was busy stitching a little shoe. He hardly ever nibbled the leather any more, and Bob could leave his beeswax on the bench and only find two or three toothmarks when he came back.

 'Look,' said the boy. 'Is that neat? I think it is. I stitched it ever so tight all the way round.'

'Just right,' said Bob, peering through his glasses. 'I reckon you're going to be a good cobbler.'

'Roger, love,' said Joan, 'come here a minute. I want to ask you something.'

The little boy came and stood on the hearth in front of her. He had new clothes on, and his brown hair was neatly brushed, and his black eyes shone.

'Yes?' he said politely.

'What really happened when the Princess came and saw you?' she said. 'All this stuff about miracles and so on. No-one's told us the truth, and no-one ever will unless you do.'

'We just talked,' said Roger. 'And she remembered who I was, because she used to know me when I was a rat. Then I was made into a page-boy when she went to the Ball, only I missed the coach back through getting up to mischief. If I'd gone back on that coach I'd've been made back into a rat. I suppose that might have been better, except I might have remembered being a boy and I'd've wanted to be a boy again, for ever.

'But she's changed too now, Mary Jane has. I mean the Princess. She ain't so happy now. It all come about because of her wish, and that goes to show,' he said.

'What's it go to show?' said Bob.

'I dunno. It's what she said. But she made me promise to be as good a boy as I could, and she promised me she was going to be as good a princess as she could, and that was the consequence.'

'Ah,' said Bob. 'And do you want to be a rat now?'

'It'd be easier,' said Roger. 'You have less trouble being a rat, except for being sterminated. I wouldn't want that. It's hard being a person, but it's not so hard if they think you *are* a person. If they think you ain't a person, then it's too hard for me. I think I'll stick to cobbling.'

'That's a wise decision,' said Bob. 'There's always a demand for good craftsmanship. If I hadn't made them slippers, well, I don't like to think what would have happened.'

The kettle came to the boil, so Joan made them all a cup of tea, and Bob toasted some cheese, and they all sat down comfortably around the hearth. The world outside was a difficult place, but toasted cheese and love and craftsmanship would do to keep them safe.

# PHILIP PULLMAN

## Clockwork

### or All Wound Up

Illustrated by Peter Bailey

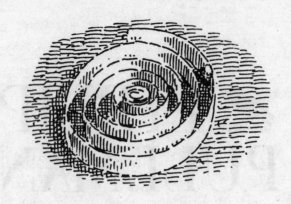

# CLOCKWORK: A PREFACE

In the old days, when this story took place, time used to run by clockwork. Real clockwork, I mean, springs and cogwheels and gears and pendulums and so on. When you took it apart you could see how it worked, and how to put it together again. Nowadays, time runs by electricity and vibrating crystals of quartz and goodness knows what else. You can even buy a watch that's powered by a solar panel, and sets itself several times a day by picking up a radio signal, and never runs a second late. Clocks and watches like that might as well work by witchcraft for all the sense I can make of them.

Real clockwork is quite mysterious enough.

Take a spring, for instance, like the mainspring of an alarm clock. It's made of tempered steel, with an edge that's sharp enough to draw blood. If you play about with it carelessly it'll spring up and strike at you like a snake, and put out your eye. Or take a weight, the kind of iron weight that drives the mighty clocks they have in church towers. If your head were under that weight, and if the weight fell, it would dash out your brains on the floor.

But with the help of a few gears and pins, and a little balance wheel oscillating to and fro, or a pendulum swinging from side to side, the strength of the spring and the power of the weight are led harmlessly through the clock to drive the hands.

And once you've wound up a clock, there's something frightful in the way it keeps on going at its own relentless pace. Its hands move steadily round the dial as if they had a mind of their own. Tick, tock, tick, tock! Bit by bit they move, and tick us steadily on towards the grave.

Some stories are like that. Once you've wound them up, nothing will stop them; they move on forwards till they reach their destined end, and

Philip Pullman

no matter how much the characters would like to change their fate, they can't. This is one of those stories. And now it's all wound up, we can begin.

# PART ONE

O nce upon a time (when time ran by clockwork), a strange event took place in a little German town. Actually, it was a series of events, all fitting together like the parts of a clock, and although each person saw a different part, no-one saw the whole of it; but here it is, as well as I can tell it.

It began on a winter's evening, when the townsfolk were gathering in the White Horse Tavern. The snow was blowing down from the mountains, and the wind was making the bells shift restlessly in the church tower. The windows were steamed up, the stove was blazing brightly, Putzi the old black cat was snoozing on the hearth; and the air was full of the rich smells of sausage and sauerkraut, of tobacco and beer. Gretl the little barmaid, the landlord's daughter, was hurrying to and fro with foaming mugs and steaming plates.

The door opened, and fat white flakes of snow swirled in, to faint away into water as they met the heat of the parlour. The incomers, Herr Ringelmann the clockmaker and his apprentice Karl, stamped their boots and shook the snow off their greatcoats.

'It's Herr Ringelmann!' said the Burgomaster. 'Well, old friend, come and drink some beer with me! And a mug for young what's his name, your apprentice.'

Karl the apprentice nodded his thanks and went to sit by himself in a corner. His expression was dark and gloomy.

'What's the matter with young thingamajig?' said the Burgomaster. 'He looks as if he's swallowed a thundercloud.'

'Oh, I shouldn't worry,' said the old clockmaker, sitting down at the table with his friends. 'He's anxious about tomorrow. His apprenticeship is coming to an end, you see.'

'Ah, of course!' said the Burgomaster. It was the

custom that when a clockmaker's apprentice finished his period of service, he made a new figure for the great clock of Glockenheim. 'So we're to have a new piece of clockwork in the tower! Well, I look forward to seeing it tomorrow.'

'I remember when my apprenticeship came to an end,' said Herr Ringelmann. 'I couldn't sleep for thinking about what would happen when my figure came out of the clock. Supposing I hadn't counted the cogs properly? Supposing the spring was too stiff? Supposing – oh, a thousand things go through your mind. It's a heavy responsibility.'

'Maybe so, but I've never seen the lad look so gloomy before,' said someone else. 'And he's not a cheerful fellow at the best of times.'

And it seemed to the other drinkers that Herr Ringelmann himself was a little down-hearted, but he raised his mug with the rest of them and changed the conversation to another topic.

'I hear young Fritz the novelist is going to read us his new story tonight,' he said.

'So I believe,' said the Burgomaster. 'I hope it's not as terrifying as the last one he read to us. D'you know, I woke three times that night and found my hair on end, just thinking about it!'

'I don't know if it's more frightening hearing them here in the parlour, or reading them later on your own,' said someone else.

'It's worse on your own, believe me,' said another. 'You can feel the ghostly fingers creeping up your spine, and even when you know what's going to happen next you can't help jumping when it does.'

Then they argued about whether it was more terrifying to hear a ghost story when you didn't know what was going to happen (because it took you by surprise) or when you did (because there was the suspense of waiting for it). They all enjoyed ghost stories, and Fritz's in particular, for he was a talented storyteller.

The subject of their conversation, Fritz the writer himself, was a cheerful-looking young man who had been eating his supper at the other end of the parlour. He joked with the landlord, he laughed with his neighbours, and when he'd finished, he called for another mug of beer, gathered up the untidy pile of manuscript beside his plate, and went to talk to Karl.

'Hello, old boy,' he said cheerfully. 'All set for

# Clockwork or *All Wound Up*

THE GREAT CLOCK OF GLOCKENHEIM WAS THE MOST AMAZING PIECE OF MACHINERY IN THE WHOLE OF GERMANY. IF YOU WANTED TO SEE ALL THE FIGURES YOU WOULD HAVE TO WATCH IT FOR A WHOLE YEAR, BECAUSE THE MECHANISM WAS SO COMPLEX THAT IT TOOK TWELVE MONTHS TO COMPLETE ITS MOVEMENT. THERE WERE ALL THE SAINTS, EACH COMING OUT ON THEIR OWN DAY; THERE WAS DEATH, WITH HIS SCYTHE AND HOURGLASS; THERE WERE OVER A HUNDRED FIGURES ALTOGETHER. HERR RINGELMANN WAS IN CHARGE OF IT ALL. THERE NEVER WAS A CLOCK LIKE IT, I PROMISE.

tomorrow? I'm looking forward to it! What are you going to show us?'

Karl scowled and turned away.

THE ARTISTIC TEMPERAMENT! WHAT NONSENSE! THERE'S NO SUCH THING. ONLY AMATEURS HAVE TEMPERAMENTS. REAL ARTISTS GET ON WITH THE JOB AND DON'T FUSS ABOUT IT. IF YOU HEAR ANYONE TALKING ABOUT THE ARTISTIC TEMPERAMENT, YOU CAN BE SURE THEY DON'T KNOW WHAT THEY'RE TALKING ABOUT.

'The artistic temperament,' said the landlord wisely. 'Drink up your beer, and have another on the house, in honour of tomorrow.'

'Put poison in, and I'll drink it then,' muttered Karl.

'What?' said Fritz, who could hardly believe his ears. The two of them were sitting right at the end of the bar, and Fritz moved so as to turn his back on the rest of the company and speak to Karl in private. 'What's the matter, old fellow?' he went on quietly. 'You've been working at your masterpiece for months! Surely you're not worried about it? It can't fail!'

Karl looked at him with a face full of savage bitterness.

'I haven't made a figure,' he muttered. 'I couldn't

do it. I've failed, Fritz. The clock will chime tomorrow, and everyone will be looking up to see what I've done, and nothing will come out, nothing . . .' He groaned softly, and turned away. 'I can't face them!' he went on. 'I should go and throw myself off the tower now and have done with it!'

'Oh, come on, don't talk like that!' said Fritz, who had never seen his friend so bitter. 'You must have a word with old Herr Ringelmann – ask his advice – tell him you've hit a snag – he's a decent old fellow, he'll help you out!'

'You don't understand,' said Karl passionately. 'Everything's so easy for you! You just sit at your desk and put pen to paper, and stories come pouring out! You don't know what it is to sweat and strain for hours on end with no ideas at all, or to struggle with materials that break, and tools that go blunt, or to tear your hair out trying to find a new variation on the same old theme – I tell you, Fritz, it's a wonder I haven't blown my brains out long before this! Well, it won't be long now. Tomorrow morning you can all laugh at me. Karl, the failure. Karl, the hopeless. Karl, the first apprentice to fail in hundreds of years of clockmaking. I don't care. I shall be lying at the bottom of the river, under the ice.'

Fritz had had to stop himself interrupting when Karl spoke about the difficulty of working. Stories are just as hard as clocks to put together, and they can go wrong just as easily – as we shall see with Fritz's own story in a page or two. Still, Fritz was an optimist, and Karl was a pessimist, and that makes all the difference in the world.

Putzi the cat, waking from his snooze on the hearth, came and rubbed his back against Karl's legs. Karl kicked him savagely away.

'Steady on,' said Fritz.

But Karl only scowled. He drank deeply and wiped his mouth with the back of his hand before banging the mug on the counter and calling for more. Gretl the young barmaid looked anxiously at Fritz, because she was only a child, and wasn't sure whether she should be serving someone in Karl's condition.

'Give him some more,' said Fritz. 'He's not drunk, poor fellow, he's unhappy. I'll keep an eye on him, don't you worry.'

So Gretl poured some more beer for Karl, and the clockmaker's apprentice scowled and turned away.

Fritz was worried about him, but he couldn't stay there any longer, because the patrons were calling for him.

'Come on, Fritz! Where's that story?'

'Sing for your supper! Come on! We're all waiting!'
'What's it about this time, eh? Skeletons, or ghosts?'

'I hope it's a nice bloody murder!'

'No, I hear he's got something quite different for us this time. Something quite new.'

'I've got a feeling it's going to be more horrible than anything we could imagine,' said old Johann the woodcutter.

While the drinkers ordered more mugs of beer to see them through the story, and filled their pipes and settled themselves comfortably, Fritz gathered up his manuscript and took up his place by the stove.

To tell the truth, Fritz was less comfortable himself than he had ever been before at one of these story-telling evenings, because of what Karl had just told him, and because of the theme of his story – of the start of it, anyway. But after all, it wasn't about Karl. The subject was really quite different.

(There was another private reason for Fritz to be nervous. The fact was, he hadn't actually finished the story. He'd written the start all right, and it was terrific, but he hadn't been able to think of an ending. He was just going to wind up the story, set it going, and make up the end when he got there. As I said just now, he was an optimist.)

'We're all ready and waiting,' said the Burgomaster. 'I'm looking forward to this story, even if it does make my hair stand on end. What's it called?'

'It's called –' said Fritz, with a nervous glance at Karl – 'it's called "Clockwork".'

'Ah! Very appropriate!' cried old Herr Ringelmann. 'Did you hear that, Karl? This is a story in your honour, my boy!'

Karl scowled and looked down at the floor.

'No, no,' said Fritz hastily, 'this story isn't about Karl, or the clock in our town, no, not at all. It's quite different. It just happens to be called "Clockwork".'

'Well, set it going,' said someone. 'We're all ready.'

So Fritz cleared his throat and arranged his papers and began to read:

### FRITZ'S STORY

'I wonder if any of you remember the extraordinary

business at the palace a few years ago? They tried to hush it up, but some details came out, and a bizarre mystery it was, too. It seems that Prince Otto had taken his young son Florian hunting, together with an old friend of the royal family, Baron Stelgratz. It was the dead of winter – just like now. They'd set off in a sledge for the hunting lodge up in the mountains, well wrapped up against the cold, and they weren't expected back for a week or so.

'Well, what should happen but that only two nights later, the sentry on duty at the palace gate saw a commotion down the road, and heard the whinnying of horses – whinnying in panic – making a terrible racket; and it looked, though he couldn't be sure, as if a sledge was being driven towards the palace by a madman.

'The sentry raised the alarm, and called for lights, and when the sledge got close enough, they could see that it was the royal sledge, the very one the prince had set off in only two nights before. It was hurtling up the road behind those terrified horses, and it wasn't going to stop; and the sergeant of the guard gave orders to drag the palace gates open quickly before it crashed.

'They got them open just in time. The sledge rushed through, and then drove round and round the courtyard, for the horses were mad with fear and couldn't stop. The poor beasts were covered with foam and their eyes were rolling, and the sledge would be going round that courtyard still if one of the runners hadn't caught on a mounting block and turned the whole thing over.

'Out fell the driver, and out fell a bundle from the back of the sledge. A servant hastened to pick it up, and found little Prince Florian wrapped in a fur rug, safe and warm and half asleep.

'But as for the driver . . .

'Well, as soon as the sentries came close, they saw who it was. It was none other than Prince Otto himself, stark dead, as cold as ice, with his eyes wide and staring ahead of him, his left hand gripping the reins so tight they had to be cut loose, and (this was the strangest part) his right hand still moving, lashing the whip up and down, up and down, up and down.

'They covered him up so the princess wouldn't see him, and took little Prince Florian to her to prove he was alive and well, because he was their only child.

'But what was to be done with Prince Otto? They

took his body into the palace and sent for the Royal Physician, a worthy old man who'd studied in Heidelberg and Paris and Bologna, and who'd published a treatise on the location of the soul; he'd studied geology, and hydrology, and physiology, but he'd never seen anything like this before. A dead body that wouldn't keep still! Imagine that! Stretched out icy-cold on a marble slab, with its right arm lashing and lashing and lashing with no sign that it was ever going to stop.

THERE WAS A LOT OF ARGUMENT ABOUT THE LOCATION OF THE SOUL IN THOSE DAYS. SOME PHILOSOPHERS THOUGHT IT WAS LOCATED IN THE BRAIN, SOME IN THE HEART, SOME IN THE PINEAL GLAND, WHATEVER THAT IS. THEY EVEN USED TO WEIGH PEOPLE BEFORE AND AFTER THEY DIED, TO SEE WHETHER THEY WEIGHED LESS WHEN THE SOUL HAD LEFT THEM. I DON'T KNOW WHETHER THEY DID OR NOT.

'The physician locked the door to keep the servants out, and brought the lamp closer, and bent low to look, and then his eye was caught by something in the clumsy arrangement of the clothes. So, avoiding that lashing right arm, he carefully unfastened the cloak and the fur coat and the under-jacket and the shirt, and laid the prince's chest bare.

315

'And there it was: a gash across his breast just over the heart, crudely sewn up with a dozen stitches. The physician got his scissors and snipped them away, and then he nearly fainted with surprise, because when he opened the wound, there was no heart there. Instead, there was a little piece of clockwork: just a few cogs and springs and a balance wheel, attached in subtle ways to the prince's veins and tick-tick-ticking away merrily, in perfect time with the lashing of his arm.

'Well, you can imagine how the physician crossed himself and took a sip of brandy to calm his nerves. Who wouldn't? Then he carefully cut the attachments and lifted out the clockwork, and as he did so, the arm fell still, just like that.'

As he got to that point in his story, Fritz paused for a sip of beer, and to see how his audience was taking it. The silence in the inn was profound. Every single customer was sitting so still they might have been dead themselves, except for their wide eyes and expressions of tense excitement. He had never had such a success!

He turned the page and read on:

### Fritz's Story (continued)

'Well, the physician sewed up Prince Otto's wound, and let it be known that the prince had died of apoplexy. The servants who'd carried the body in thought differently; they knew a dead man when they saw one, even if his arm was moving; at any rate, the official version was that Prince Otto had suffered a contusion of the brain, and that his love for his son had kept him alive just long enough to drive him safely home. He was buried with a good deal of ceremony, and everyone was in mourning for six months.

'As for what had happened to Baron Stelgratz, the other member of the hunting party, no-one could guess. The whole affair was shrouded in mystery.

'But the Royal Physician had an idea. There was one man who might be able to explain what had happened, and that was the great Dr Kalmenius of Schatzberg, of whom very few people had heard; but those who did know of him said he was the cleverest man in Europe. For making clockwork, he had no equal, not even our good Herr Ringelmann. He could make intricate pieces of calculating apparatus that worked out the positions of all the stars and the planets, and answer any mathematical question.

'Dr Kalmenius could have made his fortune if he'd wanted to, but he wasn't interested in fortune or in fame. He was interested in something far deeper than that. He would spend hours sitting in grave-yards, contemplating the mysteries of life and death. Some said he experimented on dead bodies. Others said he was in league with the powers of darkness. No-one knew for certain. But one thing they did know was that he used to walk about at night, pulling behind him a little sledge containing what-ever secret matter he was working on at the time.

'What did he look like, this philosopher of the night? He was very tall and thin, with a prominent nose and jaw. His eyes blazed like coals in caverns of darkness. His hair was long and grey, and he wore a black cloak with a loose hood like that of a monk; he had a harsh grating voice, and his expression was full of savage curiosity.

'And that was the man who—'

Fritz stopped.

He swallowed, and his eyes moved to the door. Everyone followed his gaze. The parlour had never

THERE WAS SOMETHING UNCANNY ABOUT DR KALMENIUS'S
CLOCKWORK. HE MADE LITTLE FIGURES THAT SANG AND SPOKE AND
PLAYED CHESS, AND SHOT TINY ARROWS FROM TINY BOWS, AND
PLAYED THE HARPSICHORD AS WELL AS MOZART. YOU CAN SEE SOME
OF HIS CLOCKWORK FIGURES TODAY IN THE MUSEUM AT SCHATZBERG,
BUT THEY DON'T WORK ANY MORE. IT'S ODD, BECAUSE ALL THE PARTS
ARE IN PLACE, AND IN PERFECT ORDER, AND THEY <u>SHOULD</u> WORK; BUT
THEY DON'T. IT'S ALMOST AS IF THEY HAD . . . DIED.

been so still. No-one moved, no-one dared to breathe, for the latch was lifting.

The door slowly opened.

On the threshold stood a man in a long black cloak with a loose hood like a monk's. His grey hair hung down on either side of his face: a long, narrow face with a prominent nose and jaw, and eyes that looked like burning coals in caverns of darkness.

Oh, the silence as he stepped inside! Every single person in the parlour was gaping, mouth open, eyes wide; and when they saw what the stranger was pulling behind him – a little sledge with something wrapped in canvas – more than one crossed themselves and stood up in fear.

The stranger bowed.

'Dr Kalmenius of Schatzberg, at your service,' he said, in a harsh, grating voice. 'I have come a long way tonight, and I am cold. A glass of brandy!'

The landlord poured it hastily. The stranger drained it at once and held out the glass for more. Still nobody moved.

'So silent?' said Dr Kalmenius, looking around

mockingly. 'One might think one had arrived among the dead!'

The Burgomaster swallowed hard and got to his feet.

'I beg your pardon, Dr – er – Kalmenius, but the fact is that—'

And he looked at Fritz, who was staring at Dr Kalmenius with horror. The young man was as pale as the paper in his hand. His eyes were nearly starting from his head, his hair was standing on end, and a ghastly sweat had broken out on his forehead.

'Yes, my good sir?' said Dr Kalmenius.

'I – I—' said Fritz, and swallowed convulsively.

The Burgomaster intervened: 'The fact is that our young friend is a writer of stories, Doctor, and he was reading us one of his tales when you arrived.'

'Ah! How delightful!' said Dr Kalmenius. 'I should greatly enjoy hearing the rest of your story, young sir. Please don't feel inhibited by my presence – carry on as if I weren't here at all.'

A little cry broke from Fritz's throat. With a sudden movement he crumpled all his sheets of paper together and thrust them into the stove, where they blazed up high.

'I beg you,' he cried, 'have nothing to do with this man!'

And like someone who has seen the Devil, he ran out of the inn as fast as he could.

Dr Kalmenius broke into a wild and mocking laugh, and at that, several other good citizens followed Fritz's example, and left their pipes and their mugs of beer, grabbed their coats and hats, and were off, not even daring to look the stranger in the eye.

Herr Ringelmann and the Burgomaster were almost the last to leave. The old clockmaker thought he should say something to a fellow craftsman, but his tongue was mute, and the Burgomaster thought he should either welcome the eminent Dr Kalmenius or send him on his way, but his nerve failed; and the two old men took their sticks and hurried away as fast as they could.

Little Gretl was clinging to her father the landlord, watching it all with wide eyes.

'Well!' said Dr Kalmenius. 'You keep early hours in this town. I will take another glass of brandy.'

The landlord poured with a shaking hand, and ushered Gretl out, for this was no company for a child.

Dr Kalmenius drained the brandy at once, and called for yet another.

'And perhaps this gentleman will join me,' he said, turning to the corner of the bar.

For there sat Karl still. In the rush of all the other customers to leave, he had not moved. He turned his glowering face, now flushed with drink and sullen with self-hatred, to glare at the stranger, but he could not meet those mocking eyes, and he dropped his gaze to the floor.

'Bring a glass for my companion,' said Dr Kalmenius to the landlord, 'and then you may leave us.'

The landlord put the bottle and another glass on the bar, and fled. Only five minutes before, the parlour had been full to bursting; but now Dr Kalmenius and Karl were alone, and the inn was so quiet that Karl could hear the whisper of flames in the stove, and the ticking of the old clock in the corner, even over the beating of his own heart.

Dr Kalmenius poured some brandy, and pushed the glass along the bar. Karl said nothing. He bore the stranger's stare for nearly a minute, and then he banged his fist on the counter and cried:

'God damn you, what do you want?'

'Of you, sir? I want nothing from you.'

'You came here on purpose to jeer at me!'

'To jeer at you? Come, come, we have better clowns than you in Schatzberg. Should I come all this way to laugh at a young man whose face shows nothing but unhappiness? Come, drink up! Look cheerful! It is your morning of triumph tomorrow!'

Karl groaned and turned away, but Dr Kalmenius's mocking voice continued:

'Yes, the unveiling of a new figure for the famous clock of Glockenheim is an important occasion. Do you know, I tried to find a bed in five different inns before I came here, and they were all full up. Visitors from all over Germany – gentlemen and ladies – craftsmen, clockmakers, experts in all kinds of machinery – all come to see your new figure, your masterpiece! Isn't that something to be joyful about? Drink, my friend, drink!'

Karl snatched the glass and swallowed the fiery liquor.

'There won't be a new figure,' he muttered.

'What's this?'

'I said there won't be a new figure. I haven't made one. I couldn't. I wasted all my time, and when it was too late I found I couldn't do it. There you are. Now you can laugh at me. Go on.'

'Oh, dear, dear,' said Dr Kalmenius solemnly. 'Laugh? I wouldn't dream of it. I've come here to help you.'

'What? You? How?'

Dr Kalmenius smiled. It was like a flame suddenly breaking out of an ash-covered log, and Karl recoiled. The old man came closer.

'You see,' he said, 'I think you may have overlooked the philosophical implications of our craft. You know how to regulate a watch and repair a church clock, but had you ever considered that our lives are clockwork, too?'

'I don't understand,' said Karl.

'We can control the future, my boy, just as we wind up the mechanism in a clock. Say to yourself: I *will* win that race – I *will* come first – and you wind up the future like clockwork. The world has no choice but to obey! Can the hands of that old clock in the corner decide to stop? Can the spring in

NOW WE'RE GETTING TO THE HEART OF IT. THIS IS DR KALMENIUS'S PHILOSOPHY. THIS IS WHAT HE WANTS KARL TO BELIEVE. WELL, THERE MAY BE SOMETHING IN IT. THERE ARE PLENTY OF PEOPLE WHO THINK THEY ONLY HAVE TO WISH FOR SOMETHING, AND IT'LL COME TRUE. DOESN'T EVERYONE THINK LIKE THAT WHEN THEY BUY A LOTTERY TICKET? AND THERE'S NO DOUBT, IT'S A PLEASANT THING TO IMAGINE. BUT THERE'S A FLAW IN IT . . .

your watch decide to wind itself up and run backwards? No! They have no choice. And nor has the future, once you have wound it up.'

'Impossible,' said Karl, who was feeling more and more light-headed.

'Oh, but it's easy! What would you like? Wealth? A beautiful bride? Wind up the future, my friend! Say what you want, and it will be yours! Fame, power, riches – what would you like?'

'You know very well what I want!' cried Karl. 'I want a figure for the clock! Something to show for all the time I should have spent in making it! Anything to avoid the shame I'll feel tomorrow!'

'Nothing could be easier,' said Dr Kalmenius. 'You spoke – and there is what you wished for.'

And he pointed to the little sledge he'd pulled behind him into the parlour. The runners stood in a

. . . AND HERE IT IS: YOU DON'T WIN RACES BY WISHING, YOU WIN THEM BY RUNNING FASTER THAN EVERYONE ELSE. AND TO DO THAT YOU HAVE TO TRAIN HARD AND STRIVE YOUR UTMOST, AND SOMETIMES EVEN THAT ISN'T ENOUGH, BECAUSE ANOTHER RUNNER JUST MIGHT BE MORE TALENTED THAN YOU ARE. HERE'S THE TRUTH: IF YOU WANT SOMETHING, YOU <u>CAN</u> HAVE IT, BUT ONLY IF YOU WANT EVERYTHING THAT GOES WITH IT, INCLUDING ALL THE HARD WORK AND THE DESPAIR, AND ONLY IF YOU'RE WILLING TO RISK FAILURE. THAT'S THE PROBLEM WITH KARL: HE WAS AFRAID OF FAILING, SO HE NEVER REALLY TRIED.

puddle of melted snow, and the canvas cover was damp.

'What is it?' said Karl, who had suddenly become very afraid.

'Uncover it! Take off the canvas!'

Karl got unsteadily to his feet and slowly untied the rope holding the cover down. Then he pulled the canvas off.

In the sledge was the most perfect piece of metal sculpture he had ever seen. It was the figure of a knight in armour, made of gleaming silvery metal, holding a sharp sword. Karl gasped at the detail, and walked round looking at it from all angles. Every piece of armour-plating was riveted in such a way that it would move smoothly over the one below, and as for the sword—

He touched it, and drew his hand back at once, looking at the blood running down his fingers.

'It's like a razor,' he said.

'Only the best will do for Sir Ironsoul,' said Dr Kalmenius.

'Sir Ironsoul . . . What a piece of work! Oh, if this were in the tower among the other figures, my name would be made for ever!' said Karl bitterly. 'And how does he move? What does he do? He does work by clockwork, I suppose? Or is there some kind of goblin in there? A spirit or a devil of some kind?'

With a smooth whirr and a ticking of delicate machinery, the figure began to move. The knight raised his sword and turned his helmeted head to look for Karl, and then stepped off the sledge and moved towards him.

'No! What's he doing?' said Karl in alarm, backing away.

Sir Ironsoul kept going. Karl moved aside, but the figure turned too, and before Karl could dodge away, he was pinned in the corner, with the little knight's sword moving closer and closer.

'What's he doing? That sword is sharp – stop it, Doctor! Make it stop!'

Dr Kalmenius whistled three or four bars of a simple, haunting little tune, and Sir Ironsoul fell still. The point of the sword was right at Karl's throat.

The apprentice eased his way past the figure and sank onto a chair, weak with fear.

'What – who – how did it start? This is uncanny! Did you set it off?'

'Oh, I didn't start him,' said Dr Kalmenius. 'You did.'

'I did? How?'

'It was something you said. His mechanism is so delicate, so perfectly balanced, that one word and one word alone will start him moving. And he's such a clever little fellow! Once he's heard that word, he won't rest until his sword is in the throat that uttered it.'

'What word?' said Karl fearfully. 'What did I say? Clockwork . . . goblin . . . move . . . work . . . spirit . . . devil . . .'

Once again Sir Ironsoul began to move. He

turned round implacably, found Karl, and set off towards him. The apprentice was out of his chair in a flash and cowering in the corner.

'That was it!' he cried. 'Stop it again, please, Doctor!'

Dr Kalmenius whistled once more, and the figure stopped.

'What is that tune?' said Karl. 'Why does he stop for that?'

'It's a little tune called "The Flowers of Lapland",' said Dr Kalmenius. 'He likes that, bless him. He stands still to listen to it, and that tips his balance wheel the other way, and then he stops. What a marvel! What a piece of work!'

'I'm afraid of him.'

'Oh, come, come! Afraid of a little tin man who likes a pretty tune?'

'It's uncanny. It's not like a machine at all. I don't like it.'

'Well, that's a great shame. What will you do without him tomorrow? I shall be watching with great interest.'

'No, no!' said Karl, in anguish. 'I didn't mean . . . Oh, I don't know what I mean!'

'Do you want him?'

'Yes. No!' cried Karl, beating his fists together. 'I don't know. Yes!'

'Then he is yours,' said Dr Kalmenius. 'You have wound up the future, my boy! It has already begun to tick!'

And before Karl could change his mind, the clockwork-maker gathered his long cloak around him, swept the hood up over his head, and vanished out of the door with his sledge.

Karl ran to the door after him, but the snow was so thick that he could see nothing. Dr Kalmenius had vanished.

Karl turned back into the parlour and sat down weakly. The little figure stood perfectly still, with its sword upraised, and its blank metal face gazing at the young apprentice.

'He wasn't a man,' Karl muttered. 'No man could make this. He was an evil spirit! He was the dev—'

He clapped his hands over his mouth and looked in terror at Sir Ironsoul, who stood motionless.

'I nearly said it!' Karl whispered to himself. 'I mustn't ever forget – and the tune! How does it go? If I can remember that, I'll be safe . . .'

He tried to whistle it, but his mouth was too dry; he tried to hum it, but his voice was shaking. He held out his hands and looked at them. They were trembling like dry leaves.

'Perhaps if I have another drink . . .' he said.

He poured some more brandy, splashing most of it on the counter before he got some in the glass. He swallowed it quickly.

'That's better . . . Well, after all, I *could* put him in the clock. And if I bolted him to the frame, he'd be safe enough. He wouldn't be able to get out of that, no matter what words anyone said . . .'

He looked around him fearfully. The parlour was as silent as the grave. Then he lifted the curtain and peered through the window, but there was not a single light in the town square. Everyone in the world seemed to have gone to bed, and the only beings awake were the clockmaker's apprentice and the little silvery figure with the sword.

'Yes, I'll do it!' he said.

So he threw the canvas over Sir Ironsoul, hastily pulled on his coat and hat, and hurried out to unlock the tower and prepare the clock.

Now, as it happened, there was one other person awake, and that was Gretl, the landlord's little daughter. She couldn't sleep at all, and the reason for that was Fritz's story. There was one thing she couldn't get out of her mind. It wasn't the clock-work in the dead prince's breast; it wasn't the horses foaming with terror or the dead driver behind them; it was the young Prince Florian.

She thought: poor little boy, to travel home in that frightful way! She tried to imagine what terrors he must have faced, alone in the sledge with his dead father, and she shivered under her blankets, and wished that she could comfort him.

And because she couldn't sleep, she thought she'd go down and sit by the stove in the parlour for a while, because her bed was cold. So she wrapped a blanket around her shoulders and tiptoed down the stairs just as the great clock in the tower was chiming midnight. There was no-one in the parlour, of course, and the lamp was burning low, so she didn't notice the little canvas-covered figure in the corner, and sat down to warm her hands at the stove.

'What a strange story that was going to be!' she said to herself. 'I'm not sure that people ought to tell

333

GRETL WAS KIND-HEARTED, YOU SEE. HER HEART WAS IN THE RIGHT PLACE. HER HEART WAS WARM, HER HEART WAS TENDER, SHE HAD A HEART OF GOLD. YOU KNOW THOSE EXPRESSIONS? THERE ARE SOME PEOPLE, LIKE GRETL, WHO CAN'T HEAR OF ANYONE ELSE'S PROBLEMS WITHOUT SUFFERING ALMOST AS MUCH AS THEY DO. THE WORLD IS A CRUEL PLACE SOMETIMES, AND WARM-HEARTED PEOPLE DO MOST OF THE GOOD IN IT. AND MUCH OF THE TIME, THEY'RE MOCKED AND SCORNED FOR THEIR PAINS.

stories like that. I don't mind ghosts and skeletons, but I think Fritz went too far that time. And didn't everyone jump when the old man came in! It was as if Fritz conjured him up out of nothing. Like Dr Faust, conjuring up the devil . . .'

And the sheet of canvas fell softly to the floor, and the little metal figure turned his head, and raised his sword, and began to move towards her.

OH, NO! GRETL, BE CAREFUL! STOP! DON'T SAY IT! ... AH! TOO LATE ...

# Part Two

When Prince Otto married his Princess Mariposa, the whole city rejoiced: fireworks were lit in the public gardens, bands played all night in the ballrooms, and flags and banners waved from every rooftop.

'At last we'll have an heir!' the people said, for they had been afraid that the dynasty would come to an end.

But time went by, and more time, and no child came to Prince Otto and Princess Mariposa. They sought the opinions of the finest doctors, but still no child came. They made a pilgrimage to Rome to seek the blessing of the Holy Father, but still no child came. Finally, as Princess Mariposa stood at the

337

THE PRINCESS WAS CALLED MARIPOSA. SHE WAS VERY BEAUTIFUL,
BUT WHAT PRINCESS ISN'T? BEING BEAUTIFUL IS THEIR PROFESSION.
PRINCESS MARIPOSA SPENT MOST OF HER TIME SHOPPING. THE DRESS
DESIGNERS LET HER BUY DRESSES AT HALF-PRICE, BECAUSE SHE WORE
THEM AT FASHIONABLE PARTIES AND MADE THE DESIGNERS FAMOUS.
IF YOU WANT TO BUY THINGS CHEAP, IT HELPS TO BE RICH, STRANGE AS
IT SEEMS. POOR PEOPLE ALWAYS HAVE TO PAY THE FULL PRICE.

palace window, she heard the chiming of the cathedral clock, and said, 'I wish I had a child as sound as a bell and as true as a clock'; and when she had said those words, she felt her heart lift.

And before the year was out, she did have a child. But alas for her and for everyone, her labour was hard and painful, and when the baby had taken one breath in this world, he could take no more, and he died in the arms of the nurse. Princess Mariposa knew nothing of that, for she was in a dreadful swoon, and no-one could say whether she would live or die. As for Prince Otto, he was nearly out of his mind with fury. He snatched the dead child from the nurse's arms and said, 'I will have an heir, come what may!'

He ran down to the stables and ordered the grooms to saddle his fastest horse, and with the dead child clasped to his breast he galloped away.

Where was he going? North, and further north, until he came to the workshop of Dr Kalmenius, near the silver mines of Schatzberg.

There it was that the great clockwork-maker created his wonders, from the celestial clocks that told the position of every planet for the next twenty-five thousand years to the little figures that danced, and rode miniature ponies, and shot tiny arrows, and played the harpsichord.

'Well?' said Dr Kalmenius.

Prince Otto stood in his riding-cloak with the snow still white on his shoulders, and held out the body of his child.

'Make me another child!' he said. 'My son is dead, and his mother lies between life and death! Dr Kalmenius, I command you to make me a child of clockwork who will not die!'

Even Prince Otto, in his madness, didn't believe that a clockwork toy could resemble a living child; but the silver they mined in Schatzberg was not the same as other metals. It was malleable and soft and lustrous, with a bloom on it like that on a butterfly's wing. And as for the great clockwork-maker, the task was a challenge to his artistry that he couldn't resist, and so, while Prince Otto buried the dead child, Dr Kalmenius set to work to make the new one. He smelted the ore and refined the silver, and beat it into a subtle thinness; he spun gold into filaments finer than spiders' silk, and attached each one separately to the little head; he cast and filed and tempered, he soldered and riveted and bolted, he timed and adjusted and regulated, until the little mainspring was tight, and the little escapement on its jewelled bearings was ticking back and forth with perfect accuracy.

When the clockwork child was ready, Dr Kalmenius gave him to Prince Otto, who scrutinized him carefully. The baby was breathing and moving and smiling and even, by some secret art, warm. In every way he looked exactly like the child who had died. Prince Otto wrapped his cloak around the baby, and rode back to the palace, where he laid the child in the arms of Princess Mariposa; and the princess opened her eyes, and the joy of seeing her own child, as she thought, alive and well, brought her back from the brink of the grave. And besides, she looked so pretty with a child in her arms; she had always known she would.

They named him Florian. A year went by, two years, three, and the little boy grew up beloved by everyone, happy and sturdy and clever. Prince Otto took him riding on a little pony, taught him to shoot a bow and arrow; he danced, he picked out tunes on the harpsichord; he grew stronger and bigger, more merry and lively all the time.

But in the fifth year of his life, the little prince began

to show signs of a disturbing illness. There was a painful stiffness in his joints, he had a constant feeling of chill, and his face, which was normally so lively and expressive, was becoming mask-like and rigid. Princess Mariposa was worried to distraction, for he no longer looked nearly so handsome next to her.

'Can't you do something to cure him?' she demanded of the Royal Physician.

The physician tapped the boy's chest, and looked at his tongue, and felt his pulse. It was like no disease he had ever seen. If he hadn't known the prince was a little boy, he'd have said he was seizing up like a rusty clock, but he could hardly say that to Princess Mariposa.

'Nothing to worry about,' he said. 'It's a condition known as inflammatory oxidosis. Give him two spoonfuls of cod-liver oil three times a day, and rub

THAT'S A TYPICAL DOCTOR'S ANSWER. HE MAKES UP A MEDICAL-SOUNDING NAME (ALL OXIDOSIS MEANS IS RUSTY DISEASE) AND PRESCRIBES SOME MEDICINE THAT AT LEAST WON'T DO ANY HARM. THAT'S ONE OF THE FIRST THINGS THEY TEACH THEM IN MEDICAL SCHOOL – OR IT USED TO BE. BUT THE ROYAL PHYSICIAN HAD A VERY GOOD BEDSIDE MANNER, AND EVEN IF HE DIDN'T ALWAYS KNOW HOW TO CURE HIS PATIENTS, HE SOOTHED AND FLATTERED THEM BEAUTIFULLY.

his chest with oil of lavender.'

The only one to suspect the truth was his father, and so Prince Otto set off once again for the mines of Schatzberg, and knocked at the door of Dr Kalmenius's workshop.

'Well?' said the clockwork-maker.

'Prince Florian is ill,' said Prince Otto. 'What can we do?'

He described the symptoms, and Dr Kalmenius shrugged his shoulders.

'It's in the nature of clockwork to run down,' was the answer. 'His mainspring was bound to weaken, his escapement to become clogged with dust. I can tell you what will happen next: his skin will stiffen and crack, and split from top to bottom to reveal nothing but dead, seized-up metal inside him. He will never work again.'

'But why didn't you tell me this would happen?'

'You were in such a hurry that you didn't ask.'

'Can't you just wind him up?'

'Impossible.'

'But what can we do?' said Prince Otto in his rage and despair. 'Is there nothing that can save his life? I must have an heir! The survival of the Royal

Family depends on it!'

'There is one thing,' said Dr Kalmenius. 'He is failing because he has no heart. Find him a heart, and he will live. But I don't know where you'll find a heart in good condition that its owner is willing to part with. Besides—'

But Prince Otto had left already. He didn't stop to hear the rest of what Dr Kalmenius was going to say. That's often the way with princes; they want instant solutions, not difficult ones that take time and care to bring about. What the great clockwork-maker had been going to say was this: 'The heart that is given must also be kept.' But quite possibly Prince Otto wouldn't have understood anyway.

He rode back to the palace, turning the problem over in his mind. And what a dilemma! To save his son, he had to sacrifice another human being! What could he do? And whom could he ask to make such a great sacrifice?

And then he thought of the Baron Stelgratz.

Of course! There was no-one better. Baron Stelgratz was an old, trusted adviser, a staunch friend, faithful, brave, and true. The little prince loved him, and he and the baron used to play for hours at mock-battles with

Prince Florian's toy soldiers, and the good old nobleman would teach him how to handle a sword or fire a pistol, and tell him all about the animals of the forest.

The more Prince Otto thought about it, the better a choice it seemed. Baron Stelgratz would leap at the chance to give his heart for the family. Better not tell him yet, though; better wait till they were at Dr Kalmenius's workshop; then he would see the necessity quite clearly.

When Prince Otto arrived back at the palace, he found that the little prince had got worse. He could hardly walk without falling over stiffly, and his voice, which had been so full of life and laughter, was becoming more and more like a musical-box; he said very little, but he sang the same few songs over and over. It was clear that he wouldn't last very long.

So Prince Otto went straight to the princess, and persuaded her that a few days' hunting, some brisk exercise in the forest, would do the little child a power of good. Furthermore, he said, Baron Stelgratz would come too; no harm would come to Florian in the baron's company.

So Prince Otto wrapped the little boy up well, and set him in the sledge with Baron Stelgratz beside him, and off they set.

But on the way through the forest, as darkness was falling, the sledge was attacked by wolves.

Maddened by hunger, the great grey beasts poured out of the trees and sprang up at the horses. Prince Otto lashed his whip furiously, and the sledge leapt forward, with the wolves tearing after. Prince Florian sat beside the baron, gripping the side of the sledge, and watched fearfully as the wolf-pack raced closer and closer. Baron Stelgratz emptied his rifle at the pack of leaping, slavering beasts, without deterring them in the least, and the sledge bumped and swayed from side to side on the rough track. At any moment they might crash, and then they would all perish.

'Highness!' cried the baron. 'There is only one thing to do, and I do it with all my heart!'

And the good old man threw himself off the sledge. To save his friends, he sacrificed himself.

Instantly the wild wolves turned on him and tore him to pieces, and the sledge drove on into the silent forest, leaving the snarling, howling beasts far behind.

And *now* what could Prince Otto do?

Drive on, was the only answer; drive on! And hope

THE ONLY THING TO DO WHEN YOU'RE CHASED BY WOLVES IS TO THROW THEM SOMETHING TASTY, AND HOPE YOU GET AWAY WHILE THEY EAT IT. BARON STELGRATZ KNOWS THIS. HE'S JUST FIRING HIS LAST BULLET. HE KNOWS THAT TOO.

to find some lonely huntsman or woodcutter, and compensate their family later on. But not a single human being came into view. Behind Prince Otto, the little child, wrapped in furs, was huddled alone on the bouncing seat of the sledge, stiffening, growing colder, changing back into a machine minute by minute. Occasionally the movement of the sledge would shake a little song out of him, but he spoke no more.

Finally they arrived at the mines of Schatzberg, and the house of the clockwork-maker.

And there was only one solution. Prince Otto realized that he had to sacrifice himself, and he was ready. The dynasty was more important than anything else: more important than happiness, than love, than truth, than peace, than honour; far more important than his own life. Prince Otto would give up his heart, cold, fanatical, and proud as it was, for the sake of the future glory of the Royal House.

'You're quite sure this is what you want?' said Dr Kalmenius.

'Don't argue with me! Take out my heart, and put it in my child's breast! It doesn't matter if I die, as long as the dynasty lives!'

The problem now was not the heart, it was the return: how could the child drive back on his own? So, for an extra payment, Dr Kalmenius agreed to animate the dead body of Prince Otto with a small degree of purpose just enough to drive the sledge back to the palace.

The operation was performed. Prince Otto's heart was detached from his breast with subtle instruments, and transferred into the weak and failing body of the silver boy. Instantly, a bright flush of health took the place of Prince Florian's metallic pallor, his eyes opened, and a lively vigour spread through all his limbs. He was alive.

Meanwhile, Dr Kalmenius prepared a simple piece of clockwork apparatus to put in the breast of Prince Otto. It was very crude; when it was wound up, it would make his body drive to the palace. That was all it would do. But it would do it for a long, long time. If Prince Otto's body had been taken to the other side of the world, he would have set off at once for home, though the flesh rotted and fell off his bones, and would never stop until many years later, when his skeleton drove the sledge into the courtyard, with the clockwork ticking in his ribs.

So Dr Kalmenius placed the sleeping body of Prince Florian in the sledge, well wrapped up against the cold, and put the whip into the hand of his dead father, who began at once to lash and lash and lash; and the horses, foaming with terror, began their mad gallop homewards.

And a strange homecoming they had of it. You might have heard the tale of how the sledge drove in at the palace gates, and how the Royal Physician found the clockwork heart. The servants whispered about the dead man whose arm wouldn't keep still, and rumours and guesses flew through the palace and the city like shuttles in a loom, weaving a story of corpses and ghosts, of curses and devils, of death and life and clockwork. But no-one knew the truth.

So time passed. They searched for the baron, they mourned for Prince Otto, Princess Mariposa wept very fetchingly in her widow's black, and Prince Florian grew. Five more years went by, and everyone said how handsome the little prince was, how merry and good, how lucky they were to have such a child as the heir of the family!

But as the winter of the prince's tenth year set in, the dreaded symptoms returned. Prince Florian complained of pains in his joints, of a stiffness in his arms and legs, of a constant chill; and his voice lost its human expressiveness and took on the tinkling sound of a musical-box.

Just as before, the Royal Physician was baffled.

'He has inherited this disease from his father,' he said. 'There can be no question about that.'

'But what disease is it?' said Princess Mariposa.

'A congenital weakness of the heart,' said the physician, sounding as if he knew. 'Combined with inflammatory oxidosis. But if you remember, Your Highness, we cured that last time by means of healthy exercise in the forest. What Prince Florian needs is a week at the hunting lodge.'

'But last time he went with his father and Baron Stelgratz, and you know what happened then!'

'Ah, medical science has advanced wonderfully in the past five years,' said the physician. 'Have no fear, Your Highness. We shall arrange a hunting trip for the little prince, and he will come back glowing with health, just as he did before.'

But it seemed that the courtiers had less faith in the advance of medical science than the physician, for they all remembered what had happened last time, and none of them wanted to risk a journey through the forest, even if it was to save Prince Florian. This one had gout, that one had an urgent appointment in Venice, another had to visit his aged grandmother in Berlin, and so on, and so on. There was no question of the physician himself going; he was needed every moment at the palace, in case of an emergency. And Princess Mariposa could not possibly go, because the winter air was so bad for her complexion.

Finally, because there was no-one else to do it, they called up one of the grooms and offered him ten silver pieces to take little Prince Florian to the hunting lodge.

'In advance?' the man said, because he had heard the story of what had happened before, and wanted to be sure of his money if anything went wrong.

So they gave him the silver in advance, and the groom tucked Prince Florian into the sledge and harnessed the horses. Princess Mariposa waved from the window as they drove away.

When they had gone some way into the forest, the groom thought: I don't think this kid can last another day; he looks pretty bad to me. And if I go back and tell them he's died, they're bound to punish me. On the other hand, with ten silver pieces and this sledge I can make my way over the border and set up in business on my own account. Buy a little inn, maybe find a wife and have some children of my own. Yes, that's what I'll do. There's nothing that can save this little fellow; I'm doing him a kindness, really; it's a mercy, that's what it is.

So he stopped the sledge at a crossroads and put Prince Florian out.

'Go on,' the groom said, 'go on, you're on your own now, I can't look after you any more. Have a good brisk walk. Stretch your legs. Off you go.'

And he drove away.

Prince Florian obediently started to walk. His legs were very stiff, and the snow lay thickly on the road, but he kept going till he turned a bend and looked down at a little town silent under the moon, where a bell in a church tower was chiming midnight.

A light was glowing in the window of an inn, and an old black cat watched from the shadows. Prince Florian struggled up to the door and opened it. Being unable to speak, he politely began to sing his one remaining song.

# Part Three

Sir Ironsoul stopped at once, with a whirr and a click. His sword was inches from Gretl's throat. The prince's song rang out sweetly through the parlour.

Gretl could only stare: in horror at Sir Ironsoul and his sword, in wonder at the prince.

'Where did you come from?' she said. 'Are you the little prince in the story? I think you must be. But how cold you are! And who is this? How sharp his sword is! I don't like him at all. Oh, what must I do? I feel I'm supposed to do something, but I don't know what it is!'

There was no-one to help. She was alone with the two little figures, one all malice, the other all sweetness. Gretl touched the prince's cheek gently, and found it cold, but her touch awoke something in his machinery for an instant, and he turned his eyes to hers and smiled.

'Oh, you poor thing!' she cried.

He opened his lips, and sang one or two notes.

'I know what it is,' said Gretl. 'You're not well. And I don't like that little knight one bit, and I don't want to leave you here with him, but I know whose fault this is. It was Fritz who made the story up. If only we could find out how it finished . . .'

She looked at the stove, where Fritz had thrown the sheets of paper on which his story was written. She had thought they were all destroyed, but crumpled up on the floor, in the shadow, there was one piece left unburnt.

She picked it up and straightened it out. It was the very page he had been reading when the stranger had come in. On it were the words:

*He was very tall and thin, with a prominent nose and jaw. His eyes blazed like coals in caverns of darkness.*

*His hair was long and grey, and he wore a black
cloak with a loose hood like that of a monk;
he had a harsh grating voice and his
expression was full of savage curiosity.
And that was the man who —*

There was no more. The story stopped at that point.

'That was exactly when he came in!' said Gretl to herself. But there were another few words scribbled below, and, peering closely, she managed to make them out.

*Oh, this is impossible! How can I write an
ending to this story? I'll have to make it up
when I get there, and hope I do it well.
If I come up with something good,
the devil can have my soul!*

Gretl's eyes widened, and she bit her lip in horror. People shouldn't say things like that! 'Well,' she said to herself, 'he started it all off, and I'm going to make him finish it. You sit in here and keep warm, Prince Florian, if that's who you really are, and

I'll go and fetch Fritz. He's the only one who can sort it out.'

So she threw on her cloak, and set off to the house where Fritz the storyteller had his lodging.

Meanwhile, Karl had been preparing the place in the mechanism of the great clock that was set aside for his masterpiece. Feverish with excitement, he hurried down the staircase of the clock tower and across the square to the inn. The old cat Putzi was still outside, sitting on the window sill, watching everything as he licked his paws and cleaned his ears. It was cold out there, and he was wondering about coming in for a snooze by the stove.

But Karl didn't notice him. He had other things than cats on his mind. He went in quietly and shut the door, and then he stopped in alarm, for there was the canvas, thrown aside, and there was Sir Ironsoul, sword upraised, on the other side of the room.

Karl's heart missed a beat. Had someone else come in and disturbed the little knight? There was no-one dead, at least, but why had the figure moved? Karl looked around, and then he saw the little prince sitting politely in his chair, watching him. A thousand strange fears ran over his skin.

Karl opened his mouth to speak, and then realized that the child wasn't alive after all. It was another clockwork figure like Sir Ironsoul! And a far finer one, by the look of it. He peered at it closely. The hair, the finest gold wires he had ever seen; the bloom on the silver cheeks, like a butterfly's wing; the eyes, bright blue jewels, almost alive in the way they seemed to look at him!

Only Dr Kalmenius could have created this. And he must have brought it for Karl. What did the figure do?

Karl reached out and lifted the prince's hand from his lap. With a little flicker of his energy, Prince Florian shook Karl's hand, and sang a bar of music for him. Karl's hair stood on end, for an idea had just come to him. Why not put *this* figure in the clock instead of Sir Ironsoul? It was more finely finished, and a handsome little boy who sang a pretty tune would be far more popular with the crowds than a faceless knight who did nothing but threaten people with a sword.

And then he could keep Sir Ironsoul for himself.

And then . . . Oh, how his mind raced. He could travel the world. He could become famous giving exhibitions and demonstrations.

He became quite dizzy as he thought of the uses to which he could put the metal knight. The gold he could steal, the forbidden treasures that could be his, if he had a secret accomplice, like Sir Ironsoul, who could be relied on always to kill and never to give him away! All he would have to do would be to trick his intended victim into saying the word 'devil', and leave Sir Ironsoul nearby to play his part. He, Karl, could be somewhere else entirely, playing cards with a dozen witnesses, or even in church surrounded by the faithful. No-one would ever know!

So excited did he become that he lost all sense of what was right. The church, his father and mother and brother and sister, Herr Ringelmann, every influence for good he'd ever known was whirled away into the darkness, and all he could see was the wealth and power that would be his if he used Sir Ironsoul in that way.

And before he could change his mind, he threw the canvas over the knight, tucked the stiffening figure of Prince Florian under his arm, and set off back to the clock tower.

Meanwhile, Gretl was struggling through the snow towards the house where Fritz lodged. She could see from the end of the street that all the windows were dark except one in the attic where Fritz often used to work throughout the night. She had to knock half a dozen times before the landlady came grumbling to open the door.

'Who is it? What do you want at this time of night? Oh, it's you, child; what in the world are you after?'

'I've got to speak to Herr Fritz! It's very important!'

Mumbling and frowning, the old lady stepped aside and said, 'Yes, I heard all about that business at the inn. Making up wicked stories! Frightening people! I'll be glad when he's gone. In fact I've got half a mind to give him notice.

Go on up, child, top of the stairs and keep going. No, you can't have a candle, this is the only one I've got and I need it myself. You've got sharp eyes; make do.'

So Gretl climbed the four staircases to the top of the house, each one darker and narrower than the one below, and came at last to a tiny landing where a line of light glowed beneath a door. There she knocked, and a nervous voice answered:

'Who is it? What do you want?'

'It's Gretl, Herr Fritz! From the inn! I've got to speak to you!'

'Come in, then – as long as you're by yourself . . .'

Gretl opened the door. She found Fritz standing in the light of a smoky lamp, throwing paper after paper into a leather bag which was bulging with his clothes and books and other bits and pieces. A glass of plum brandy stood on the table beside him. He had already drunk quite a lot, by the look of him, for his eyes were wild, his cheeks were flushed, and his hair was standing on end.

'What is it?' he said. 'What do you want?'

'That story you told us,' Gretl began, but she got no further, for the young man put his hands over his ears and shook his head violently.

'Don't speak of it! I wish I'd never begun it! I wish I'd never told a story in my life!'

'But you've got to listen to me!' she said. 'Something dreadful's going to happen, and I don't know what it is because you didn't finish writing the story!'

'How do you know I didn't finish it?' he said.

She showed him the sheet of paper she'd found. He groaned, and put his face in his hands.

'Groaning won't help,' she said. 'You've got to finish the story properly. What happens next?'

'I don't know!' he cried. 'I dreamed the first part of it, and it was so strange and horrible that I couldn't resist writing it down and pretending it was mine . . . But I couldn't think of any more!'

'But what were you going to do when you got to that part?' she said.

'Make it up, of course!' he said. 'I've done that before. I often do it. I enjoy the risk, you see. I start telling a story with no idea what's

THIS IS FRITZ: USELESS, YOU SEE. QUITE IRRESPONSIBLE. BUT
THEN FRITZ WAS ONLY PLAYING AT BEING A STORYTELLER. IF HE WAS
A PROPER CRAFTSMAN LIKE A CLOCKWORK-MAKER HE'D HAVE KNOWN
THAT ALL ACTIONS HAVE THEIR CONSEQUENCES. FOR EVERY TICK
THERE IS A TOCK. FOR EVERY ONCE UPON A TIME THERE MUST BE A
STORY TO FOLLOW, BECAUSE IF A STORY DOESN'T, SOMETHING ELSE
WILL, AND IT MIGHT NOT BE AS HARMLESS AS A STORY.

going to happen at the end, and I make it up when I get there. Sometimes it's even better than writing it down first. I was sure I could do it with this one. But when the door opened and the old man came in, I must have panicked . . . Oh, I wish I'd never begun! I'll never tell a story again!'

'You must tell the end of this one, though,' said Gretl, 'or something bad will happen. You've got to.'

'I can't!'

'You must.'

'I couldn't!'

'You *have* to.'

'Impossible,' he said. 'I can't control it any more. I wound it up and set it going, and it'll just have to work itself out. I wash my hands of it. I'm off!'

'But you can't! Where are you going?'

'Anywhere! Berlin, Vienna, Prague – as far away as I can get!'

And he poured himself another glass of plum brandy and swallowed it all in one go.

So Gretl sighed and turned to leave.

At the same time as she was feeling her way down the dark stairs in Fritz's lodging-house, Karl was going back into the inn. He had taken little Florian up to the clock tower and fastened him to the frame, ignoring the prince's helpless struggles and his musical requests for mercy. When morning came, there he would be, Karl's masterpiece, on show as everyone expected. And Karl would receive everyone's congratulations, and his certificate of competence from Herr Ringelmann, and he'd be entered in the roll of master clockwork-makers; and then he could leave the town and make his way with Sir Ironsoul into the wide world, where power and fortune awaited him!

But when he opened the door of the inn to collect the little knight and hide him in his lodgings, he felt a shiver of fear. He stood on the threshold, afraid and unwilling to enter. And once again he took no notice of Putzi the cat, who jumped down from the windowsill when he saw the door open. There's no need to be superstitious about cats, but they are our fellow creatures, and we shouldn't ignore them. It would have been polite of Karl to offer his knuckles for the old cat to rub his head against, but Karl was wound up too tightly for politeness. So he didn't see the cat stalking in past his legs.

TROUBLE WILL COME OF THIS, YOU MARK MY WORDS. IT ALWAYS PAYS TO BE POLITE, EVEN TO DUMB CREATURES.

Finally Karl gathered his courage and went in. How still the room was! And how sinister that little figure under the canvas! And that sword-point: how wickedly sharp! Sharp enough to have pierced the canvas already, and be glinting in the lamplight . . .

Some coals settled in the stove, sending a little flare of red out on the floor, and making Karl jump nervously. The glow made him think of the fires of hell, and he sweated and mopped his brow.

Then the long-case clock in the corner began to whirr and wheeze, preparing to strike. Karl leapt as if he'd been discovered in the act of murder, and then leant weakly against the table, his heart beating like thunder.

'Oh, I can't bear this!' he said. 'I've done nothing wrong, have I? Then why am I so nervous? What is there to be frightened of?'

Hearing his words, old Putzi decided that here was someone who might give him a little milk, if he asked nicely; so the cat jumped up on the table beside him, and rubbed himself on Karl's arm.

Feeling this, Karl turned in shock to see a black cat who had appeared, as it seemed, out of nowhere. Naturally, this was too much for Karl. He leapt away from the table with an exclamation of horror.

HERE IT IS. HERE COMES THE TROUBLE.

'Oh! What the devil—?'

And then he clapped his hands to his mouth, as if trying to cram the word back inside. But it was too late. In the corner of the room, the metal figure had begun to move. The canvas fell to the floor, and Sir Ironsoul raised his sword even higher, and turned his helmet this way and that until he saw where Karl was cowering.

'No! No! Stop – wait – the tune – let me whistle the tune—'

But his lips were too dry. Frantic, he licked them with a dry tongue. No use! He couldn't produce a sound. Nearer and nearer came the little knight with the sharp sword, and Karl stumbled away, trying to hum, to sing, to whistle, and all he could do was cry and stammer and sob, and the knight came closer and closer.

When Gretl got back to the inn she heard Putzi miaowing inside, and said as she opened the door, 'How did you get in, you silly cat?'

THERE'S NO WAY OF AVOIDING THIS. I'D SAVE THE WRETCH IF I COULD, BUT THE STORY IS WOUND UP, AND IT MUST ALL COME OUT. AND I'M AFRAID KARL DESERVED A BAD END. HE WAS LAZY AND BAD-TEMPERED, BUT WORSE THAN THAT, HE HAD A WICKED HEART. HE REALLY WOULD HAVE USED SIR IRONSOUL TO KILL PEOPLE AND MAKE MONEY IN THE WAY HE'D THOUGHT ABOUT. SO CLOSE YOUR EYES AND THINK OF SOMETHING ELSE FOR A MOMENT; KARL IS TICKING HIS FINAL TOCK.

Putzi shot out into the square as Gretl came in, and wouldn't stop to be petted. She shut the door and looked around for the prince, but she didn't see him anywhere. Instead, a horrid sight met her eyes, and made her shiver and clutch her breast. There in the middle of the room stood Sir Ironsoul, with his helmet shining blankly and his sword slanting down. He was holding it like that because the point was in the

TIME IS RUNNING OUT, LIKE SAND IN THE HOURGLASS, WHICH IS
ANOTHER KIND OF CLOCK, AFTER ALL. WILL GRETL GET TO THE PRINCE
IN TIME? SHE'S IN TIME NOW: SHE'S RIGHT INSIDE THE CLOCK, AT
THE VERY HEART OF TIME. SHE'LL GET THERE.

throat of Karl the apprentice, who lay stark dead beside him.

Gretl nearly fainted, but she was a brave girl, and she had seen what lay in Karl's hand. It was the heavy iron key of the clock tower. With her mind in a whirl, she was still able to guess part of what had happened, if not all of it, and she realized what Karl must have done with the prince. She took the key from his hand and ran out of the inn and across the square to the great dark tower.

She turned the key in the lock and began to climb for the second time that night, but these stairs were higher and steeper than those in Fritz's lodging. And they were darker, too; and there were bats that flitted through the air; and the wind groaned across the mouths of the mighty bells, and made their ropes swing dismally.

But up and up she climbed, until she came to the lowest of the clock-chambers, where the oldest and simplest part of the mechanism was housed. In the darkness she felt her way around the huge iron cog-wheels, the thick ropes, the stiff metal figures of St Wolfgang and the devil, but she didn't find the prince; and so she climbed on. She ran her hands over the Archangel Michael, and in his armour he reminded her of Sir Ironsoul, and she took her hands away quickly. She felt up the side of a figure in a painted robe, and her fingers explored his face until she realized that it was the skull-face of Death, and she took her hands away from him, too.

The higher she climbed, the more noise the clock made: a ticking and a tocking, a clicking and a creaking, a whirring and a rumbling. She clambered over struts and levers and chains and cogwheels, and the further she went, the more she felt as if she, too, were becoming part of the clock; and all the time, she peered into the dark and felt around and listened with all her might.

Finally she clambered up through a trapdoor into the very topmost chamber, and found silver moonlight shining in on such a complexity of mechanical parts that she could make no sense of them at all. At the same moment, she heard a little song. It was the prince calling to her.

Dazzled by the moonlight, Gretl blinked and rubbed her eyes. And there was Prince Florian, with the very last of his clockwork life, singing like a nightingale.

'Oh! You poor cold thing! He's fastened you so tightly I can't undo the bolts – oh, that was wicked! He was going to leave you here and run away, I'm sure. What's the matter with you, Prince Florian? I'm sure you'd tell me if you could. I think you're ill, that's what the trouble is. I think you need warming up. You're too cold, but that's hardly surprising, seeing what they've done with you. Never mind! If I can't get you down, I'll stay up here with you. I can wrap my cloak around us both, you'll see. We're better off up here in any case, if you ask me. The things that have been going on! You'd never believe it! I won't tell you now, because you wouldn't go to sleep. I'll tell you in the morning, I promise. Are you comfortable, Prince Florian? You don't have to speak if you don't want to; you can just nod.'

Prince Florian nodded, and Gretl tucked her

cloak around them, and held the little boy in her arms as she went to sleep. The last thing she thought was: He *is* getting warmer, I'm sure; I can feel it!

The morning came. All through the town, visitors and townsfolk alike were getting dressed and eating their breakfasts hungrily, eager to see the new figure in the famous clock.

The snow-laden rooftops glittered and gleamed in the bright blue air, and the fragrance of roasting coffee and fresh-baked rolls drifted through the streets. And as time drew on towards ten o'clock, a strange rumour went round the town: the clockmaker's apprentice had been found dead! Murdered, what was more!

The police called Herr Ringelmann in to look at the body. The old clockmaker was shocked and dismayed to see his apprentice lying dead.

'The poor boy! It was his day of fame! Whatever can have happened? What a disaster! Who can have done this terrible thing?'

'Do you recognize this figure, Herr Ringelmann?' said the sergeant. 'This clockwork knight?'

'No, I've never seen it before in my life. Is that

Karl's blood on its sword?'

'I'm afraid so. Do you think he could have made this figure?'

'No, certainly not! The figure he made is up in the clock. That's the tradition, you know, sergeant: he was going to fit his new figure in the clock on the last evening of his apprenticeship, just as I did in my time. Karl was a good boy; a little quiet and morose, perhaps, but a good apprentice; I'm sure he did what he was supposed to do, and we'll see his new figure when it comes out in a minute or so. What a sad occasion, instead of a happy one! The new figure will have to be his memorial, poor boy.'

Nothing was right that morning. The innkeeper was desperately anxious, because Gretl was missing. What could have happened to her? The whole town was in a ferment. A crowd had gathered outside the inn, and they watched the policemen carrying out Karl's body on a stretcher, covered by a piece of canvas. But they didn't look that way for long, because it was nearly ten o'clock, and the time had come for the mechanism to reveal the new figure.

All eyes turned upwards. There was even more interest than usual, because of the strange circumstances of Karl's death, and the square was so crowded that you couldn't see the cobbles; people were crammed shoulder to shoulder, and every face was turned up like a flower to the sun.

The hour began to strike. The ancient clock wheezed and whirred as the mechanism came into play. The familiar figures came out first, and bowed or gestured or simply twirled on their toes; there was St Wolfgang, throwing the devil over his shoulder; there was the Archangel Michael with his glittering armour; there was the figure Herr Ringelmann had made for the end of *his* apprenticeship, many years ago: a little boy who popped out, thumbed his nose at Death, and twiddled his fingers before ducking out of sight again.

And then came the new figure.

But it wasn't one figure, it was two: two sleeping children, a girl and a boy, so lifelike and beautiful that they didn't seem to be made of clockwork at all.

A gasp of surprise went up from the crowd as the

two little figures yawned and stretched and looked down, clutching each other for fear of the height, and yet laughing and chatting together in the bright morning light, and pointing out the sights around the square.

'A masterpiece!' cried someone, and another voice said, 'The best figures ever made!'

And more voices joined in:

'A work of genius!'

'Incomparable!'

'So lifelike – look at the way they're waving at us!'

'I've never seen anything like it!'

But Herr Ringelmann had his suspicions, and peered upwards, shading his eyes. And then the innkeeper, looking up with everyone else, saw who it was, and gave a cry of joy.

'It's my Gretl! She's safe! Gretl, keep still! We'll come up and bring you down safely! Don't move! We'll be there in a moment!'

And very soon, the two children were safely on the ground. Two children, because the prince wasn't clockwork any more; he was a child as real as any other, and so he remained. 'The heart that is given

OUT OF THE NIGHT, AND OUT OF THE PAST. GRETL HAS MADE
FLORIAN A PRESENT OF HER HEART, AND WHAT THEY'RE LOOKING AT
IS THE FUTURE.

must also be kept,' as Dr Kalmenius had been about to say to Prince Otto; but the prince didn't listen, did he? No-one could guess where the little boy had come from, and Florian couldn't remember. Presently everyone accepted that he had been lost, and that they had better look after him; so they did.

As for the metal knight with the bloodstained sword, Herr Ringelmann took it away to his workshop to examine closely. When they asked him about it later, he could only shake his head.

'I don't know how anyone expected that to work,' he said. 'It's full of miscellaneous bits and pieces, and they're not even connected up properly: broken springs, wheels with cogs missing, rusty gears – worthless rubbish, all of it! I do hope Karl didn't make it; I thought better of him than that. Well, my friends, it's just a mystery, and I don't suppose we'll ever get to the bottom of it.'

Nor did they, because the one person who might have been able to tell them the truth was Fritz, and he had been so badly scared that he'd left town before the sun rose, and he never came back. He fled to another part of Germany, and he was going to stop writing fiction altogether, until he found he could earn lots of money by making up speeches for politicians. As for what happened to Dr Kalmenius, who can say? He was only a character in a story, after all.

And if Gretl knew more than anyone, she said nothing about it. She had lost her heart to the prince, and kept it too, which was how he came to be turned from clockwork into boy. So they both lived happily ever after; and that was how they all wound up.

# PHILIP PULLMAN

## The Scarecrow
### and His
## Servant

Illustrated by Peter Bailey

# LIGHTNING

One day old Mr Pandolfo, who hadn't been feeling at all well, decided that it was time to make a scarecrow. The birds had been very troublesome. Come to that, his rheumatism had been troublesome, and the soldiers had been troublesome, and the weather had been troublesome, and his cousins had been troublesome. It was all getting a bit too much for him. Even his old pet raven had flown away.

He couldn't do anything about his rheumatism, or the soldiers, or the weather, or his cousins, who were the biggest problem of all. There was a whole family of them, the Buffalonis, and they wanted to get hold of his land and divert all the springs and streams, and drain all the wells, and put up a factory to make weedkiller and rat poison and insecticide.

All those troubles were too big for old Mr Pandolfo to manage, but he thought he could do something about the birds, at least. So he put together a fine-looking scarecrow, with a big solid turnip for a head and a sturdy broomstick for a backbone, and dressed him in an old tweed suit, and stuffed him tightly with straw. Then he tucked a short letter inside him, wrapped in oilskin for safety.

'There you are,' he said. 'Now you remember what your job is, and remember where you belong. Be courteous, and be brave, and be honourable, and be kind. And the best of blooming luck.'

He stuck the scarecrow in the middle of the wheatfield, and went home to lie down, because he wasn't feeling well at all.

That night another farmer came along and stole the scarecrow, being too lazy to make one himself. And the next night someone else came along and stole him again.

So little by little the scarecrow moved away from the place where he was made, and he got more and more tattered and torn, and finally he didn't look nearly as smart as he'd done when Mr Pandolfo put him together. He stood in the middle of a muddy field, and he stayed there.

But one night there was a thunderstorm. It was a very violent one, and everyone in the district shivered and trembled and jumped as the thunder went off like cannon-fire and the lightning lashed down like whips. The scarecrow stood there in the wind and the rain, taking no notice.

And so he might have stayed; but then there came one of those million-to-one chances that are like winning the lottery. All his molecules and atoms and elementary particles and whatnot were lined up in exactly the right way to switch on when the lightning struck him, which it did at two in the morning, fizzing its way through his turnip and down his broomstick and into the mud.

The Scarecrow blinked with surprise and looked all around.

There wasn't much to see except a field of mud, and not much light to see it by except the flashes of lightning.

Still, there wasn't a bird in sight.

'Excellent,' said the Scarecrow.

On the same night, a small boy called Jack happened to be sheltering in a barn not far away. The thunder was so loud that it woke him out of his sleep with a jump. At first he thought it was cannon-fire, and he sat up terrified with his eyes wide open. He could think of nothing worse than soldiers and guns; if it weren't for the soldiers, he'd still have a family and a home and a bed to sleep in.

But as he sat there with his heart thumping, he heard the downpour of the rain on the roof, and realized that the bang had only been thunder and not gunfire. He gave a sigh of relief and lay down again, shivering and sneezing and turning over and over in the hay trying to get warm, until finally he fell asleep.

By the morning the storm had cleared away, and the sky was a bright cold blue. Jack woke up again feeling colder than ever, and hungry too. But he knew how to look for food, and before long he'd gathered up some grains of wheat and a couple of turnip tops and a limp carrot, and he sat in the doorway of the barn in the sunlight to eat them.

'Could be worse,' he said to himself.

He ate very slowly to make it last, and then he just sat there, getting warm. Someone would come along soon to chase him away, but for the moment he was safe.

Then he heard a voice calling from across the fields. Jack was curious, so he stood up and shaded his eyes to look. The shouting came from somewhere in the field beyond the road, and since he had nothing else to do, Jack stood up and walked along towards it.

The shouts came from a scarecrow, in the middle of the muddiest field in sight, and he was waving his arms wildly and yelling at the top of his voice and leaning over at a crazy angle.

'Help!' he was shouting. 'Come and help me!'

'I think I'm going mad,' said Jack to himself. 'Still, look at that poor old thing – I'll go and help him anyway. He looks madder than I feel.'

So he stepped on to the muddy field, and

struggled out to the middle, where the Scarecrow was waiting.

To tell the truth, Jack felt a little nervous, because it isn't every day you find a Scarecrow talking to you.

'Now, tell me, young man,' said the Scarecrow, as soon as Jack was close enough to hear, 'are there any birds around? Any crows, for example? I can't see behind me. Are they hiding?'

His voice was rich and sonorous. His head was made of a great knobbly turnip, with a broad crack for a mouth and a long thin sprout for a nose and two bright little stones for eyes. He had a tattered straw hat, now badly singed, and a soggy woollen scarf, and an old tweed jacket full of holes, and his rake-handle arms had gloves stuffed with straw on the ends of them, one glove leather and the other wool. He also had a pair of threadbare trousers, but since he only had one leg, the empty trouser leg trailed down beside him. Everything was the colour of mud. Jack scratched his head and looked all around.

'No,' he said, 'no crows anywhere. No birds at all.'

'That's a good job done,' said the Scarecrow. 'Now

I want to move on, but I need another leg. If you go and find me a leg, I shall be very obliged. Just like this one, only the opposite,' he added, and he lifted his trouser leg daintily to show a stout stick set firmly in the earth.

'All right,' said Jack. 'I can do that.'

So he set off towards the wood at the edge of the field, and clambered through the undergrowth looking for the right sort of stick. He found one before long, and took it back to the Scarecrow.

'Let me see,' said the Scarecrow. 'Hold it up beside me. That's it. Now slide it up inside the leg of my trousers.'

The end of the stick was broken and splintered and it wasn't easy to push it up the soggy, muddy trouser leg, but Jack finally got it all the way up, and then he jumped, because he felt it twitch in his hand.

He let go, and the new leg swung itself down beside the other. But as soon as the Scarecrow tried to move, the new foot became stuck just like the first one. The harder he struggled, the deeper he sank.

Finally he stopped, and looked at Jack. It was astonishing how much expression he could manage with his gash-mouth and stone-eyes.

'Young man,' he said, 'I have a proposition to make. Here you are, an honest and willing youth, and here am I, a Scarecrow of enterprise and talent. What would you say if I offered you the position of my personal servant?'

'What would my duties be?' said Jack.

'To accompany me throughout the world, to fetch and carry, to wash, cook, and attend to my needs. In return, I have nothing to offer but excitement and glory. We might sometimes go hungry, but we shall never want for adventure. Well, my boy? What do you say?'

'I'll do it,' said Jack. 'I've got nothing else to do except starve, and nowhere to live except ditches and empty barns. So I might as well have a job, and thank you, Mr Scarecrow, I'll take it.'

The Scarecrow extended his hand, and Jack shook it warmly.

'Your first job is to get me out of this mud,' said the Scarecrow.

So Jack heaved the Scarecrow's two legs out of the mud and carried him to the road. He hardly weighed anything at all.

'Which way shall we go?' said Jack.

They looked both ways. In one direction there was a forest, and in the other there was a line of hills. There was no-one in sight.

'That way!' said the Scarecrow, pointing to the hills.

So they set off, with the sun on their backs, and the green hills ahead.

In a farmhouse not far behind them, a lawyer was explaining something to a farmer.

'My name is Cercorelli,' he said, 'and I specialize in finding things for my employers, the distinguished and highly respectful Buffaloni Corporation, of Bella Fontana.'

The farmer gasped. He was a stout, red-faced, idle character, and he was afraid of this lean and silky lawyer, who was dressed entirely in black.

'Oh! The Buffalonis! Yes, indeed, Mr Cercorelli,' he said. 'What can I do to help? Anything! Just name it!'

'It's a small matter,' said the lawyer, 'but one of sentimental importance to my clients. It concerns a scarecrow. It was made by a distant cousin of the Chairman of the Corporation, and it seems to have vanished from its place of origin. My client Mr Giovanni Buffaloni is a very warm-hearted and family-minded man, and he would like to restore the scarecrow to its original home, in memory of his dear cousin who made it.'

The lawyer looked through some papers, and the farmer ran his finger around the inside of his shirt collar, and gulped.

'Well, I, um . . .' he said faintly.

'One might almost think that scarecrows had the power of movement!' said Mr Cercorelli, smiling in a sinister way. 'This fellow has been wandering. I've traced him through several farms already, and now I discover that he made his way to yours.'

'I – er – I think I know the scarecrow you mention,' said the farmer. 'I nick— I bought him from someone else, who didn't need him no more.'

'Oh, good. May we go and see if he is the right one?'

'Well, of course, I'd do anything for the Buffalonis, important people, wouldn't want to upset them, but . . . Well, he's gone.'

'Gone . . . *again*?' said the lawyer, narrowing his eyes.

'I went out this morning, to – er – to tidy him up a bit, and he wasn't there. Mind you, there was a big storm last night. He might have blown away.'

'Oh, dear. That is very unfortunate. Mr Buffaloni takes a dim view of people who do not look after his property. I think I can say that his degree of disappointment will be considerable.'

The farmer was quaking with alarm.

'If I ever hear anything about the scarecrow,' he said, 'anything at all, I'll report to you at once.'

'I think that would be very wise,' said Mr Cercorelli. 'Here is my card. Now show me the field from which the scarecrow vanished.'

# THE BRIGANDS

The Scarecrow and his servant set a good pace as they walked along. On the way, they passed a field of cabbages in the middle of which stood another scarecrow, but he was a mournful-looking fellow whose arms hung feebly at his side.

'Good day to you, sir!' called the Scarecrow, waving to him cheerfully.

But the scarecrow in the field took no notice.

'You see,' the Scarecrow explained to Jack, 'there's a man whose mind is on his job. He's concentrating hard. Quite right.'

'Nice-looking cabbages,' said Jack.

He left the cabbages reluctantly and ran to catch up with the Scarecrow, who was striding ahead like a champion. Presently they found the road getting steeper and the fields getting rockier, and finally there were no fields at all and the road was only a track. It was very hot.

'Unless we find something to eat and drink very soon,' said Jack, 'I'm going to peg out.'

'Oh, we'll find something,' said the Scarecrow, patting him on the shoulder. 'I have every confidence in you. Besides, we understand springs and streams and wells where I come from. Fountains, too. You take it from me, we'll find a spring before long.'

They walked on, and the Scarecrow pointed out curious features of geology, such as a rock that looked like a pigeon, and botany, such as a bush with a robin's nest in it, and entomology, such as a beetle that was as black as a crow.

'You know a lot about birds, master,' said Jack.

'I've made them my lifetime study, my boy. I do believe I could scare any bird that ever lived.'

'I bet you could. Oh! Listen! What's that?'

It was the sound of someone crying, and it came from round the corner. Jack and the Scarecrow hurried on, and found an old woman sitting at a crossroads, with a basket of provisions all scattered on the ground. She was weeping and wailing at the top of her voice.

'Madam!' the Scarecrow said, raising his straw hat very politely. 'What wicked bird has done this to you?'

The old woman looked up, and gave a great gulp of astonishment. Her mouth opened and shut several times, but not a sound came out. Finally, she struggled to her feet and curtseyed nervously.

'It was the brigands,' she said, 'begging your pardon, my lord. There's a gang of terrible brigands living in these hills, robbing travellers and making life a misery for us poor people, and they just came galloping past and knocked me over and rode away laughing, the cowardly rogues.'

The Scarecrow was amazed.

'Do you mean to say that this was the work of *human beings*?' he said.

'Indeed, yes, your honour,' said the old woman.

'Jack, my boy – tell me it's not so—'

Jack was gathering up the things that had fallen out of her basket: apples, carrots, a lump of cheese, a loaf of bread. It was very difficult to do it without dribbling.

'I'm afraid it is, master,' said Jack. 'There's a lot of wicked people about. Tell you what – let's turn round and go the other way.'

'Not a bit of it!' said the Scarecrow sternly. 'We're going to teach these villains a lesson. How dare they treat a lady in this disgraceful way? Here, madam – take my arm . . .'

He was so courteous to the old woman, and his manner was so graceful, that she very soon forgot his knobbly turnip face and his rough wooden arms, and talked to him as if he was a proper gentleman.

'Yes, sir – ever since the wars began, first the soldiers came through and took everything, and then the brigands came along, robbing and murdering and taking what they wanted. And they say the chief brigand is related to the Buffalonis, so they've got political protection too. We don't know where to turn!'

'Buffalonis, you say? I don't like the sound of them. What are they?'

'A very powerful family, sir. We don't dare cross the Buffalonis.'

'Well, fear no more,' said the Scarecrow resolutely. 'We shall scare the brigands away, and they'll never trouble you again.'

'Nice-looking apples,' said Jack hopefully, handing the old woman her basket.

'Ooh, they are,' she said.

'Tasty-looking bread, too.'

'Yes, it is,' said the old woman, tucking it firmly under her arm.

'Lovely-looking cheese.'

'Yes, I like a piece of cheese. Goes down a treat with a drop of beer.'

'You haven't got any beer, have you?' said Jack,

looking all around.

'No,' she said. 'Well, I'll be on my way. Thank you, sir,' she said, curtseying again to the Scarecrow, who raised his hat and bowed.

And off she went.

Jack sighed and followed the Scarecrow, who was already striding off towards the top of the hill.

When they reached the top, they saw a ruined castle. There was one tower that was still standing, and some walls and battlements, but everything else had tumbled down and was covered in ivy.

'What a spooky place,' said Jack. 'I wouldn't like to go near it at night.'

'Courage, Jack!' said the Scarecrow. 'Look – there's a spring. What did I tell you? Drink your fill, my boy!'

It was true. The spring bubbled out of the rocks beside the castle and flowed into a little pool, and as soon as he saw it, Jack gave a cry of delight and plunged his face deep into the icy water, swallowing and swallowing until he wasn't thirsty any more.

Finally he emerged, and heard the Scarecrow calling.

'Jack! Jack! In here! Look!'

Jack ran through the doorway at the foot of the tower, and found the Scarecrow looking around at all kinds of things: in one corner, barrels of gunpowder, muskets, swords and daggers and pikes; and in another corner, chests and boxes of gold coins and silver chains and glittering jewels of every colour; and in a third corner –

'Food!' cried Jack.

There were great smoked hams hanging from the ceiling, cheeses as big as cartwheels, onions in strings, boxes of apples, pies of every kind, bread, biscuits, and spice cakes and fruit cakes and butter cakes and honey cakes in abundance.

It was no good even trying to resist. Jack seized a pie as big as his own head, and a moment later he was sitting in the middle of the food, chewing away merrily, while the Scarecrow watched in satisfaction.

'What a stroke of luck finding this!' he said. 'And no-one knows about it at all. If only that old lady knew about it, she could come and help herself, and she wouldn't be poor any more.'

'Well,' said Jack, swallowing a mouthful of pie and picking up a spice cake, 'it's not quite like that,

master. I bet all this belongs to the brigands, and we better clear off soon, because if they catch us they'll cut our throats.'

'But I haven't got a throat.'

'Well, I have, and I don't want it cut,' said Jack. 'Look – we can't stay here – let's grab some of the food and scram.'

'Shame on you!' said the Scarecrow severely. 'Where's your courage? Where's your honour? We're going to scare these brigands away, and scare them so badly that they never come back. I wouldn't be surprised if we win a grand reward. Why, they might even make me a duke! Or give me a gold medal. No, it wouldn't surprise me a bit.'

'Well,' said Jack, 'maybe.'

Suddenly the Scarecrow pointed at a heap of straw.

'Oh – look – what's that?' he said.

There was something moving. It was a little creature the size of a mouse, which was crawling feebly around in a heap of straw on the floor. They both bent over to look at it.

'It's a baby bird,' said Jack.

'It's an owl chick, that's what it is,' said the

Scarecrow severely. 'These parents have no sense of responsibility. Look at that nest up there! Down-right dangerous.'

He pointed to an untidy bundle of twigs in a crack high up in the wall.

'Well, there's only one thing for it,' he said. 'You keep guard, Jack, while I return this infant to his cradle.'

'But—' Jack tried to protest.

The Scarecrow took no notice. He bent over and picked up the little bird, and tucked it tenderly into his pocket, making gentle clucking noises to soothe it. Then he began to clamber perilously up the sheer face of the wall, jamming his hands and feet into the cracks.

'Master! Take care!' called Jack, in a fever of anxiety. 'If you fall down, you'll snap like a dry stick!'

The Scarecrow didn't listen, because he was concentrating hard. Jack scampered to the door and looked around. Darkness was gathering, but there was no sign of any brigands. He scampered back in, and saw the Scarecrow high up and clinging to the wall with one hand while fumbling in his pocket with the other, and then reaching up and carefully putting the little bird back into the nest.

'Now you sit still,' he said sternly. 'No more squirming, you understand? If you can't fly, don't squirm. When I see your parents, I shall have a word with them.'

Then he began to clamber back down the wall. It looked so dangerous that Jack hardly dared watch, but finally the Scarecrow reached the floor again, and brushed his hands severely.

'I thought the birds were your enemy, master,' said Jack.

'Not the children, Jack! Good gracious me. Any man of honour would sooner bite off his own leg than hurt a child. Heaven forfend!'

'Blimey,' said Jack.

While the Scarecrow pottered about in the ruins, looking at everything with great curiosity, Jack gathered up a couple of pies, a loaf of bread, and half a dozen apples, and put them in a leather bag he found hanging on a hook next to the muskets. He hid it among the ivy growing over the tumbled wall outside.

The sun had set by this time, and it was nearly dark. Jack sat on the stones and thought about brigands. What did they do to people they caught? They weren't like scarecrows, or men of honour; they were more like soldiers, probably. They were bound to do horrible things, like tying you up and cutting bits off you, or dangling you over a fire, or putting earwigs up your nose. They might take all your ribs out. They might cram your trousers full of fireworks. They might—

Someone tapped him on the shoulder, and Jack leapt up with a yell.

'My word,' said the Scarecrow admiringly, 'that's a fine noise. I was just going to tell you that the brigands are coming.'

'What?' said Jack, in terror.

'Come, come,' said the Scarecrow. 'It's only a small flock – not more than twenty, I'd say. And I've got a plan.'

'Let's hear it, quick!'

'Very well. Here it is: we'll hide in the castle until they're all inside, and then we'll scare them, and then they'll run away. How's that?'

Jack was speechless. The Scarecrow beamed.

'Come along,' he said. 'I've found an excellent place to hide.'

Helplessly, Jack followed his master back into the tower, and looked all around in the dimness.

'Where's this excellent place to hide?' he said.

'Why, over there!' said the Scarecrow, pointing to a corner of the room in plain sight. 'They'll never think of looking there.'

'But – but – but—'

Jack could already hear the clop of horses' hooves outside. He scrunched himself down in the corner beside the Scarecrow, and squeezed his knees together to stop them knocking, and put his hands over his eyes so that no-one could see him, and waited for the brigands to come in.

# A STORY BY THE FIRESIDE

They were a disciplined band, those brigands. Jack watched between his fingers as they came in silently and sat around the fireplace. The chief brigand was a ferocious-looking man, with two belts full of bullets criss-cross over his shoulders, another one round his waist, a cutlass, two pistols, and three daggers: one in his belt, another strapped to his arm, and the third in the top of his boot. What's more, if he lost all his other weapons he could still stab two people with his moustache, which was waxed into long points as sharp as a pin.

His eyes glared and rolled as he looked around at his men, and Jack was almost sure they gave out sparks.

Any second now he'll see us, Jack thought. So it was despair as much as bravado that made him stand up and say:

'Good evening, gentlemen, and welcome to my master's castle!'

And he swept a low bow.

When he looked around, he saw twenty swords and twenty pistols all pointing at him, and twenty pairs of eyes, each eye just like the end of a pistol barrel.

The chief brigand roared: 'Who's this?'

'It's a mad boy, Captain,' said one of the men. 'Shall we roast him?'

'No,' said the chief, coming close and touching Jack's ribs with the point of his sword. 'There's no meat on him. He's all bone and gristle. He might flavour a stew, I suppose. Turn round, boy.'

Jack turned round and then turned back again. The chief brigand was shaking his head doubtfully.

'You say this is your master's castle?' he said.

'Indeed it is, sir, and you're most welcome,' said Jack.

'And who's your master?'

'My Lord Scarecrow,' said Jack, pointing to the Scarecrow in the corner, who was lying propped against the wall as still as a turnip, a suit of old clothes, and a few sticks could lie.

The chief brigand roared with laughter, and all his well-trained band slapped their thighs and held their sides and bellowed with mirth.

'He is mad!' cried the chief brigand. 'He's lost his wits!'

'Indeed I have, sir,' said Jack. 'I've been looking for them for months.'

'What do mad boys taste like?' said one of the brigands. 'Do they taste different from normal ones?'

'Spicier,' said another. 'More of a peppery taste.'

'No!' said the chief. 'We won't eat him. We'll keep him as a pet. We'll teach him to do tricks. Here – mad boy – turn a somersault, go on.'

Jack turned a somersault and stood up again.

'He's quick, isn't he?' said one brigand.

'Bet he can't dance, though,' said another.

'Mad boy!' roared the chief. 'Dance!'

Jack obediently capered like a monkey. Then he capered like a frog, and then he capered like a goat. The brigands were in a good mood by now, and they roared with laughter and clapped their hands.

'Wine!' bellowed the chief. 'Mad boy, stop dancing and pour us some wine!'

Jack found a big flagon of wine and went around the circle of brigands, filling up the horn cups they were all holding out.

'A toast!' the chief brigand said. 'To plunder!'

'To plunder!' the brigands shouted, and drank the wine in one gulp, so Jack had to go all the way round and fill the cups again.

Meanwhile, some of the brigands were lighting a fire and cutting up great joints of meat. Jack looked at the meat uneasily, but it looked like proper beef, and it certainly smelled good when it started to cook.

While it was roasting, the chief brigand counted out the jewels and gold coins they'd plundered and divided them all into twenty heaps, one big one and nineteen little ones; and as he was doing that, he said, 'Here, mad boy – tell us a story.'

Well, that was a hard one for Jack. However, if

he didn't do it there'd be big trouble; so he sat down and began.

'Once upon a time,' he said, 'there was a band of brigands living in a cave. They were cruel and wicked – oh, you could never imagine such terrible men. Every one of them was a qualified murderer.

'Anyway, one day they fell to quarrelling among themselves, and before they knew it, one of them lay dead on the floor of the cave.

'So the chief said, "Take him out and bury him. He makes the place look untidy."

'And they picked the dead man up and took him outside and dug a hole for him, and they put him in and shovelled the earth back on top, but he kept throwing it out.

'"You're not burying me!" he said, and he climbed out of the grave.

'"Oh yes we are!" they said, and they tried to shove him back in, but he wouldn't go. Every time they got him in the grave, he climbed out again, and he was as dead as a doornail. Finally they got him in and seven of them sat on him while the others piled rocks on top, and that did it.

'"He won't get out of that," said the chief, and

they went back in the cave and lit a fire to make supper. They had a big meal and lots of wine and then they lay down to sleep.

'But in the middle of the night, one of the brigands woke up. The cave was all silent, and the moonlight was shining in through the entrance. What woke him up was a sound, like a rock moving quietly on another rock, not loud at all, just a quiet sort of scraping noise. This man lay there with his eyes wide open, just listening as hard as he could. Then he heard it again.'

All the brigands were sitting stock-still, and they gazed fearfully at Jack with wide eyes.

Help, he thought. What am I going to say next?

But he didn't have to say anything, because into the silence there came a little scraping sound, like a rock moving quietly on another rock.

All the brigands jumped, and they all gave a little squeak of terror.

'And then,' said Jack, 'he saw . . . *Look! Look!*'

And he pointed dramatically to the corner where the Scarecrow was lying. Every head turned round at once.

The Scarecrow slowly lifted his head and stared at them with his knobbly turnip face.

All the brigands gasped, including the chief.

And the Scarecrow stretched out his arms and bent his legs, and stood up, and took one step towards them –

And every single brigand leapt to his feet and fled, screaming with terror. They fell over – they knocked one another out of the way – the ones that fell over got trampled on, and the ones that trampled on them got their feet caught and fell over themselves, to be trampled on in their turn – and some of them fell in the fire and leapt up squealing with pain, and that scattered the burning logs so that the cave was dark, and that made them even more frightened, so they shrieked and yelled in mortal fear; and those who could still see a little saw the Scarecrow's great knobbly face coming towards them, and scrambled even harder to get away –

And no more than ten seconds later, the brigands were all running away down the road, screaming with terror.

Jack stood in the doorway in amazement, watching them disappear into the distance.

'Well, master,' he said, 'it happened just as you said it would.'

'Timing, you see,' said the Scarecrow. 'The secret of all good scaring. I waited till they were feeling at their ease, lulled and comfortable, you know, and then I got up and scared them good and proper. It was the last thing they expected. I expect your story helped a little,' he added. 'It probably put them in a sort of peaceful mood.'

'Hmm,' said Jack. 'But I bet they come back, because they haven't eaten their dinner. I reckon we should scarper before they do.'

'Believe me,' said the Scarecrow solemnly, 'those rascals will never come back. They're not like birds, you see. With birds you need to keep scaring them afresh every day, but once is enough for brigands.'

'Well, you were right once, master. Perhaps you're right again.'

'You can depend on it, my boy! But you know, you shouldn't have told the brigands that I was the lord of this castle. That wasn't strictly true. I'm really the lord of Spring Valley.'

'Spring Valley? Where's that?'

'Oh, miles away. Ever so far. But it all belongs to me.'

'Does it?'

'Every inch. The farm, the wells, the fountains, the streams – all of it.'

'But how do you know, master? I mean, can you prove it?'

'The name of Spring Valley is written in my heart, Jack! Anyway, now I've had a rest, I'm eager to be on our way, and see the world by moonlight. Perhaps we'll meet the parents of that poor little owl chick. My word, I look forward to scaring them. Take as much food as you like – the brigands won't need it now.'

So Jack took the bag of food he'd hidden earlier, and added a pie and a cold roast chicken to it for good measure, and then followed his master out onto the high road, which was shining bright under the moon.

At that very moment, Mr Cercorelli the lawyer was sitting at a rough wooden table in a cottage kitchen, opposite an old woman who was eating bread and cheese.

'Like a scarecrow, you say?' he said, making a note.

'Yes, sir, horrible ugly brute he was. He leapt out of the bushes at me. Lord! I thought my last hour had come. He give me such a start that I dropped all me bread and cheese, and it was only when young master Buffaloni and his nice friends come along and chased him away that I felt safe again.'

'And did you see which way he went, this footpad who looked like a scarecrow?'

'Yes, sir. He went up into the hills. I shouldn't wonder if he's got a gang of marauding villains up there with him.'

'No doubt. Was he alone on this occasion?'

'No, sir. He had a young boy with him. Vicious-looking lad. Foreign, probably.'

'A young boy, eh?' said the lawyer, making another note. 'Thank you. That is very interesting. By the way,' he said, because he hadn't eaten all day, 'that cheese looks remarkably good.'

'Yes, it is,' said the old woman, putting it away. 'Very nice indeed. Nice bit of cheese.'

Mr Cercorelli sighed, and stood up.

'If you hear any more of this desperate rogue,' he said, 'be sure to let me know. Mr Buffaloni is offering a very generous reward. Good evening to you.'

# THE TRAVELLING PLAYERS

After a good night's sleep under a hedge, the Scarecrow and his servant woke up on a bright and sparkling morning.

'This is the life, Jack!' said the Scarecrow. 'The open road, the fresh air, and adventure just around the corner.'

'The fresh air's all right for you, master,' said Jack, removing leaves from his hair, 'but I like sleeping in a bed. I haven't seen a bed for so long, I can't remember whether the sheets go under the blankets or the blankets go under the sheets.'

'I shall just go and pay my respects to a colleague,' said the Scarecrow.

They'd woken up to find themselves close to a crossroads. A wooden sign stood where the roads met; but what the four arms were pointing to was impossible to read, for years of sun and rain had completely worn away the paint.

The Scarecrow strode up to the road sign and greeted it courteously. The sign took no notice, and neither did Jack, who was busy cutting a slice of cold meat with his little pocket knife, and folding it inside a slice of bread.

Then there came a loud *crack!*

Jack looked up to see the Scarecrow, very angry, clouting the nearest arm of the signpost as hard as he could.

'Take that, you insolent rogue!' he cried, and punched it again.

Unfortunately the first punch must have loosened something in the sign, because when he punched it for the second time, all four arms swung round, and the next one clonked the Scarecrow hard on the back of the head.

The Scarecrow fell over, shouting, 'Treachery! Cowardice!' and then bounced up at once, and seized the arm that had hit him and wrenched it off the signpost altogether.

'Take that, you dastardly footpad!' he cried, belabouring the post with the broken arm. 'Fight fairly, or surrender!'

The trouble was that every time he hit the post, it swung around again and hit him from the other side. However, he stood his ground, and fought back bravely.

'Master! Master!' called Jack, jumping up. 'That's not a footpad – that's a road sign!'

'He's in disguise,' said the Scarecrow. 'Mind out – stand back – he's a footpad all right. But don't you worry, I'll deal with him.'

'Right you are, master. Footpad he is, if you say so. But I think he's had enough now. I'm sure I heard him say, *I surrender*.'

'Did you? Are you sure?'

'Absolutely certain, master.'

'In that case—' began the Scarecrow, but stopped and looked down in horror at his own right arm, which was slipping slowly out of the sleeve of his jacket. The rake handle had come away from the broomstick that was his spine.

'I've been disarmed!' the Scarecrow said, shocked.

In fact, as Jack saw, the rake handle was so dry and brittle that it had never been much use in the first place, and the punishment it had taken in the fight with the road sign had cracked it in several places.

'I've got an idea, master,' he said. 'This fellow's arm is in better condition than your old one. Why don't we slip that up your sleeve instead?'

'What a good idea!' said the Scarecrow, cheering up at once.

So Jack did that, and just as had happened with the stick that had become his leg, the arm gave a kind of twitch when it met his shoulder, and settled into place at once.

'My word,' said the Scarecrow, admiring his new arm, trying it out by waving it around, and prac- tising pointing at things with the finger on the end. 'What gifts you have, Jack, my boy! You could be a surgeon. Or a carpenter, even. And as for you, you scoundrel,' he added severely to the road sign, 'let that be a lesson to you.'

'I don't suppose he'll attack anyone else, master,' said Jack. 'I reckon you've sorted him out for good. Which way shall we go next?'

'That way,' said the Scarecrow, pointing confidently along one of the roads with his new arm.

So Jack shouldered his bag, and they set off.

After an hour's brisk walking, they reached the edge of a town. It must have been market day, because people were making for the town with carts full of vegetables and cheeses and other things to sell. One man was a bird-catcher. His cart was piled high with cages containing little songbirds such as linnets, larks and goldfinches. The Scarecrow was very interested.

'Prisoners of war,' he explained to Jack. 'I expect they're being sent back to their own country.'

'I don't think so, master. I think people are going to buy them and keep them in cages so they can hear them singing.'

'No!' exclaimed the Scarecrow. 'No, no, people wouldn't do that. Why, that would be dishonourable. Take it from me, they're prisoners of war.'

Presently they came to the market place, and the

Scarecrow gazed around in amazement at the town hall, the church, the market stalls.

'I had no idea civilization had advanced to this point,' he said to Jack. 'Why, this almost compares to Bella Fontana. What industry! What beauty! What splendour! You wouldn't find a place like this in the kingdom of the birds, I'm sure of that.'

Jack could see children whispering and pointing at the Scarecrow.

'Listen, master,' he said, 'I don't think we—'

'What's *that*?' said the Scarecrow, full of excitement.

He was pointing at a canvas booth where a carpenter was hammering some planks together to hold up a brightly painted picture of a wild landscape.

'That's going to be a play,' said Jack. 'That's called scenery. Actors come out in front of it and act out a story.'

The Scarecrow's eyes were open as wide as they could go. He moved towards the booth as if he were being pulled on a string. There was a big colourful poster nearby, and a man was reading it aloud for those people who couldn't read themselves:

'*The Tragical History of Harlequin and Queen Dido,*' the man read out. '*To be acted by Signor Rigatelli's Celebrated Players, late from triumphs in Paris, Venice, Madrid, and Constantinople. With Effects of Battle and Shipwreck, a Dance of the Infernal Spirits, and the Eruption of Vesuvius. Daily at noon, mid-afternoon, and sunset, with special evening performance complete with Pyrotechnical Extravaganza.*'

The Scarecrow was nearly floating with excitement.

'I want to watch it *all*!' he said. 'Again and again!'

'Well, it's not free, master,' Jack explained. 'You have to pay. And we haven't got any money.'

'In that case,' said the Scarecrow, 'I shall have to offer my services as an actor. I say!' he called. 'Signor Rigatelli!'

A fat man wearing a dressing gown and eating a piece of salami came out from behind the scenery.

'Yes?' he said.

'Signor Rigatelli,' began the Scarecrow, 'I—'

'Blimey,' said Signor Rigatelli to Jack, 'that's good. Do some more.'

'I'm not doing anything,' Jack said.

'Excuse me,' said the Scarecrow, 'but I—'

'That's it! Brilliant!' said Rigatelli.

'*What?*' said Jack. 'What are you talking about?'

'Ventriloquism,' said Rigatelli. 'Do it again, go on.'

'Signor Rigatelli,' said the Scarecrow once more, 'my patience is not inexhaustible. I have the honour to present myself to you as an actor of modest experience but boundless genius . . . What are you doing?'

Signor Rigatelli was walking around the Scarecrow, studying him from every angle. Then he lifted up the back of the Scarecrow's jacket to see how he worked, and the Scarecrow leapt away, furious.

'No – it's all right, master, don't get cross,' said Jack hastily. 'It's just that he'd like to be an actor, you see,' he explained to Rigatelli, 'and I'm his agent,' he added.

'I've never seen anything like it,' said the great showman. 'I can't see how it works at all. Tell you what, we'll use him as a prop in the mad scene. He can stand there on the blasted heath when the queen goes barmy. Then if he looks all right he can go on again as an infernal spirit. Can you make him dance?'

'I'm not sure,' said Jack.

'Well, he can follow the others. First call in ten minutes.'

And Rigatelli crammed the rest of the salami in his mouth, and went back inside his caravan.

The Scarecrow was ecstatic.

'A prop!' he said. 'I'm going to be a *prop*! Do you realize, Jack, that this is the first step on the road to a glorious career? And already I'm playing a prop! He must have been very impressed.'

'Yes,' said Jack, 'probably.'

The Scarecrow was already disappearing behind the scenery.

'Master,' said Jack, 'wait . . .'

He found the Scarecrow watching with great interest as an actor, sitting in front of a mirror, put his greasepaint on.

'Good grief!' the actor said, suddenly catching sight of the Scarecrow, and leapt out of his chair, dropping his greasepaint.

'Good day, sir,' said the Scarecrow. 'Allow me to introduce myself. I am to play the part of a prop. May I trouble you for the use of your make-up?'

The actor swallowed hard and looked around. Then he saw Jack.

'Who's this?' he said.

'This is Lord Scarecrow,' said Jack, 'and Signor Rigatelli says he can take part in the mad scene. Listen, master,' he said to the Scarecrow, who was sitting down and looking with great interest at all the pots of greasepaint and powder. 'You know what a prop is, don't you?'

'It's a very important part,' said the Scarecrow, painting a pair of bright red lips on the front of his turnip.

'Yes, but it's what they call a silent role,' said Jack.

'You don't move and you don't speak.'

'What's going on?' said the actor.

'*I'm* going on!' said the Scarecrow proudly. 'In the mad scene.'

He outlined each of his eyes with black, and then dabbed some red powder on his cheeks. The actor was watching, goggle-eyed.

'That looks lovely, master,' Jack said, 'but you don't want to overdo it.'

'You think we should be subtle?'

'For the mad scene, definitely, master.'

'Very well. Perhaps a wig would make me look more subtle.'

'Not that one,' said Jack, taking a big blond curly wig out of the Scarecrow's hands. 'Just remember – don't move and don't speak.'

'I'll do it all with my eyes,' said the Scarecrow, taking the wig back and settling it over his turnip.

The actor gave him a horrified look and left.

'I need a costume now,' said the Scarecrow. 'This'll do.'

He picked up a scarlet cloak and twirled it around his shoulders. Jack clutched his head in despair, and followed the Scarecrow out behind the scenes, where the actors and the musicians and the stage hands were getting everything ready. There was a lot to look at, and Jack had to stop the Scarecrow explaining it all to him.

'Yes, master – hush now – the audience is out there, so we all have to be quiet . . .'

'There it is!' said an angry actress, and snatched the wig off the Scarecrow's head. 'What are you playing at?' she said to Jack. 'How dare you put my wig on that thing?'

'I beg your pardon,' said the Scarecrow, getting to his feet and bowing very low. 'I would not upset you for the world, madam, but you are already so beautiful that you need no improvement; whereas I . . .'

The actress was watching with critical interest as she settled the wig on her head.

'Not bad,' she said to Jack. 'I've seen a lot worse. I can't see how you move him at all. But don't you touch my stuff again, you hear?'

'Sorry,' said Jack.

The actress swept away.

'Such grace! Such beauty!' said the Scarecrow, gazing after her.

'Yes, master, but *shush*!' said Jack. 'Sit *down*. Be *quiet.*'

Just then they heard a crash of cymbals and a blast on a trumpet.

'Ladies and gentlemen!' came the voice of Signor Rigatelli. 'We present a performance of the doleful and piteous tragedy of Harlequin and Queen Dido, with pictorial and scenic effects never before seen, and featuring the most comical interludes ever presented on the public stage! Our performance today is sponsored by the Buffaloni Dried Meat Company, the makers of the finest salami in town, A Smile In Every Bite.'

The Buffalonis again, thought Jack. They get up to everything.

There was a roll of drums, and the curtain went up. Jack and the Scarecrow watched wide-eyed as the play began. It wasn't much of a story, but the audience enjoyed Harlequin pretending to lose a string of sausages, and then swallowing a fly by mistake and leaping around the stage as it buzzed inside him; and then Queen Dido was abandoned by her lover, Captain Fanfarone, and ran offstage mad with grief. She was the actress in the blond wig.

'Here! Boy!' came a loud whisper from Rigatelli. 'Get him on! It's the mad scene! Stick him in the middle and get off quick.'

The Scarecrow spread his arms wide as Jack carried him onstage.

'I shall be the best prop there ever was!' he declared. 'They'll be talking about my prop for years to come.'

Jack put his finger to his lips and tiptoed offstage. As he did, he found himself face to face with the actress playing Queen Dido, who was about to come on again. She looked furious.

'What's that thing doing?' she demanded.

'He's a prop,' Jack explained.

'If you make him move or speak I'll skin you alive,' she said. 'Manually.'

Jack swallowed and nodded hard.

The curtain rose, and Jack jumped, because Queen Dido gave a wild, unearthly shriek and ran past him on to the stage.

'Oh! Ah! Woe! Misery!' she screamed, and flung herself to the ground.

The audience watched, enthralled. So did the Scarecrow. Jack could see his eyes getting wider and following her as she grovelled and shrieked and pretended to tear her hair.

'Hey nonny nonny,' she wailed, and danced up and down blowing kisses at the air. 'There's rosemary, that's for remembrance! Hey nonny nonny! O, Fanfarone, thou art a villain, forsooth! It was a lover and his lass! There's a daisy for you. La, la, la!'

Jack was very impressed. It certainly looked like great acting.

Suddenly she sat down and began to pluck the petals out of an imaginary daisy.

'He loves me – he loves me not – he loves me – he loves me not – oh, daisy, daisy, give me your answer, do! Oh, that my heart would boil over and put out the fires of my grief! La, la, la, Fanfarone, thou art a pretty villain!'

Jack was watching the Scarecrow closely. He could see the poor booby getting more and more worried, and he whispered, 'Don't, master – it's not real – keep still!'

The Scarecrow was trying, that was clear. He only moved his head very slowly to follow what Queen Dido was doing, but he did move it, and already

one or two people in the audience had noticed and were nudging their neighbours to point him out.

Queen Dido struggled to her feet, clutching her heart. Suddenly the Scarecrow noticed that she had a dagger in her hand. She had her back to him, and she couldn't see him leaning sideways to peer round at her, a look of alarm on his great knobbly face.

'Oh! Ah! Woe! The pangs of my sorrow tear at my soul like red-hot hooks! Ahhhhhhhh . . .'

She gave a long despairing cry, beginning as high as she could squeal and descending to the lowest note she could reach. She was famous for that cry. Critics had said that it plumbed the depths of mortal anguish, that it would melt a heart of stone, that no-one could hear it without feeling the tears gush from their eyes.

This time, though, she had the feeling that the audience wasn't quite with her. Some of them were laughing, even, and what made it worse was that when she spun round to see if it was the Scarecrow they were laughing at, he instantly remembered to act, and fell still, staring out as if he was nothing but a turnip on a stick.

Queen Dido gave him a look of furious suspicion, and resolved to try her famous cry again.

'*Waaahhh – aahhh – aaaahhhh . . .*' she wailed, wobbling and quavering all the way from a bat-like squeak down to a groan like a cow with a belly-ache.

And behind her the Scarecrow found himself moving in time with her, and imitating the way she wobbled her head and waved her arms and sank gradually downwards. He couldn't help it – he was deeply moved. Of course, the audience thought it was hilarious, and they roared, they slapped their thighs, they clapped and whistled and cheered.

Queen Dido was furious. And so was Signor Rigatelli. He suddenly appeared beside Jack and shoved two actors out on to the stage, saying, 'Get him off! Get him off!'

Unfortunately, the two actors were dressed as brigands, and sure enough the Scarecrow thought they were real.

'You villains!' he cried, and leapt forward with his wooden arms held out like fists. 'Your Majesty, get behind me! I'll defend you!'

And he bounced around the stage, aiming blows at the actors. Queen Dido, meanwhile, had stamped in rage and hurled her wig to the ground before

storming offstage to shout at Rigatelli.

The audience was loving it.

'Go it, Scarecrow!' they shouted, and 'Whack 'em, Turnip! Look behind you! Up the Scarecrow!'

The two actors didn't know what to make of it, but they kept on chasing the Scarecrow and then having to run away when he fought back.

Suddenly the Scarecrow stopped, and pointed in horror at the blond wig on the boards in front of him.

'You cut her head off when I wasn't looking!' he cried. 'How dare you! Right, that does it. I'm really angry now!'

And waving his wooden arms like a windmill,

436

he leapt at the two actors and belaboured them mercilessly. The audience went wild. But the actors were getting cross now, and they fought back, and then Rigatelli himself came bustling up to try and restore order.

Jack rushed onstage as well, to try and pull the Scarecrow away before he got hurt. Unfortunately one of the actors had got hold of the Scarecrow's left arm, and was tugging and tugging at it, while the Scarecrow was whacking him around the head; and when Jack seized the Scarecrow around the middle and tried to tug him backwards, his master's left arm came away entirely, and the actor holding it fell back suddenly into Rigatelli, knocking him back into the other actor, who grabbed at the scenery to save himself; but the combined weight of the three of them was too much for the blasted heath, and it all came down with a screech of wood and a tearing of canvas, and in a moment there was nothing to be seen but a heap of painted scenery heaving and cursing, with arms and legs waving and disappearing and emerging again.

'This way, master!' Jack said, hauling the Scarecrow off the stage. 'Let's run for it!'

'Never!' cried the Scarecrow. 'I shall never surrender!'

'It's not surrendering, master, it's beating a retreat,' said Jack, dragging him away.

Everyone in the market place had heard what was going on, and they'd left their stalls to go and laugh at the actors and the collapsing theatre. Among them was the bird-catcher. All his cages with their linnets and goldfinches were glittering in the sun, and the little birds were singing as loud as they could, and the Scarecrow couldn't resist.

'Birds,' he said very sternly, 'I accept that a state of war exists between your kingdom and me, but there is such a thing as justice. To see you imprisoned in this cruel way makes the blood rush to my turnip with indignation. I am going to set you free, and I charge you on your honour to go straight home and not eat any farmer's grain on the way.'

Jack didn't notice what his master was doing, because he'd spotted an old man sitting at a stall selling umbrellas. He was too rheumaticky to run over to the theatre with everybody else, and he was pleased to sell one of his umbrellas to Jack, who had found a gold coin in a corner of the brigands' bag.

Then someone shouted, 'Stop thief! Get away from my birds!'

Jack turned round to see the Scarecrow opening the last of the cages.

A flock of little birds was wheeling around his head, chirping merrily, and he was waving his one arm, the one that pointed nowhere.

'Fly!' he shouted. 'Fly away!'

'Come on, master!' called Jack. 'They're all after us now!'

And he dragged the Scarecrow away, and the two of them fled as fast as they could. The cries of anger, the shouts of laughter, the full-throated singing of the liberated birds all gradually faded behind them.

When they reached the open country again, they stopped. Jack was out of breath. The Scarecrow was looking at himself, trying to work out what was wrong, and then he cried, 'Oh no! My other arm's gone! I'm falling to pieces!'

'Don't worry, master, I've thought of that. I bought you a new arm – look,' said Jack, and he slipped the umbrella up the Scarecrow's sleeve, handle first.

'Good gracious,' said the Scarecrow. 'I do believe – I think I – yes, yes, I can! Look at this! Just look at this, Jack!'

And he shook his new arm, and the umbrella opened. His great turnip-face, with its bright red mouth and black-rimmed eyes, was radiant.

'Aren't I clever!' he said, marvelling. 'Look at the ingenuity of it! It goes up – it comes down – it goes up – it comes down—'

'You can keep the sun off us, master,' said Jack. 'And the rain.'

The Scarecrow looked at him proudly. 'You'll go a long way, my boy!' he said. 'I was going to think of those things in a minute, but you beat me to it.

And what a triumph we had on the stage! We saw everything they said on the poster.'

'We didn't have the Shipwreck, though, or the Eruption of Vesuvius.'

'Oh, we will, Jack,' said the Scarecrow confidently. 'I'm sure we will.'

# SCARECROW FOR HIRE

When the lawyer reached the town next morning, he found it full of strange rumours. After interviewing Mr Rigatelli and the actress who played Queen Dido, who were both convinced that the Scarecrow was an automaton controlled by mesmeric waves as part of a plot organized by a rival theatre company, Mr Cercorelli found his way to the elderly umbrella salesman.

'Yes, I seen it all,' said the old man. 'It was a boy with a horan-gatang. I seen one of 'em before. They live in the trees in Borneo. Almost human they are, but you wouldn't mistake him close up. What d'you want him for? Has he escaped from a zoo?'

'Not exactly,' said Mr Cercorelli. 'Which way did they go?'

'That way,' said the old man, pointing. 'You'll recognize 'em easy enough. They bought one of my umbrellas.'

The Scarecrow and his servant walked a long way that day. They spent the night under a hedge by an olive grove, and the moment they woke up, Jack knew something was wrong.

He sat up and looked all around. The sun was shining, the air smelled of thyme and sage, there was the sound of little bells around the necks of a herd of goats browsing nearby; but something was missing.

'Master! Wake up! Our bag's been stolen!' Jack cried in despair, as soon as he realized what had happened. 'All the food's gone!'

The Scarecrow sat up at once, and opened his umbrella in alarm. Jack was lifting stones, peering under the hedge, running backwards and forwards to look up and down the road.

The Scarecrow peered into the ditch, frowning at a lizard. It took no notice. Then he bent over and looked at something among the leaves.

'A clue!' he called, and Jack came running.

'What, master?'

'There,' said the Scarecrow, using his pointing hand to indicate something small and unpleasant at his feet.

'What is it?'

'An owl pellet. You can take it from me, this was left by the culprit. No doubt about it, the thief is an owl.'

'Oh,' said Jack, scratching his head.

'Or a jackdaw,' the Scarecrow went on. 'In fact, now I think of it, it must have been a jackdaw, and he left the owl pellet to throw us off the scent. Can you believe the villainy of these birds! They have no shame.'

'No,' said Jack. 'None at all. Anyway, we haven't got any money, and we haven't got any food. I don't know what we're going to do.'

'We shall have to work for our living, dear boy,' said the Scarecrow cheerfully. 'But we are full of enterprise and both in the pink of health. Ow! Ow! What are you doing?'

His last words were spoken to a goat, which had come up behind him and started to make a meal of his trousers.

The Scarecrow turned and clouted the goat with his road sign. But the goat objected to this, and butted him hard, knocking him over before Jack could catch him. The Scarecrow was astonished.

'How dare you! What a cowardly attack!' he said, struggling up.

The goat charged him again. This time the Scarecrow was prepared. He opened his umbrella suddenly, and the goat skidded to a halt and started to eat that instead.

'Oh, really,' said the Scarecrow, 'this is too much!'

And then a tug-of-war began, with the goat at one end and the Scarecrow at the other. The rest of the goats came over to see what was happening, and one of them started nibbling at the Scarecrow's coat tails, another at his trousers, and a third began to

browse on the straw coming out of his chest.

'Go on! Scram! Clear off!' Jack shouted, clapping his hands, and reluctantly the goats slouched away.

'You expect that sort of behaviour from people with feathers,' the Scarecrow said severely, 'not people with horns. I'm very disappointed.'

'They were taking a consuming interest in you, master,' said Jack.

'Well, you can't blame them for that,' said the Scarecrow, brushing his lapels and shaking out the remains of his coat. 'But I must say, Jack, they shouldn't be allowed out without a goatherd. We shan't let that happen in Spring Valley.'

'Spring Valley? Oh, I remember. How did you manage to get a big estate, all full of – what was it?

– a farm and streams and wells and so on?'

'Well, it's a puzzle, Jack,' the Scarecrow admitted, as they set off along the road. 'I've always had an inner conviction that I was a man of property. A sort of gentleman farmer, you know.'

'And is that where we're going, Spring Valley?'

'In good time, Jack. We have to make our fortunes first.'

'Oh, I see. Well, look,' said Jack, pointing ahead of them, 'there's a farm, and a farmer. Let's go and ask him for a job. That'll be a start.'

The farmer was sitting disconsolately outside his house, sharpening a scythe.

'You want a job?' he said to Jack. 'You couldn't have come at a better . . . you know. The soldiers took all my, umm, away, and the birds are eating the, er, as fast as it comes up. You set up your, that, him, in the top field, and you can take the rattle and work in the orchard.'

'The thing is,' said Jack, 'he's getting a bit tattered. If you had a spare pair of trousers he'd look a lot more realistic.'

'There's a dirty old pair of, umm, you know, in the woodshed. Help yourself. There'll be a bite to, er, at sunset, and you can sleep in the barn.'

Soon afterwards, they were at work. The Scarecrow shooed away all the birds from the cornfield, and from time to time he opened and shut his umbrella, just to teach them a lesson. Jack roamed up and down the orchard, rattling hard whenever he saw a finch or a linnet.

It was hard work. The sun was hot and there were plenty of birds to scare. Jack found himself thinking about Spring Valley, and the Scarecrow's great estate. The poor noodle must have made it up and found himself believing it, Jack thought. He was good at that. It sounded like a nice place, though.

At sunset Jack stopped rattling, and went to call the Scarecrow in. His master was very impressed by the rattle.

'Formidable!' he said when Jack showed him how it worked. 'What a weapon! I don't suppose I could use it tomorrow?'

'Well, if you do, master, I won't have anything to scare the birds with. You're an expert, and you can do it just by looking at them, but I need all the help I can get. Now you go and sit down in the barn, and I'll fetch us some supper.'

The farmer's wife gave Jack a pot of stew and a big hunk of bread, and told him not to come in the kitchen with that monster of his. New-fangled bird-scarers were all very well, but this was a respectable farm, and she couldn't be doing with mechanical monsters in the house.

'Righto, missus,' said Jack. 'Any chance of a drink?'

'There's a bucket in the well,' she said, 'and a tin cup on a string next to it.'

'Thank you,' said Jack, and took his pot of stew to the barn, pausing for a good long swig of water on the way.

But before he went into the barn, he stopped outside, because he could hear voices.

'Oh, yes,' the Scarecrow was saying, 'we fought off a dozen brigands, my servant and I.'

'Brigands?' said someone else. It was a female voice, and it was full of admiration.

Jack walked in to find the Scarecrow sitting on a bale of straw, surrounded by a dozen rakes and hoes and broomsticks and spades and pitchforks. They were all leaning on the wall, listening respectfully.

At least, that's what it looked like until they

realized Jack was there. Then they went back to looking like rakes and hoes and so on.

'Ah, Jack, my boy!' said the Scarecrow.

'The farmer's wife gave me a bowl of stew for us,' said Jack doubtfully, looking around.

'You have most of it,' said the Scarecrow. 'I don't eat a great deal. A small piece of bread will be quite sufficient.'

So Jack sat down and tucked into the stew, which was full of peppers and onions and bits of gristly sausage.

'I thought I heard voices, master,' he said with his mouth full.

'And so you did. I was just telling these ladies and gentlemen about our adventures.'

Jack looked around at the rakes and hoes and brooms. None of them moved or said a word.

'Ah,' said Jack. 'Right.'

'As I was saying,' the Scarecrow went on, 'the brigands were a fearsome crew. Armed to the teeth, every single one. They trapped us in their cave and—'

'I thought you said it was a ruined castle,' said a rake.

'That's right, a ruined castle,' said the Scarecrow cheerfully.

Jack's hair was standing on end. It certainly seemed as if one of the rakes had spoken, but it was getting dark, and he was very tired. He rubbed his eyes, and felt them closing as fast as he could rub them open again.

'Well, which?' demanded the rake.

'Castle. Next to a cave. My servant and I went in to investigate, and the next thing we knew, in came two dozen brigands. Or three dozen, probably. I hid in the corner, and Jack told them a story to send them to sleep, and then I loomed up like an apparition – like this—'

The Scarecrow raised his arms and made a hideous face. Some of the smaller brooms flinched

451

away, and a little fork squeaked in terror.

'And the brigands turned tail and fled,' the Scarecrow went on. 'I've thought about it since, and I've worked out the reason why. I think they were birds, and they were only disguised as brigands. Big birds,' he explained. 'Sort of ostrich-sized. Very dangerous,' he added.

'You must be very brave,' said a broom shyly.

'Oh, I don't know,' said the Scarecrow. 'One gets used to danger in this line of work. But soon after that, I entered a new profession. I went on the stage!'

Jack was lying down now. The last thing he noticed before he fell asleep was the Scarecrow beginning to act out the role he had taken in the play; only it seemed a much more important role than Jack remembered, and when it got to the point where Queen Dido fell in love with the Scarecrow and made him Prime Minister, Jack realized he'd been asleep for some time.

He woke up to find the sun in his eyes and the Scarecrow shaking him.

'Jack! Wake up! Time for work! The birds have been up for some time. But Jack – I need to have a

word with you. In private.'

Jack rubbed his eyes and looked around.

'We *are* in private,' he said.

'No! I mean *more* private,' the Scarecrow said, in an urgent whisper. 'Away from – you know . . .'

He gestured over his shoulder and nodded backwards in a meaningful way.

'Ah, I see,' said Jack, who had no idea what he was talking about. 'Just give me a moment, and I'll meet you out by the well, master.'

The Scarecrow nodded and strode out of the barn. Jack scratched his head. The rakes and hoes and brooms were perfectly still and silent.

'Must have been dreaming,' Jack said to himself, and got up.

The farmer's wife gave him some bread and jam for breakfast, and Jack took it out to the well, where the Scarecrow was waiting impatiently.

'What is it, master?' he said.

'I've decided to get married,' the Scarecrow told him. 'As a matter of fact I've fallen in love. Oh, Jack, she's so beautiful! And such a delicate nature! You'd never believe it, but I feel almost clumsy beside her. Her grace! Her charm! Oh, my heart is lost, I love her, I worship the ground she brushes!'

'Brushes?' said Jack, his mouth full.

'She's a broom,' the Scarecrow explained. 'You must have noticed her. The very pretty one! The lovely one! Oh, I adore her!'

'Have you told her?'

'Ah. That's what I was going to tell you. I haven't got the nerve, Jack. My courage fails me. As soon as I look at her I feel like a – like a – like an onion.'

'An onion?'

'Yes, just like an onion. But I can't think of a thing to say. So *you'll* have to tell her.'

Jack scratched his head.

'Well,' he said, 'I'm not as eloquent as you are, master. I'd probably get it all wrong. I'm sure she'd rather hear it from you.'

'Well, of course she would,' agreed the Scarecrow. 'Anyone would. But I'm struck dumb when I see her, so it'll have to be you.'

'I don't understand why you feel like an onion,' Jack said.

'No, neither do I. I had no idea that love would have that effect. Have you ever been in love, Jack?'

'I don't think so. If I fell in love, I'd probably feel

like a turnip. Listen, I tell you what, master—'

'I know! You could pretend to be a bird, and attack her, and I could pretend to come and fight you off. I bet she'd be impressed by that.'

'I'm not a good actor like you, master. She'd probably guess I wasn't a real bird. Listen, let's go and do some work, and you can think about her all day long, out in the cornfield. We'll talk about it later, before we come in.'

'Yes! That's a good idea,' said the Scarecrow, and marched off proudly to start the day's work.

# A Serenade

Jack worked hard all morning. At midday the farmer came into the orchard to see how he was getting on, and looked around approvingly.

'That other fellow,' he said, 'your mate . . .'

'My master,' said Jack.

'As you like. Him. He's a good worker, and no mistake. But . . . well . . . you know.'

'Oh, he's good at scarecrowing,' said Jack.

'No doubt about it. But – umm – he's a bit, er, well, isn't he?'

'Only if you don't know him.'

'Oh, is that right? Then he's . . . mmm . . . is he?'

'He's a deep character,' said Jack, rattling at a blackbird.

'Ah,' said the farmer. 'Thing is, he looks almost – well, if I didn't know better, I'd even say . . . you know.'

'That's part of his cleverness. See, when he's working, he never . . . kind of thing.'

'No,' said the farmer. 'Wouldn't do to . . . umm.'

'I mean, there'd be no end of a – you know.'

'Too true. You're right there. All the same, eh? I mean . . .'

'Yes,' agreed Jack. 'No. It'd be terrible if . . . er.'

'A word to the wise, eh?' said the farmer, and winked and tapped the side of his nose. Jack did the same, in case it was the private signal of a secret society. The farmer nodded and went away.

Well, it's a good thing he didn't go and say all that to the master, Jack thought. The poor booby wouldn't have understood a word.

He rattled away busily all afternoon, and as the sun was setting he went to call the Scarecrow from the top field.

'Jack,' said the Scarecrow, 'I've been thinking about her all day long, just as you suggested, and I've come to the conclusion that if she won't marry me, I'll have to do something desperate.'

'Oh dear,' said Jack. 'What would that be, master?'

'I'm saving that till tomorrow to think about.'

'Good idea. I wonder what's for supper?'

The farmer's wife gave them another bowl of stew, and she gave the Scarecrow a long hard suspicious look, too, which he didn't see, because he was gazing at the barn with a dopey expression on his turnip.

'Thank you, missus,' Jack said.

'You mind you keep him locked up at night,' said the farmer's wife. 'I don't like the look of him. If I find any hens missing . . .'

Jack and his master sat down beside the well, and once again the Scarecrow let Jack have all the stew, and only nibbled at a piece of bread.

'You ought to eat something, master,' said Jack. 'I bet she'd like you just as much if you had a full belly. You'd feel better, anyway.'

'No, I've got no appetite, Jack. I'm wasting away with love.'

'If you're sure, then,' said Jack, finishing off the stew.

'I know!' said the Scarecrow, sitting up suddenly and opening his umbrella with excitement. 'I could serenade her!'

'Well—' said Jack, but the Scarecrow was too excited to listen.

'Yes! That's it! Here's the plan. Wait till dark, and then pick her up and pretend to sweep the floor. And sweep her outside, and then sort of casually lean her against the wall, and then I'll sing to her.'

'Well—' Jack began again.

'Oh, yes. When she hears me sing, her heart will be mine!'

'You better not sing too loud. I don't think the farmer'd like it. I'm sure his old lady wouldn't.'

'Oh, I shall be very discreet,' said the Scarecrow. 'Tender, but ardent, is the note to strike.'

'That sounds about right,' said Jack.

'Start sweeping as soon as the moon shines into the farmyard. I think moonlight would show me to advantage, don't you?'

'Maybe you better let me tidy you up,' said Jack, and he dusted the Scarecrow's shoulders, and put some fresh straw in his chest, and washed his turnip. 'There – you look a treat. Remember – not too loud, now.'

The Scarecrow sat down outside the barn, and Jack went inside to lie down. Before he did, though,

he found the broom and put
her beside the door, so that
he'd be able to find her in
the dark.

'Excuse me,' he found
himself saying, 'but I
hope you don't mind if
I put you over here.
You'll find out why when
the moon comes up.'

She didn't reply, but
she leant against the
wall very gracefully. Jack thought she
must be shy, until he caught himself and shook his
head.

He's got me believing she's alive, he thought. I
better be careful, in case I go as mad as he is.

He lay down on the straw and closed his eyes. The
old donkey and the cow were asleep on their feet,
just breathing quietly and chewing a bit from time
to time, and it was all very quiet and peaceful.

Jack woke up when the moonlight touched his
eyes. He yawned and stretched and sat up.

'Well,' he said to himself, 'time to start brushing

the floor. This is a daft idea. Still, he's a marvel, the master, no doubt about it.'

He took the broom and swept the floor, brushing all the straw and dust casually towards the door where the moonlight was shining through. Once he was outside, he leant the broom against the wall and yawned again before going back to lie down.

And almost at once he went back to sleep. He must have started dreaming straight away, because it seemed as if he were watching the Scarecrow sweeping the ground outside, singing to the broom as he did so:

> 'Your handle so slender,
> Your bristles so tender,
> I have to surrender
>   My heart to your charms;
> Retreating, advancing,
> And secretly glancing,
> Oh, never stop dancing
>   All night in my arms!'

Jack blinked and rubbed his eyes, but it made no difference. The Scarecrow and the broom were waltzing around the barnyard like the most graceful dancers at a ball.

> 'Your gentle demeanour
> Sweeps everything cleaner!
> I never have seen a
>    More elegant Miss;
> So gracious, so charming,
> Completely disarming,
> Oh where is the harm in
>    A maidenly kiss?'

Jack thought, He's going to marry her, and then he won't want a servant any more. Mind you, he does look happy. But I don't know if I'll ever find a master I'd rather serve . . .

And while he was lying there puzzled by all those thoughts, he was woken up all of a sudden by a horrible raucous yell.

*'Hee-haw! Hee-haw!'*

He sat up, and realized first that it *had* been a dream; and second, that the old donkey in the barn was braying and stamping and creating no end of a fuss; and third, that outside in the barnyard the

Scarecrow was roaring and howling and bellowing with anger, or distress, or misery.

Jack scrambled to the door of the barn to see the farmer's wife, in a long nightdress, running out of the kitchen door with a frying pan held high above her head. Behind her, the farmer, in a long night-shirt, was fumbling with a blunderbuss. The Scare-crow was clutching the broom to his heart, and real tears were streaming down his turnip.

'No, missus! No! Don't!' Jack shouted, and ran out to try and hold off the farmer's wife, who was about to wallop the Scarecrow with the frying pan. There was no danger from the farmer; as soon as he tried to aim the blunderbuss, all the lead shot fell out of the end of the barrel, and bounced on the flagstones like hail.

Jack reached the Scarecrow just as the farmer's wife did, and stood between them with his arms held wide.

'No, missus! Stop! Let me explain!' he said.

'I'll brain him!' she cried. 'I'll teach him to go caterwauling in the middle of the night and terrify-ing honest folk out of their beds!'

'No, don't, missus, he's a poor zany, he doesn't

mean any harm – you leave him to me—'

'I told you!' said the farmer, staying safely behind his wife. 'Didn't I? Eh?'

'Yes, you did,' Jack agreed. 'You told me some-thing, anyway.'

'None of this . . . you know,' the farmer added.

'You take that horrible thing away,' said the farmer's wife, 'and you get out of here right now, and don't you come back!'

'Certainly, missus,' said Jack, 'and what about our wages?'

'Wages?' she said. 'You're not getting any wages. Clear off, you and your monster both!'

Jack turned to the Scarecrow, who hadn't heard any of what the farmer's wife had said. In fact, he was still sobbing in despair.

'Now then, master, what's the trouble?' he said.

'She's already engaged!' the Scarecrow howled. 'She's going to marry a rake!'

'Oh, that's bad luck,' said Jack. 'Still, look on the bright side—'

'I shall do the decent thing, of course,' the Scarecrow went on, struggling to control his emotions. 'My dear young lady,' he said to the broom, 'nothing would make me stand between you and your happiness, if your heart is already given to the gentleman in the barn. But I warn him,' he said, raising his voice and looking in at all the tools leaning on the wall, 'he had better treat this broom like the precious creature she is, and make her happiness the centre of his life, or he will face my wrath!'

With a last choking sob, he handed the broom gently to Jack. Jack took her into the barn and stood her next to the rake.

When he got back outside, the Scarecrow was speaking to the farmer and his wife.

'I am sorry for waking you up,' he said, 'but I make no excuses for the passionate expression of my feelings. After all, that is the one thing that distinguishes us from the animals.'

'Mad,' said the farmer's wife. 'Barmy. Go on, get out, clear off down the road and don't come back.'

The Scarecrow bowed as gracefully as he could.

'Well, dear,' the farmer said, 'mustn't . . . you know. Not so many, umm, about these days, eh? Sort of thing . . .'

'He's raving mad, and I want him gone!' she said.

'Also he's a horrible-looking monster, and he's frightened the donkey. Scram!' she said again, raising the frying pan.

'Come on, master,' said Jack. 'We'll seek our fortune somewhere else. We've slept under hedges before, and it's a nice warm night.'

So side by side the Scare- crow and his servant set off down the moonlit road. From time to time the Scarecrow would sigh heavily and turn to look back with such a look of anguish on his turnip  that Jack felt sure the broom would leave her rake and fall in love with him, if she could; but it was too late.

'Oh, yes,' said the farmer, 'he was definitely . . . you know.'

'Mad as a hatter!' said his wife. 'A dangerous

lunatic. Foreign, too. Shouldn't have been let out.'

'I see,' said Mr Cercorelli. 'And when did he leave?'

'When was it now?' said the farmer. 'About . . . er . . .'

'Middle of the night,' snapped his wife. 'What d'you want to know for, anyway? You his keeper?'

'In a manner of speaking, that is so. I am charged by my employer to bring this scarecrow back where he belongs.'

'Ah,' said the farmer. 'So it's a case of, umm, is it?'

'I beg your pardon?'

'You know, touch of the old, er, as it were. Eh?'

Mr Cercorelli gathered his papers and stood up.

'You put it very accurately, sir,' he said. 'Thank you for your help.'

'You going to lock him up when you catch him?' demanded the farmer's wife.

'Oh, I can assure you,' said Mr Cercorelli, 'that is the least of it.'

# THE MISTY CART

'Jack,' said the Scarecrow next morning, 'now that my heart is broken, I think we should set out on the open road and seek our fortune.'

'What about your estate in Spring Valley, master?'

'Ah, yes, indeed. We must earn enough money to set the place in order. Then we shall go back and look after it.'

I hope there's plenty of food there, Jack thought.

The Scarecrow strode out briskly, and Jack trotted along beside him. There were plenty of things to look at, and although the Scarecrow's heart was broken, his curiosity about the world was undimmed.

'Why has that building burned down?' he'd say, or 'I wonder why that old lady is climbing a ladder,' or 'D'you know, Jack, it's an extraordinary thing, but we haven't heard a bird for hours. Why would that be, do you think?'

'I think the soldiers have been here,' Jack told him. 'They probably burned the house down, and took all the farm workers away so the old lady's got to mend the roof herself. As for the birds – why, the soldiers must have eaten up all the food and left none for the birds, not even a grain of wheat.'

'Hmm,' said the Scarecrow. 'Soldiers, eh? Do they do that sort of thing?'

'They're the worst people in the world, soldiers,' said Jack.

'Worse than birds?'

'Much worse. The only thing to do when the soldiers come is hide, and keep very very quiet.'

'What do they look like?'

'Well—'

But before Jack could answer, the Scarecrow's attention was caught by something else.

'Look!' he cried, pointing in excitement. 'What's that?'

471

There was a caravan coming towards them, pulled by an ancient horse that was so skinny you could count all its ribs. The caravan was covered in painted stars and moons and mystic symbols, and sitting on the box holding the reins was a man almost as skinny as the horse, wearing a long pointed hat and a robe covered in more stars and moons.

The Scarecrow gazed at it all with great admiration.

As soon as he saw them, the man waved and shook the reins to make the horse stand still. The poor old beast was only too glad to have a rest. The man jumped off the box and scampered over to the Scarecrow.

'Good day to you, sir! Good day, my lord!' he said, bowing low and plucking at the Scarecrow's sleeve.

'Good day to *you*, sir,' the Scarecrow said.

'Master,' said Jack, 'I don't think—'

But the stranger with the mystic robes had seized the Scarecrow's road-sign hand, and was scrutinizing it closely.

'Ah!' he said. 'Aha! Ha! I see great fortune in this hand!'

'Really?' said the Scarecrow, impressed. 'How do you do that?'

'By means of the mystic arts!'

'Oh!' said the Scarecrow. 'Jack, we must get a misty cart! Just like this gentleman's one. Then *we'd* know things too. We could make our fortune and find our way to Spring Valley and take it—'

'Spring Valley, did you say, sir?' said the stranger. 'Would you be a member of the celebrated Buffaloni family, my lord?'

'I don't think so,' said the Scarecrow.

'Ah! I understand! They've called you in as a consultant, to take it in hand. I hear that the Buffalonis are doing splendid things in the field of industry. Draining all those springs and wells and putting up wonderful factories! Yes? No?'

Seeing that the Scarecrow was baffled, the astrologer smoothly went on:

'But let me read your horoscope and look deep into the crystal ball. Before the power of my gaze, the veil of time is drawn aside and the mysteries of the future are revealed. Come into my caravan for a consultation!'

'Master,' Jack whispered, 'this'll cost us money,

and we haven't got any. Besides, he's an old fraud—'

'Oh, no, my boy, you've got it wrong,' said the Scarecrow. 'I'm a pretty good judge, and this gentleman's mind is on higher things than fraud. His thoughts dwell in the realm of the sublime, Jack!'

'Quite right, sir! You are a profound and perceptive thinker!' said the mystic, beckoning them into the caravan, and uncovering a crystal ball on a little table.

They all sat down. Waving his fingers in a mystical way, the astrologer peered deeply into the crystal.

'Ah!' he said. 'As I suspected. The planetary

fluminations are dark and obscure. The only way of disclarifying the astroplasm is to cast your horoscope, my dear sir, which I can do for a very modest fee.'

'Well, that's that then,' said Jack, standing up, 'because we haven't got a penny between us. Good day—'

'No, Jack, wait!' said the Scarecrow, banging his head.

'What are you doing, master?' said Jack. 'Stop it – you'll hurt yourself!'

'Ah – there it is!' cried the Scarecrow, and out of a crack in his turnip there fell a little gold coin.

Jack and the mystic pounced at once, but the mystic got there first.

'Excellent!' he said, nipping the coin between his long horse-like teeth. 'By a remarkable coincidence, this is exactly the right fee. I shall consult the stars at once.'

'Where did that gold coin come from, master?' said Jack, amazed.

'Oh, it's been in there for a while,' the Scarecrow told him.

'But – but – if – if –' Jack said, tearing his hair.

The Scarecrow took no notice. He was watching

the astrologer, who took a dusty book from a shelf and opened it to show charts and columns of numbers, and ran a finger swiftly down them, muttering learnedly.

'You see what he's doing?' whispered the Scarecrow. 'This is clever, Jack, this is very deep.'

'Ahhhhh!' said the astrologer, in a long quavering wail. 'I see great fortune in the stars!'

'Go on, go on!' said the Scarecrow.

'Oh, yes,' said the mystic, licking a dirty finger and turning over several pages. 'And there is more!'

'You see, Jack? What a good thing we met this gentleman!' said the Scarecrow.

The astrologer suddenly drew in his breath, peering at the symbols in his book. So did the Scarecrow. They both held it for a long time, until the astrologer let it out in a long whistle. So did the Scarecrow.

Then, as if it was too heavy a burden to bear, the astrologer slowly lifted his head.

The Scarecrow's little muddy eyes were as wide as they could get – his straw was standing on end – his great gaping mouth hung open.

'I have never seen a destiny as strange and profound

as this,' said the astrologer in a low, quavery voice. 'The paranomical ecliptic of the clavicle of Solomon, multiplied by the solar influence in the trine of the zaphoristical catanastomoid, divided by the meridian of the vernal azimuth and composticated by the diaphragm of Ezekiel, reveals . . .'

'Yes?'

'Means . . .'

'Yes? Yes?'

'Foretells . . .'

'Yes? Yes? Yes?'

The mystic paused for a moment, and his eyes swivelled to look at Jack, and then swivelled back to the Scarecrow.

'Danger,' he said solemnly.

'Oh no!' said the Scarecrow.

'Followed by joy –'

'Yes!'

'And then trouble –'

'No!'

'Leading to glory –'

'Yes!'

'Turning to sorrow –'

'No, no, no!'

The Scarecrow was in mortal fear.

The astrologer slowly closed the book and moved it out of Jack's reach. Then his upper lip drew back so suddenly that it made Jack jump. Beaming like a crocodile in Holy Orders, the old man said:

'But the suffering will be crowned with success –'

'Hoorah!' cried the Scarecrow.

'And the tears will end in triumph –'

'Thank goodness for that!'

'And health, wealth and happiness will be yours for as long as you live!'

'Oh, I'm so glad! Oh, what a relief!' said the Scarecrow. 'There you are, Jack, you see, this gentleman knows what he's talking about, all right. Oh, I was worried there! But it all came right in the end. Thank you, sir! A thousand thanks! We can go on our way with confidence and fortitude. My goodness, what an experience.'

'My pleasure,' said the mystic, bowing low. 'Take care as you leave. The steps are rickety. Good day!'

He gave Jack a suspicious look, and Jack gave him one in return.

'Just think of that, Jack,' said the Scarecrow in an awed and humble voice as the caravan slowly drew away. 'We have been inside a misty cart, and we have heard the secrets of the future!'

'Never mind that, master,' said Jack. 'Have you got any more money in your head?'

'Let me see,' said the Scarecrow, and he banged his turnip vigorously. Then he shook it hard. 'Hmm,' he said, 'something's rattling. Let me see . . .'

He turned his head sideways and shook it. Something fell out and bounced on the road.

The two of them bent over to look at it.

'It's a pea,' said Jack.

'Ah, yes,' said the Scarecrow modestly. 'That's my brain, you know.'

But before either of them could pick it up and put it back, a blackbird flew down, seized the pea in his beak, and flew up and perched on a branch.

The Scarecrow was outraged. He waved his road sign, he opened and shut his umbrella, and he stamped with fury.

'You scoundrel! You thief!' he roared. 'Give me my brain back!'

The blackbird swallowed the pea, and then, to

Jack's astonishment, said, 'Get lost. I saw it first.'

'How dare you!' the Scarecrow shouted in reply. 'I've never known such unprincipled behaviour!'

'Don't shout at me,' whined the blackbird. 'You're cruel, you are. You got a horrible cruel face. I'll have the law on you if you shout at me. It's not fair.'

In fury, the Scarecrow opened and shut his umbrella several times, but in his rage he couldn't find any words, so the things he said sounded like this:

'Rrrowl – nnhnrrr – eeee – mnmnm – ngnnmmg-grrnnnggg – bbrrr – ffff – ssss – gggrrrssschhttt!'

The blackbird cringed, and uttering a feeble squeak, he flew away.

Jack scratched his head.

'I knew parrots could talk, master, but not blackbirds,' he said.

'Oh, they all can, Jack. You should hear the insolent way they speak to me when they think nobody else can hear. I expect that young scoundrel thought you were a scarecrow too, and he could get away with it.'

'Well, I'm learning new things all the time,' said Jack. 'Anyway, it seems to me, master, that until we find you a new brain, you'll have to try and get on without one. We managed to find you some new arms all right, remember.'

The Scarecrow had been stamping up and down, still furious, but he stopped and looked at Jack when he heard that, and calmed down at once.

'Do you think we could find another one?' he said.

'Can't be too hard,' said Jack. 'See how you get on without it at first. You might not need one at all. Like an appendix.'

'It's very personal, though,' said the Scarecrow doubtfully.

'We'll find something, don't worry.'

'Ah, Jack, my boy, employing you was the best decision I ever made! I can do without a brain, but I don't think I could do without my servant.'

'Well, thank you, master. But I don't think I can do without food. I hope we find something to eat soon.'

Since there was nothing to eat there, they set off along the road again. But it was a bleak and deserted sort of district; the only farms they passed were burned down, and there wasn't a single person in sight.

'No birds,' said the Scarecrow, looking around.

'It's a curious thing, Jack, but I don't like it when there aren't any birds.'

'I don't like it when there isn't any food,' said Jack.

'Look!' said the Scarecrow, pointing back along the road. 'What's that?'

All they could see was a cloud of dust. But there was a sound as well, and Jack recognized it at once: a regular tramp-tramp-tramp and the beats of a snare drum accompanying it. It was a regiment of soldiers.

# The Pride Of The Regiment

Jack tugged at the Scarecrow's sleeve.

'Come on, master!' he said urgently. 'We'll hide till they've gone past!'

The Scarecrow followed Jack into a clump of bushes.

'Are we allowed to look at them?' he said.

'Yes, but don't let them see us, master, whatever you do!' Jack begged.

The beating of the drums and the thudding of the feet came closer and closer. The Scarecrow, excited, peered out through the leaves.

'Jack! Look!' he whispered. 'It's astonishing! They're all the same!'

The soldiers, with their bright red coats and white

trousers, their black boots and bearskin caps, their muskets all held at the same angle and their brass buckles gleaming, *did* all look the same. There were hundreds of them marching in step, all big and strong and well-fed.

'Magnificent!' exclaimed the Scarecrow.

'Hush!' said Jack desperately.

Ahead of the column of soldiers rode several officers on grey horses, prancing and trotting and curvetting; and behind came a dozen wagons drawn by fine black horses, all gleaming and beautifully groomed.

'What style! What panache! What vigour!' said the Scarecrow.

Jack put his hands over his ears, but the thudding of the soldiers' boots made the very earth shake. Tramp! Tramp! Tramp! Like a great mechanical monster with hundreds of legs, the regiment moved past.

When Jack dared to look, the Scarecrow was standing in the middle of the road, gazing after them with wonder and admiration.

'Jack!' he called. 'Have you ever seen anything so splendid? Tramp, tramp, tramp! And their red coats

– and their shiny belts – and their helmets! Oh, that's the life for me, Jack. I'm going to be a soldier!'

'But, master—'

'Off we go! Tramp tramp tramp!'

Swinging his arms briskly, the Scarecrow set off on his wooden legs at such a pace that Jack had to run to keep up.

'Master, please listen to me! Don't be a soldier, I beg you!'

'Remember what the man in the misty cart said, Jack – great fortune! Fame, and glory!'

'Yes, and trouble and danger too – don't forget those!'

'And I'll tell you something else,' added the Scarecrow. 'The regiment is bound to have lots of food. They're such a fine-looking band of men, I'll bet they eat three times a day. If not four.'

That did it for Jack. At the thought of food, he set off after the regiment as fast as his master, soldiers or no soldiers.

It didn't take them long to catch up, because the soldiers had stopped for their midday meal, and the rich smell of beef stew made poor Jack's mouth water from several hundred yards away.

The Scarecrow strode into the camp and marched up to the cook, who was dishing out stew and potatoes to the soldiers as they stood in a smart line holding out their plates.

'I want to be a soldier,' the Scarecrow announced.

'Get away with you, turnip face!'

'I've got all the qualifications—'

'Go on, scram!'

The Scarecrow was about to lose his temper, so Jack said:

'Excuse me, sir, but who's the officer in charge?'

'Colonel Bombardo, over there,' said the cook, pointing with his ladle. 'At least, he's the commanding officer. It's the sergeant who's in charge.'

'Oh, right,' said Jack. 'I don't suppose I could have a potato?'

'Clear off! Get out of it!'

Nearly howling with hunger, Jack tugged at the Scarecrow's sleeve.

'We have to speak to the officer,' he explained. 'This way, master.'

The colonel was sitting on a canvas chair, trying to read a map upside down.

'Colonel Bombardo, sir,' said Jack, 'my master

Lord Scarecrow wants to join your army. He's a good fighter, and—'

'Lord Scarecrow?' barked the colonel. 'Knew your mother. Damn fine woman. Welcome, Scarecrow. Go and speak to the sergeant over there. He'll sort you out.'

'He knew my mother!' whispered the Scarecrow, awestruck. 'Even *I* didn't know my mother. How clever he is! What a hero!'

The sergeant was a thin little man with a wrinkled face that looked as if it had seen everything there was to see, twice.

'Sergeant,' said Jack, 'this is Lord Scarecrow. Colonel Bombardo sent us over to join the regiment.'

'Lord Scarecrow, eh,' said the sergeant. 'Right, your lordship, before you join the regiment you'll have to pass an examination.'

Jack thought: Thank goodness for that! As soon as they find out what a ninny he is, they'll send us packing. But I'd love some of that stew . . .

The Scarecrow was sitting down already, with a big bass drum in front of him to write on. He looked at the exam paper, took up the pencil at once, and began to cover the page with an energetic scribble.

'What sort of questions are they?' Jack asked.

'Ballistics, navigation, fortification, tactics and strategy,' said the sergeant.

'Oh, good. I don't suppose I could have anything to eat?'

'What d'you think this is? A soup kitchen? This is an army on the march, this is. Who are you, anyway?'

'I'm Lord Scarecrow's personal servant.'

'Servant? That's a good'un. Soldiers don't have servants.'

'Colonel Bombardo's got a servant,' said Jack, looking enviously at the colonel, who was sitting with several other officers at a table outside his tent, tucking in to stew and dumplings, while a servant poured wine.

'Well, he's an officer,' said the sergeant. 'If they didn't have servants, they wouldn't be able to put their trousers on, some of 'em.'

'They get a lot to eat,' Jack said.

'Oh, for crying out loud,' said the sergeant, scribbling on a piece of paper. 'Take this chitty to the cook, go on.'

'Thank you! Thank you!' said Jack, and ran back to the cook, just in time to see the last soldier in the queue walking away with a full plate.

The cook inspected the chitty.

'Bad luck,' he said. 'There's none left.'

He showed Jack the empty stewpot. Jack felt tears springing to his eyes, but the cook winked and said:

'None of *that* rubbish, anyway. You duck under here, and I'll give you some proper Catering Corps tucker.'

Jack darted into the wagon in a moment, and was soon sitting down with the cook and his two assistants, eating braised beef *à la bourguignonne*, which was rich and hot and peppery and had little oniony things and big pools of gravy and delicate new potatoes and parsley and mint. Jack felt as if he was in heaven.

He didn't say a word till he'd finished three whole platefuls.

'Thank you!' he said finally. 'Can I take some to my master?'

'He's lunching with the colonel,' said the cook. 'While you was gobbling that up, we had a message to send over another officer's meal. So you're joining the regiment, then?'

'Well, Lord Scarecrow was taking the exam,' said Jack, 'but I don't think he can have passed it. I better go and see.'

'No hurry,' said the cook. 'They'll be there for a while yet, with their brandy and cigars.'

'Cigars?' said Jack in alarm, thinking of the Scarecrow's straw.

'Don't worry. There's a bucket-wallah to put 'em out if they catch fire to theirselves.'

'The regiment thinks of everything,' Jack said.

'Oh, it's a grand life, being a soldier.'

Jack began to think that maybe it was, after all. He thanked the cooks again, and strolled over to the sergeant, who was trimming his nails with a bayonet.

'How did Lord Scarecrow get on in the exam?' he said.

'He answered all the wrong questions. He doesn't know anything at all.'

'So he won't be able to be a soldier, then?' said Jack, relieved.

'Not a private, no, nor a sergeant, not in a hundred

years. He's nowhere near clever enough. He's going to be an officer.'

'*What?*'

'Captain Scarecrow is taking his lunch with his fellow officers. You'll need to find him a horse and polish his boots and wash his uniform and keep him smart, and by the look of him you'll have your work cut out.'

'But he doesn't know how to command soldiers!'

'None of 'em do. That's why they invented sergeants. You better go and get him a uniform. The quartermaster's in that wagon over there.'

Jack explained to the quartermaster that the Scarecrow needed a captain's uniform. The quartermaster laid a set of clothes and boots on the counter.

Jack gathered them up, but the quartermaster said, 'Hold on. He'll need a sword as well if he's an officer. And a proper shako. And a pistol.'

The shako was the tall cap that the officers wore. It had a white plume in it, and a shiny black peak. Jack's heart sank as he staggered over to the officers' table. Once he gets all this on, he'll want to be a soldier for ever, he thought.

'Ah, Jack, my boy!' said the Scarecrow happily as the officers left their table. 'Did you hear the wonderful news? I'm a captain, no less! I did so well in the examination that they made me an officer at once.'

Then he saw what Jack was carrying, and his turnip beamed with an expression of utter delight.

'Is that for me? Is that my uniform? This is the happiest day of my life! I can hardly believe it!'

Jack helped the Scarecrow put on the red coat and the white trousers, and the shiny black boots, and two white belts that went over his shoulders and crossed on his chest, and another belt to hold his trousers up just in case. The poor Scarecrow was transfigured with joy.

'Just let the birds try their tricks now!' he said, waving his sword around. 'I bet no blackbird would dare to eat my brain if he saw me like this!'

'Mind what you're doing with the sword, master,' said Jack. 'It's just for decoration, really. Now you stay here and I'll go and find a horse for you.'

'A *horse*?' said the Scarecrow. He stopped looking joyful and looked nervous instead.

'I'll get you a slow old one,' said Jack.

'He won't want to eat me, will he? I mean, you know . . .' said the Scarecrow, delicately twiddling at the straw poking out of his collar.

'I don't think there's any hay in you, master,' said Jack, 'only straw. You'll just have to show him who's boss. Or her.'

The farrier, who was in charge of the horses, was busy putting some horseshoes on a docile old grey mare called Betsy. He said she'd be just the job for an inexperienced rider.

'Captain Scarecrow's a good fighter,' said Jack. 'He's fought brigands and actors and all sorts. But he hasn't done much riding.'

'Nothing to it. Shake the reins to make her go, pull 'em back to make her stop.'

'What about turning left and right?'

'Leave that to her. *Actors*, did you say?' said the farrier.

'Yes, he fought three of them at once. On a stage.'

'Stone the crows.'

'Yes, he can do that too,' said Jack, leading Betsy over to Captain Scarecrow.

'He's very big,' said the Scarecrow doubtfully, when he saw her.

'He's a she. She's called Betsy. She's all ready to ride. Put your foot in the stirrup – there it is – and I'll lift you up.'

They tried it three times. The first time the Scarecrow went straight over the top and down the other side, landing on his turnip and denting his shako. The second time he managed to stay there, but he was facing the wrong way round. The third time he managed to stay in the saddle, facing the right way, but he'd lost his shako and dropped his sword, and his umbrella had come open in alarm.

'Stay there, master, and I'll pick up the bits and pieces,' said Jack.

He gathered up the sword and the shako, and

soon he had the Scarecrow looking very proud and martial. Around them the regiment was striking camp ready to move on, and presently the drums began to beat and the sergeant gave the order to march.

Old Betsy pricked up her ears and began to amble forward.

'Help!' cried the Scarecrow, swaying wildly.

'Look, master,' said Jack, 'I mean Captain, sir, I'm holding the bridle. She won't go any faster while I'm here.'

So they moved along behind the column of marching soldiers and the wagons and the horses, old Betsy keeping up a steady walk and the Scarecrow hanging onto the saddle with both hands.

Presently he said:

'By the way, where are we going, Jack?'

'Dunno, master. I mean Captain, sir.'

'We're off to fight the Duke of Brunswick!' said

another officer, a major, riding up alongside.

'Really?' said the Scarecrow. 'And what sort of bird is he? A great big one, I expect?'

'I expect so, yes,' said the major.

'Has he got a regiment too?' said Jack.

'Oh, dozens.'

'But we're just one!'

'Ah, the King of Sardinia's army is coming to join us.'

'So there's going to be a great big battle?'

'Bound to be.'

'And when are we going to fight them?' said the Scarecrow.

'Don't know. They could attack at any moment. Ambush, you know.'

The major galloped away.

'Jack,' said the Scarecrow. 'This battle . . .'

'Yes?'

'I suppose I might get damaged?'

'Yes. We all might.'

'Could you by any chance find me some spare arms and legs? In case, you know . . .'

'I'll make sure we've got plenty of spare parts, don't you worry, master.'

'And you know, you were quite right about my brain,' the Scarecrow said reassuringly. 'I don't miss it at all.'

And on they marched, towards battle.

Some way behind, Mr Cercorelli had caught up with the astrologer.

'I warn you,' he was saying sternly, 'telling fortunes without a licence can lead to a severe penalty. What do you know of this scarecrow?'

The mystic bowed very deeply, and said in a humble voice, 'I cast his horoscope, your honour, and saw evidence of the deepest villainy. The planetary perfluminations—'

'Don't waste my time with that nonsense, or I'll have you up in front of the magistrate. What did he tell you, and where did he go?'

'He said he was going to Spring Valley, your honour.'

'Did he indeed? And did he set off in that direction?'

'No, your worship. Quite the opposite.'

'Did he say what he was going to do in Spring Valley?'

Philip Pullman

'Yes, my lord. He said he was going to make a fortune, and then go and take Spring Valley in hand. His very words! Naturally, I was going to report him as soon as I arrived at the nearest police station.'

'Naturally. Here is my card. I expect to hear at once if you see him again, you understand?'

# THE BATTLE

Mr Cercorelli wasn't the only person looking for the Scarecrow. High up above the countryside where the Scarecrow and his servant had been wandering, an elderly raven was gliding through the blue sky. She was a hundred years old, but her eyes were as sharp as they'd ever been, and when she saw a group of her cousins perching on a pine tree near a mountain top, she flew down at once.

'Granny!' they said. 'Haven't seen you for fifty years. What have you been up to?'

'Never you mind,' she said. 'What's going on over the other side of the hill? There are cousins of ours flying in from all over the place.'

'The soldiers are coming,' they explained. 'There's going to be a big battle. The red soldiers are going to fight the blue soldiers, and the green soldiers are coming along tomorrow to join in. But how are things over in Spring Valley?'

'Bad,' said Granny Raven. 'And getting worse. Have you seen a scarecrow? A walking one?'

'Funnily enough, we heard a young blackbird complaining about something like that just the other day. Shouldn't be allowed, he said. What d'you want to find him for?'

'None of your business. Where did you meet this blackbird?'

They told her, and she flew away.

That evening, after raiding six farms and commandeering all their food, the regiment camped by the side of a river. On the other side of the river there was a broad green meadow, and it was there that they were going to fight the Duke of Brunswick's army the next day.

While the Scarecrow joined his brother officers in a high-level discussion about tactics and strategy, Jack went to help the cooks prepare the evening meal.

'Is this how you always get food?' said Jack. 'You just take it from the farmers?'

'It's their contribution to maintaining the army,' explained the cook. 'See, if we weren't here to defend them, the Duke of Brunswick would come and take everything from them.'

'So if you didn't take their food, he would?'

'That's it.'

'Oh, I see,' said Jack. 'What are we having for supper?'

They were going to have roast pork, and Jack sat and peeled a mound of potatoes to go with it. When he'd done that, he wandered through the camp and looked at everything.

'How are we going to get across to the battlefield?' he asked one of the gunners, who was polishing a big brass cannon.

'There's a ford,' said the gunner. 'We just hitch up the guns and drive 'em in the water and up the other side. We'll do it after breakfast.'

'Where's the Duke of Brunswick's army now?'

'Oh, they're on their way. Only we got here first, so we got what's called tactical advantage.'

'But if he gets to the meadow before we're across,

then *he'll* have tactical advantage.'

'Ah, no, you don't understand,' said the gunner. 'Now clear off, I'm busy.'

So Jack went to look at the river instead. It was wide and muddy, and there might have been a ford, and there might not; because normally where there was a ford you saw a track or a road going down to the river on one side and coming out of it on the other.

He went and asked the farrier.

'No, there's no ford,' said the farrier, lighting his pipe with a glowing coal in a pair of tongs.

'Then how are we going to get across the river?'

'On a bridge. It's top secret. The Sardinians have got this new kind of bridge, movable thing, all the latest engineering. When they come, they'll put this bridge up in a moment – well, about half an hour – and we'll go straight across, form a line of battle, and engage the enemy.'

'Oh, I see. But suppose the Duke of Brunswick decides to fire all his cannons at the bridge while we're crossing it?'

'He wouldn't do that. It's against all the rules of engagement.'

'But supposing—'

'Go on, hop it. Scram. And you keep your trap shut about that bridge. It's top secret, remember.'

Jack decided not to puzzle any more, but to collect some sticks instead, so that he could repair the Scarecrow next day if he needed to.

When it was supper time, he and the other servants had to wait on the officers in their tent. Captain Scarecrow was behaving with great politeness, engaging his neighbours in lively and stimulating conversation, and sipping his wine like a connoisseur. The only thing that went wrong was when the officers took snuff after their meal. The proper way to take it was to put a little pinch on the back of your hand, sniff it briskly up your nose, and try not to sneeze; but the Scarecrow had never come across snuff before, and he sniffed up too much.

Jack could see what was going to happen, and he ran up with a tea towel – but it was too late. With a gigantic explosion, the Scarecrow sneezed so hard that all the buttons popped off his uniform, his umbrella opened in surprise, and bits of straw flew everywhere. Not only that; his turnip itself came loose, and lolled on his neck like a balloon on a stick. If Jack hadn't been there to hold it, it might have come off altogether and rolled right across the table.

As soon as the Scarecrow recovered his wits, he looked at Jack in horror.

'Dear me, what a ghastly exprience!' he said. 'Was that the Duke of Brunswick attacking us? There was a terrible explosion, I'm sure of it!'

'Just a touch of gunpowder in the snuff,' said Colonel Bombardo. 'Better than snuff in the gunpowder, what? Cannons'd be sneezing, not firing. Damn poor show.'

Presently the sergeant came in and said it was time for all the officers to go to bed. Jack helped the Scarecrow to their tent.

'It'll be an exciting day tomorrow, Jack!' said the Scarecrow, as Jack tucked him up in the camp bed.

'I'm sure it will, master. I better sew all those buttons on extra tight in case you sniff some gunpowder. Goodnight!'

'Goodnight, Jack. What a good servant you are!'

So they all went to sleep.

When they woke up, there was no sign of the Sardinians, but the Duke of Brunswick's army had turned up during the night and made camp in the meadow across the river. There were lots of them.

'He's got a big army,' said Jack to the cook as they made breakfast.

'It's all show,' said the cook. 'Them big cannons they've got, they're only made of cardboard. Anyway, the Sardinians'll be here soon.'

But the Sardinians didn't show up at all. While the Duke of Brunswick's soldiers lined up their cannons pointing straight across the river, the officers of the Scarecrow's regiment rode up and down, waving their swords and shouting orders. Meanwhile, the sergeant was drilling the troops. He marched them along the riverbank and then made them about-turn and march back the other way.

Not many of them fell in.

And while they were doing that, the gunners got their cannons all lined up one behind the other to go across the famous secret bridge that the Sardinians were going to bring. The Duke of Brunswick's soldiers kept looking at them and pointing and laughing.

'They won't be laughing when the Sardinians come,' said the chief gunner.

But there was no sign of the Sardinians. Finally, at about tea time, a messenger came galloping up with some shocking news. Jack was close by, and he heard the sergeant telling Colonel Bombardo all about it.

'Message here from the King of Sardinia, sir,' he said. 'He's changed his mind, and he's joining

forces with the Duke of Brunswick.'

'I say! What do you think we should do, Sergeant?'

'Run away, sir.'

'Just what he'll be expecting. Very bad idea, if you ask me. We'll do just the opposite – we'll go across the ford, and before the Duke of Brunswick knows what's hit him, we'll give him a sound thrashing!'

'Very good, sir. This ford, sir—'

'Yes?'

'Where is it, sir?'

'In the river, Sergeant. Right there.'

'Right you are, sir. You're going first, are you, sir, to lead the way?'

'D'you think I should?'

'It's the usual thing, sir.'

'Then *charge*!'

And Colonel Bombardo galloped his horse right off the bank and into the water, and disappeared at once. No-one else moved.

No-one except Jack, that is. He saw the Scarecrow looking in an interested way at the river, where Colonel Bombardo's shako had just floated to the surface; and he ran through all the ranks of soldiers and past the guns and seized hold of Betsy's bridle.

It was a good thing he did, because at that very moment, there came a terrific volley of firing from the Duke of Brunswick's army across the river, and almost at once there came another volley from the other direction altogether: from behind them.

'It's the Sardinians!' someone said.

And then there were cannons going off all over the place. The regiment was trapped on the river-bank, with the Sardinians behind them and the Duke of Brunswick's army on the other side, and there was no ford at all.

The air was full of gunpowder smoke, and no-one could see anything. Soldiers were shouting and crying and running in all directions; bullets were

whizzing through the air from every side; cannon-balls were smashing into the tents and the wagons; and the Scarecrow was waving his sword and shouting, 'Charge!'

Luckily, no-one took any notice.

Then a stray cannonball whizzed past Betsy's flanks, giving her a nasty fright and taking some of the Scarecrow's trousers with it.

'Whoah! Help!' cried the Scarecrow.

'It's all right, master, just hold on,' said Jack.

And then a bullet clipped the Scarecrow's head, sending bits of turnip everywhere.

'Charge!' shouted the Scarecrow again, waving his sword so wildly that Jack was worried in case he cut Betsy's head off by mistake; but then another bullet came along and knocked the sword out of his hand with a loud *clang*.

'Now look what you've done!' cried the Scarecrow.

He scrambled down from Betsy's back, and he was about to run straight at the nearest soldiers and join in the fight, when Jack saw him suddenly stop and peer into a bush.

'What is it, master?' he said. 'Look, you can't

hang around here – it's dangerous—'

But the Scarecrow took no notice. He was reaching right in among the leaves, and then he very carefully lifted out a nest. Sitting in the nest was a terrified robin.

'This is quite intolerable,' the Scarecrow was saying to her. 'Madam, I offer my apologies on behalf of the regiment. It is no part of a soldier's duty to terrify a mother and her eggs. He owes a duty of care and protection to the weak and defenceless! Sit tight, madam, and I shall remove you at once to a place of safety.'

Tucking the nest into his jacket, the Scarecrow set off. There was a short pause when a stray bullet shot his leg off, and he had to lean on Jack's arm, but slowly they made their way through the battlefield. All around them soldiers in red uniforms were fighting with soldiers in blue uniforms, waving swords, firing pistols and muskets; and then along came some soldiers in green uniforms as well. The thunder of the explosions, and the groans and screams, and the crack of muskets and the whine of bullets and the crackle of flames were appalling, and the things Jack saw going on were so horrible that he just closed his eyes and kept stumbling forward, leading Betsy with one hand and holding the Scarecrow up with the other, until the worst of the noise had faded behind them.

There was a bush close by, and before he did anything else the Scarecrow lifted the nest out of his jacket, with the robin still sitting on it, and placed it gently in among the leaves.

'There you are, madam,' he said politely, 'with the compliments of the regiment.'

Then he fell over.

Jack helped him up again, stuffing back the straw that was coming out all over the place.

'What a battle!' said the Scarecrow. 'Bang, crash, whiz!'

'Look at the state of you,' said Jack. 'You're full of bullet-holes, and you've only got one leg, and part of your turnip's gone. I'm going to have to tidy you up – you're badly wounded.'

'I shouldn't think anyone's more wounded than I am,' said the Scarecrow proudly.

'Not unless they're dead. Sit still.'

Jack took a good strong stick from the bundle of spare parts he'd tied onto Betsy's saddle before the battle began. He slid it inside the remains of the Scarecrow's trouser leg. The Scarecrow sprang up at once.

'Back to the battle!' he said. 'I want to win a medal, Jack, that's my dearest wish. I wouldn't mind losing all my legs and my arms and my head and everything, if only I could have a medal.'

Jack was busy tying the rest of the sticks together to make a raft.

'Well, master,' he said, 'if you turned up at that farm with no legs and no arms and no head and no sense, but with a medal shining on your chest, I don't suppose the broom would be able to resist you.'

'Don't remind me, Jack! My broken heart! In the excitement of battle I'd almost forgotten – oh! Oh! I loved her so much!'

While the Scarecrow was lamenting, Jack gave Betsy a carrot.

'Go on, old girl, you can look after yourself,' he said, and Betsy ambled away and disappeared in the bushes.

'Now, master, you come with me,' Jack went on, finishing the raft, 'because we've got a secret mission. It's very important, so just keep quiet, all right?'

'Ssh!' said the Scarecrow. 'Not a word.'

And Jack pushed the raft out onto the water, and he and the Scarecrow scrambled on board; and a few minutes later, they were floating down the river, with the sound of battle and the cries of the wounded soldiers fading quickly behind them.

# MAROONED

While the Scarecrow and his servant were floating down the river, two important conversations were taking place.

The first one took place on the riverbank, where Mr Cercorelli was talking to the sergeant of the Scarecrow's regiment amid the wreckage of the battlefield.

'The last I seen of him, sir, he was charging into battle like a good'un,' the sergeant told him. 'He made a fine figure of an officer.'

'An officer, you say?'

'Captain Scarecrow was one of the most gallant officers I ever saw. Fearless, you might say. Or else you might say thick as a brick. But he did his duty by the regiment.'

'Did he survive the battle?'

'I couldn't tell you that, sir. I haven't seen him since.'

Mr Cercorelli looked at the devastation all around them.

'By the way,' he said, 'who won?'

'The Duke of Brunswick, sir, according to the morning paper. Very hard to tell from here. It was the King of Sardinia changing sides at the last minute that did for us.'

The lawyer made a mental note to congratulate his employers. The Buffaloni Corporation had important financial interests in Sardinia; no doubt they had reminded the King about them.

'Mind you,' the sergeant went on, 'we got a return battle next month.'

'Oh, really?'

'Yes, sir. And it'll go different next time, because the King of Naples is coming in with us.'

The lawyer made a mental note to tell his employers that as well.

'If you hear any more of Captain Scarecrow,' he said, 'here is my card. Good day.'

*

The other conversation took place through a window in a little farmhouse.

'Hey! You!' called Granny Raven, perching among the geraniums in the window box.

An old man and his wife were sitting at the table, wrapping their crockery in newspaper and putting it in a cardboard box. They both looked up in astonishment.

'Here,' said the old man to his wife, 'that's old Carlo's pet, the one what escaped!'

Granny Raven clacked her beak impatiently.

'Yes, that's me,' she said, 'even if you've got it the wrong way round. He was my pet. And I didn't escape, I flew off to find a doctor, only I was too late. Now stop gaping like a pair of flytraps, and pay attention.'

'But you're *talking*!' said the old woman.

'Yes. This is an emergency.'

'Oh,' said the old man, gulping. 'Go on, then.'

'Not long before old Carlo died,' Granny Raven said, 'he asked you both to go over and do something for him. Do you remember what that was?'

'Well, yes,' said the old woman. 'He asked us to sign a piece of paper.'

'And did you?'

'Yes,' said the old man.

'Right,' said Granny Raven. Then she clacked her beak again, and looked at the table. 'What are you doing with that crockery?' she said.

'Packing,' said the old woman. 'Ever since the Buffaloni factory opened, our spring's dried up. We can't live here any more. They're taking everything over, them Buffalonis. It's not like what it used to be. Poor old Carlo's well out of it, I reckon.'

'Well, d'you want to fight the Buffalonis, or give in?'

'Give in,' said the old man, and 'Fight 'em,' said

the old woman, both at once.

'Two to one,' said Granny Raven, looking at the old man very severely. 'We win. Now listen to me, and do as I say.'

When Jack woke up, the raft was floating along swiftly, together with lots of broken branches and shattered hen-coops and one or two dead dogs and other bits and pieces. The water was muddy and turbid, and the sun was beating down from a hot sky, and the Scarecrow was sitting placidly watching the distant banks go by.

'Master! Why didn't you wake me up before we drifted this far down the river?'

'Oh, we're making wonderful progress, Jack. You'd never believe how far we've come!'

'I don't think it's taking us to Spring Valley, though,' said Jack, standing up and shading his eyes to look ahead.

Very soon he couldn't even see the banks any more, and the water, when he dipped his hand in, turned out to be too salty to drink.

'Master,' he said, 'we're drifting out to sea! I think we've left the land altogether!'

The Scarecrow was astonished.

'Just like that?' he said. 'We don't have to pay a toll, or anything? How clever! I never thought I'd go to sea. This will be very interesting.'

'Why, yes, it will, master,' said Jack. 'We don't know whether we'll drown before we starve to death, or starve to death before we drown. Or die of thirst, maybe. It'll be interesting to find out. We'd be better off getting shot to pieces by cannonballs, if you ask me.'

'Now then, you're forgetting the man in the misty cart, Jack! Fame and glory, remember!'

'I think we've had that already, master. We're on to the danger and suffering now.'

'But it ends in triumph and happiness!'

Jack was too fed up to say anything. He sat on the edge of the raft and stared glumly all around. There was not a speck of land anywhere, and the sun glared like a furnace in the burning sky.

The Scarecrow saw his unhappiness, and said, 'Cheer up, Jack! I'm sure that success is just around the corner.'

'We're at sea, master. There aren't any corners.'

'Hmm,' said the Scarecrow. 'I think I'll scan the horizon.'

So Jack held on to his master's legs, and the Scarecrow held on to Jack's head, and peered this way and that, shading his eyes with the umbrella; but there was nothing to be seen except more and more water.

'Very dull,' said the Scarecrow, a little disappointed. 'There isn't even a seagull to scare.'

'I don't like the look of those clouds, though,' said Jack, pointing at the horizon. 'I think we're going to have a storm. Well, this is just what we need, I must say.'

The clouds got higher and bigger and darker as they watched, and presently a stiff wind began to blow, making the water lurch up and down in a very unpleasant way.

'A storm at sea, Jack!' said the Scarecrow eagerly. 'This will be a noble spectacle! All the awe-inspiring powers of nature will be unleashed over our very heads. There – you see?'

There was a flash of lightning, and only a few seconds later, the loudest crash of thunder Jack had ever heard. And then came the rain. The heavy drops hurtled down as fast as bullets, and almost as hard.

'Never mind, my boy,' shouted the Scarecrow over the noise. 'Here – shelter under my umbrella!'

'No, master! Put it down, whatever you do! We'll be struck by lightning, and that'll be the end for both of us!'

The two of them clung together on their fragile raft, with the waves getting higher and rougher, and the sky getting darker, and the thunder getting closer, and the wind getting fiercer every minute.

And then Jack felt the sticks of the raft beginning to come loose.

'Master! Hold on! Don't let go!' he cried.

'This is exciting, Jack! Boom! Crash! Whoosh! Splash!'

Then the biggest wave of all swept over them, and the raft collapsed completely.

'Oh no – it's coming apart – help! Help!'

Jack and the Scarecrow fell into the water, among the loose sticks and bits of string that were all that was left of the raft.

'Master! Help! I can't swim!'

'Don't worry, my boy. I can float. You can hold onto me! I shan't let you down!'

Jack didn't dare open his mouth again in case he swallowed more sea. In mortal terror, he clung to his master as the waves hurled them this way and that.

How long they floated he had no idea. But eventually, the storm passed over; the waves calmed down, the clouds rolled away, and the sun came out. Jack was trembling with the effort of holding tight, and weak from hunger and thirst, and still very frightened, so when the Scarecrow said something, he had to reply:

'What's that, master? I didn't hear you.'

'I said I can see a tree, Jack.'

'What? Where?'

The Scarecrow twisted around a bit in the water and stood up. Jack was too amazed to do more than lie there and look up as his master stood above him, shaking the water out of his clothes and pointing ahead.

Then Jack realized that he wasn't floating any more. In fact, he was lying in very shallow water at the edge of a beach.

'We're safe!' he cried. 'We haven't drowned! We're still alive!'

He jumped to his feet and skipped ashore, full of joy.

It didn't matter that he was cold and wet and hungry – nothing like that mattered a bit. He was alive!

The Scarecrow was ahead of him, peering about with great interest. The tree he had seen was a palm tree, with one solitary coconut hanging high up among the leaves, and as Jack found when he joined his master, it was the only tree to be seen.

'We're on a tropical island,' he said. 'We're shipwrecked!'

'Well, Jack,' said the Scarecrow, 'I wonder what we'll find on this island. Quite often people find buried chests full of treasure, you know. I think we should start digging right away.'

'We'd be better off looking for food, master. You can't eat doubloons and pieces of eight.'

The Scarecrow looked all around. It was a very small island indeed; they could see all the way across it, and Jack reckoned that even if he walked very slowly, it would only take him ten minutes to walk all the way round the edge. 'Never despair,' said the Scarecrow. 'I shall think of something.'

Jack thought he'd better look for some water before he died of thirst, so he wandered into the middle of the island, among the bushes, to look for something to drink.

But there was no stream, no pond, nothing. He found some little fruits, and ate one to see if it was juicy; but it was so sour and bitter that he had to spit it out at once, although he  thought it was a waste of spit, because he didn't have any to spare. He looked at every different kind of leaf in case there was a cup-shaped one that had kept a drop of dew from the night before; but all the leaves were either flat and floppy or dry and hairy or thin and spiny, and none of them held a single drop of water.

'Oh, dear,' he said to himself, 'we're in big trouble now. This is the biggest trouble we've seen yet. This is a desperate situation, and no mistake.'

With a slow unhappy tread, Jack continued his short walk around the island. Less than five minutes later, he came back to the coconut palm. He tried to climb the trunk, but there were no branches to hold onto; he tried to throw stones at the coconut, but it was too high; he tried to shake the trunk, but it didn't move.

He moved into the shade and lay down, feeling so hungry and miserable and frightened that he began to cry. He found himself sobbing and weeping, and he couldn't stop, and he realized that although he was partly crying for himself, he was partly crying for the poor Scarecrow too, because his master wouldn't understand at all when he found his servant lying there dead and turning into a skeleton; he wouldn't know what to do, he'd be so distressed; and with no-one to look after him, he'd just wander about the island for ever until he fell apart.

'Oh, Jack, Jack, my dear boy!' he heard, and he felt a pair of rough wooden arms embracing him. 'Don't distress yourself! Life and hope, you know! Life and hope!'

'I'm sorry, master,' Jack said. 'I'll stop now. Did you have an interesting walk?'

'Oh, yes. I found a bush that looks just like a turkey, and another bush with little flowers the same colour as a starling's egg, and a stone exactly as big as a duck. It's full of interesting things, you know, this island. Oh! And I found a little place that looks just like Spring Valley, in miniature.'

'Spring Valley, master? I'd like to have a look at that.'

'Then follow me!'

The Scarecrow led him to a spot near the middle of the island, where the ground rose up a little way, and some bare rocks stood above the surface. In between them there was a little grassy hollow.

'You see,' said the Scarecrow, 'the farmhouse is *here*, and *there's* the orchard, and *that's* where the vines grow, and the olives are over *there*, and the stream runs down *here* . . .'

'Nice-looking place, master. I wish there was a real stream here, though.'

'Then we shall just have to dig a well, Jack. There's bound to be some fresh water under here. That's what we do in Spring Valley.'

'Well . . .' said Jack.

'Yes! A well. You dig there, and I'll dig here,' said the Scarecrow, and he began to scrape vigorously at the ground with a dry stick.

There was nothing better to do, so Jack found a stick too, and scratched and poked and scrabbled at the earth. The sun was hot, and the work made him even thirstier than he was to begin with, and besides, the end of his stick soon got wedged under the corner of a big rock.

He found a stone to jam under the stick so he could lever the rock out. The Scarecrow was happily scratching away further down the miniature Spring Valley, singing to himself, and Jack heaved down on his stick with all his might.

The big rock shifted a bit. He heaved again, and it shifted some more.

It looked a bit funny for a rock. The corner was perfectly square, for one thing, and for another, it wasn't made of rock at all. It was made of wood, and bound with iron. Jack felt his eyes grow wider and wider. The iron was rusty and the wood was decaying, and there was a great big padlock holding it shut, which fell off as soon as he touched it.

Then he lifted the lid.

'Master!' he cried. 'Treasure! Look! You were right!'

The box was packed with coins, jewels, medals,

necklaces, bracelets, pendants, rings for ears and rings for fingers, medallions, and every kind of gold ornament. They spilled out of the top of the box and jingled heavily as they fell on the ground. The Scarecrow's muddy little eyes couldn't open wide at the best of times, but they were fairly goggling.

'Well, that's amazing, Jack,' he said.

The Scarecrow picked up an earring and felt around the side of his turnip for an ear, but there wasn't one. Then he picked up a necklace and tried to put it on, but it wouldn't go over his turnip at all; so he put a golden bracelet on his signpost wrist, and it fell straight off. Jack plunged his hands into the chest and filled them with coins and jewels, holding them high and letting them fall down through his fingers.

'We must be millionaires, master!' he said.

But his mouth was so dry that he couldn't speak properly.

'All the same,' he croaked, 'I'd rather have some water.'

'Would you, my boy? There should be enough in the well by now. Come and see.'

Jack thought he was hallucinating. He scrambled

to his feet and ran after the Scarecrow, and sure enough, in the spot where he'd been digging, a little stream had started bubbling up.

'Oh, master! Oh, thank you! Oh! Oh! Oh!'

Jack flung himself to the ground and plunged his face into the muddy water, and drank and drank and drank until his belly could hold no more.

The Scarecrow was watching him with quiet satisfaction.

'There you are, you see,' he said. 'We understand water in Spring Valley.'

Jack lay back, bloated, and let the blessed feeling of not being thirsty any more soak him from head to feet.

When he got up, the spring was still bubbling away, and the water was trickling down towards the beach. It didn't look as if it would get there, because most of it sank straight down into the dry earth. The Scarecrow was busy somewhere else – Jack could hear him singing to himself – so, looking carefully at the way the earth sloped and where the rocks were, Jack found another stick and began to dig.

'What are you doing, Jack?' called the Scarecrow.

'I'm making a reservoir, master. What are you doing?'

'Sorting out the treasure,' came the answer.

'Good idea.'

So Jack went on digging until there was a hole as deep as his arm and about the same size across, and he patted the earth smooth and tight all around inside it. Then he scraped a trench in the soil, and led the water from the spring down into his new hole. The Scarecrow came to watch.

'See, master, once the water's in there, all the mud will sink to the bottom, and it'll be nice and clear to drink from,' Jack explained.

'Excellent!' said the Scarecrow. 'A splendid piece of civil engineering, Jack.'

Jack scraped another trench at the other side, for the water to run away once the reservoir was full. They stood and watched the hole filling up.

'Now come and see what I've done!' said the Scarecrow proudly.

He had made a little grotto with some stones and some mud, and he'd stuck diamonds and pearls and rubies and emeralds all over it with some sticky gum from a bush. He'd made a pretty pattern in the ground with some gold coins, and another pattern with the silver ones, and then he'd made some pretend trees out of bits of stick, and draped the necklaces over them like icicles.

'That's lovely, master,' said Jack.

'And I haven't even begun to study the pictures on the coins yet. Oh, there's endless food for the mind here, Jack!'

'Food . . .'

Jack looked longingly at the coconut palm, but the coconut still hung there high up among the leaves, as if it was mocking him. He tried to put it out of his mind. At least he had something to drink.

So while the Scarecrow worked on his grotto, Jack went down to the beach and walked up and down, looking for a fish to catch. But there wasn't a fish to be seen. He could feel himself going a little crazy from hunger.

'Maybe I could eat one of my toes,' he said to himself. 'I wouldn't really miss it, not a little one. But there wouldn't be enough meat on just one. I'd need a whole foot, or two, maybe.'

He paddled up and down at the edge of the sea, sunk in misery. In the middle of the afternoon he went to the reservoir to have another drink, and the Scarecrow showed him the grotto, with great pride, pointing out all the architectural and decorative effects.

'There, Jack! What d'you think of that? Do you see how I've arranged the stones, with all the light ones here and all the dark ones there? I think I'll go and look for some shells now, to stick round the edge. But Jack – what's the matter, my boy?'

'I'm sorry, master. I've tried not to give in to despair – but I'm starving to death – I think what you're making there must be my burial place, and a very nice one too, but I don't want to starve to death . . . I don't know what to do, master, really I don't . . .'

And poor Jack sank down to the ground, too weak to stand up any longer. In a moment the Scarecrow was kneeling by his side.

'Jack, Jack, what was I thinking of! If that blackbird hadn't stolen my brain, you could have made some pea soup. But as it is, the rest of my head is at your disposal, my dear servant. Cut yourself a slice of my turnip, and feast to your heart's content!'

So Jack struggled up and, not wanting to hurt the Scarecrow's feelings, took his little pocket knife and tried to find a place to cut a slice of his master's turnip. The poor thing was so battered and bruised and dried out that it was

scarcely a vegetable any more, and it was as hard as a piece of wood; but Jack managed to find a bit round the back where he could cut a little slice, and he did, and crammed it into his mouth.

'Not all at once, my boy – you'll choke!' said the Scarecrow. 'Nibble, that's the thing to do. And drink plenty of water.'

The turnip was hardly edible at all. It was dry and woody and bitter, and it took so much chewing that every mouthful took five minutes to soften and swallow.

Nevertheless, Jack ate it, and even thought he felt it doing him good.

By the time he'd finished, the Scarecrow had come back with some pretty shells from the beach. They spent an hour or so sorting them out, and then they stuck them on the ceiling of the little grotto. Then they dug a lake around it, and led some water into it from the stream, and that kept them going until sunset, and by then Jack's belly was so empty that he kept on making little moaning sounds, and the Scarecrow offered him another slice of turnip.

But there was hardly anything left to hack. A few bitter shreds were all Jack had for supper. And while he hugged his empty belly and tried to fall asleep, the Scarecrow pottered about in the moonlight, fitting every gem and every gold ornament and every piece of priceless jewellery into the grotto palace until it was perfect, and it glittered over its reflection in the tiny lake, looking fit for the queen of the fairies.

# An Invitation

Just before he woke up in the morning, Jack had a dream.

He dreamed he was just lying there on the sand, listening to a conversation in the air above. He couldn't see who was talking, but they had rusty voices, like old barbed wire being pulled through holes in a tin can.

'I'll bet you the small one goes before the day's out,' said one voice.

'I reckon the big one's gone already,' said the other.

'No. He's a monster, and they go on for ever.'

'Thin pickings these days, brother!'

'I heard there was a great battle on the mainland. Feasting for days, my cousin said.'

'All gone when I got there. Bones, nothing but bones.'

'The land's bare, brother. The soldiers move on, and who knows where they go?'

'Aye, who knows? Did you hear of the factories they're building in Spring Valley? They're making poisons, brother, poisons for the land. Is that little feller dead yet?'

Jack had been listening in his dream, and all of a sudden, with a horrible shock, he realized that it wasn't a dream at all, and that two vultures were sitting in the palm tree directly above him.

'Go away!' he managed to shout, in a voice almost as hoarse as theirs. 'Go on! Scram!'

His cry awoke the Scarecrow, who leaped up at once.

'Leave this to me, Jack!' he cried. 'This is scarecrow's work!'

And he uttered a bloodcurdling cry, and opened and shut his umbrella several times. The vultures, duly scared, spread their wings and lumbered away.

'My dear servant!' the Scarecrow said, full of compassion, as he turned to Jack. 'How long had those two villains been sitting up there?'

'I dunno, master. I heard them talking and I thought it was a dream. I wish it had been – they said I was almost a goner – Oh, master, ever since we began there's been people talking about eating me, and now the birds are at it too – and *I'm* the one that needs to eat!'

'Have another slice of my head, Jack. As long as I have a turnip on my shoulders, you shall not want for nourishment, dear boy!'

So Jack sawed away and cut himself another little scrap of his master's head, and chewed it hard with lots of water. But the poor Scarecrow was looking a great deal the worse for wear by now; Jack's knife had left deep gouges in the turnip, and the bits that were too tough to cut stuck out like splinters.

While Jack sat there gnawing the bitter root and trying to make it last a bit longer, the Scarecrow went off to inspect the grotto. He had an idea for improving the southern frontage, he said; but he'd only been gone a minute when Jack heard a furious yell.

He struggled to his feet, and hurried to see what was the matter. He found the Scarecrow stamping with fury and shouting:

'You flying fiends! How dare you! I'll bite your beaks off! I'll fill you full of stones! I'll boil you! You vagabonds, you housebreakers! Squatting – *squatting* in our *grotto*! Shoo! Begone!'

'Calm down, master! You'll do yourself a mischief,' said Jack. 'What's going on?'

He got down on his knees and peered into the grotto.

'Blimey!' he said.

For right in the centre there was a nest, and sitting on the nest was a little speckled bird. As Jack watched, another little bird flew in with a worm and gave it to the one on the nest, and as the one on the

543

nest reached up for the worm, Jack saw that there were four eggs beneath her.

Eggs, thought Jack. *Eggs!*

'Jack?' called the Scarecrow from behind him. 'Be careful – they go for the eyes, these fiends – stand back and let me deal with them!'

The two little speckled birds were looking at Jack. He licked his lips, and swallowed. Then he sighed.

'I suppose,' he said reluctantly, 'you better stay there, since you've got some eggs to look after.'

They said nothing.

'Jack?' said the Scarecrow anxiously.

'It's all right, master,' said Jack, standing up and feeling dizzy, so that he had to hold onto the Scarecrow for a moment. 'They're sitting on some eggs.'

'Eggs, eh?' said the Scarecrow severely. 'Well, that obviously means that hostilities are suspended until they hatch. Very well,' he called, 'you, you birds in there, in view of your impending parenthood, I shall not scare you away. But you must keep the place tidy, and leave as soon as your chicks have flown.'

The male bird flew out and perched on a nearby twig.

'Good morning,' he said. 'And what do you do?'

The Scarecrow blinked, and scratched his turnip.

'Well, I, um—' he began.

'Lord Scarecrow's in the agricultural business,' said Jack.

'Jolly good,' said the bird. 'And have you come a long way?'

'All the way from Spring Valley,' said the Scarecrow.

'Splendid. Well done,' said the bird, and flew away.

Now Jack was sure he was hallucinating. As a matter of fact, he didn't feel at all well.

'Jack, my boy,' said the Scarecrow, 'I wonder if

I could ask you to adjust my turnip a fraction. I think it's coming loose.'

'Let's go down to the beach, master,' Jack said. 'It's too bright to see here. There's a bit of shade there, under the coconut tree.'

Leaning on his digging stick, Jack made his way through the scrubby bushes with the Scarecrow holding the umbrella over him. It really was almost too hot to bear.

When they reached the coconut tree, they had a surprise, because a flock of pigeons rose out of it noisily, making the leaves wave. And just as the pigeons flew away, the coconut fell onto the sand with a thud.

'Oh! Thank goodness!' cried Jack, and ran to pick it up.

He turned it over and over, feeling the milk sloshing this way and that. He took out his knife and dug a hole in the end, and drank every drop. There wasn't actually as much as he'd thought, and what's more, it was going rancid.

'Jack – my boy – help—'

The Scarecrow was tottering and stumbling over the sand, trying to hold his turnip on. But it had

been so bashed and hacked about
that it wasn't going to stay on,
and besides, as Jack saw when
he helped his master to sit
down in the shade, the broomstick he'd had for a spine was
badly cracked.

'Dear oh dear, master, you're in
a worse state than me,' Jack said.
'At least we can do something
about you. Lie still, and I'll take
your spine out first, and then
put my digging stick there
instead.'

'Is it a dangerous operation?' said
the Scarecrow faintly.

'Nothing to it,' said Jack. 'Just don't wriggle.'

As soon as the new spine was in place, Jack picked
up the turnip – but alas! It fell apart entirely.

And now what could he do?

There was only one thing for it.

'Here we go, master,' he said. 'Here's a new head
for you.'

He jammed the coconut down onto the end of

the digging stick, and at once the Scarecrow sat up.

He turned his new head from side to side, and brushed the tuft of spiky hair on the top. Oddly enough, the expressions of surprise and delight and pleasure that passed over the coconut were exactly the same as the ones Jack remembered from the turnip. The Scarecrow looked just like himself again; in fact he looked much better than before.

'You look very handsome, master,' said Jack.

'I *feel* handsome! I don't think I've ever felt so handsome. Jack, my boy, you are a wonder. Thank you a thousand times!'

But the wandering about, and the hot sun, and the rancid coconut milk on his empty stomach were all too much for Jack.

'Can I sit under your umbrella for a minute, master?' said Jack. 'I'm feeling ever so hot and dizzy.'

'Of course!'

So they sat side by side for a few minutes. But Jack couldn't keep upright; he kept slipping sideways and leaning on the Scarecrow's chest. His master let him rest there until he fell asleep.

And once again Jack had a dream, and heard voices. This time one of them belonged to the Scarecrow himself, and he was speaking quietly, but with a great deal of force:

'It's just as well for you that my servant is asleep on my breast, because otherwise I'd leap up and scare you in a moment. But I don't want to wake him. You chose your moment well, you scoundrel!'

'No, no, you've got it wrong,' said the other voice, a light and musical voice which seemed to come

from a bush nearby. 'I've got a message for you, from the Grand Congress of All the Birds.'

'Grand Congress of All the Birds!' said the Scarecrow, with bottomless scorn. 'I've never heard of it.'

'Your ignorance is legendary,' said the bird.

'Well, thank you. But don't think you can get round me with your flattery. Since I can't move, I suppose I shall have to listen to your preposterous message.'

'Then I shall read it out. *The Eighty-Four Thousand Five Hundred and Seventy-Eighth Grand Congress is hereby convened on Coconut Island, that being the place chosen by Their Majesties the King and Queen of All the Birds. The President and Council send their greetings to Lord Scarecrow, and invite him to attend as principal guest of honour, to receive the thanks of the Congress for his gift of a Royal Palace, and to discuss the matter of Spring Valley, and—*'

'Spring Valley!' cried the Scarecrow. 'What's all this?'

'I haven't finished,' said the bird. '*– To discuss the matter of Spring Valley, and to make common* *purpose in order to restore the good working of the land, to our mutual benefit.* There,' he concluded. 'That's it.'

'Well, I'm astonished,' said the Scarecrow. 'Spring Valley is a very important place. And if you're going to start deciding what to do about it, I insist that I have the right to speak on the subject.'

'But that's exactly what we're inviting you to do!'

'Well, why didn't you say so? Now, you understand, I shall have to bring my servant with me.'

'Out of the question.'

'What!'

'He is a human being. We birds were meeting in Congress for hundreds of thousands of years before human beings existed, and they have brought us nothing but trouble. You are welcome, as our guest of honour, because we're not scared of you, whereas we're all scared of humans. And—'

The Scarecrow leapt to his feet.

'Not scared of *me*? How dare you not be scared of me! I've got a good mind to make war on the whole kingdom of the birds!'

And he stamped away, waving his arms in a fury. Jack couldn't keep his eyes closed any longer.

He sat up and blinked in the burning sunlight, and the messenger bird flew to another bush a bit further off.

Jack said quickly, 'No, please, listen. Don't let my master's manner put you off. He's highly strung, Lord Scarecrow is, he's got nerves like piano wires. The fact is,' he added quietly, looking around to see the Scarecrow stumping up and down and gesticulating in the distance, 'I don't think he'd manage very well without me. He's a great hero, no doubt about it, but he's as simple as a baby in some ways. Ever since his heart was broken by a broomstick he's been desperate, just desperate. His brain even fell out. I'll see if I can get him to change his mind.'

'Don't be long,' said the bird testily.

Squinting against the glare, Jack stumbled through the bushes and out onto the beach. He fell over three times before the Scarecrow saw him. His master came hurrying over the sand, his anger forgotten.

'Jack! Jack! My boy, are you ill?'

'I think I'm going to croak, master. I think I'm going to kick the bucket. But listen – I have given you good advice, haven't I? What I've said to you made sense, didn't it?'

'The best sense in the world!' said the Scarecrow warmly. 'No sense like it!'

'Then do as I suggest, and say thank you very much to this bird, and go and attend their Grand Congress. And maybe you can get to Spring Valley even if I don't.'

'Without you, my faithful servant?'

'I don't think I'll ever see it, master. I'm done for, that's what I think.'

'I shall never leave your side! And you may tell that crested charlatan so, in no uncertain terms.'

So poor Jack had to haul himself up and stagger back to the bird.

'He says he'd be delighted to accept your invitation,' he said, 'and he sends his compliments to the President and Council.'

'I should think so too,' said the bird.

'Did I . . .' Jack tried to say, but he could hardly get any words out. 'Did I hear you right, or was I dreaming? Those two little speckled birds that made their nest in the grotto – you said they were the King and Queen of all the birds?'

'That is correct.'

'Oh, good,' said Jack.

But he couldn't say anything else, because he felt himself falling sideways, and then he felt nothing at all.

# The Grand Congress

J ack woke up to find himself lying on his back and gazing up at a bright blue sky. He was lying on something soft and comfortable, so he naturally thought he was dead.

But the angels were making a lot of noise. In fact he wondered why St Peter, or the Holy Ghost, or someone, didn't come along and tell them all to stop quarrelling. They sounded like a lot of squawking birds.

Birds!

He sat up, rubbed his eyes, and looked around.

He was sitting in the middle of the island, a little way from the reservoir and the grotto palace, and under the shade of a bush whose leaves and branches

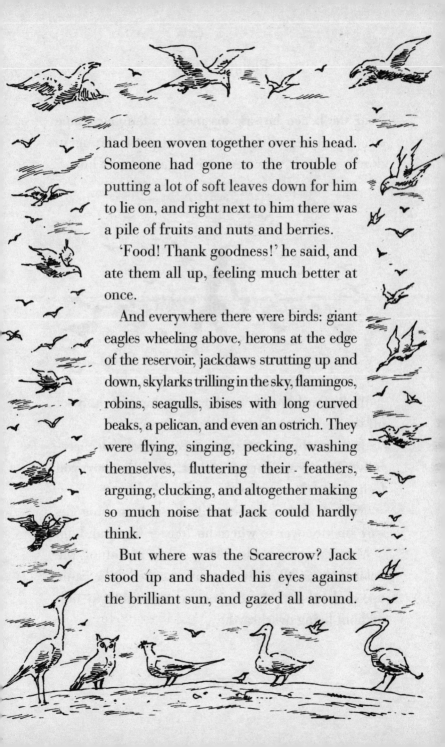

had been woven together over his head. Someone had gone to the trouble of putting a lot of soft leaves down for him to lie on, and right next to him there was a pile of fruits and nuts and berries.

'Food! Thank goodness!' he said, and ate them all up, feeling much better at once.

And everywhere there were birds: giant eagles wheeling above, herons at the edge of the reservoir, jackdaws strutting up and down, skylarks trilling in the sky, flamingos, robins, seagulls, ibises with long curved beaks, a pelican, and even an ostrich. They were flying, singing, pecking, washing themselves, fluttering their feathers, arguing, clucking, and altogether making so much noise that Jack could hardly think.

But where was the Scarecrow? Jack stood up and shaded his eyes against the brilliant sun, and gazed all around.

Philip Pullman

Near the beach he saw his master's familiar shape striding along stiffly, talking and gesticulating to dozens of birds who were moving along with him.

'Well, I'm blowed,' said Jack to himself, and set off through the bushes to find out more.

'Jack, my boy!' said the Scarecrow, waving cheerfully. 'You've woken up at last! And how are you feeling, my dear servant?'

'Well, I dunno, master,' Jack said, making his way shakily over to where his master was standing.

Although the birds didn't seem afraid of the Scarecrow at all, they flew away when Jack came up, and he and the Scarecrow were able to talk without being overheard.

'I suppose I'm still alive,' Jack went on, 'and my arms and legs are all working, so I reckon I must be all right. But what's going on, master? Where did the birds come from?'

'Ah. What happens is that every ten years, the King and Queen choose somewhere to make a nest, and then they summon all the birds to the Grand Congress. Very simple, you see; primitive, really – suits their childish minds. But they were so pleased with the palace we built for them that they just wouldn't go anywhere else. Oh, and I made them let you stay, and bring you some fruit and nuts and so on. I said I wouldn't accept their gold medal otherwise.'

'They're going to give you a gold medal? That's wonderful, master!'

'Yes, they were thrilled. But look – they're calling everyone together.'

On the topmost branch of a shrub near the grotto palace, a chaffinch was calling loudly. All the other birds stopped what they were doing and flew, or strutted, or waddled, or glided into the space in front of her, and settled down to listen.

'Birds of every degree!' the chaffinch called.

Philip Pullman

'Waders, swimmers, fliers and walkers! Welcome to the Eighty-Four Thousand Five Hundred and Seventy-Eighth Congress of All the Birds! I call upon our noble President to open the proceedings and welcome our guests.'

An elderly pelican hopped onto a rock and spoke in a deep and sonorous voice.

'I declare this Congress open,' he said. 'We have much urgent and important business to discuss. But our first task is the pleasant one of announcing the winner of our gold medal. We have acclaimed many distinguished laureates in the past, but few whose accomplishments were as varied as those of our guest today. With no regard for his personal safety, he clambered high up a stone wall to restore the fallen chick of Dr and Mrs Owl to his parents' nest. Secondly, ignoring the danger of riot and pursuit, he bravely set free five linnets, six goldfinches, and seven blackbirds from their sordid and miserable captivity. Thirdly, in the midst of a deadly battle, and at great personal risk, he carried the nest of Signora Robin to a place of safety.'

Lots of little birds were gazing in admiration at the Scarecrow, who stood beside Jack with a pleased expression on his coconut.

'And finally, using the utmost resources of his architectural skill, our gold medallist built a palace of jewels for Their Majesties our King and Queen to nest in. I am happy to report the appearance of four chicks this morning. The parents and the chicks are all very well.'

The birds cheered loudly. Several took off and flew around in delight before landing again.

The chaffinch called for silence. All the birds fell still once more, and then he said:

'I now invite Lord Scarecrow to come forward and receive the gold medal, and to say a few words.'

The Scarecrow moved with great dignity between the ranks of watching birds and stood beside the President, while four hummingbirds flew up over the Scarecrow's head and dropped a scarlet ribbon very neatly around his neck. The medal hanging from it gleamed proudly on his tattered chest.

The Scarecrow cleared his throat and began, 'Your Majesties! Mr President! Birds of every kind and degree!'

Everyone fell still. Jack crossed his fingers.

'It gives me great pleasure,' the Scarecrow went

on, 'to stand here today and receive this tribute. It is true, in the past we may have had our disagreements; some of your people may have stolen—'

The President coughed disapprovingly and said, 'We don't refer to it as stealing, Lord Scarecrow. Please confine yourself to general remarks of a friendly nature.'

'Oh, you're trying to censor me, are you?' said the Scarecrow, bristling. 'I must say that's typical. I come here in a spirit of friendship to do you the honour of accepting this paltry bauble, and you treat me like—'

The birds were squawking with indignation and raising their wings and shaking their heads. The President clattered his beak loudly for silence, and said:

'Paltry bauble? How dare you! I never heard such insolence!'

The Scarecrow was about to lose his temper. There was only one thing to be done.

'Excuse me,' Jack called out, 'excuse me, Your Majesties, Mr President, Lord Scarecrow and everyone, I think there's just been a bit of trouble with the translation.'

'But we're all speaking the same language!' protested the President. 'There's no doubt whatso- ever about the monstrous and unpardonable insult that this *thing* has just expressed. No doubt at all!'

'*Thing*, sir? *Thing*, did you call me?' cried the Scarecrow, and his umbrella opened and closed in a passion.

'Well, you see, that's just what I mean,' said Jack, carefully making his way through the ranks of the birds. 'Mr President, sir, it's clear to me that you're speaking in different languages. You're talking Bird, which is a rich and noble tongue worthy of the great nation of feathered heroes who speak it, and Lord Scarecrow is talking Coconut, which is a subtle and mysterious language full of wisdom and music. So if you'd let me translate for you—'

'And who are you? You're a human being. What are you doing here?' demanded the President.

'Me, sir? My name is Jack, sir, just a boy, that's right, no more than a lowly servant, sir. But I humbly offer my services, at this most dangerous time in world affairs, in the interests of peace and harmony. So if you'd just let me tell Lord Scarecrow what you're saying, and tell you what *he's* saying, I'm sure this Congress will get on very happily.'

'Hmph,' the President snorted. 'Well, you can begin by saying that unless Lord Scarecrow apologizes for that intolerable insult, we shall have no alternative but to strip him of his gold medal and declare war.'

'Certainly,' said Jack, bowing low.

He turned to the Scarecrow and said, 'Lord Scarecrow, the President offers you his profound apologies, and begs you to regard this little exchange of words as merely a storm in a teacup.'

'Oh, does he?' said the Scarecrow. 'You can tell him in return that I am a proud and free scarecrow, unused to tyranny and the despotic rule of a set of feathered popinjays, and I shall never submit to censorship.'

'Righto, master,' said Jack.

He turned to the President and said, 'Lord Scarecrow presents his most cordial and earnest compliments, and begs the Congress to regard his hasty words of a moment ago as being merely the natural and warm-hearted exuberance of one who has all his life cherished the highest and most passionate regard for all the nation of the birds. He asks me to add that he has never in his whole life received an honour that means as much to him as this gold medal, and he is already the holder of the Order of the Emerald Wurzel, the Beetroot Cup, and the Parsnip Challenge Trophy. What's more, he's a Knight of the Broomstick. But he'd gladly relinquish all those honours in favour of your gold medal, which he intends to wear with a full and grateful heart for the rest of his days.'

'He said all that, did he?' said the President suspiciously.

'It's what they call a compressed language, Coconut,' said Jack.

'Is it. Well, if that is the case, then I am happy to accept his apology,' said the President, bowing stiffly to the Scarecrow.

'He says he offers his most humble apology,' Jack told the Scarecrow.

'It didn't sound like that to me,' said his master. 'In fact—'

'No, he was speaking in Bird.'

'Ah, I see,' said the Scarecrow. 'What an extraordinary language.'

'That's why you need an interpreter, master.'

'Indeed. How lucky that you speak it so fluently! Well, in that case, I am happy to accept his apology.'

And the Scarecrow bowed very stiffly to the President.

Seeing this display of mutual respect, all the birds broke into a storm of singing and shouting and flapping and squawking and chirping and cooing. The Scarecrow responded by beaming widely and bowing in all directions. And thus everyone, for the moment, became the best of friends; but Jack thought that they would probably need a good interpreter for some time to come.

After the formalities, the Congress moved on to discuss the business of Spring Valley. But the Scarecrow didn't seem able to keep his mind on it. Several birds gave reports on the Buffaloni Corporation's poison factory, and the way they'd diverted the streams, and drained the wells, and dried up the fountains; but all the Scarecrow could do was fidget and scratch and pluck at his clothes.

When they broke for a recess, Jack said, 'Are you all right, master? You look a little out of sorts.'

'I think I'm leaking, my boy,' said the Scarecrow. 'I'm suffering a severe loss of straw.'

Jack had a look.

'It's true, master,' he said. 'Something must have loosened your stuffing. We'll have to get you some more.'

'What are you doing?' said the chaffinch, flying down to look. 'What's going on? What's the matter?'

'Lord Scarecrow's leaking,' Jack explained. 'We've got to find some more stuffing for him.'

'Nothing to it! You leave it to us!' said the chaffinch, and flew away.

'I'll take all this old straw out, master,' said Jack. 'It's been soaked and dried and battered about so much that you could do with a new filling. You'll feel much better for it, you take my word.'

He pulled out handfuls of dusty old straw, bits of twig, scraps of rag, and all the other bits and pieces the Scarecrow was so full of.

'I feel very hollow,' said the Scarecrow. 'I don't like it a bit. I can hear myself echoing.'

'Don't worry, master, we'll soon have you filled up again. Hello! What's this?'

Tucked into the middle of all the straw was a little packet of paper wrapped in oilskin.

'That's my inner conviction,' said the Scarecrow. 'Don't throw that away, whatever you do.'

Jack unwrapped the oilskin. Inside it there was a sheet of paper covered in writing.

'Oh, dear,' said Jack. 'I hoped there'd be a picture. I can't read this, master, can you?'

'Alas, no,' said the Scarecrow. 'I think my education was interrupted.'

By that time, a flock of birds had begun to fly down, each carrying a piece of straw or a twig or a bit of moss, and under the chaffinch's direction they packed them securely in the Scarecrow's inside. Each bird flew in, wove its contribution into the rest, and darted out again.

'They're doing some good stuffing, master,' said Jack. 'I'll put this back now, and then they can finish it off.'

'What's that?' said the chaffinch. 'What have you got there? What is it?'

'It's my inner conviction,' said the Scarecrow.

'What's it say? What's it all about?'

'We don't know,' said Jack. 'We can't read.'

With a loud chirrup of impatience, the chaffinch flew away. The other birds went on packing the Scarecrow, but word had got around, and the President himself came along to have a look. While

the little birds flew in and out, the Scarecrow displayed his inner conviction proudly.

'You see, it's bound in oilskin,' he said proudly. 'So all through our adventures, it's been perfectly preserved. I knew it was there,' he added. 'I've been certain of it all my life.'

'Yes, but what does it say, you booby?' demanded the President. 'Are you too silly to know what your own inner conviction is?'

The Scarecrow opened his mouth to protest, but then remembered and looked at Jack for the translation.

But Jack didn't have time to say a word, because a harsh *Caw!* from behind him made him jump, and he turned round to see an elderly raven fly down and land on the grass.

She nodded to the President, who bowed very respectfully back at her.

'Good day, Granny Raven,' he said.

'Well, where is it?' she said. 'This paper from inside the Scarecrow. Come on, let's have a look.'

Jack unfolded it for her, and she put a big claw on it and read it silently.

Then she looked up.

'You, boy,' she said to Jack. 'I want a word with you. Come over here.'

Jack followed her to a quiet spot a little way away.

'I heard about your so-called translating,' she said. 'You're a bright lad, but don't push your luck. Now tell me about the Scarecrow, and don't leave anything out.'

So Jack told her everything that had happened from the moment he heard the Scarecrow calling for help in the muddy field to the moment when he'd fainted from hunger the day before.

'Right,' she said. 'Now, there's going to be big trouble coming, and the Scarecrow's going to need that inner conviction of his more than ever. Fold it up, and put it back inside him, and don't let him lose it.'

'But why, Granny Raven? What's this trouble? And is he going to be in any danger? I mean, he's as brave as a lion, but he's not all there in the head department, if you see what I mean.'

'Not that sort of trouble. Legal trouble. Buffaloni trouble.'

'Well, we can run away!'

'No you can't, not any more. They're on your trail. We've got a couple of days' advantage, so we've got to make the most of it.'

'I don't like the sound of this at all.'

'There's a chance,' said Granny Raven, 'but only if you do exactly as I tell you. And hurry up – we haven't got a moment to lose.'

# THE ASSIZES

The first thing Granny Raven told them to do was get themselves back to the mainland. This turned out to be quite easy. Some seagulls who lived by the nearest fishing port found a rowing boat that wasn't being used, and they hitched it up to a team of geese, who towed it across to the island in less than a day. Once Jack and his master were on board, the birds towed it back the same way, and that very evening, the two wanderers settled down under a hedge.

'Who knows, Jack,' said the Scarecrow, 'this could be one of our last nights in the open air! We'll be sleeping in our very own farmhouse before long.'

Or jail, Jack thought.

The next thing they had to do was make their way to the town of Bella Fontana, which was the nearest town to Spring Valley. By walking hard, they did it in less than a week. Granny Raven had had to go elsewhere on urgent business, she said, but she'd see them in the town.

'You know, Jack,' the Scarecrow said as they walked towards the market place, 'I might have been mistaken about these birds. They're very good-hearted, fundamentally. No brains to speak of, but full of good intentions.'

'Now then, master,' said Jack, 'just remember: Granny Raven said she'd meet us by the fountain. And while we're in the town, I think you'd better leave the talking to me. You'll be much more impressive if you keep silent and mysterious.'

'Well, that's exactly what I am,' said the Scarecrow.

On the way, he'd managed to lose his gold medal eleven times and the oilskin package containing his inner conviction sixteen. Jack thought it would be a good idea to put them in a bank, and keep them safe till they were needed. So as soon as they got to the town centre, with its dried-up basin which had once been the municipal fountain, they looked around for the bank.

They were about to go inside when a big black bird flew down and perched on the dusty basin and gave a loud *Caw!*

'Granny Raven!' said Jack. 'Where've you been? We were just going into the bank.'

'I've been busy,' she said. 'What d'you want a bank for?'

The Scarecrow explained: 'We're going to deposit my inner conviction. Don't worry. We know what we're doing.'

'You're luckier than you deserve,' said Granny Raven. 'D'you know what that bank's called? It's the Banco Buffaloni.'

The Scarecrow stared at it in dismay.

'These Buffalonis are everywhere!' he said. 'Well, we can't trust this bank, it's obvious. I shall have to look after my inner conviction myself. Where is it? Where's it gone? Where did I put it?'

'You've got it, master,' said Jack. 'It's safe in your straw. But what do we do now, Granny Raven? And what's going on? There's a lot of people around.'

'It's the Assizes,' she said, 'when the judge comes around judging court cases. He tries all the criminals and judges all the civil cases. There he is now.'

As Jack and the Scarecrow watched, the great doors of the town hall opened and out came an elderly man wearing a long red robe, at the head of a procession of men carrying maces and scrolls. Behind him came several men in black robes, who were the lawyers, and finally came the town clerk in a top hat. Escorted by a procession of policemen in their best uniforms, they crossed the square and went up the steps into the law court.

'Right,' said Granny Raven. 'You go in after them, and get a move on.'

'But what are we going to do in there?'

'You're going to go to court and register the Scarecrow's claim to Spring Valley.'

'An excellent idea, Jack!' said the Scarecrow. 'Let's do it at once.'

And before Jack could hold him back, the Scarecrow set off up the steps and in through the

577

doors, with Granny Raven sitting on his shoulder.

Jack darted up behind him, and found the Scarecrow arguing with an official behind a desk.

'But I demand the right to have my case heard!' the Scarecrow was saying, banging his umbrella on the desk. 'It is an extremely important matter!'

'You're not on my list,' said the official. 'What's your name? Lord Scarecrow? Don't be ridiculous. Go away!'

Jack thought he'd better help. They were in such deep trouble already that they might as well dig a bit deeper.

'Ah, you don't understand,' he said. 'This case is a matter of extreme urgency. It all turns on the ownership of Spring Valley, and it won't take long. If it's not settled, you see, all the water'll dry up. Just like the fountain out there. Stick him on the list, and we can get through it in five minutes, and then all the water in the valley will be safe.'

'Go on!' said a man in the queue for the public seats. 'I'd like to see a scarecrow in court.'

'Yeah, let him go first,' said a woman with a shopping bag. 'He's got a nice face.'

'He's got a face like a coconut!' said the official.

'Well, it *is* a coconut,' the Scarecrow agreed.

'Go on, put him on first,' people were saying. 'It's the only laugh we'll have today.'

'Yes! Let the scarecrow have his case heard!'

'Good luck, scarecrow!'

So the man had no choice. He wrote at the top of the list:

*Lord Scarecrow in the case of the ownership of Spring Valley.*

No sooner had he done that than the door burst open, and in came a squad of policemen. At the head of them was a lean man in a black silk suit. It was the lawyer, Mr Cercorelli, and he said:

'One moment, if you please. Inspector, arrest this person at once.'

The Scarecrow looked around to see who was going to be arrested, only to find the chief policeman seizing his road sign and trying to put handcuffs on him.

'What are you doing? Let me go! This is an outrage!' he cried.

'Go on, boy,' said Granny Raven quietly to Jack. 'Do your stuff.'

'Oh, excuse me,' said Jack to the lawyer, 'but you can't arrest Lord Scarecrow, being as he's already in the process of going to law.'

'I beg your pardon?'

'It's true, Mr Cercorelli, sir,' said the official, showing him the list of cases to be tried.

The Scarecrow shook off the handcuffs, and dusted himself down with great dignity as a bell rang to summon everyone into the courtroom.

Mr Cercorelli withdrew to talk urgently to a group of other lawyers in a huddle by the door. Jack watched them closely, and saw them all leaning over Mr Cercorelli's shoulder to read the name of the Scarecrow's case; but as soon as they read it, they all smiled and nodded with satisfaction.

Oh blimey, he thought.

Then he heard the man at the desk say something, and turned to say, 'I beg your pardon?'

'I said you're in luck,' said the official to Jack. 'This is a very distinguished judge you're up in front of. He's the most learned judge in the whole of the kingdom.'

'What's his name?' said Jack, as the doors opened and the Clerk of the Court called for silence.

'Mr Justice Buffaloni,' said the official.

'*What?*'

But it was too late to withdraw. The crowd behind them was surging and heaving to get in, and Jack saw a lot of whispering and pointing and hurrying in and out of side doors. Soon the courtroom was full to bursting, and the Scarecrow and Jack were crammed behind a table right in the middle, with lawyers to left and right, the judge's bench high up in front of them, and a jury filing into the jury box along the side.

Everyone had to stand up as the judge came in. He bowed to the court, and everyone bowed back to him, and then he sat down.

'I'm getting a bit nervous,' Jack whispered. 'And Granny Raven's vanished. I don't know what to do.'

'No, no, Jack,' the Scarecrow whispered back. 'Have confidence in the law, my boy! Right is on our side!'

'Silence!' bellowed the Clerk. 'First case. Scarecrow versus the United Benevolent Improvement Society Chemical Works.'

The Scarecrow smiled and nodded his coconut. Jack put his hand up.

'What? What?' said the judge.

'Excuse me, your worship,' said Jack, 'but it's all going a bit fast. Who are these United Benevolent Improving people?'

'Well, if it comes to that,' said the judge, 'who are *you*?'

And he beamed at all the lawyers, and they all slapped their sides and roared with laughter at the judge's sparkling legal wit.

'I'm Lord Scarecrow's legal representative,' said Jack, 'and my client wants to know who these United Improvers are, because we never heard of them till now.'

'If I may explain, my lord,' said Mr Cercorelli, rising smoothly to his feet. 'I act for the United Benevolent Improvement Society, which is the body that holds a majority shareholding in the company known as the United Benevolent Improvement Chemical and Industrial Company, which is the operating organization that runs the United Benevolent Improvement Chemical Works, which owns and operates several factories situated in Spring Valley for the beneficial exploitation of certain mineral and water rights granted to the United Benevolent Improvement Society, which is a registered charity under the Act of 1772, and acts as a holding company in the case of the United Benevolent Improvement Chemical Works by *tenendas praedictas terras.*'

'There you are,' said the judge to Jack. 'Perfectly clear. Now be quiet while we hear this case and find for the defendant.'

'Oh, right,' said Jack. 'Well, my lord, I'd like to ask Lord Scarecrow to be a witness.'

All the other lawyers went into a huddle. Long words came buzzing out like wasps around a fruit tree. The Scarecrow smiled at everyone in the court, gazing all round with great pride and satisfaction.

Finally Mr Cercorelli said, 'We have no objection, your lordship. He will, of course, be subject to cross-examination.'

'Scarecrow to the witness box!' called the Clerk of the Court.

The Scarecrow stood up and bowed to the judge, to the jury, to the clerk, to the lawyers, and to the public.

'Stop bobbing up and down like a chicken and get into the witness box!' snapped the judge.

'A *chicken*?' said the Scarecrow.

'It's a legal term, master,' said Jack hastily.

'Oh, in that case it's perfectly all right,' said the Scarecrow, and bowed again all round.

The members of the public, watching from the gallery, were enjoying it a great deal. They settled down comfortably as Jack began.

'What is your name?' he said.

The Scarecrow looked puzzled. He scratched his coconut.

'It's Lord Scarecrow,' said Jack helpfully.

'Leading the witness!' called one of the lawyers.

'Strike it from the record,' said the judge. 'You, boy, confine yourself to questions. Don't tell the witness what to say.'

'All right,' said Jack. 'He's called Lord Scarecrow. I'm his servant, by the way.'

'And a very good one!' said the Scarecrow.

'Silence!' called the judge. 'Get on with the examination, boy, and as for you, you scoundrel, hold your tongue.'

The Scarecrow nodded approvingly, and beamed at everyone. The people in the public gallery began to giggle.

'Now then,' said Jack, 'I put it to you, Lord

Scarecrow, that this United Benevolent Improvement Society is not the legal owner of Spring
Valley.'

'Quite right,' said the Scarecrow.

'Then who is?'

'I am!'

'And can you prove that?'

'I hope so,' said the Scarecrow doubtfully.

The people in the gallery began to laugh.

'Silence in court!' said the judge, and glared
furiously. When everyone was quiet again, he said to
Jack, 'If you don't get to the point, I shall have you
both arrested for wasting the court's time. Has your
witness got anything useful to say, or has he not?'

'Oh, indeed he has, your lordship. Let me just ask
him again.'

'You can't go on asking him the same question!'

'Just once more. Honest.'

'Once, then.'

'Thank you very much, your lordship. Right.
Here goes. Lord Scarecrow, how do you know that
you are the owner of Spring Valley?'

'Ah!' said the Scarecrow. 'I've got an inner
conviction. I've always had it. In fact I've got it

587

here,' he went on, fumbling in his chest. 'I know it's here somewhere. Yes! Here it is!'

'Yes, that's it,' said Jack. 'Your lordship, members of the jury, ladies and gentlemen, this piece of paper proves beyond any doubt whatsoever that Spring Valley belongs to Lord Scarecrow, and these United Benevolizers are being illegal. I rest my case.'

'But what does it say, you stupid boy?' snapped the judge. 'Get your client to read it out to the court.'

'Well, he's never learned to read, your lordship.'

'Well, *you* read it then!'

'But I never learned to read either. It's a big drawback, and if I'd known then what I know now, I'd have arranged to be born into a rich family and not into a poor one. I'm sure I'd have learned to read then.'

'If you don't know how to read,' demanded the judge, 'how do you know what's on that paper? I warn you, boy, you're in great danger!'

'My lord,' said one of the lawyers, 'all he has to do is hand it to your lordship, and your lordship can read it out for the benefit of the court.'

'Oh no, you don't,' said Jack at once. 'We want

separate verification, according to the principles of *non independentem judgi nogoodi*. So there.'

This was getting more and more difficult. But just then, Jack saw a movement out of the corner of his eye, and looked up at a high window to see Granny Raven making her way in, accompanied by a very nervous-looking blackbird. She made the blackbird sit in the corner of the window-sill, and didn't let him move.

'However,' Jack went on, relieved, 'I think I can see a way out of this legal minefield. I'd like to invite my associate Granny Raven to come and take over this part of the case.'

Granny Raven glided down and perched on the table next to Jack, causing great excitement among the public, and great consternation on the part of the lawyers. They went into a huddle, and then Mr Cercorelli said:

'My lord, it is quite impossible to allow this, on the grounds of *ridiculus birdis pretendibus lawyerorum*.'

But Jack said at once, 'My client is only a poor scarecrow, without a penny to his name. Is the law of the land designed only for the rich? Surely not! And if, out of the goodness of her heart, this raven – this poor, elderly, shabby, broken-down old bird – offers to represent the Scarecrow, because she is all he can afford, then surely this great court and this noble judge will not deny my client the meagre help that she can bring? Look at the vast wealth, the profound resources, the eminent legal minds ranged against us! Your lordship, members of the jury, ladies and gentlemen of the public – is there no justice to be had in the Assizes of Bella Fontana? Is there no mercy—?'

'All right, all right,' sighed the judge, who could see that everyone in the public gallery was nodding in sympathy. 'Let the bird speak on behalf of the Scarecrow.'

'I should think so too,' said Granny Raven, and then added quietly to Jack, 'Shabby and broken-down, eh? I'll have a word with you later.'

The Scarecrow was watching everything with great interest.

'Well, go on then,' said the judge.

'Right,' said Granny Raven. 'Now pay attention. You, Scarecrow, step down from the witness box. I want to summon two more witnesses before I speak to you again. Mr and Mrs Piccolini, into the witness box.'

Nervously, arm in arm, the elderly couple who'd been packing to leave their cottage came through the courtroom and stepped up into the box.

Once they'd given their names and addresses, Granny Raven said:

'Now tell the court what happened just before your neighbour died.'

'Well, our neighbour, Mr Pandolfo,' said Mrs Piccolini, 'he hadn't been well, poor old man, and when he asked us to step over to his house we thought he was going to ask us to call the doctor. But instead he just asked us to watch him sign a piece of paper, and then to sign it as well. So we did.'

'Did he tell you what was on the paper?'

'No.'

'Would you recognize the paper again?'

'Yes. Mr Pandolfo was drinking some coffee, and he spilled a drop or two on the corner of the paper. So it would have a stain on it.'

Granny Raven turned to Jack and said, 'Go on, open it up.'

Jack opened the oilskin package and held up the paper. As the old woman had said, there was a coffee-stain on the corner. Everyone gasped.

All the lawyers rose to their feet at once, protesting, but Granny Raven clacked her beak so loudly that they all fell still.

'Don't you want to hear what the paper says?' she said. 'Because everybody else does.'

They went into a huddle, and after a minute one of them said, 'We are willing to agree to the letter's being read out by an independent witness.'

'In that case,' said Jack, 'we nominate that lady in the jury box.'

He pointed to an old lady in a blue dress. The Scarecrow stood up and bowed to her, and she looked very flustered and said, 'Well, if you like, I don't mind . . .'

She put on a pair of glasses, and Jack handed her the letter. She quickly skimmed it through, and

said, 'Oh, dear. Poor old man!'

Then the old lady read in a clear voice:

'*This letter was written by me, Carlo Pandolfo, being of sound mind, but not very well in the legs, and is addressed to whom it may concern.*

'*As I am the legal owner of Spring Valley, and I can dispose of it however I please, I choose this manner of settling the ownership after I peg out.*

'*And I particularly want to keep the farm and all the springs and wells and watercourses and ponds and streams and fountains out of the hands of my cousins those rascal Buffalonis because I don't trust any of them and they are a pack of scoundrels every one.*

*'And I have no wife or children or nieces or nephews.*

*'And no friends either except Mr and Mrs Piccolini down the hill.*

*'So I shall make a scarecrow and place him in the three-acre field by the orchard and in him I shall put this letter.*

*'And this letter shall be my last will and testament.*

*'And I leave Spring Valley with all its buildings and springs and wells and watercourses and ponds and streams and fountains to the said scarecrow and it shall belong to him in perpetuity and I wish him good luck.*

*'That is all I have to say.*

*'Carlo Pandolfo.'*

When the lady reached the end of the letter, there was a silence.

Then the Scarecrow said, 'Well, I did tell you I had an inner conviction.'

And then there was an uproar. All the lawyers began talking at once and all the people in the public gallery turned to one another and said, 'Did you hear that? Well I never – have you ever heard? – and what about—?'

The Clerk of the Court called for silence, and everyone stopped to see what the judge would say. But it was Granny Raven who spoke.

'There you are,' she said. 'That's the long and the short of it. The will is legal, and properly witnessed, and Spring Valley belongs to the Scarecrow, and we can all—'

'One moment,' said Mr Cercorelli. 'Not so fast. We haven't finished yet.'

# A Surprise Witness

And everyone looked at the judge. The look on his face was enough to make Jack feel that all his ribs had come loose and fallen into the pit of his stomach.

'The first witness has yet to be cross-examined,' he said. 'Mr Cercorelli, you may proceed.'

'Thank you, my lord,' said the lawyer.

Jack looked at Granny Raven. What was going to happen now? But he couldn't read any expression on the old bird's face.

The Scarecrow climbed back up into the witness box, smiling all around. Mr Cercorelli smiled back, and the two of them looked like the best of friends.

Then the lawyer began:

'You are the scarecrow mentioned in the letter we have just heard?'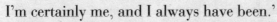

'Oh, yes,' said the Scarecrow.

'You are sure of that?'

'Absolutely sure.'

'No doubt at all?'

'No. None whatsoever. I'm certainly me, and I always have been.'

'Well, Mr Scarecrow, let us examine your claim a little more closely. Let us examine *you* a little more closely!' he said, smiling at everyone again.

The Scarecrow smiled back.

'Let's examine your left hand, for example,' said the lawyer. 'It's a remarkable hand, is it not?'

'Oh, yes. It keeps the rain off!' said the Scarecrow, opening his umbrella, and closing it again quickly when the judge frowned at him.

'And where did you get such a splendid hand?'

'From the market place in the town where I starred in *The Tragical History of Harlequin and Queen Dido*,' said the Scarecrow proudly. 'It was a great performance. First I came on as—'

597

'I'm sure it was enthralling. But we're talking about your hand. You lost your original hand, did you?'

'Yes. It came off, so my servant got me this one.'

'Splendid, splendid. Now can you show us your right hand?'

The Scarecrow stuck his right hand in the air.

'It looks like a road sign,' said the lawyer. 'Is that what it was?'

'Oh, yes. It points, you see. As soon as my servant got this for me, I became very good at pointing.'

'And why did your servant get you a new right hand?'

'Because the first one broke off.'

'I see. Thank you. So you have neither of the arms you were – ahem – born with?'

Jack jumped up to protest. He could see where this was leading.

'Your lordship, it doesn't make any difference which bits have been replaced – he's still the same scarecrow!'

'Oh, but it does, your lordship,' said Mr Cercorelli. 'We are seeking to establish how much of the original scarecrow created by Mr Pandolfo still remains. If there is none, then the will is null and void, and the estate of Spring Valley passes to the United Benevolent Improvement Society, according to the principle *absolutem absurditas scaribirdibus landlordum.*'

'Quite right,' said the judge. 'Carry on.'

And in spite of Jack's protests, Mr Cercorelli went through the Scarecrow's whole story, showing how every bit of him had been replaced, including the very straw inside him.

'And so, members of the jury,' he concluded, 'we can see clearly that the scarecrow made by Mr Pandolfo, the scarecrow to whom he intended to leave Spring Valley, no longer exists. Every component particle of him has been scattered to the four winds. There is nothing left. This gentleman in the witness box, so proud of his left hand that keeps the rain off and his right hand that points so well, is no more than a fraud and an impostor.'

'Hey!' said Jack. 'No, no, wait a minute!'

'Silence!' said the judge. 'Members of the jury, you have heard an account of the most shameless attempt at fraud, deception, malfeasance, embezzlement, and theft that it has ever been my misfortune to hear about. Your duty now is very simple. You have to retire to the jury room and make up your minds to do as I tell you. You must find for the defendants, and decide that the United Benevolent Improvement Society are the true owners of Spring Valley. The court will—'

'Hold on,' said a harsh old voice. 'What did that scoundrel say a minute ago? Not so fast, he said. We haven't finished yet.'

Every head turned to look at Granny Raven.

'Everybody listening?' she said. 'I should think so too. We've got three more witnesses to call. It won't take long. The next witness is Mr Giovanni Stracciatelli.'

Jack had never heard of him, and neither had anyone else. The lawyers all huddled together and whispered, but they didn't know what to do, and when Mr Stracciatelli came to the witness box carrying a large leather-bound book, all they could do was watch suspiciously.

'You are Giovanni Stracciatelli?' said Granny Raven.

'I am.'

'And what is your occupation?'

'I am the Commissioner of Registered Charities.'

At once all the lawyers rose to their feet and protested, but Granny Raven's voice was louder than all of them.

'You stop your fuss!' she cawed. '*You* brought up the subject of charities, and *you* claimed that the United Benevolent Improvement Society was a proper charity registered under the Act, so let's have a good look at it. Mr Stracciatelli, would you please read out the names of the trustees of the United Benevolent Improvement Society?'

Mr Stracciatelli put on a pair of glasses and opened his book.

'*Trustees of the United Benevolent Improvement Society,*' he read. '*Luigi Buffaloni, Piero Buffaloni, Federico Buffaloni, Silvio Buffaloni, Giuseppe Buffaloni, and Marcello Buffaloni.*'

Gasps from the public gallery – more protests from the lawyers.

'Thank you, Mr Stracciatelli, you can step down,' said Granny Raven. 'I'd like to remind the court of Mr Pandolfo's opinion concerning the Buffalonis. This is what his letter says: *I particularly want to keep the farm and all the springs and wells*

*and watercourses and ponds and streams and*
*fountains out of the hands of my cousins those rascal*
*Buffalonis because I don't trust any of them and they*
*are a pack of scoundrels every one.'*

Still more protests. The judge was looking very
sour indeed.

'Now you may say,' said Granny Raven, 'that Mr
Pandolfo was wrong about the Buffalonis. You may
claim that every Buffaloni born is a perfect angel.
That is all beside the point. The point is that Mr
Pandolfo did *not* want his land to go to the Buffalonis,
and he *did* want to leave it to the scarecrow.'

'But the scarecrow no longer exists!' shouted Mr
Cercorelli. 'I've just proved it!'

'You were concerned with his component
particles, not with the whole entity,'
said Granny Raven. 'So let us
take you at your word, and
assume that all that matters
is the stuff he's made of.
I call our next witness, Mr
Bernard Blackbird.'

The blackbird flew down
and perched on the witness

box. He was very nervous of the Scarecrow, who was watching him closely.

'Name?' said Granny Raven.

'Bernard.'

'Tell the court about your dealings with the Scarecrow.'

'Don't want to.'

Granny Raven clacked her beak, and Bernard squeaked in terror.

'All right! I will! Just let me think. It's all gone dark in me mind.'

'You wake your ideas up, my lad,' said Granny Raven, 'or you'll be flying home with no feathers. Tell the court what you told me.'

'I'm scared of *him*,' said Bernard, looking at the Scarecrow.

'He won't hurt you. Do as you're told.'

'All right, if I have to. It was on the road some-where. I was ever so hungry. I seen him coming out of a caravan, and then I seen him banging his head. Mind you, that was a different head. That was a turnip.'

'Never mind what sort of head it was. What was he doing?'

'Banging it. He was whacking hisself on the bonce. Then summing fell out, and him and the little geezer bent down to look at it, and—'

'My brain!' cried the Scarecrow. 'So it was *you*, you scoundrel!'

'Silence!' shouted the judge. 'Witness, carry on.'

'I forgot what I was saying,' whined the blackbird. 'When he shouts at me I get all nervous. I'm highly strung, I can't help it. You shouldn't let him shout like that. It's not fair. I'm only young.'

'Stop complaining,' said Granny Raven. 'What

happened next? Something fell out of his head. What was it?'

'It was a pea. A dried pea.'

'It was my *brain*,' said the Scarecrow passionately.

'Stop him!' cried Bernard, flinching. 'He's gonna hit me! He is! He give me a really cruel look!'

'You'll get worse than that from me,' said Granny Raven. 'Tell the court what you did.'

'Well, I thought he didn't have no more use for it, so I ate it. I was hungry,' he said piteously. 'I hadn't had nothing for days, and when I seen that pea I thought he was just throwing it away. So I come down and pecked it up. I never knew it was important. It didn't taste very nice, either. It was ever so dry.'

'That'll do.'

'It give me a belly-ache.'

'I said that's enough!'

'It might have been poisoned.'

'How dare you!' said the Scarecrow.

'Stop him! Stop him!' cried Bernard, fluttering in terror. 'You seen the look he give me? You heard him? Help! He's going to murder me!'

'That's quite enough,' snapped Granny Raven.

'I need compensation, I do,' said Bernard. 'I need counselling. It's stolen all my youth and happiness away, this has. I'll never be the same. I need therapy.'

'Clear off home and stop whining,' said Granny Raven, 'or I'll give you some therapy that'll sort you out for good.'

Bernard crept along the edge of the witness box, flinching dramatically as he came near the Scarecrow, although the Scarecrow didn't move. Then he flew straight for the open window and vanished.

'Our final witness,' said Granny Raven, with a look of distaste after Bernard, 'is the Scarecrow's personal attendant.'

'What, me?' said Jack.

'Yes, boy, you. Get a move on.'

So Jack went into the witness box. The lawyers were busily objecting, but the judge wearily said, 'Let the boy give evidence. The jury will soon see what rubbish it is.'

Granny Raven said, 'Tell the jury what happened on the island where you were marooned.'

'Oh, right,' said Jack. 'We were left on this island, and there wasn't any food, and I was going to starve to death. So Lord Scarecrow very generously let me eat his head. All of it, except the brain, obviously, being as that was eaten already. So I started to eat it, and bit by bit I ate almost all of it, and it kept me alive. And then that coconut fell down and I stuck it on his neck, and very good he looks too. If it wasn't for Lord Scarecrow's generosity in letting me eat his head, I'd be nothing now but a skeleton.'

'So there, your lordship, members of the jury,' said Granny Raven, 'there is our entire case. The United Benevolent Improvement Society, which is currently running poison factories in Spring Valley, and draining all the wells, is a front organization for the Buffaloni family. Mr Pandolfo wanted to keep Spring Valley out of the hands of the Buffalonis, and leave it to the Scarecrow. The only remaining particles of the original Scarecrow are now indissolubly mingled with those of Bernard the blackbird and Jack the servant; and I shall obtain power of attorney to act for Bernard on behalf of all the birds, since he is a feckless wretch; but we maintain that the kingdom of the birds, together with Jack the servant, are now the true and undisputable owners of Spring Valley, in perpetuity.'

'The jury haven't heard my summing-up yet,' said the judge. 'They can begin by forgetting everything they have just heard. The testimony of the Scarecrow's witnesses is to be disregarded, on the grounds that it is more favourable to the Scarecrow than to the United Benevolent Improvement Society, a charity of the utmost worthiness, whose trustees are gentlemen of the highest honesty and integrity, besides employing a large number of *you*. Ladies and gentlemen of the jury, you know what's good for you – I mean, you know your duty. Go to the jury room, and decide that the Scarecrow should lose this case.'

'No need, your lordship,' said the foreman. 'We've already decided.'

'Excellent! It only remains for me to congratulate the United—'

'No,' said the foreman, 'we reckon the Scarecrow wins.'

'*What?*'

All the lawyers were on their feet at once, protesting loudly, but the foreman of the jury took no notice.

'We don't care about all that,' he said. 'It's common sense. Don't matter if he is all different bits from what he was, he's still the same Scarecrow. Any fool can see that. And we're all fed up with the fountains being dry. So what we decide is this: Spring Valley is to be owned by the birds *and* by the servant *and* by the Scarecrow equally. And that's it. That's the voice of the people.'

A great cheer broke out from the public gallery. The judge called for silence, but no-one took any notice. The lawyers were still arguing, but no-one took any notice of them either.

The Scarecrow and Jack were both lifted on the shoulders of the crowd and carried out to the square.

Granny Raven went to perch on the fountain while the Scarecrow made a speech.

'Ladies and gentlemen!' he said. 'I am heartily grateful for your support, and I give you my word of honour that as soon as we have closed the poison factories, we shall let all the springs flow again, so that this fountain will run with fresh water for everyone.'

More cheers from the crowd – but then they all fell silent and looked around. From the town hall a group of men, all wearing expensive clothes and dark glasses and looking stern, were walking towards the Scarecrow.

Jack heard whispers from the crowd.

'Luigi – Piero – Federico – Silvio – Giuseppe – Marcello! It's the whole Buffaloni family . . .'

'Well, master,' said Jack, 'it looks like a fight. Let's run away, quick.'

'Certainly not!' said the Scarecrow, and he faced the Buffalonis boldly, coconut high, umbrella poised, the very model of a people's hero.

The Buffalonis stopped right in front of him, six of them, big rich powerful men in shiny suits. Everyone held their breath.

Then the Buffaloni in the middle said, 'Our

congratulations to you, my friend!' and held out his hand to shake.

The Scarecrow shook it warmly, and then all the other Buffalonis gathered round, slapping him on the back, ruffling his coconut, patting him on the shoulder, shaking his hand, embracing him warmly.

'So we lose a law case!' said the chief Buffaloni. 'It's a big world – there are plenty of other enterprises! Plenty of room in this beautiful world for Buffalonis *and* Scarecrows!'

'Good luck to you, Lord Scarecrow! Our best wishes for all your business ventures!'

'If you ever need our help – just ask!'

'We respect a brave opponent!'

'Buffalonis and Scarecrows are good friends from now on – the best of friends!'

And then a café owner produced some wine, and the Buffalonis and the Scarecrow drank a toast to friendship, and happy laughter filled the square; and presently someone brought out an accordion, and in a moment the whole crowd was singing and dancing and laughing and drinking and throwing flowers, with the Scarecrow at the heart of the celebrations.

# MURDER BY TERMITES

They slept that night in the farmhouse in
Spring Valley. Jack woke up next morning to
hear his master calling.

'Jack! Jack! Help! I don't feel at all well!'

'That's all right, master,' said Jack, hurrying
along to help. 'You had too much wine last night.
Come for a walk – it'll clear your head.'

'No, it's not my head,' the Scarecrow told him.
'It's my legs and my arms and my back. I've been
poisoned. Help!'

And he did look in a bad way, it was perfectly
true. Even his coconut had gone pale. When he stood
up he fell over, when he lay down he groaned, and
he was getting twitches in his arms and legs.

613

'Twitches, master?'

'Yes, Jack! Dreadful ghastly twitches! It's horrible! It feels as if I'm being eaten alive! Call the doctor at once!'

So Jack ran to the town and called the doctor. The Scarecrow was a celebrity now, thanks to the trial, and the doctor gathered up his bag and hurried along straight away, followed by several onlookers.

They found the Scarecrow twitching badly, and groaning at the top of his voice.

'What is it, Doctor?' said Jack. 'Listen to him! He's in a terrible state! What can it be?'

The doctor took his stethoscope and listened to the Scarecrow's chest.

'Oh, dear me,' he said. 'This is bad. Let me take your temperature.'

'No, no! Don't do that!' protested the Scarecrow. 'If you take my temperature away, I'd be cold all through. As it is, I'm hot *and* cold, both together. Oh, it's horrible! Oh, no-one knows what I'm suffering!'

'What other symptoms are you feeling?'

'Internal conniptions. And a nameless fear.'

'A nameless fear? Dear me, that's not good at all. A fear of what?'

'I don't know! Horses! Eggs! Heights! Oh! Oh! I feel terrible! Help! Help!'

And the Scarecrow leapt all over the room, capering and skipping and prancing like a goat.

'What's he doing, Doctor?' said Jack. 'I've never seen him like this. Is he going to die?'

'He's clearly been bitten by a spider,' explained the doctor. 'Dancing is quite the best cure, all the medical authorities agree.'

The Scarecrow overheard him, and sank to the floor with terror.

'A spider! Oh, no, Doctor, anything but that! I'll go mad with despair!'

'Better keep on dancing then, master,' said Jack.

But the poor Scarecrow couldn't dance another step.

'No, I can't move!' he cried. 'All the strength has drained from my body – my nameless fear is going all the way down to my toes—'

'Let me feel your pulse,' said the doctor.

The Scarecrow held out his left hand. As soon as the doctor took his wrist, the umbrella opened, startling the doctor, who stepped back in alarm.

'Try the other one,' said Jack. 'Here, master, point at something.'

The doctor took his road sign in one hand, and a large silver watch in the other. Jack watched the Scarecrow, and the Scarecrow watched the doctor, and the doctor watched the watch.

After a minute the doctor solemnly declared, 'This patient has no signs of life at all.'

The Scarecrow let out a piercing yell.

'Oh no! I'm dead! Help! Help!'

'You can't be dead yet, master,' said Jack, 'not if you're making a racket like that. Can't you find anything that you can cure, Doctor?'

'Dear me, this is a very bad case, a very poor case indeed. There's only one thing for it,' said the doctor.

'What?' said the Scarecrow and Jack, together.

'I shall have to operate. Lie down on the bed, please.'

The poor Scarecrow was quivering with terror.

'Aren't you going to put him to sleep first?' said Jack.

'Of course I am,' said the doctor. 'My goodness, do you take me for a quack?'

The Scarecrow heard the word *quack* and looked around for the duck, but the doctor took a rubber hammer and knocked him on the coconut. The Scarecrow fell down, stunned.

'Now what?' said Jack.

'Undo his clothing,' said the doctor. 'Then hand me my penknife.'

Everyone gasped, and craned closer to look. Jack unfastened the Scarecrow's coat, and laid bare his shirt, with the straw sticking stiffly out of every gap, and his poor wooden neck sticking out of the top.

His master was lying so still that Jack thought he really must be dead, and before the doctor could do anything, Jack flung himself across the Scarecrow and cried and sobbed.

'Oh, master, don't be dead! Please don't be dead! I don't know what I'd do without you, master! Please don't die!'

He sobbed and howled and clung to the poor old Scarecrow, and nothing would move him. Several of the bystanders began to cry too, and before long the room was filled with weeping and wailing, and every eye was gushing with tears. Even the doctor had to find his handkerchief and blow his nose vigorously.

The birds had heard the news, and a great lament went up from all the fields round about, and the bushes and trees were full of piteous cries:

'The Scarecrow's dying!'

'He's been poisoned!'

'He's been assassinated!'

And the loudest wails of lamentation came from the room in the farmhouse in Spring Valley where the doctor and Jack and all the townsfolk were gathered around the Scarecrow. But they didn't come from the people, they came from the Scarecrow himself, because all the noise had woken him up.

He leapt off the bed and cried:

'Oh! Oh! I'm dying! I'm poisoned! Oh, what a loss to the world! Treachery! Assassination! Murder! Oh, Jack, my dear boy, has he cut me open yet?'

'He was just about to.'

'Oh! Oh! Oh! I feel terrible! I've got conniptions all up and down my spine! I feel as if a million little ghosties were nibbling me! Oh – oh – there goes my leg – I'm falling apart, Jack! Help! Help!'

The Scarecrow was running around the room in terror, and the doctor was running after him trying to hit him with the rubber hammer, to put him to sleep again. Jack was running behind them gathering up all the bits that fell on the floor – some string, a bit of wood from somewhere up his trousers, lots of straw – and everyone else was wailing and sobbing.

Then Jack heard a loud *Caw!* and looked round in relief.

'Granny Raven!' he said. 'Thank goodness you've

come back! Lord Scarecrow's been taken ill, and the doctor says—'

'Never mind the doctor,' she said, perching on the window-sill. 'He doesn't need a doctor. What he needs is a carpenter. So I've gone and fetched one. Here he is.'

In came an old man wearing a carpenter's apron and carrying a bag of tools.

'Hold still, Lord Scarecrow,' he said. 'Let's have a look at you.'

'He's my patient!' said the doctor. 'Stand back!'

'I want a second opinion,' cried the Scarecrow. 'Let him look!'

Jack helped the Scarecrow back onto the bed. The carpenter put some glasses on and peered closely at the Scarecrow's legs, and then at the digging stick Jack had put in to replace his spine. He tapped them with a pencil, he felt all round them, he looked all the way up and down the faded road sign.

Then he stood up with a solemn expression. Everyone fell silent.

'In my professional opinion,' said the carpenter, 'this gentleman is suffering from an acute case of woodworm.'

The Scarecrow gave a shriek of horror. Everyone gasped.

'And if I'm not mistaken,' the carpenter went on, 'he's got termites in his stuffing, and an infestation of death-watch beetle in his backbone.'

The Scarecrow looked at Jack in despair, and reached for his hand.

'Can we save him?' Jack said.

'He needs an immediate transplant,' said the carpenter. 'He's got to have a whole new backbone, and he needs his insides cleaning out completely. This is a fresh infestation, mind. It's deeply suspicious. In my professional opinion, all them beetles and insects and woodworms got tipped down his neck yesterday.'

'The Buffalonis!' Jack cried. 'When they all came crowding round to pat him on the back! Assassins! Murderers!'

The Scarecrow was paralysed with terror. All he could do was lie there and whimper.

So Jack ran all through the farm looking for a broomstick, but the only ones he could find were already infested with woodworm, or split down the middle, or soft with dry rot.

He looked for a stick of any kind, but the only ones he could find were too short, or too bent, or too flimsy.

Then he ran back to the Scarecrow, who was lying pale and faint on the bed, twitching and whimpering.

And there were a lot more people in the room. The first visitors had now been joined by several elderly women dressed in black, weeping and wailing and tearing their hair. In those days, every town had a band of professional mourners, and these were the mourners of Bella Fontana. They'd heard about the impending death of Lord Scarecrow, and had come to offer their services. Besides,

they'd missed the death of poor old Mr Pandolfo, and they wanted to make amends.

'Ladies,' Jack said, 'I know you mean it for the best, but the thing about scarecrows is that what they really like is jolly songs. You got any jolly songs you can sing?'

'That would be disrespectful!' one of the old ladies said. 'We were always told that when someone was on the brink of death, we had to weep and wail, to remind them of where they were going next.'

'Well, that's very cheerful,' said Jack, 'and I'm sure they all appreciate it no end. But it's different with scarecrows. Songs, dances, jokes and stories, else you all go home.'

'Humph,' said the oldest old lady, but then Jack found a bottle of Mr Pandolfo's best wine, and they all agreed to try singing and dancing, just to see how it went.

'Oh, Jack,' whispered the Scarecrow, 'I'm not long for this world!'

'Well, cheer up, master, it could be worse. You're in your own bed, in your own house, on your own farm, and you might have been stuck in a muddy field or lying in splinters on a battlefield or floating about in the sea getting nibbled by fishes. Here you've got clean sheets, and these nice ladies to sing to you, and people looking high and low for a new backbone. But oh, master, don't die! Oh, oh, oh!'

And poor Jack started to wail and cry again, and flung his arms around the Scarecrow, ignoring the danger of catching woodworm.

And that started the old ladies off again. They'd been singing and dancing to 'Funiculi, Funicula', and 'Papa Piccolino', and they'd just started on 'Volare', but Jack's wails and sobs had them howling and screeching along with him, and then the Scarecrow himself joined in, and there was such a row that they didn't hear the doctor and the carpenter coming back. Only when dozens of birds flew around their heads, and Granny Raven cawed at the top of her voice, did all the crying and howling stop.

'We got a broomstick,' said the carpenter, 'and it's a good 'un. This old raven found it for us, and me and the doctor's going to transplant it right away. Everyone's got to go out of the operating theatre, for reasons of concentration and hygiene. When the operation is over, Lord Scarecrow'll need quiet and rest and recuperation, and until then, keep your fingers crossed.'

So all the townspeople left the room, and the doctor and the carpenter, with Jack's help, detached the old worm-eaten spine and emptied out all the beetle-infested straw, and gently and delicately inserted the new stick that Granny Raven had found, and packed the Scarecrow tightly with handfuls of clean fresh straw from the barn.

'Well,' said the doctor when they'd finished and washed their hands, 'we have done all that medical science can do. Now we have to rely on Mother Nature. Keep the patient warm, and make sure that his dressings are changed twice a day. If all goes well—'

'Jack, my boy,' said a well-known voice behind them, 'I feel a great deal better already! I believe I would like a bowl of soup.'

# Spring Valley

They never managed to get the Buffalonis charged with attempted murder by termites, so the case was never solved; but they didn't have any more trouble from them.

The poison factory was closed down, and re-opened as a mineral water bottling plant. Spring Valley water is famous now; every smart restaurant has it on the menu.

They cleaned up the land and cleared out all the ditches, and re-dug the wells, and opened the clogged-up drains, and now the fountains in the town are splashing good clear water all day and night, and the children play in the paddling pools and the birds wash themselves in the municipal birdbaths. Spring Valley water flows to every house, and all the houses have three kinds of tap: hot, cold, and sparkling.

As for the Scarecrow, he was the happiest of anyone. The broomstick that Granny Raven had found, the one that was transplanted to save his life, turned out to be the very one he'd fallen in love with all that time ago. Her fiancé the rake had left her for a feather duster, and, unhappy and abandoned, she had passed from hand to hand, lamenting the loss of the handsome Scarecrow who had proposed marriage to her. When the two of them found themselves united, their happiness was complete.

The Scarecrow spends all his days wandering around Spring Valley, playing with Jack's children, shooing the greedy birds away from the young corn, and enjoying the fresh air. But he only shoos the birds away to a special box of birdseed that he keeps behind the barn, and what's more, there's always a nest in his coat pocket. The little birds, the sparrows and robins, queue up for the honour; there's a waiting list. The Scarecrow and his broomstick are as proud of the eggs as if they'd laid them themselves.

'Jack's children?' I hear you say.

Yes, a few years later, when he was grown up, Jack got married. His wife is called Rosina, and their children's names are Giulietta, Roberto and Maria. They're all as happy as fleas. Granny Raven is godmother to the children, and she stands no nonsense from any of them, and they love her dearly.

And on winter evenings, as they sit by the fire with some good soup inside them, and the children are playing on the hearth and the wind is roaring round the rooftops, the Scarecrow and his servant talk about their adventures, and bless the chance that brought them together. There never was a servant, Jack is sure, who had such a good master; and in all the history of the world, the Scarecrow is certain, there never was a scarecrow who had so honest and faithful a servant.

# EPILOGUE

Of all the stories I've written, the four in this volume are especially dear to me. As I said in the prologue, I sometimes call them fairy tales, though there are no fairies anywhere near them; we use that term in English because we have no precise equivalent of the German *Märchen* or the Russian *skazka*, though to be perfectly accurate, those words really mean a short story, which these tales are not. And when we're talking about fairy tales it's important to distinguish between the ones that come from folklore, like those of the Brothers Grimm, and those that are literary in origin, like these.

What I mean by fairy tale is a story in which all kinds of improbable and sometimes funny, sometimes gruesome things happen, and in which a hero or heroine is tested and found worthy, and in which it all comes right in the end. Nothing like a novel, in fact, because in a novel it can all be as dull as mud and everything ends in misery. The stories in this book might not be all that short, but they're still fairy tales. I just like to get these things right.

In the prologue I wrote about one fairy-tale idea you're allowed to use whenever you need to, and there are many others, so many that there wouldn't be space to list them all in six books this size. But one idea I'll mention here, because I find it interesting, is that fairy-tale characters are more like masks than people. Another way of putting it is that they are the same all the way through. It's a rare thing in a fairy tale when a character does something unexpected; someone false is always false, someone true is always true. That's another difference from the novel, where the more psychology you have, the better. Most of the time I write novels, and I like psychology, myself, but occasionally I want a change; I want to live for a while among the charming constancy of the masks. So I write a fairy tale. Here are four of them, and I hope we all live happily ever after.

*Philip Pullman*

# ABOUT THE AUTHOR

Philip Pullman was born in Norwich and educated in England, Zimbabwe, Australia and Wales. He studied English at Exeter College, Oxford.

His first children's book, *Count Karlstein*, was published in 1982. To date, he has published thirty-three books, read by children and adults alike. His most famous work is the *His Dark Materials* trilogy. These books have been honoured by several prizes, including the Carnegie Medal, the Guardian Children's Book Award, and (for *The Amber Spyglass*) the Whitbread Book of the Year Award – the first time that prize was given to a children's book. Pullman has received numerous other awards, including the 2002 Eleanor Farjeon Award for children's literature and the 2005 Astrid Lindgren Award.

www.philip-pullman.com
@PhilipPullman